Suffragette
Autumn
Women's
Spring

Suffragette Autumn Women's Spring

Ian Porter

Matador
9 Priory Business Park
Kibworth Beauchamp
Leicestershire LE8 0RX, UK
Tel: (+44) 116 279 2299
Fax: (+44) 116 279 2277
Email: books@troubador.co.uk
Web: www.troubador.co.uk/matador

ISBN 978 1783063 437

British Library Cataloguing in Publication Data.
A catalogue record for this book is available from the British Library.

Typeset in Aldine401 BT Roman by Troubador Publishing Ltd
Printed and bound in the UK by TJ International, Padstow, Cornwall

Matador is an imprint of Troubador Publishing Ltd

To the brave women and men who fought for
Votes for Women

"We must be free or die, who speak the tongue That Shakespeare spoke – the faith and morals hold Which Milton Held. – In everything we are sprung Of Earth's first blood, have titles manifold."
William Wordsworth

"Democracy is the worst form of government, except for all those other forms that have been tried from time to time."
Winston Churchill

"Rebellion against tyranny is obedience to God – Deeds, not words."
Women's Social and Political Union

Preface

The fight for the vote for women in Britain effectively began when John Stuart Mill tabled an amendment to the 1867 Reform Act which would have given women the same political rights as men, a large section of whom were enfranchised for the first time by the Act. The amendment was defeated and there followed almost 40 years of lobbying by an increasingly large section of women throughout a number of suffrage societies. But progress was slow and limited.

Frustrated by this lack of success, Mrs Emmeline Pankhurst set up her own women's suffrage society, the Women's Social and Political Union. When her private members' bill on the vote was talked out in the House of Commons amidst laughter by MP's she decided it was time to take more direct action.

In 1905, her daughter Christabel and supporter Annie Kenny disrupted a large Liberal meeting, by shouting from the audience. They were thrown out but eager to gain publicity Christabel allegedly spat at a policeman. The two women were arrested, and in court were fined and required to be bound over on their own recognizances. They refused to pay the fine and refused to be bound over, making them guilty of contempt of court, which carried a custodial sentence. The women went to prison. The newspapers, which had hitherto mostly ignored women's fight for the vote, reported the incident on their front pages the following morning. Publicity would now be the oxygen of the WSPU movement.

When the Liberals won a landslide victory at the 1906 General Election, with a majority of their MP's reputed to be in favour of votes for women, there was much optimism. But these hopes were dashed when leading members of the new Cabinet showed themselves to be opposed to women gaining the vote.

From this time the WSPU became a militant organisation. Members deliberately got themselves arrested to gain publicity for the cause, but eager to highlight their cause further they refused to pay whatever fine was imposed upon on them by the courts, and duly went to prison. The Home Office treated them as common criminals so the protesters started hunger-striking for political prisoner status. The widely condemned use of force-feeding of Suffragettes in prison soon followed.

The non-militant suffragists, such as the National Union Of Women's Suffrage Societies, which had a membership that far outnumbered that of the relatively small WSPU, initially applauded the militants for bringing the fight for the vote more into the public domain. But once the WSPU introduced violence into their tactics, their actions were deplored by the vast majority of women fighting for the vote. The militant and non-militant factions essentially went their separate ways.

Emmeline Pankhurst was the figurehead of the WSPU; the great charismatic speech-maker. Her daughter Christabel was the decision-maker of the organisation. And it was the principle of the vote for women, rather than who actually got it which interested Christabel. She favoured limited suffrage, for just propertied women; effectively middle-class women. The 1910 Conciliation Bill, which the Suffragettes supported, would have given only propertied women the vote. Its first reading was passed by a huge majority but Prime Minister Asquith blocked its progress.

Mrs Pankhurst continued to successfully politicise women all around the country but frustrated by the government's false promises and delaying tactics Christabel decided to increase the Suffragettes' level of violence from March 1912. This stepped over the line which the public and press were willing to tolerate and they turned against the women. Suffragettes became pariahs.

******

Suffragettes would use the time when Parliament was in recess to sail abroad to spread the word. Mrs Pankhurst visited the United States on several occasions. And the amount of publicity surrounding the maiden voyage of the RMS Titanic would have been just the sort of thing into which she would have liked to have tapped. But the British parliamentary season was still in full swing in April 1912, so such a trip would have to wait for a couple of months.

It was just as well…

Part One

Chapter 1

"I am a civil servant, sir, and custom guides us a bit."
Captain Maurice Clarke, Titanic Safety Officer

0100am April 15th 1912:

Alexander Nash had been the hardest man in London's East End during the latter part of the nineteenth century, and he had not softened much with age. He had always been able to intimidate even the toughest of men by sheer menace, allied it must be said to the ability to back up this threat with violence when the occasion warranted. Ironically, it was the weakest of men whom he could not intimidate. They did not understand well enough the consequences of what would happen if they did not accede to his demands. And there was nothing weaker than a panic stricken little pipsqueak of a steward aboard the RMS Titanic.

The ship had hit an iceberg an hour and twenty minutes earlier, and with it now about to sink, Nash, along with all the other male passengers in third class, otherwise known as steerage, was imprisoned behind locked gates. The staircase up from steerage and the ladder from the aft well deck to second class, which eventually led through to the deck from where the lifeboats were being launched, remained blocked and guarded. Stewards were resisting all pleas and threats.

They were prepared to do their duty, but only to their orders rather than their fellow man. Nash gave the gates one last push of exasperation before turning and shoving his way through the surrounding crowd. He climbed a stairwell on to the only section of deck available to steerage passengers and looked around for alternatives. He spotted the deck had cargo crane jibs on it, so barked the shortest of advice to any men around him who wanted to listen.

"Cranes! Climb 'em!"

Nash led a group of men to the cranes and started to shin along one. Reaching the top got him into a position from where he clambered over a railing and then made his way up to the second class passenger entrance to the boat deck. In no time he had progressed to the lifeboat launching area. He had expected there to be a mass of women and children getting into lifeboats but there were few to be seen. He looked over the side and saw half full lifeboats rowing away from the ship, some with plenty of men in them. He grabbed a passing steward by the arm.

"Women and nippers orf are they? Every man for 'isself is it?"

It was fairly obvious from Nash's clothes and accent to which class he belonged. The steward tried to break free of Nash's grasp.

"I'm a steward for first class, if you'll forgive me."

Nash tightened his grasp and threw the man against the side wall of a walkway, then dragged him towards the rail. Nash nodded over the rail towards the sea.

"I won't arst yer again."

The stunned steward understood the threat.

"First and second class women and children are off; some

steerage I imagine. Rest are amidships towards the stern."

"Don't give me none of that sea talk; what's amidships when it's at 'ome?"

"It's below decks," and just to make absolutely sure the menacing man understood him, the steward added in landlubber-speak, "downstairs in the middle of the ship towards the back."

Nash looked at the steward as if he was something unpleasant he had just found stuck to the sole of his boot.

"Trapped like the men are they? Show me."

Another steward rushed to the aid of his colleague.

"I say, is this rough fellow causing trouble?"

Nash spoke quietly into the ear of the man still in his grasp.

"I can frow two over as soon as one."

The steward did not doubt it.

"No, I was just about to show him amidships, he is looking for some people," replied the steward to his cohort. He turned to Nash. "Follow me sir."

Nash was shown through the gymnasium, where men exercised on bicycles to keep warm. They had been there since before the collision and were still wearing their exercise clothes. The steward barged past an assortment of passengers and crew heading in the opposite direction. The former's initial indifference after the iceberg had struck had turned to bewilderment amongst the less well informed, whilst those who understood enough to feel fear were heading for the lifeboats. The latter were a mix of the redundant, overstretched and panic stricken. Out of work stokers, eyes red from fire staring out of faces black with soot, had made it above decks and now headed in the same direction as little pantry boys, who followed strict orders to take hot baked bread from the kitchen ovens to the lifeboats. And everywhere stewards and other crew ran about in all directions, following a stream of piecemeal, uncoordinated orders. Beneath the Titanic's surface layer of competence lay an underbelly of slapdash.

The steward and his charge passed by the forward staircase and the first class promenade. The window that usually enclosed the promenade to protect first class passengers from sea-spray, had just been unlocked to allow a small group of very affluent looking passengers to climb through to a lifeboat which had been lowered from the boat deck. A man attempting to board was being refused by an officer.

Nash wondered why a lifeboat had so few people getting in to it.

"Woss goin' on there?" he asked.

It's no business of yours thought the steward. But he wisely chose to relay something different.

"It is the Astors. They have been waiting for the promenade window to be opened so that a lifeboat may be lowered for them but until now the officer in charge of such things has been too busy to assist them. It appears Mr Astor wants to board but it is women and children only I'm afraid."

"Should 'ave fought of that before yer let all the rest of the soddin' boats off shouldn't yer," commented Nash. "Now, show me this amidships a yourn. We could get some women up 'ere in that boat before it goes."

The two men headed along a corridor then down several stairwells as they made their way through the first class stateroom area. The steward hopped down the steps far quicker than the bulky Nash could manage and quickly increased the distance between them. Nash was slow to spot what the steward was up to, but he was powerless to do anything about it in any case. He reached the bottom of a stairwell to find himself alone. The steward had disappeared.

"You lit'le cowson!" shouted Nash to an eerily empty passageway.

He peered about him, down a corridor that looked identical to all the others he had just passed. He had absolutely no idea where he was.

"Can I help you?"

It was a young woman's voice and the haughtiness and suspicion in her tone was unmistakable. Nash's noisy assessment of the steward's parentage had been heard by Ruby Martin, one of the ship's a la carte restaurant's two cashiers. Nash turned to see a young woman who looked as attractive as anyone could who had donned the most unflattering garb of bulky white lifejacket. She was staring at him with an expression not unlike the one of disgust he had recently given the steward. Nash spotted that she was wearing crew uniform which, as much as could be seen of it, was a surprisingly elegant full length dress. He was of the opinion that women who knew too well that they were good looking, and he was immediately convinced this one surely did, needed to be brought down a peg or two. Thus he made a point of returning her glare with interest and nodded curtly in the direction he had been headed.

"Lookin' for amidships," he said flatly.

"I see. Are you looking for anything in particular; the first class staterooms perhaps? A fur stole? Or should that be a fur steal?"

Nash became aware that in fixing her gaze he was staring deep into his inquisitors' dark eyes, guilty of the very thing he was trying to avoid. He looked away, looked down the corridor and chose to ignore her slight.

"I 'eard there's women and children still down 'ere trapped."

"Did you now?" she said cynically. "Well, that is as may be but it is hardly any concern of yours. Now, I do not know how you got down here, I thought all third class male passengers were still aft, but I suggest you return there, await further orders and leave these matters to the crew."

Ordinarily Nash would have been impressed by the spirit and wit of this young woman. She might even have been forgiven her good looks. But he did not like the snooty assumption, albeit an obvious and correct one, that he was steerage class. He gave her his gravest expression, which was enough to scare the roughest of men let alone a young woman.

"Crew," he growled, cramming the optimum amount of contempt into the word. "Is that the same crew who are sinking this unsinkable boat an' 'ave people locked up to drown like rats in a trap while they does it? Now, yer gonna show me where steerage is or do I 'as to find it meself?"

She was not sure whether this huge man was a plunderer or not, but she was certainly intimidated by him and not a little afraid for her personal safety, so she did as she was told. Not that she let him know that.

"Very well, as I am looking for my father, a ship's baker who, like a lot of third class women and children, is billeted in this part of the ship, I shall allow you to assist me to look for both him and the families."

She did not know this part of the ship at all, and as a result the two of them spent some time roaming corridors. It was a maze not made any easier by cabin doors having been locked, which Ruby assumed was to prevent people from returning to rescue trinkets and the like. The two of them shouted out the obvious questions but all they received in reply was an eerie silence save for the groans and creaks of a dying ship and the sound of water cascading nearby. Nash appreciated he had frightened this young woman with his demeanour, so interspersed his shouts with bizarre attempts at inappropriate small talk. If the silence was eerie, given the circumstances in which it was taking place, the conversation was downright surreal. What was her job? What was the pay like? Had she always been on the ships? That was no London accent he could hear, was she from Southampton? Saw them play West Ham in September. He was from the East End of London. Had she ever been to London?

This attempted badinage was met by little more than monosyllables to begin with, as the young woman concentrated on her task at hand, but she could not help but query what the man had meant by people being locked up. Nash told of his failed attempt at grille-breaking and more successful crane-climbing exploits. From what she knew of the officers and stewards on board Ruby thought his story had the ring of truth to it. The conversation eventually led on to her telling him that previous to ship work she had been in domestic service, yes she was from Southampton and no she had never been to London.

She concluded that this big Londoner was simply rough and ready rather than anything more sinister, and his desire to rescue people appeared genuine. And there was nothing to steal down here in any case thanks to the zealousness of the stewards tasked with locking up everything. No, this chap was no thief. She was warming to him. He was about fifty, and must have had a tough life in the famously poverty stricken East End of London, but he appeared to have weathered well, both in body and mind. He seemed so much more chipper than she remembered her father had been at the same age. And it was good of this chap to be down here looking out for poor women. He seemed to be the only man on this ship who was; so much for women and children first. One of the few rights a woman has is to get off a sinking ship first, and they do not even get that when it comes right down to it.

These dark thoughts were interrupted by signage to third class cabins coming in to view.

"At last," she muttered under her breath.

A sudden marked decrease in the quality of the fixtures and fittings around them made it clear they had now entered steerage. Ruby started towards what would have been the last stairwell down before reaching the third class cabins. But water had already flooded halfway up the steps. She stared down the stairwell for several seconds, taking in the enormity of the scene below, before she turned and stared at Nash, horror in her eyes.

"It's gone."

"Wot yer mean gone? Woss gone?" asked Nash, peering over Ruby's shoulder at the water before continuing. "Ain' there no uvver way down?"

"You don't understand. Anyone below us in the bow is drowned. Father is perished. They all are."

"Bow?" asked Nash.

"The front of the ship; the ship is going down by the head," said Ruby, voice breaking with both grief for her father and hopelessness at the situation in which she and this stranger now found themselves.

She motioned haphazardly to the floor with a hand to help her audience grasp more fully the magnitude of what she was saying.

"Look at the tilt of the floor," she said, the shrillness in her voice telling her she was losing the battle to hang on to her self-control in front of this man. "I don't know this part of the ship terribly well. I work in first class, on B-deck, and my quarters are also in a different area. But one thing is for certain we have to get higher or we too shall perish soon enough."

As if to prove her point, water started cascading down the stairwell from above. Their escape route was now an impassable waterfall. Water also began streaming down the walls the length of the corridor, like a giant urinal, as well as pouring on to their heads through the ceiling above. The first class state rooms above them were clearly underwater. They were trapped. There was water above and below them. The ship must be going down. It was the end.

Ruby crouched down on her haunches, wincing as the sub-zero ocean poured over and around her, cutting in to her like a knife. She lent her back against the side of the corridor, a mix of gravity and despair sliding her down into the rising water, buried her head in her hands and started to sob. Nash knew the sound only too well. It was common amongst women in the slums of the East End; the whining, snivelling cry of hopelessness and defeat.

Nash looked down and around at the in-rushing water,

which was already nipping at his ankles, feeling the same despair. The corridor lights went out, as the ship's dynamos started to come under pressure, entombing the two of them in total darkness for a second, before the lights flickered back on.

The lights set off an avalanche of thoughts in Nash's head. Had he survived the guilt he felt at not killing the Whitechapel Murderer when he had the chance; lived through the appalling overcrowding of Spitalfields in the 1890's; suffered through a further twenty years of sweated near-slave labour in the docks while he 'bettered himself'; for this? Drowning like a rat in the bottom of a ship. A ship sailed by arrogant, uncaring fools who were just like the men who left people to rot in slums; who promised social reform but did nothing.

These men were going to win after all. They will have killed him. A surge of anger coursed through him. He wanted to hit someone. He wanted to hit a lot of people. He bent down and thrust a huge hand down between Ruby's lifejacket and her dress-front, unconcerned with any lack of protocol as the back of his arm touched her breast. She gasped for a moment before he got a grip on the lifejacket and pulled her roughly to her feet. It certainly brought the young cashier to her senses. He motioned to a door at the end of the corridor.

"We ain' tried that yet. Know where it goes do ya?"

"No I don't. It's hopeless anyway."

Ruby had given up. Nash hadn't.

"We're tryin' it any 'ow."

Nash pulled Ruby off her feet with ease, threw her across his right shoulder fireman-style and waded through the deepening water to the end of the corridor. He set his cargo down and spoke to her sternly.

"Stay on yer feet. Now, woss yer name gell?"

"Ruby. Ruby Martin."

"I'm Nashey. Now listen Ruby, I know someone who was on the Alice, a boat wot sunk in the river a time back. 'e said wot saved 'im were 'e followed the bubbles. They float up to the surface see. So when the water comes over yer, mark my words now, follow the bubbles. If there's a way out, that'll be it."

"I know you were not down here stealing. It was good to know you Nashey," replied a now soft, doleful voice.

Nash ignored her. He had never understood his fellow working class' love of sentimentality. Music hall songs reeked of it. He did not care for it at the best of times and he certainly wasn't interested in this young woman displaying it now. He took the door handle in his hand and looked at her grimly.

"Now, take a good breff."

She did as she was advised, they shared meaningful nods to each other and Nash pulled.

★★★★★★

A barefoot young Irish steerage passenger had been hammering at a gate, officially locked as required by international immigration laws as much as the rules of class structure, when the order to unlock the barrier had been given. But free from her immediate prison, the panic stricken Annie Kelly had then to negotiate the rabbit warren of corridors and stairwells that eventually led up to an open deck. With no stewards on hand to assist, she had gone the wrong way, heading towards the stern and found herself at a stairwell heading only down. With no other option available Annie took it and headed along a corridor past the post office and then a first class baggage hold. Another down-only stairwell had her enter a cargo bay which contained amongst other things a Renault automobile. The incongruous object drew her attention for a moment before the far end of the hold forced itself into her line of vision. It was underwater. It was only the great tilt of the ship that was stopping the water from engulfing her. The spot from where the water was gushing in was completely submerged, muffling the noise of pouring ocean, the water-line eerily moving near-silently across the floor towards her like a liquid monster coming to get her in a nightmare. An inch of water ran into her toes like the last few feet of a wave at the seaside, but unlike spent surf, this water did not recede. The inch of water became two inches. It was time to run.

Annie tried to retrace her steps upwards but took a wrong turn and ended up in the mailroom, which she thought must surely be close to the post office passed earlier. Another corridor and a further ascending stairwell and she found herself back at the first class baggage area. She felt a surge of relief at passing the post office door which told her where she was, but the reprieve was short lived. Water had been escaping sneakily under the groaning door but now the ocean lost patience with its captor, flinging the door open and off its hinges, the flying wood just missing her. A torrent of water plunged out of the open doorway and smashed into her legs, rugby tackling her to the floor. The blow and its arctic blast knocked all the breath out of her body. She tried to exhale but, as if punched in the stomach, there was nothing there.

An attempt to scramble to her feet was similarly unsuccessful, a loss of coordination in increasingly cold toes being the culprit. She slipped and fell flat on her face, the freezing water leaping on her and biting into her like a rabid dog. The drenched, shivering, gasping young woman finally staggered upright and made her way along the rapidly filling corridor.

Being alone in the bowels of the ship had been frightening enough, but having paddled back to the third class cabins, she now ran into a more terrifying scene. It was the pandemonium of panicking women screaming as they searched for lost husbands, missing children and an escape route. Annie was about to join the chaos when Steward Hart hove into view.

The officers in charge of despatching the lifeboats, having almost run out of women and children to put in them, had sent Hart and two other stewards below decks to look for steerage class women and guide them up to the boat deck, from where the last few boats were to be launched imminently. The three stewards did not do a systematic search of corridors, cabins or public rooms. It was sheer luck if a woman happened to come across one of them.

Hart already had a small entourage of third class women passengers in single file snaking behind him. Some held on to the woman in front, more for comfort and reassurance than anything. Half a minute later Annie was thankfully bringing up the rear of the file, her numb feet causing her to stumble along like the latest drunken addition to a conga line.

Hart dropped his charges at a lifeboat which was about to be launched, and returned below decks looking for more women to rescue. In the melee the silent, demoralised, terrified women were ignored by the harassed Officer

Lightoller, and the lifeboat was sent off half full with the last of the first and second class women passengers. Annie and her fellow steerage travellers waited till Hart returned with another group. It was then that the two sets of women were put in lifeboats despatched full from the other side of the ship by Officers Murdoch and Lowe.

******

The door flew open. Nash and Ruby stood and stared. A couple of seconds passed, neither of them blinking or breathing. The ocean was flooding through the ship at differing speeds in different places. One spot could be submerged whilst the level beneath it was still dry. The only place this deep in the ship that remained free of the ocean was the swimming pool, which now stared at them literally dryly. The irony was not lost on the two saturated people. They turned and look at each other for a moment before their shivering heads increased in oscillation to shakes of disbelief at the most unfunny of jokes being perpetrated upon them. They splashed through the doorway, following the water pouring out of the corridor into the pool and its surrounding area.

"'ere, woss the time Ruby?" asked Nash.

"How should I know?" replied Ruby frowning. "What do you want to know for?"

Nash motioned to a list of charges just inside the door.

"Says 'ere it's only free for gentleman from six to nine o'clock; ladies from ten till twelve, otherwise it's a bob each; yer get a towel an' all for that mind. Got any money on yer gell?"

16

This very poor attempt at humour may have been inappropriate but it released some tension in both of them. Ruby snorted, not a little hysterically.

"Actually sir, you're no gentleman. It is first class passengers only," she replied in mock officious tone. "I'll have to ask you to lea…"

"We 'ave to go, now!" shouted an abruptly serious Nash, who had suddenly realised the in-rushing water was flowing in at such a rate that their perilous position had only been postponed for the briefest of periods. They needed to find an exit and quickly.

This speedily refocused Ruby's thoughts.

"That way!" she shouted, pointing. "I know where we are now. It's the Turkish bath there, and that's a stairwell up next to it."

Ruby led them past the swimming pool then took the steps at a gallop to reach the reception room at the foot of the forward first class staircase. There were plenty of people milling about there, which gave Ruby a momentary surge of reassurance, before reality pushed her on up the remainder of the staircase, with Nash hot on her heels. They arrived up on deck, an Arctic blast of air slicing through their clothing to make them feel even colder if that were possible, and looked across at where the lifeboats were being launched, some distance away.

Ruby watched as Captain Smith shouted orders through a megaphone to a lifeboat in the water to come back and take on more passengers. They were ignoring him, rowing away from the ship as quickly as their oars could take them. Ruby shook her head slowly, disbelieving what she was seeing.

The lifeboats were clearly being launched half full by his

manic, error prone senior officers so why did he not communicate with them? Why did the captain not take control of the situation? A junior officer could shout the odds through a megaphone.

Nash turned to Ruby, nodding at the lifeboats, but saw she was seemingly staring in to space. He assumed she was thinking about her father.

"I saw some bakers just before I bumped into yer, bringin' up bread to put in the lifeboats," he shouted, over the growing din of a ship in its death throes.

His breath was giving a good impersonation of the steam escaping from the ship in the sub-zero air as he continued in an attempt to reassure her.

"Your ol' man was one of 'em I shouldn't wonder."

This brought Ruby away from her captain-spotting.

"They would have just been the pantry boys," corrected Ruby, body shivering, teeth chattering, her soaked uniformed arms grasped fruitlessly around her lifejacket.

"Nah," countered Nash. "Boys would have been in the lifeboats by now."

"They are only boys when it comes to their wages. They are male crew."

At this point Ruby's broad white hairband with bow, which was part of her uniform and held her bun in place, collapsed under the weight of saturated hair. Freed from captivity, hair cascaded forward and a thick glossy black curl flopped into an eye. Ruby winced and cursed before scraping a hand back over her forehead to push the offending hair back. Her gaze headed downwards causing her to notice a vital piece of Nash's apparel was missing.

"What has happened to your lifebelt?"

"Only two lifebelts to a third class cabin, and there were four of us in mine. They ain' no good any'ow. Any as goes in that freezin' water catches their deffs before they drowns. 'member wot I said about the Alice? I lost a cousin on it when I were a lad. 'e could swim but sewage got 'im. They'd just dumped tons of it in the river. Shit or cold, yer just as dead. Better not to 'ave a lifebelt on; least yer can swim quick to a boat. Yer can't swim in no lifebelt, just bob up an' down like some ruddy great cork. I ain' goin' that way. An' if their ain' no boats, least it's over with quick."

Nash turned away to look at the scene in front of them. All but one of the full size lifeboats had already been launched. This plus the four collapsible lifeboats were all that was left on board. Collapsible C was being launched from the starboard side. Nash was surprised to see it full of women and children. He wondered where they had come from. He saw from their clothing that they were clearly third class passengers. Elbowing Ruby lightly in her side to attract her attention Nash nodded towards the women.

"Looks like some steerage women got orf after all."

But Ruby did not need her attention to be brought to the lifeboat. She was already staring wildly at it.

"Bastard," said Ruby quietly with disbelief in her voice.

Nash didn't catch what Ruby had said due to the noise from the ship intensifying as it listed further. The sound of water plunging out of the side of the ship from the exhaust of the condensers had been a constant din for some time but it was now drowned out by far bigger, sharper sounds such as thousands of pieces of crockery smashing to the floor.

"Eh?"

But Nash's question fell on deaf ears as Ruby turned to him.

"Come on move!" she barked, glaring at Nash with a look as black as the night, as she grabbed him by the pullover momentarily before releasing her grip to start running towards the collapsible.

Blimey she's recovered her senses all right, thought Nash, rather impressed. He was not used to anyone, let alone a slip of a girl, barking orders at him with a look that could kill, but he followed without question. They barged their way unceremoniously through the crowds milling around the remaining lifeboats before both of them were stopped by a line of seamen with linked arms.

"No men, no men," shouted the seamen, who would not unlink their arms to let Ruby through while Nash was at her side.

"Ismay's a man isn't he!?" shouted Ruby. "Coward! You coward Ismay!" she shrieked at the top of her breaking voice over the heads of the cordon, as she tried to break through it.

"Here, that is no talk from crew! You look to yourself young woman. What is your name? You will go on report," shouted a ship's officer.

Nash was too confused to know how to react. He wondered what was going on. But as soon as the officer gripped Ruby roughly by the arm and started shaking her like a rag doll, he knew what to do. A moment later the man was horizontal, kissing the deck. Nash looked defiantly at the seamen linking arms but they had their work cut out holding back the hordes. The panic was now well and truly on to get in one of the last lifeboats. They were not about to come to the aid of some jumped up little officer who simply got what he deserved. Nash turned to Ruby.

"Woss all this in aid of?"

"I just saw one of the owners of this tub get in a lifeboat. He pushed his way on to it," shouted Ruby.

Nash didn't know what she was so affronted by. He had assumed all the toffs, men as well as women, would be first off the ship. That's what they do. It's the poor people who always have to suffer. That was the way of the world. When the steward had led him through the first class area earlier he had been surprised to see very wealthy people getting in to a lifeboat so late in the proceedings, and likewise he was shocked that an owner of the ship had taken so long to make his escape. But he could see that Ruby was in no mood to discuss the matter.

"Well we can't do nuffin' aboud it now can we," replied Nash loudly. "There's only a few boats left so far as I can make out and we've gotta get you in one of 'em sharp."

Crew shouted orders and replies as Ismay's escape route was launched. "Lower away!" "Shove her off!" "Level!" "Aft!" "Stern!" "Both together!" "When you're afloat, row round to the companion ladder and stand by with other boats for orders!" "Aye aye sir!"

Shouts were going out from officers and stewards to anyone, anywhere.

"Any more ladies? Any more ladies? Any more ladies on your deck?"

"Oi trouseys, over 'ere!" shouted back Nash.

"Ladies they said. Not women," corrected Ruby with a bitter sneer.

Second Officer Lightoller barked orders for her to be let through the cordon. Nash eased her forwards.

"Go 'ed gell."

"I shouldn't get in. I am only a cashier," said Ruby to the officer.

"No matter, you are a woman, take your place," replied Lightoller, unaware of his own pomposity.

While Ruby hesitated, five or six men who had got into the lifeboat before it had been swung out had crewman pull them out by their legs. Another man jumped into the boat, inflicting great pain on the woman on whom he had landed. He too was pulled out as more men lined up to jump into the boat. Three pistol shots cracked into the still night air accompanied by a warning.

"You will be shot like dogs!" shouted an officer.

"We have to lower away now!" shouted Lightoller, motioning to his launch crew to do the necessary.

Ruby looked back at Nash, still hesitating. She saw him cup his hand over his mouth and speak into the ear of one of the men holding back the crowd. The man nodded and opened his link in the chain of the cordon for a moment to let Nash and Ruby scurry through to the boat launching area.

"What did you say to that seaman?" she asked.

Nash ignored the question, instead sweeping Ruby off her feet to hold her in his arms. He bent to one knee to lessen the distance between his cargo and the bottom of the lifeboat, which had already been lowered a few feet. He looked for the bulkiest person in the boat. An officer had just climbed in. He would be a good target. With the ship listing badly to port, the side they were on, Nash was kneeling immediately above the officer.

Nash winked at Ruby.

"Keep yer 'and on yer 'apenny gell!"

He then turned his attention to Fifth Officer Lowe, who was busying himself putting the plug in the lifeboat.

"Oi, Jack Hobbs, catch this at mid-wicket if yer can!"

Lowe looked up and as he did, Nash dropped Ruby unceremoniously on top of him. Ruby let out a yelp in the brief moment she was airborne, before her lifejacket bounced off Lowe's. They were each a little stunned by their collision but pulled themselves upright in a second or two, uninjured.

"You're big enough and ugly enough to 'ave a slip of a gell land on yer," shouted Nash. And shifting his gaze to Ruby, he added, "Wot I said to 'im were let me frew so I can chuck this soppy lit'le cow in that boat before I freeze to deff. They can shoot me quick enuff if I go to jump in."

Having posted Ruby by airmail into the last remaining full size lifeboat, Nash immediately turned away before his package had a chance to reply or swop glances with him. After all, they had exchanged their final nods down by the swimming pool. He gave the seaman who had allowed him through to the lifeboat a curt nod of appreciation as he ducked beneath the interlinked arms of the man and his neighbour in the cordon, back through to the other side of the human barrier. He then pushed through the throng that was surrounding the cordon before heading back purposefully towards the gymnasium that he had seen earlier. The gym was the highest enclosed spot on the ship, and still safely above the waterline.

Nash felt that he needed to supplement the small swimming advantage he believed that not wearing a life-jacket would give him over others in the water. He would attempt to don white clothes that might more readily be spotted by a lifeboat. He had remembered how several of the men he had seen exercising in the gymnasium were wearing all white and wondered if there might be some cast offs lying around.

Sure enough a white exercise vest had been abandoned on the floor of the now empty gym, and there were plenty of white towels around too. He threw off his saturated old jacket, pullover, shirt and vest, and sucked in a sharp breath of complaint as the cold night air stabbed at his flesh. His new ensemble proved way too small as he struggled to get it over his huge shoulders, so it was wrenched off. His only upper body attire were to be a couple of towels; one tied around his neck muffler-style, the other pulled over the top of his head and fastened beneath his chin like a woman would a shawl. He removed the leather belt of his trousers, complete with big heavy buckle, untied his huge boots and slipped them off. He didn't wear socks. He winced, partly because his already soaking, freezing feet just got even colder by touching the deck, and partly because he saw himself in a mirror on the gym's wall. He looked quite a sight. But after all, that was the whole point.

He headed back outside and saw a man throwing deckchairs overboard, no doubt with a view to joining them in the water and using them to cling to. The splashes of the furniture came quickly. The ocean was almost upon them. Collapsible lifeboat D had just been launched and was being rowed away from the ship as quickly as possible. Nash looked to see where the nearest other lifeboats were, but could not see any in the moonless dark of night. Fearful of the suction when the ship went down, they had rowed out of sight. Nash nodded. It's what he would have done. At least Ruby was safely away.

The band now started what time was likely to decree would be their swan song, the waltz 'Songe d'Automne'.

******

Officer Harold Lowe cursed under his breath in his Welsh accent as he extracted himself from the bottom of the lifeboat, but reddened cheeks of anger were replaced by those of embarrassment as he came to appreciate that he had just surfaced from beneath a woman's dress. She in turn shifted awkwardly to one side and looked away, glancing up to whence she had come. Lowe got to his feet and followed her gaze up at the Titanic, but there was no sign of the man who had thrown the woman on top of him.

"Damned impudent fellow! Couldn't understand a word he said. Coward Italian I'll wager!" said Lowe.

Ruby, complete with saturated clothes, bedraggled hair and the stunned expression of someone who was probably never going to see her father again, looked the epitome of misery. But she couldn't help but smile inwardly to herself. She considered Lowe for a moment. Dark haired, about her age, strong jaw, he would be good-looking if it were not for those tiny little eyes of his. She recognised him as the man who had fired the warning pistol shots above the heads of the men threatening to jump in to the lifeboat. The object of her appraisal reached down to make sure the plug of the lifeboat was still safely in, and swept up his white officer's cap, knocked off his head by Ruby's arrival. He placed it back in its rightful place and pulled it down into position with an overzealous wrench of the peak.

"I believe he's a damned impudent cockney fellow," said

Ruby with undisguised contempt, pronouncing 'fellow' sarcastically in the same affected manner as Lowe. She thought she may as well correct the officer, although she appreciated it would merely allow him to replace the language of race with that of class.

Lowe looked her up and down, noting her ship's uniform.

"Your name?" he asked haughtily with menaces.

Ruby had to admit that he had a presence about him. He was the sort of man who commanded respect. Just like many of the officers on board. And out of respect had come trust. But there was no more respect or trust left in Ruby. She guessed why he wanted her name. Just before she had gone below to look for her father she had seen a first class passenger whom she had served, Mrs White, complaining to an officer that there had been crewmen openly smoking in front of passengers. They would be going on report. If they lived that is.

"Ask that cockney fellow to tell you when you see him," she said with chin-pointing defiance.

She then looked away, her attention drawn by the gasps from her fellow lifeboat passengers. They were seeing for the first time the true horror of the situation. It was far more evident from over the side of the ship just how desperate was the Titanic's position. The bow of the liner was barely above water with many decks now submerged, yet their lighting continued to work, the eeriest of shimmering light coming up from the depths. Ruby looked down and estimated the original seventy foot drop from the lifeboat's davits to the ocean of an hour and a half ago was now only about a fifth of that distance. But nevertheless it would still be a fair distance to fall. She returned her gaze to Lowe. He did not know how lucky he was. Had they started lowering his lifeboat a minute earlier, she would have been landing on him from a rather greater height. She didn't doubt for a moment the tough East Ender would still have dropped her into the boat.

It was clear that the Titanic would sink before any rescue ships arrived, so the sixteen lifeboats would have to rescue those in the water who had not been sucked down with the ship. What she would not give for their lifeboat to be the one that rescued Nashey. She could just imagine Lowe engaging him.

"You there, cockney fellow, I have a bone to pick with you."

The officer would slip down nicely with Nashey's morning cup of tea and two slices. But she feared the big cockney would be one of those to perish. She thought his choosing not to wear a lifebelt was clearly foolhardy, and unless a rescue ship's lights appeared out of the darkness immediately, she would not be seeing him again.

Lowe had not had time to register disapproval at Ruby's insubordination, his attention drawn to far more pressing needs. The lifeboat was being lowered towards a torrent of water pouring out of the side of the Titanic from its pumps. Such was the force of the deluge that if they did not use the lifeboat's oars to push against the side of the ship to move themselves away from it, the craft would be flooded. But the oars of the lifeboat had stupidly not been stowed with use in an emergency in mind. The only other crewman in the boat, stoker Jenkins, was having to waste precious seconds untying the oars from overzealously knotted twine that stowed them securely beneath the lifeboat's seats.

Ruby spotted that once this job was done, the oars still needed to be extracted from beneath the seats and that could take seconds they did not have. She jumped up, grabbed a pair of oars and as soon as Jenkins had untied them, swung them out with alacrity, giving the woman on the opposite side of the boat a nasty whack on the ankle with one of the blades. The woman grimaced and bent down to massage her injury whilst the woman sitting next to her gasped in indignation on her neighbour's behalf. But any complaint that was about to issue forth towards the reckless young crewwoman was stopped in its tracks by Lowe.

"Well done!" he shouted in his matter-of-fact manner.

Lowe rushed forward to pick up the oars as he barked orders.

"Same again! You man, help her!" was shouted at Jenkins as he finished unknotting another couple of oars.

Ruby and the crewman followed orders. Moments later Lowe, Jenkins, Ruby and a young female steerage passenger, inspired by the deeds of her fellow woman, were pushing against the side of the Titanic with all their might. The lifeboat swayed on its fall ropes like a giant marionette just enough to avoid the cascade, though the spray ensured all members of the boat were doused with a salty souvenir of the night. The obstacle duly circumvented, with the boat now about to touch down on the ocean, the oars were needed elsewhere.

"Rest oars!" shouted Lowe, the two men immediately withdrawing theirs from the side of the Titanic. The two women had no idea what he meant but their hesitation had the benefit of the boat not banging back against the side of the ship as hard as it might have.

The heavy listing of the ship meant the lowering of the lifeboat had become more difficult. And during the puppetry part of the descent to the ocean the falls had become twisted and would not now release them. Lowe shouted at Jenkins to retrieve a knife from a box under the seat by the tiller, which was duly done and within seconds the stoker had cut the ropes and they floated free. Lowe had taken an oar and ordered Jenkins to do likewise, and the two men started to row. The sixty five seat capacity lifeboat was full, and consequently too heavy for only two people to row at any speed. It was clear that the death of the Titanic was imminent and Lowe was becoming increasingly concerned that they would not be able to get sufficiently far away to avoid the suction of the ship when it went down.

"Need volunteers for rowing!" he shouted.

Not surprisingly it was the same two women who had used the oars a few minutes earlier that were soon rowing in a mixed four. Not a word was said but the two women were well aware of the danger and joined the two men in rowing like galley slaves. Minutes later they were at Lowe's prescribed safe distance, one hundred and fifty yards from the doomed ship.

******

The ocean was now pouring into the Titanic at many tons a minute which started to pull the ship apart. The strain on the ship wrenched off the substantial port stay of the forward funnel. The starboard one soon followed and the funnel broke away from the ship, crashing over the side, falling in to the water with immense force. It crushed some of the people who had already jumped into the water hoping in vain to be rescued by a lifeboat. A massive crash followed as some of the boilers left their beds and went smashing down through the ship. With a huge groan the aft of the ship started to rise out of the water. Three huge bronze propellers rose above the waves, dripping water made fluorescent in the darkness by the ship's lights reflecting on them. The great ship stood to attention for a minute, before breaking in two between the third and fourth funnels, close to the aft expansion joint. This was a natural weakness because of inch-wide gaps which extended down two decks to allow the ship to flex in rough seas. The aft smashed back on to the ocean; the ship now only in one piece along the keel.

But it was only a temporary stay of execution. The ship soon returned to the vertical, lights still remarkably ablaze. It stayed there for half a minute or so, unwavering like a gymnast holding a perfect balance, before starting its inexorable slide to the depths, slowly at first before increasing its velocity.

Nash had wedged himself against a rail running across the deck which became a barrier against gravity when the ship went vertical, and then he jumped just before his part of the deck plummeted into the ocean. The shock of the freezing water took his breath away so he was struggling to make it back to the surface even though the much feared ship's suction was conspicuous by its absence. He was getting his wish; he was going to drown rather than freeze to death. He managed to get to the surface and had just taken a couple of huge breaths when a ship's boiler exploded. The Titanic, in an act of final defiance as it started its dive to the depths, had literally gone out with a bang. The explosion blew Nash out of the water. Second Officer Lightoller had been in the water a few feet away, and had joined Nash on the short haul flight.

On touchdown the gasping, spluttering, disorientated Nash looked about him. The ship had disappeared. He thought he saw a vapour trail on the surface but it was gone in an instant. There had not been time to launch two of the collapsible lifeboats before the ship had gone down. One of them, Collapsible B, was nearby, turtled, with several men already climbing aboard. Nash set off towards it. Lightoller, who was wearing a life-jacket, also spotted the collapsible but Nash left him in his wake. His theory about the advantages of not having a life-jacket looked like it might pay dividends.

It was not a long swim but the water was teeming with people and Nash's swimming ability only amounted to an amateurish head-out-of-the-water breaststroke cum doggy-paddle. And it did not help that the sub-zero ocean was seemingly using his lungs like a pair of bellows to squeeze the life out of him. By the time he had negotiated his way through the throng via the odd well placed elbow and shove, there were close to thirty men on board the upturned lifeboat. They were trying desperately to retain their balance as they stood up on the raised planking of the boat's underside, which was now its topside. He heard the cultured voice of what he assumed was a first or second class male passenger shout out.

"Grab that oar floating there someone! Don't let any more on! We'll capsize for sure!"

Nash, his poor swimming technique leaving him no longer able to draw breath, was seconds from disappearing beneath the waves to his death when his two hands made contact with the sides of the collapsible. He kept one arm on the boat and reached up with the other for help but instead got buffeted with an oar as a hint that his presence was not welcome on board. The curvature of the boat initially protected his head, his huge forearms taking all the blows while his lungs wheezed like those of a sixty-a-day man having his first cough and a spit of a new day. He made no attempt to protect himself from the blows, for he needed every bit of his great arm strength to clamber on to the boat. He simply ignored the punishment as he slowly hauled his body out of the water and up the planking, his head coming into oar-range as he made progress upwards to a point where his legs and feet were clear of the water.

Oars being difficult things for the uninitiated to handle at the best of times meant that a panicking man trying to use one as a weapon, whilst also maintaining his precarious balance on board an upside down boat, did not make the best of marksman. That said the two most accurate strikes on Nash had drawn blood, though the assault had barely registered with the tough East Ender. Nash noticed blood from his mouth had leaked on to the white muffler towel. He reached up with a hand to inspect damage to his head, and felt stickiness in his hair. He had lost the headscarf towel.

Never could tie a proper soddin' knot could ya boy.

Not with-standing the basic animal instinct for self-preservation, this was the first lucid thought Nash had had since entering the water. He scraped the back of his hand across his whiskered chin and lower lip, and spat a blood oyster onto the planking in front of him, but otherwise sat quietly, or as quietly as a man could who was getting his breath back after almost drowning. He did not look at the man who had tried to send him to his death or those who stood by and watched the attempt. Considering their behaviour was simply a matter of the survival of the fittest, he would not seek retribution, though he held them all in complete contempt.

The sea water had ensured Nash got an unwanted saline drip into his ears, nose and throat. He was thinking that if he coughed much harder he would bring his lungs up, when Lightoller, who had followed Nash, swam up towards the boat. Nash snatched the oar from his attacker with contemptuous ease, taking the opportunity to meet the man's eye with the grimmest of expressions before he held the end of the oar hard against the planking, the blade sticking out into the water for the swimmer to grab. Once it had been duly taken, Nash eased the oar gently back towards himself to assist the man further. Nash's balance on the planking was too precarious to reach forward to offer the man a hand to help him up onto the boat, so he turned to face the planking and shinned up to a point where he was able to grip the apex of the upturned boat. This done he proffered the back of a leg.

"Reach 'old steady now ovverwise I'll kick yer away!" shouted Nash over his shoulder.

Lightoller was just able to reach high enough to grab one of Nash's feet and did as he was told. Nash gritted his teeth as he applied huge pressure on the apex to counter the effect of Lightoller using his foot for a moment's leverage before gaining sufficient purchase on the boat's underbelly to scramble further on board under his own steam. There was no argument from the other men. Perhaps it was because they recognised the second officer. Perhaps there was another reason.

Once he had paid back his oxygen debt, Lightoller offered thanks to his saviour but Nash wasn't interested and did not respond. Nash had not done it for him as such; he had done it to do the right thing in front of those who had not.

A few more men were allowed to clamber half on to the boat, but they were not to be as lucky as the officer Nash had helped. The boat really was up to full capacity now, so they had to cling on the best they could, their lower bodies still in the freezing water. One man swam up and was told there was no room. He accepted his fate with moving grace.

"That's all right boys. God bless you. Carry on."

Nash nodded in silent respect to the well-spoken man, who drifted away and was not seen again.

★★★★★★

Ruby and her fellow lifeboat passengers had been in front row seats at the horrifying spectacle. They sat in silence save for the sound of the four rowers panting from their exertions, as everyone was transfixed by the sight of the ship in its death throes. The giant glow-worm had become Excalibur, thrown into the water only to be caught by the lady of the ocean and thrown back, the glittering scabbard sparkling and flashing a second time before slipping beyond the reach of the mysterious hand beneath the waves.

The screaming of the Titanic passengers still on board, as they hurtled into the ocean, was replaced by a moment of silence and then, as if the ship was still fighting for its life beneath the waves, there was a heavy explosion under the water, then a second, and a third.

Clouds had covered the moon during the evening, and now with the lights of the Titanic removed, the scene had been transformed into one of total darkness. And out of the pitch black, the cold still night air magnifying every sound, the great but fleeting noise of the explosions was replaced by an awful cacophony of fifteen hundred souls thrashing and screaming.

But terrible though the scene was, Ruby felt a flash of optimism course through her as it became evident that there was no suction from the sinking ship. And with plenty of space in many of the lifeboats, some of those in the water could be saved immediately and others transferred on to nearby ice floes to await a rescue ship to arrive.

Lowe was the first to react. He grabbed the tiller and told his oarsman and women to restart their efforts, before telling Ruby to swop places with the big stoker, so they had more balance to their rowing. After a few pulls it became clear that Lowe was not guiding the boat back towards the screaming mass.

"What are you doing?!" shouted Ruby between grunts of exertion.

Lowe did not see why he needed to answer this question. He did not have to justify his actions to anyone. But the young woman had been something of a brick in dealing with the outflow and rowing problems, and most of the other women in the boat probably had men in the water, so it would be churlish not to make the situation clear to everyone.

"I appear to be the highest ranking officer to have escaped in any lifeboat within sight, so I am in charge, not just of this lifeboat but of all those we can see. It is my decision that I will redistribute people in these lifeboats, to ready this boat to return empty, save for oarsmen, to pick up survivors in the water."

It seemed reasonable. Ruby had to admit that Lowe appeared to be more impressive than the rest of the headless chickens who had masqueraded as the Titanic's officers. She nodded and kept silent.

Lowe gathered several boats together and started the redistribution. It was a time-consuming affair, the bobbing boats having to be held together on a strengthening sea. And landlubber first and second class women passengers, whose fashionable attire was far from suited to clambering about on small sea-craft in the middle of the Atlantic, found it a particularly awkward transition from one lifeboat to another.

The screaming and thrashing had quickly faded to whimpering and soon enough Ruby became aware that even this had faded to an eerie silence. This redistribution business was taking too long.

"They're dying! We can't wait any longer! We have to go back! And we have to take all the boats back! Now!"

Lowe looked askance at her. This young woman clearly did not know her place.

"That is out of the question. I will take this boat back after I have removed all women and children from it. And when that moment arises I will wait again for if I return too soon they'll flood the boats and take us all down with them! They have lifebelts after all."

Ruby had expected Lowe's pompous, unfeeling outburst to be met with a chorus of derision from the women within earshot, but there was silence. The glow of a lantern in the closest of the lifeboats within the linked flotilla allowed Ruby to see some of its occupants staring out of the darkness. All she could see was face upon face of women, some peeping out from the blankets they were huddled in, either looking blankly back at her or down at their laps, mortified.

"Lifebelts! They're not drowning, they are freezing to death! For pity's sake!" she screamed at both Lowe and the women. "They'll all be too bloody cold to take anyone down with them!"

"He knows best." "Let the officer decide." "The man is only doing what is right." And other words to that effect reached her ears. The blanks were having their say. The mortified stayed silent.

It was not the women's passivity that appalled her most. It was their trust. They trusted men to do the right thing, when the history of this night, if it taught them anything, was that it was time for women to make their own decisions. Ruby slumped down, her head in her hands, and left Lowe to continue.

All the redistribution bar Ruby's own transfer duly took place. Some crewmen had transferred across into Lowe's boat. Ruby had not stirred as Lowe had gone about his business so he left her till last.

"It is time," he said abruptly.

Ruby brought her head up.

"I have an idea if you will hear me sir," she said in a quiet, subservient tone she thought Lowe would appreciate.

She did not wait for a reply, fearful of a negative answer, and continued.

"Instead of waiting, we take the boat back now but sail around the edge of the people, picking off anyone who has drifted away from the main…"

She hesitated. She had been about to say 'body'.

"The main bulk; that way we will not be swamped."

Lowe had to admit it was a good idea. One he should have thought of himself. Feathers duly ruffled, he was as much annoyed as thankful for the suggestion from a woman.

"I had already considered that a prompt start would at least have the men stave off the cold with rowing," he lied before adding. "And what do you mean, we?"

"Surely you have to tend the thing at the end of the boat to steer it sir."

Ruby was well aware of the words 'tiller' and 'bow', but thought she should pander to his ego. He needed to feel superior, hence also the 'sir'. But now it was time for her to tell a bare-faced lie.

"And as you so rightly pointed out sir you have got your men there to row, but you will want someone, a lightweight is best of course, with a lamp to spot when people are alive. No point wasting time on the dead. I am a trained nurse. I only took the position on the Titanic to work my passage to America. I have a position lined up in the Manhattan Hospital in New York."

She had no idea what any of New York's hospitals were called, but Manhattan was the only New York place name which sprang to mind on the spur of the moment. And she had never even been in a hospital. Her father's tales of workhouse infirmaries becoming hospitals meant nobody in his family ever set foot in such a place. But Ruby was past being told by men what she could and could not do. She was not going to stand by and let this man decide who was to live or die. She could be the lady of the lamp for this night at least.

Lowe was not sure whether he believed the young

woman or not. It could be a cock and bull story but her being a nurse certainly explained the haughty attitude and she was clearly not concerned about going on report, which she would not if she already had another position arranged. She also appeared to be the sort who might have plenty to say at any later inquiry. He doubted anyone would take any notice of a woman but Jenkins had heard everything she'd had to say. He might back her up. There was no point in leaving oneself open to any criticism, and besides her idea seemed sensible enough so it could not do any harm to take her along.

Lowe took the tiller and set off. He kept close to the wreckage, away from the main mass of people, ready to save anyone who had become detached from the crowd. It quickly became clear that they were not going to be bringing large numbers aboard.

"There's one!" shouted Ruby with an air of desperation in her voice, pointing at a South-East Asian man who had strapped himself to a wooden door.

Lowe thought the man looked lifeless.

"What's the use," he retorted, "he's dead likely, and if he isn't there's others better worth saving than a Jap."

Ruby ignored the xenophobia and shone her lantern into the man's face, which jolted him into life.

"He's alive, get 'im!" shouted Ruby.

Lowe momentarily forgot who was in charge of the lifeboat, and followed orders. They pulled next to the man as he unstrapped himself from the door with surprisingly dexterity. He was manhandled into the boat, after which he jumped up, stretched frozen limbs, stamped frozen feet, and then much to everyone's amazement took over on an oar.

"By Jove I'm ashamed of what I just said about the little blighter! I'd save the likes of him six times if I got the chance!"

Lowe was clearly impressed. This incident gave him a more positive attitude to the rescue mission, and he started moving further into the mass. They soon brought another three into the boat alive but by the time dawn broke they had not found anyone else to bring aboard for some time and all daylight achieved was highlight the full horror of what was before them. When Lowe abandoned the search, Ruby turned to those whom they had saved to see if there was anything she could do for them. There was. She provided the arms in which one of them died.

******

Such were the limitations on space that all those able to do so had to stand up on the turtled lifeboat, moving with the swell in the slowest of waltzes to keep balanced in the strengthening sea. Nash had what would be the start of frostbite beginning to eat in to him so had to remain seated. He did not want to take up more space than anyone else but appreciated the loss of feeling in his legs meant attempting to stand up on the slippery planking might result in a fall which could knock others into the water and endanger everyone by unbalancing the boat.

Four hours into the vigil Nash found a job to do. The barely conscious crewman sitting next to him, the eighteen year old ship's junior wireless operator Harold Bride, who was severely weakened by numbness, started slipping slowly down the boat's planking towards his death. Nash threw a hand around him to stop the slide before pulling the lad into a less precarious position. Bride's weight then rested against the big East Ender, who also kept a grip on his young charge, for an hour and a half while dawn shed light on an arriving ocean liner.

Chapter 2

"All he said was that he had a jolly good breakfast
and he never thought I would make it."

Mrs W. Carter at her divorce hearing, on her
husband greeting her aboard the Carpathia.

Officer Lowe was the only person in any of the sixteen
lifeboats who had the knowledge or ingenuity to make use
of the mast and sail which was provided in each boat. Using
the breeze which had sprung up, he was able to move his
craft through the water with more speed and manoeuvrability
than any of the other boats. When dawn broke and the rescue
ship was spotted, he headed for the upturned sinking
Collapsible A and transferred everyone across from it to his
vessel. This took some time so his was the last of the lifeboats
to arrive at the Carpathia, a Cunard vessel which had been
heading for Europe.

The survivors in some of the first lifeboats to arrive at the
rescue ship had had to brave climbing a rope ladder dropped
from its gangway doors, many feet above, but now a bosun's
chair had been rigged up. Being a slight woman, Ruby
banged against the ship's side as she was hauled up on the
chair. On one occasion she was spun around in the swing-
like device and could see down to Officer Lowe shipping the
mast and stowing everything neatly in the lifeboat. She was

pleased that Lowe had rescued the people in the sinking collapsible, but she was cold, wet and in mourning, and in no mood to feel thankful. The lowest form of wit rose within her.

That is correct Officer Lowe, must do the right thing; have everything ship shape and Bristol-fashion. Pity you did not do the right thing a few hours ago and save the lives of those people in the water.

On board she was ushered to a dining room, given a hot water bottle and blankets and shown a bunk room where she could remove her saturated clothes and life-jacket. Carpathia passengers passed round pyjamas and other clothing. This was all done in virtual silence save for the odd 'here you are my dear' and other such phrases. Ruby soon went back on deck and asked the first Carpathia seaman she came across what was to happen now. She was informed that apparently they were doing a brief cruise around the area looking for survivors on the ice or clinging to wreckage. There were deckchairs, wood and a large volume of cork from the collapsed bulkheads floating, so they were hopeful of finding some survivors. Ruby had neither the will nor inclination to tell the sailor that they were wasting their time.

As it became more and more evident that the search was indeed hopeless, the sound of the ship began to change. Just as hours before the terrible thrashing in the water had soon become a sepulchral silence, so now the shocked quiet was replaced with the sound of pathetic hopelessness and misery as people started to appreciate that their worst fears were being confirmed. Their family and friends were lost.

Survivors were gathered in the saloon and a roll call taken. It was only then that the full horror hit everyone. It was apparent that there were no more than several hundred people present. There had been well over two thousand souls on board the Titanic. The saloon became a sea of darting eyes, everyone looking around desperate to see a face they knew, or better still a face they loved. Ruby was not surprised to see how many men and how few steerage class women were evident. So much for women and children first, she thought bitterly. It had been ladies, children and gentlemen first. She spent some time pushing through the crowd to look for her father but there was no sign of him. Likewise Nashey had not made it either. But he had been right. Having a lifebelt had meant nothing.

There was a memorial service on the spot where the Titanic had gone down and then the rescue ship left, eager not to distress everyone further. All public rooms and officers' cabins were given to survivors. The Carpathia's third class passengers, men and women, were placed together in one section and their vacant berths given to Titanic's steerage survivors. Makeshift mattresses were put down on the floor of the library and saloons for second and some first class women, children and female crew. The ship's officers vacated their cabins for use by the highest ranking of the Titanic's ladies.

On her way to the library, Ruby saw a cabin with a 'Do Not Knock' sign on it. She suddenly thought of the three people she had helped save from the water and those her lifeboat had later rescued from the collapsible. Some were surely too poorly to have been at the roll call. Could they have been allocated cabins such as this? She had also heard there was another collapsible that had over thirty people swim to it and survive. Some of them must be the worst for wear. There was just a chance that her father could be one of them and was now in a cabin. She spotted a Carpathia officer carrying a clipboard. Perhaps he would know something.

"Oh, no miss. That's Mr Ismay's cabin. He's not to be disturbed. There are a couple of young women with frostbite who have beds in the Smoking Room. It is the men's section actually but there is more space for them there. And there are a few chaps from the collapsible lifeboats with frostbite who have cots in there too. Crewmen and the gentlemen passengers from your ship are on the floor with blankets. What is your father's name? I have a list of survivors here."

Ruby gave him the name and for good measure, her father's job on board. When the shake of the head, kind expression and negative confirmation came, it was no less painful for being expected. Ruby thanked the officer and turned away. She stared with disgust and loathing at the sign on the cabin door for a moment then walked slowly to the library.

The Carpathia had abandoned its journey to Europe and was heading for what had been the Titanic's destination, New York. By the evening a committee had been formed from the first class Titanic passengers on board to raise funds to help destitute steerage travellers reach their onward destinations in America. One of the three committee members, American, Margaret Brown was touring the ship, fund-raising. She spotted Ruby, who was wearing an ensemble loaned to her by a Carpathia first class passenger. She was bedecked in a wide brimmed hat, pleated blouse with stand collar, the sleeves gathered at the elbow, double-breasted waistcoat, sleeveless bolero, pleated skirt and leather boots. Ruby felt a little self-conscious, not just for wearing such finery but because of the admiring looks she was receiving from men and women alike. Mrs Brown made the obvious incorrect assumption and asked for a contribution before Ruby put her right. Apologetic and a little embarrassed, Margaret, who was effusive at the best of times, was keen to engage in a little small talk to extricate herself from the awkward situation.

"Do you know a Miss Norton? A stewardess; she was in my lifeboat. Boy, was she the cat's pyjamas when it came to rowing! She needed to be too, what with near getting swamped by the outflow from the pumps or something and then rowing round those icebergs to get to this ship. You have the same trouble?"

"No I do not know a Miss Norton. It is a big ship…was. Yes we had the same trouble with the outflow but I only had to row to get away from the suction," answered Ruby quietly. "The suction that never was that is", she added resentfully. "Then we had a lot of crewmen transfer to us for rowing and we had an officer in charge of our lifeboat, Officer Lowe, who knew how to use the sail."

"You were on the boat that went back?" asked Mrs Brown quietly, looking suddenly crestfallen.

"Yes," said Ruby, barely getting the one word out before bursting into tears.

She had only been speaking to this stranger for a few seconds, but the emotion river had swelled to the point where it burst its banks. And she couldn't wait for the tears to subside. She had to tell somebody and she had to tell them that second; words, whimpers and tears jumbling the syntax.

"We… could… saved… saved all."

Margaret buried the young woman's face into her

shoulder and heard it all come out. And Ruby was not the only one with tears in her eyes. Two ladies in such torment on board an ocean liner would normally have attracted an officer or two, along with other well-wishers, keen to know what had upset them and offer assistance. But this was the ship of sighs. Tears were commonplace. The two women were left to their grief.

On the now terribly overcrowded ship, it was difficult to find a quiet, private spot but the two women found one in the corner of a nearby lounge. They swopped detailed accounts of their lifeboat journeys. Ruby told the tale of her battle with Lowe. Margaret's foe was very different but her story had certain similarities. The crewman in charge of her lifeboat, a man called Hichens, had been a thorough coward, crazed with fear. Once they were on the ocean he had refused to follow orders from the captain to go alongside the ship and pick up more passengers, and made a series of panic-stricken observations and given ridiculous orders that the women on board ignored. When the ship sank there had been a heated argument between Hitchens and the women about rescuing those in the water. But to what Margaret believed would be her eternal shame, they eventually acceded to his argument that they would be swamped by people in the water, so they did not go back.

The conversation eventually moved on and the two women found themselves discussing their respective lives. Amongst other things Margaret told Ruby that she had helped establish the Colorado chapter of the National American Woman Suffrage Association and been a founder member of the Denver Woman's Club, whose mission was the improvement of women's lives.

"Miss Paul and Miss Burns are causing quite a stir in the fight for the vote for women in my country I can tell you. They're sure ruffling feathers, and all because of what they learnt working in England as Suffragettes for your Mrs Pankhurst! What do you say to that young lady?" asked Margaret, mock accusatory.

"I do not know, I am sure," said Ruby. "I hear Suffragettes are very rough. I should not like to be one. What difference does it make, I ask you, if a woman puts a cross in a box every few years. That won't get the baby washed will it? It is more important for women to have a better life in the home; not have husbands knock them about, and divorce the so-and-sos and get an allowance out of them when they do; get better paid at work and do less hours; get better looked after when they're in the family way; young girls get fed the same and have as much schooling as their brothers."

Ruby paused for breath. Margaret was impressed with both her passion and her lungs.

"Voting will not bring about any of that," concluded Ruby with confidence.

There followed the first of several conversations between the two women over the next few days during which Margaret explained to her new young British friend the error of her thoughts. She also introduced her to a couple of British Suffragettes, Elsie Bowerman, a young woman of a similar age to Ruby, and Edith Clubnall, who was a generation older. These genteel first class Titanic passengers were as far from being 'very rough' as they were unpersuasive about their cause.

Chapter 3

"It was the universal rule in cases of shipwreck that women and children should be saved first. It was merely a matter of rule. There was no special chivalry attached to it."

Sylvia Pankhurst, Women's Social and Political Union

The Statue of Liberty was in view, illuminated for an instant by periodic lightning flashes across the night sky. The suitably sombre weather had thunder barely audible above the sound of heavy horizontal rain driving against the side of the ship. The liner, slowed for the briefest moment to pick up the port doctor off Staten Island quarantine station. It could not afford what would have been an appropriately funereal pace, as several reporters had earlier tried unsuccessfully to clamber aboard with the harbour pilot, on to whose boat they had bribed their way. Undeterred, eager, animated newspapermen in small boats shouted questions up at the ship through megaphones. Magnesium flares and flash-powder supplemented nature's scene-lighting efforts.

The cold, wet public stood silent watching Cunard's Pier 54, thirty thousand of them jammed into the police cordon surrounding 14th to 8th Avenues. A further ten thousand filled the Battery to watch the Carpathia arrive at her berth. Almost the entire New York police force was deployed. Patrolmen, mounted police, detectives and a squad specifically tasked to counter pickpockets and petty thieves. There was a series of ropes dotted with green lanterns, seventy five feet either side of the pier's entrance. Portable wooden slatted fences had been set up to clear spaces at the foot of each gangway to the pier building. Only closest relatives or friends were admitted to the pier, two per survivor. The scene was lit by huge spotlights directed on to the crowd so survivors could identify their people. All customs formalities had been waived; the usual Federal Immigration inspection of steerage passengers likewise. The stage was set.

The Carpathia turned in a great circle towards the New Jersey shore, before the huge crowd gasped as one as the liner steamed silently past its home Cunard pier. It continued on to stop at the piers of the Titanic's owners, the White Star Line, to lower the lost ship's lifeboats, another multi-explosion of photography lighting the scene as it did so. The rescue ship then crept back to the Cunard pier in eerie silence to unload its passengers.

Those in need of medical treatment were promptly stretchered off the ship and were soon in a fleet of ambulances, mostly heading for St Vincent's Hospital in Greenwich Village. Thereafter passengers disembarked in class order. As the first class passengers began to emerge on to the gangways, the awed quiet that had enveloped those on the pier was suddenly replaced by excitement, confusion, pandemonium and crush, as those meeting survivors called out names, waved frantically and pushed forwards. Some missed their relatives in the melee. One man learned all his family had been lost, and became hysterical. Reporters complete with pencil, pad and photographer, mopped up any survivor who wasn't instantly claimed like an anteater in a termite mound.

A telegram received aboard the rescue ship from friends or relatives who intended to meet a survivor was effectively a landing card. Survivors who did not have anyone meeting them were not allowed to disembark unattended. This fraternity of the friendless tended to be third class passengers and crew. By the time these emerged, the press had disappeared and the crowd on the pier was sparse. A few relatives of higher class passengers remained, anticipation having turned to sorrow, hopelessness and despair.

Representatives of the White Star Line, and various charities provided temporary assistance to the survivors who needed it. Ruby was put in an automobile, and shared her first motor car ride with a couple of other female crew members she didn't know, and the Deaconess of the Mothers of St Barnabas. This mission had kindly offered its services to the White Star Line as an unpaid hostel for female crew, and it was here that Ruby and her colleagues in the car were to be accommodated, fed and watered whilst they remained in New York.

Margaret Brown was spending a night in a New York hotel prior to getting a train home to Denver. She had offered to pay for her new young British friend to stay there too, but Ruby had declined, not only because she felt awkward about accepting such an expensive offer, but there were the logistics of getting back to England to consider. Ruby was no longer in employment. The White Star Line and their sub-contractors, through whom some restaurant crew including Ruby were employed, had stopped all pay to crew from the moment the Titanic had disappeared beneath the waves. Ruby's efforts spent rowing passengers in a lifeboat, had thus been done on her own time. But the liner company accepted a certain responsibility to their ex-crew. Before Ruby and her fellow work colleagues left the Carpathia they had been informed by telegram that free transportation home was being arranged. They would receive further details in due course at their respective designated New York lodgings.

The ex-crew were paid some expenses and had complimentary sightseeing laid on. They had also been offered work. The Imperial Theatre was to employ survivors to go on stage and recount their experiences to an audience. And there was a new Woolworth store opening, which had invited Titanic crew to work behind the counters for a day, and whatever money they took from sales, was theirs to keep. Ruby had also been badgered by souvenir hunters for her uniform and any other Titanic memorabilia she might possess.

It took a grief-stricken, traumatised mind some effort to take all this in. Sightseeing as if one was on holiday; being on display like an animal in the zoo; begging or selling your clothes. Which was the most appalling? She initially thought that surely the theatre would be the worst, recounting the horror; of those terrible sounds of thousands thrashing in the water; the even worse silence that soon followed; the stiff upper lips held out of the water care of lifebelts on stiff upper bodies. But there were people to whom she would like to talk about it. A couple were dead; another, her mother, was thousands of miles away. None were there. Perhaps shouting to strangers from a stage would be no worse than keeping it to herself. She certainly wanted to shout. She wanted to scream.

As for Woolworth's, she had an image of her cashier's ledger, credit side money paid in; debit side self-respect paid out. It would leave an overdraft she was not prepared to accrue. But far worse were the offered excursions to a Kodak Eastman factory, an oyster farm and an apparently famous bridge. But the worst offer of all was of a sightseeing trip back to that statue in New York harbour. Liberty, Equality, Fraternity. None of them existed in her life.

Chapter 4

"In London it was very necessary to keep one's hand on the whitewash brush."
Second Officer Charles Lightoller, RMS Titanic

Nash had refused what he considered would have been the indignity of being hauled up to the Carpathia on a child's swing. He heaved himself up the ladder despite his freezing cold hands having difficulty gripping it. His great upper body strength provided most of the power, taking the strain off his numb legs. But this act of pride soon brought the requisite fall. He had to spend his days on the rescue ship, along with the other frostbitten people on board, confined to bed for the duration of the trip. When the liner had docked in New York he had been one of the first of the hospital-bound to be taken off the ship.

He now lay prostrate in bed when four men walked into his ward in St Vincent's Hospital. They approached Nash but no sooner had they tried to speak to him, than a nurse appeared and started to usher them away.

"This patient has had to be sedated. You will have to come back in a couple of days if you wish to speak to him. Are you family; friends?"

"No nurse, we're…"

One of them speedily offered White Star Line

identification and just as readily flashed an accompanying broad smile. He was a young man, as were the other three, all neatly suited and brogued, carrying Derby hats in their hands. All four were smiling now.

"I see," said the nurse craning her neck briefly to see if anyone else was within earshot before continuing. "It's not for me to say of course, but to be candid I would not recommend you speak to this gentleman unless it is absolutely necessary."

The word 'gentleman' had been uttered with such sarcastic haughtiness accompanied by a glare at the seemingly unconscious figure that it was clear she thought her patient was anything but. The apparent leader of the quartet, clearly thinking himself something of a ladies' man, gave the young woman a well-rehearsed, oft used wink.

"This wise guy given you something of a what-to-do has he nurse? Not surprising you knocked him out. Well he shouldn't talk to a lady like that. We do have to return to speak to him I'm afraid, so we'll be sure and tell him off, nurse er?"

"Nurse Palmer. Oh, there's no need for that," said the woman in uniform, returning the smile.

"Very well Nurse Palmer. You're the boss."

He touched his temple with index finger and thumb together in a mock tug of the forelock accompanied by a cheeky smile. He looked around casually and appeared to spot the woman in the next bed for the first time.

"Mixed ward huh?" he commented.

"It was decided to have the Titanic patients in the same wards," confirmed the nurse. "Same problems, same treatment, and togetherness, they may appreciate it. It's all third class passengers in this ward."

"Sure makes it easy for us Nurse Palmer. We have to speak to all the steerage passengers. Is it alright if we speak to this young lady? Save us having a wasted journey."

The nurse's smile faded and she suddenly looked slightly uncomfortable. She started to speak hesitantly.

"Well…"

But before she had a chance to continue, the smooth operator quickly cut in.

"Might be a right fine and dandy idea to speak to her while this gentleman here isn't compos mentis. Heh listen to me! Have I said that right Nurse Palmer? But seriously, sounds like he could be unpleasant. Sure wouldn't be nice for the poor little lady to listen to him when she's unwell. Better if we spoke to her today, and perhaps she could then be moved away from this man before we return?"

"Well, I would have to speak to others about moving beds, but I sure think it would be preferable for you to speak to the young lady today. Go ahead. It should only be one around the bed at a time you understand but I guess if it's White Star business I can make an exception for you boys. I'll make myself scarce. But please call me immediately if she attempts to move. It's real important she stays completely still."

"Of course Nurse Palmer; and we'll only take a few moments, I promise."

More smiles were exchanged by all concerned as the young nurse disappeared, leaving the four White Star Line employees to crowd around the bed. The lothario sat on the only chair thumbing through several sheets of paper looking for the one with a name on it which matched that on the clipboard hanging from the foot of the bed. His colleagues bent over the bed and hovered.

The young woman was well sedated to stop the suffering from second degree frostbite in one of her feet. She was semi-conscious, her brain almost as numb as her toes. She had spent a night sitting with water swilling around her already freezing feet thanks to her lifeboat being drenched by the Titanic's outflow. This had been followed by days and nights aboard the cramped rescue ship with little but pain-killers administered by the rescue ship's doctor to help her. This had left one of her feet with hard waxy skin and purplish blood-filled blisters which were turning black. And the nerve damage suffered had resulted in a loss of feeling.

Her semi-conscious mind managed only the vaguest of thoughts and made out words rather than full sentences.

Man from Titanic… Give me money… Told Mrs Brown need money… Chicago…Man must have ticket.

The man sitting on the chair put a pen in her hand and asked her to sign something. He guided her hand.

…Must be receipt…

And then they were gone.

★★★★★★

The following morning the drugs had worn off and Nash was now fully conscious. He had never been at his best in the mornings so had been content to lie quietly and look about him for a while. But with full consciousness now came the pain, numbness and itching of frostbite.

Nurse Palmer was back on duty. The hospital as a whole, and her ward in particular, was much busier than usual due to the disaster. She had only had a twelve hour break between shifts and was not in the best of moods. She glared at Nash as she passed him to tend to his next bed neighbour.

"'ere nurse, any grub goin'?" asked Nash in his usual abrupt manner.

"Nurse Palmer. That is my name if you wish to address me. I am a nurse. I am not a member of the catering department. I would have thought your breakfast should be a bar of soap. You could sure wash your mouth out with it."

Nash was amused. Women telling him in no uncertain terms what they thought of him, something that no man who knew him would ever dare do, always tickled his funny bone.

"'ere, what's a matter duck?"

"You had to be restrained by five medical staff last night, before being sedated for your own and everyone else's safety. And then once under the influence of the medication, used the utmost foul language I ever did hear."

"Five little lads in white coats? That all? Blimey I must be gettin' old!" chirped a smiling Nash.

But Nash obviously did not have the same charm as the young White Star Line man as far as Nurse Palmer was concerned.

"Sir, it is nothing to be proud of I can assure you. You should be ashamed of yourself."

Nash misunderstood how an American might use the word 'sir' in an aggressive, ironic manner.

"Don't call me sir gell. Cur more like," he said with a self-deprecating smile which was met with the stoniest of faces.

He realised he needed to continue.

"Well, where I come from we got some'ing called the work'ouse. I ain' scared of nuffin' or nobody but I am scared of the 'ouse. Me ol' man and ol' gell died in one, see. And 'ospitals an' work'ouses ain' much different in my eyes. And yer can't 'old what I said when I was orf me 'ead with drugs against me, can yer? Come on gell, giss a smile."

And with that Nash started to tug at his numerous tightly fitted blankets with a view to getting out of bed. He had always had a high pain threshold, and as far as he was concerned chilblains were not going to stop him escaping from this place as soon as he could.

"Will you keep still Mr Nash!"

"Everyone calls me Nashey."

"You must remain in bed and be kept as warm as possible until Dr Grist has finished observing you."

"No, it's not for me, gell. I 'ave to get out of 'ere," said Nash as he swung his feet, which had been tightly wrapped to protect his frostbitten areas, on to the floor.

"Please Mr Nash, excessive movement can cause ice crystals to do further damage", said the nurse as she placed her hands firmly on his shoulders to stop his movement any further.

"Leave orf, I've 'ad chilblains before gell."

"You do not have chilblains Mr Nash, you have frostbite and we need to ascertain whether you have first, second or third degree frostbite."

"That's as maybe, but I'm orf oud of it."

Nash pushed upwards, easily resisting the nurse's attempt to restrain him, and tried a couple of steps. They were very painful, not that he allowed the pain to enter his face. He appreciated that he may need more time in this hospital after all.

"Any more of this nonsense and you won't be off

anywhere," scolded the nurse. "If it is third degree frostbite you could lose toes."

Nurse Palmer instantly realised that her bad temper had caused her to say too much. It was not in the patient's interest at this stage for him to know how serious his condition may be. She looked around, concerned a more senior member of medical staff may have heard her. But thankfully she was the only staff member in that section of the ward at that moment.

"Me toes might drop orf yer says. Well, lucky that water never reached 'igher up, eh nurse? Gawd only knows what might drop orf."

Nash accompanied the remark with a cheeky Cockney double entendre wink. As a fan of burlesque, the young nurse enjoyed saucy humour rather more than her patients would realise from her prim young nurse act. But she feigned indignation with a rise of the eyebrows and click of the tongue.

"Really Mr Nash this simply will not do. Dr Grist needs to decide whether or not you need splints. But we need to continue the rewarming and thawing process first. I need to immerse you in a hot bath."

No sooner had the words left her mouth and she realised that her demand had left her wide-open to an even more cheeky remark, so she quickly spoke again, holding up a hand as if she were a policeman directing traffic.

"Please, Mr Nash, do not try to break the ice with me."

He would normally have let it pass but it was perfect. This was just what he could use. If he had to stay in this hospital for a while, he needed this nurse on his side. She could be useful. He lowered his eyes.

"I broke enough ice a few nights gone to last a lifetime nurse," he said staring at the floor apparently bereft.

Nurse Palmer's jaw dropped.

"Mr Nash, I am so…"

He didn't let her go any further.

"No 'arm done, gell. And me friends call me Nashey. Wot yours call you?"

"Er," she hesitated.

She would not normally tell a patient her first name but her gaffe caused a lowering of the shields.

"Jennifer."

He gave her a grim smile and short nod. She nodded back with a sad smile, and they shared a moment. The silence was broken by a noise from the next bed. Nash's next-bed neighbour was awake. Nash got back into bed, trying but failing to disguise a hobble as a walk. Nurse Palmer headed for patient Annie Kelly.

Annie had been awoken, partly by pain because the drugs that had made her so woozy the night before were starting to wear off, and partly by something irritating her upper leg. Though in pain, she was at least now much clearer in the head, and the itchiness of her frostbite made her extra sensitive below the waist. She had moved her hand to the irritation. Something had been pinned to the top of her underwear. She unclasped it and brought it out from beneath the sheets and blankets. $25 – a twenty and a five note, and a piece of paper had been attached. Mystified, she handed it to her nurse.

"It's twenty five dollars. How on this God's earth did this get here?" said the nurse frowning, before turning her attention to the piece of paper. "Oh, this appears to be some sort of legal document, you better read this yourself."

The nurse motioned to hand back the note.

"Can't read" said Annie in a soft friendly Irish brogue. "You read it for me."

"Perhaps you should wait for a relative or friend?"

"There's no one coming to be sure. I'm on my own. It's probably just a voucher for my train to Chicago. Go on."

"Very well."

Nurse Palmer read it to herself silently to begin with. Annie could tell from the nurse's puzzled expression that it was not a simple train voucher.

"It's not something I can read out as a letter. It's a document; a form. Something you have signed. It states that you exonerate…"

"What's that yer say?" interjected Annie. "Exonerate? What's that mean?"

"I don't know. Shall I continue?"

Annie spotted Nash looking her way.

"And who might you be?" she asked, but before he had a chance to answer she continued. "Know what exonerate means do yer?"

Nash was surprised by his own knowledge. He did know. He racked his brains to remember how he knew. Something a magistrate had said to him once when he had been found not guilty. He remembered asking a clerk of the court afterwards what it meant. Annie mistook Nash's frowning expression and turned back to the nurse.

"He doesn't know. Go on with it."

"'ere not so fast Irish; I knows alright. It means let orf. If you exonerate some cove you've let 'em orf what they've been up to; forgiven 'em so to speak."

Annie turned to her nurse, who was looking down at the document with glassy eyes.

"That makes sense," said Nurse Palmer quietly, sadly. "You have signed to say that you exonerate the White Star Line from all blame for the Titanic sinking, and that you accept $25 as payment in full for any inconvenience caused and for any out of pocket expenses. Then it says 'without' and then I don't understand the next word."

"Giss a butchers', Jenny," said Nash, motioning with a hand.

Neither of the women had any idea what the man actually meant, but it was fairly obvious. The nurse looked at Annie for affirmation, who nodded. The note was taken over to his bed.

"It says 'without prejudice'. Gawd knows what that means. Then there's a cross signed above the name Annie Kelly, that's you I'm surmising Irish, and four uvver names signed under it. One by a fella called Michael Littlejohn representative of White Star Line, and the others by witnesses one, two and free and their names."

Nash looked at his nurse.

"I 'eard some fellas in 'ere last night Jen; wanted to speak to me, did they?"

"Yes. I thought you were unconscious!" answered Nurse Palmer, incredulity and irritation seeping into her voice.

"I 'ad bin right enough but the noise when they came in must 'ave woke me up and got me earwiggin'."

There was a short silence as Nash mulled things over while his nurse wondered if the next time he referred to her it would simply be as J. Nash then continued, his words now coming out slower, his voice taking on a deeper, more solemn tone.

"Four of 'em weren't there? From the White Star Line mob I'll wager? Speak to Irish did they?"

The nurse stared at the floor as she gave a barely perceptible nod, an efficient replacement for thrice yes.

"Comin' back to see me are they?"

"Yes, but not till tomorrow evening. I told the gentlemen that you needed forty eight hours complete bed-rest before they could see you. I made that real clear."

Nash nodded gravely, and then after a moment's quiet contemplation his expression brightened and his voice changed to a lighter tone.

"Well, that gives us a chance to ast 'em what without prejudice means I reckon. And it looks like I'll be gettin' meself twenty five dollar. That's twenty five dollar more than I fought I'd get out of 'em if the troof be told. That's five pound in real money. An' I'll get more as I'm a man, I shouldn't wonder."

Annie looked at Nash with disgust.

"Why should a man get any more than a woman? I paid the same fare as you, you bastard. Five pounds for nearly dying, being crippled with frostbite and watching thousands die. It ain't right I tell yer. And they won't pay you what's right, neither. You English just take it up the arse from your man every time, so you do!"

The word 'English' had been spat out with venomous emphasis. Nash did not respond. He just shrugged and looked at his bemused nurse. She barely knew him of course but she was convinced there was something about Nash's behaviour that was not quite right. When he had asked her those questions in quick succession about the men from White Star, there had been an ominous tone in his voice and expression on his face that had made her blood run cold, which did not accord with this sudden indifference. She looked back into his eyes, searching for a clue but he looked slightly away and took up the cudgels again.

"I'll 'ave that bath now gell an' anyfin' else you and the sawbones wants to do for me. But no more drugs, mind. I needs me 'ead on proper when them White Star boys come knockin'."

Nurse Palmer returned to her prim and proper act.

"Treatment of patients is determined by the medical staff Mr Nash, not the patients. You will be given whatever your doctor deems appropriate for you."

She awaited a response, but got nothing but another shrug. This man Nash was a strange one all right.

Chapter 5

"Aboard the Titanic we saw what men can be at the highest; at Westminster we see what they can be at their lowest and most greedy."

Votes for Women newspaper

Shortly after the morning's turmoil, Nurse Palmer had spoken to Dr Grist. She had explained that patient Kelly was very upset about the way she had been treated by the White Star Line, and that given they were returning tomorrow to speak to patient Nash on a similar matter, it may be advisable to move her to another ward, at least temporarily. The doctor had huffed and puffed, and torn Nurse Palmer off a strip for allowing the men to see the patient in the first place. But having been one of the medical staff who had subdued patient Nash the night before, he agreed that the less unpleasantness when that man was conscious the better for all concerned.

When Nash had been admitted, the doctor, furious with his patient for the trouble he had caused, had warned him mid-scuffle that if it were third degree frostbite it may take months to assess the extent of the damage to his feet. But over the past couple of days, Grist had developed a grudging respect for this tough man who had refused to have any medication administered yet stayed cheerful and never complained or showed any signs of the discomfort he must have been feeling. And on the last of his visits, the physician had expressed how pleased he was with his patient's progress. He had never seen such a speedy response to treatment, and it was clear that his patient had no worse than second degree frostbite so expected him to heal within a month.

Nash would normally have responded by saying something along the lines of 'they make us tough down the East End' but on this occasion he took the opportunity to tell the doctor, in front of his nurse that it was the first class nursing he had received that had been behind the transformation. Miss Palmer had looked suitably embarrassed and continued to play the part of nurse prim and proper to the end of her twelve hour shift.

Nash had conceded to himself that all the medical treatment he had received had made a big difference. The very hot baths had worked wonders. And being kept warm for two days with his frostbitten feet wrapped tight, and his obedience to strict orders not to move any more than was absolutely necessary, had really done the trick. He had decided that he would like another twenty four hours of this treatment before he met the men from the White Star Line, and had asked the doctor if this would be possible. Dr Grist had expected this patient, who had caused such a fuss when admitted, to start demanding to know when he could be released from the hospital, so had been surprised by the request. But he was only too pleased to acquiesce and arranged for the White Star Line to be contacted to rearrange their visit.

Twenty four hours later and Nash had only moved twice to any degree in three days, both times just as Nurse Palmer was going off shift, passing on Dr Grist's instructions to her replacement in the nurses' office. The office was just out of sight from Nash's section of the ward. Nash had taken the opportunity to get out of bed, quickly reconnoitre the temporarily unattended area and it surrounds, and on the first sortie stop for a short chat with another patient to glean information about where patients' clothing was kept. He had been spotted by the new woman on duty, Nurse Wadey, as she arrived from the office, and duly admonished. On the second trip he tracked down a clothing cupboard and purloined a pair of trousers and a shirt that looked like they would more or less fit him. He managed to return without being seen, hiding his contraband between his sheets, stuffing them down the far edge of the bed, out of sight from the nurse. These trips had also enabled him to get some circulation into his legs. With this came itchy pain, but it was a necessary evil.

The three days since they had swarmed over their previous victim were almost at an end and Nash guessed that the White Star men would turn up on the dot, as they duly did. The front-man smiled and asked after him. Nash went into salt-of-the-earth Cockney Sparrow mode; thankful to everyone and everything, to the hospital, to God, lady luck and most of all the White Star Line. Where would he be but for them? He made a point of asking the name of the young man who was showing so much interest in him. It was Michael Littlejohn. The niceties completed, Littlejohn got down to business. Nash nodded in all the right places. He had been right about being offered more money than Annie, but he doubted it was purely because he was a man as he had told her. It was because he was not semi-conscious as she had been. Littlejohn looked intently into the right breast pocket of his smart suit, and wiggled fingers within the pocket for a few seconds before carefully pulling out an envelope. Fifty dollars was the going rate, it would seem, for a thankful conscious man. A pen and document were produced. It was at this point the kindly Cockney looked embarrassed. He was in sudden urgent need of the lavatory. It was the first time in his life Nash had passed the word 'lavatory' into his vocabulary.

Nurse Wadey, proffered the inner-bed facilities that he had been using throughout his stay to date, but the patient was adamant he had to use the toilet on this occasion. The nurse showed her disapproval, advising that unnecessary movement could be detrimental to recovery. But she had been warned of this patient's previous behaviour and at the very least cantankerousness appeared to have set in so she grudgingly allowed him to do as he wished. Nash groaned and moaned as he got slowly out the bed, before picking up what appeared to be his toiletries bag from inside the sheets. The nurse went to his assistance but he waved her away telling her he didn't want any slip of a girl taking him.

"'ere, boys, give us 'and would ya?"

One of Littlejohn's partners in crime took an elbow and started guiding him.

"Nah, you won't do, yer too small lad, yer makin' me bend over too much. Mickey, you're the tallest, come an' give us 'and."

Michael Littlejohn hated being called 'Mickey', and he was actually only the second tallest of the four men, but he smiled condescendingly and did what was asked of him. The toilets were down a long corridor, well out of sight and sound from the ward. The two men entered the communal, wash-basin section of the toilets. Littlejohn released Nash from the hold of his arm.

"There you are Mist…"

At this point Littlejohn's breath left his body as Nash's left fist made contact with the White Star man's solar plexus at great velocity. Nash had waited for the door to the toilet area to swing shut, then pivoted, crouched slightly and let go a haymaker. Littlejohn, gasping in silence as if he were trying to breath in a vacuum, went down like a sack of potatoes, wondering if he would ever inhale again. Nash had a delicate balancing operation to mount. He needed to render the man near senseless so his prey was unable to call for help, but at the same time he didn't want Littlejohn losing consciousness. He wanted him to hear every word of what he was about to say. Consequently Nash hit his victim just once more, bending down to deliver a vicious right cross that spread the man's nose across his face with a splash of red.

Nash kicked his bag under a cubicle door, grabbed the man by a lapel, pulled him across the floor into the same cubicle and locked the door behind them. Nash sat on the toilet seat, bent down and peeled away a suit lapel to gain access to the man's inside breast pocket. He grabbed the contents and removed them. Nash now held several envelopes in his left hand. He licked his right index finger and pawed through them. Each one had an amount written on it – $25, $50, $75, $100, $150, $200. He tipped out the contents of the $200 envelope. Ten crisp $20 notes fell onto the barely conscious man crumpled at his feet. Nash grabbed the money, rolled up the other envelopes, put his hand down his underpants and stuffed the lot under his scrotum. He then opened his bag, which contained the clothing he had stolen earlier and quickly donned them, trampling on Littlejohn as he got to his feet to pull on the trousers. Nash grabbed his victim by the hair and pulled his face up to check he was still conscious. He saw that he was and nodded grimly with satisfaction, before grabbing the man around the throat with both hands to get better purchase so he could hold the man up in the confined space while he looked into his eyes as he spoke to him.

"Know 'ow much it were to buy the cheapest ticket on that boat a yours do yer? More than twenty five dollar I can tell yer. More than you paid that lit'le gell frew there. So she paid *you* for the pleasure of seeing fousands die and gettin' crippled. Fink your chiefs wouldn't do the same to your own muvver if it suited 'em do yer? I were drugged up when you came before but I do remember you smilin' at the poor little cow as yer robbed 'er. Even I wouldn't do that to no cove and I'm a *real* bastard."

Nash fought a near overwhelming urge to sign off his little speech with a vicious blow to the main's nether regions. But this was not his retribution; it was that of the young Irish woman.

"I ain' robbin' yer, understand. I'm takin' this 'ere money for that little gell. It's 'ers by rights ain' it?"

Littlejohn stared and gurgled at his attacker.

"Ain't it!?"

Added menace had been added to the question, and Littlejohn had enough of his senses left to know to nod his agreement. Satisfied, Nash then stuffed his victim onto the toilet seat and wedged him roughly against the side of the cubicle so there was room to open the cubicle door and leave.

Once out into the communal area, Nash looked in a mirror and saw flecks of the man's blood on his face. There was a washbasin in front of him but he chose to spit on his fingers, rubbed the red off his chin whiskers and wiped the remains down his new trousers.

During the afternoon he had ascertained from Nurse Palmer to which ward Annie had been moved. Fortunately he was able to make a beeline towards it without passing by his old ward complete with a nurse and three men who were starting to wonder to where their respective people had disappeared.

The adrenalin was coursing round Nash's body, assisting his feet to remind him that at the moment he really should not be spending his time attacking people in toilets, or anywhere else for that matter. He shuffled into Annie's ward and asked the nurse on duty if she could point him in the right direction for the young Irish woman's bed. The nurse took one look at the hobbling, clothed patient in front of her and took a big breath as her eyes widened. Nash knew he was about to be told, like a naughty little boy caught in mid-mischief by teacher, the error of his ways, but he did not have time to bandy words with a chiding nurse. He cut her off before she got out her first 'Mr Nash!' using a serious but unthreatening tone.

"Jus' tell me where that Irish girl is nurse and let that be an end of it. I ain' gonna 'urt 'er. I jus' got some dollar notes 'ere for 'er thas all."

The nurse felt a little intimidated but she would have stuck to her guns and refused to tell this man where her patient was, even if the young woman had still been in the hospital. So it was with not a little relief that the nurse was able to tell him honestly that she was not.

"That young lady has discharged herself," she said, shaking her head disapprovingly. "Real stupid if you ask me. She has a condition which needs further rest and recuperation but she was distraught and there was nothing we could do. This was some hours ago. She was getting a train. To Washington she said. I guess she'll have left the city by now. I can show you my log if you don't believe me."

"You're a gell ain' yer," said an impressed Nash. "Washington indeed. Chicago. It were Chicago. But I believe yer about the rest of it. Any'ow I've missed 'er and that's that. Well, I'm orf oud of it now meself, an' I don't want no arguments neiver."

Nash held an index finger to his lips. He would have turned on his heel but his feet were far too painful. He padded slowly around and made for the exit. The hospital corridors and signage were confusing but he eventually found his way out on to the streets of New York City.

The disaster had knocked the desire for pastures new out of him. He would buy himself a passage back to England on the first available liner out of New York. He had no idea where he could make enquiries about getting a ship home and although he might be able to get the information from stopping people on the street, there was also the problem of getting to wherever it was. He had heard New York was as big as London. It might be miles away, like getting from Whitechapel to Waterloo. A motor bus passed by, its destination Seventh Avenue and West Twelfth Street. What did that mean? Where were the place names? He wondered if New York had trams or tube trains. Trams would no doubt have the same confusing destination boards and even if there was a tube he had not used the London Underground for over twenty years, and it had been more luck than judgement that he had not got lost then. What chance did he have in New York? There was nothing for it, he would have to get a taxi cab and the cabbie would at least know exactly where to drop him. Of course the sharp eared cabbie would note his accent and his ignorance of New York so will 'see him coming'. No doubt the cabbie will give him a nice expensive little tour of the city but so be it. Thanks to Mr Littlejohn he could afford it, and it would be his once in a lifetime chance to be a foreign tourist.

He looked down at his bandaged feet. They needed support and protection. And if New York cabbies were anything like their London counterparts, they would not stop for a man who could not even afford a pair of boots. He had only ever bought his boots second-hand in Petticoat Lane market, but there was nothing for it, he would have to make his first ever foray into a shoe shop. A newsboy was asked where the nearest such establishment was located, and a couple of minutes later a shop assistant was looking askance at the bandage-footed man who had just walked into her world.

Nash had expected this, and was already holding a large denomination bill in his hand. He waved it and the shop assistant's face, ignorant of from where Nash had just extracted the money, transformed into a toothy smile. She asked if 'sir' would like some socks too. She could send a boy to pick some up for him. It was a very different 'sir' to the one he had received from Nurse Palmer. He replied that he had never worn socks in his life. The shocked young woman checked with her manager. The man did have money to spend, and his bandages were incredibly clean. Smiley service was resumed.

Trying on brand new stiff boots for the first time in his life would have been uncomfortable enough under normal circumstances, but his painful feet were making the whole thing quite an operation. The shop assistant had noticed how her strange new customer with the barely understandable, Australian perhaps, accent, was wincing through clenched teeth each time he tried on a different pair. Nash noticed her bemusement and told her matter-of-factly that he had been on the Titanic, and as a result had a bit of frostbite in his feet. Thirty seconds later, the assistant had been replaced at his feet by the shop manager, and every assistant and customer in the shop, of which there were several of each, had stopped what they had been doing and gathered round to ask questions. Nash was not easily shocked by anything, but his new found celebrity status astounded him. He quickly realised he had some power so used it by answering each question politely, immediately following his answer with a query of his own.

He had gone down with the ship when an explosion had blown him close to a collapsible lifeboat which he had got on. Where could he buy a ticket on an ocean liner? No he never saw Captain Smith in the water. Is there a shipping office nearby? No he didn't have any souvenirs from the Titanic. Given that he didn't know New York would it be best to get a taxi cab to the shipping office? Ten minutes later he had gleaned as much information about New York as he thought he would ever need, and had made a mental note that Titanic souvenirs were very highly sought after. No doubt he could avail himself of some bits and pieces from New York's equivalent of Petticoat Lane and pass them off as Titanic souvenirs for a nice profit. He had also been offered a ride in a motor car to the shipping office if he didn't mind answering a few more questions about the disaster en-route. But now that he knew where he could buy a ticket home and it wasn't too far away, he politely declined the offer.

He extricated himself from his fan club having settled for some soft-leather shoes, which were far more bearable than what would have been his preferred hard boots. His new purchase, discounted to a Titanic survivor, reminded him of the little shoes he used to wear back in the 1880's, to move silently over the cobbled streets of Whitechapel in order to glide up on unsuspecting gentlemen to relieve them of their valuables. When the crowd had asked him what part of Australia he hailed from, he had told them he was English, a London Cockney no less, but stopped short of mentioning Whitechapel. There was only one thing Whitechapel was internationally known for, and he was not prepared to talk about that.

Within seconds of leaving the shop Nash appreciated that even if he kept his feet bandaged, the shoes were going to chafe painfully for a while at least. He thus decided to keep the bag which contained his shoe box and some free shoe-polish compliments of the shop manager, in case he decided to return the shoes to their box and go barefoot.

En-route to the shipping office Nash concluded that he had tried but failed to help the young Irish woman and had to accept that he would go down in her history as that English so-and-so who seemed to think it was the nature of things for men to be treated better than women.

He shrugged and a rueful smile came across his face as he remembered his tough old matriarch of a mother when he was a boy. She had ensured that any ideas of male superiority he might otherwise have entertained had been knocked out of him at a very early age.

His thoughts turned to another feisty woman; the one he had thrown off the Titanic into a lifeboat, who had made a far bigger impression on him than Annie. Before he left New York he would endeavour to track down Ruby. She had not answered his question to her about how much she was paid, but as a woman crew member he guessed that it would have been a pittance. And judging by how the White Star Line was now treating its passengers, he could not imagine their crew getting a penny out of them. Ruby had also no doubt lost what little she had when the ship went down, so would be in need of money. After he had bought his ticket home, he would keep two thirds of the remaining balance of the money he acquired from Littlejohn for himself, and give the rest to Ruby. It would keep the wolf from her door for a while at least.

Chapter 6

"The new woman would rather be without exceptional treatment."

Mrs Mildred Mansel, Women's Social & Political Union

The communiques issued by the White Star Line had made no mention of what had happened to any of the bodies of the dead, how someone could retrieve them or if repatriation expenses would be paid by the Titanic's owners.

Ruby therefore found herself jostling in a crowd of people besieging the White Star Line's New York office who wanted these and countless other questions answered. When she had finally queued her way to the front of the crowd at the entrance of the building, one of the policemen on guard asked her for identification. All she had was what she had left the Titanic with, namely nothing except the cashier's uniform she was wearing. It was a full length dress in a sailor-boy style, white with blue trim cuffs, collars, hem and waistband, large lapels and a blue and white hoop-striped blouse. The gathered-in waist showed off her figure, and Ruby had thought it not only striking but rather fetching on board ship. But now she felt it made her stand out like a sore thumb on the sober streets of New York, and looked frankly rather silly. So it was with a little embarrassment that Ruby held out her arms a little to accompany her telling the policeman that her uniform was the only identification she had. But at least it had the desired effect.

"Gee, you'll get a few bucks for that ma'am. Everyone wants a souvenir from the Titanic," said the cheerful officer before he remembered the reason he was there. "What is your business here today?"

She fought the impulse to tell him that she was looking for a souvenir of the Titanic herself, namely her dead father's body.

"I wish to find out about the work being offered here in New York to Titanic crew members," she said politely.

This was partly true in as much as she thought she may as well find out more details of the work on offer while she was enquiring about her father. The policeman nodded and ushered her in. She soon received information about the jobs available at Woolworth's and the Imperial Theatre, before spending an hour watching lots of the suited and booted running about like headless chickens. Somewhere between a pillar and a post she eventually ascertained that ships chartered at great expense by the White Star Line had left Halifax, a town in Nova Scotia, Canada, to search for and pick up bodies and return them to Halifax. The office did not have any information about what would happen to the bodies on arrival, how one could claim them or what the repatriation or funeral arrangements were. And no, crew would not receive expenses for trips to Halifax because they needed to be on hand in New York in case they were required to give testimony to the Committee of Inquiry. But once any crew member was surplus to requirements they would be put on the next available ship back to England.

The meagre pocket-money received from the White Star Line left Ruby unable to afford bus fares so she did her second long walk of the day, this time to Grand Central Station to enquire about the cost, timings and frequency of trains to Halifax. The male ticket clerk informed her that she had come to the wrong station, but her bedraggled good looks were enough to have him telephone Penn Station on her behalf to find that not surprisingly there had been a clamour for seats to Halifax so consequently there was no availability for the next day. But that was not of any immediate concern to Ruby as it would in any case take her several days to earn the cost of a ticket.

A third long walk and she was presenting herself to the Imperial Theatre. As with the policeman earlier, her salt-stained, colour-run, wrinkled Titanic uniform which had shrunk so it clung to her in a most uncomfortable and unflattering manner was effectively her passport to acceptance. And yes, Ruby confirmed, she could start immediately.

An hour later, having been on her feet all day, she was making her debut under footlights. There had been none of the usual stage make-up applied. The management wanted their new recruits looking suitably dishevelled, and Ruby's pathetic appearance was just great as it was. She and her fellow crew members each in turn introduced themselves. Name, job, briefly what the job involved if it was not obvious, location on the ship, number of their lifeboat. The audience were then invited to shout out general questions which any of those on the stage might answer. The crew members were made up essentially of three types. Firstly the shy, who would not have spoken up even if they had not just seen and heard fifteen hundred people die in front of them; secondly the desolate and humiliated such as Ruby, who were wondering if life could get any worse than this; and thirdly the stage-struck who appeared to be actually enjoying their new found spot in the limelight.

Crew from this final section were more than happy to answer the questions thrown at them, most of which involved the size of the iceberg; how the ship actually went down; was it true that the band played hymns to the end and if so what was the last hymn played?; and had they seen Capt. Smith go down with his ship? Such were the exaggerations and inaccuracies in the answers given by overexcited young crew members keen to entertain their audience that Ruby almost started to wonder if she had been on the same ship. She had heard only waltzes played by the orchestra and the hymn 'Nearer My God to Thee' would never have been played to people who were becoming increasingly aware that they were indeed about to meet their maker. But who would ever query the answers. All but a few who were still on the ship when it went down were dead.

The audience were then asked to hold up their hands if they wanted to ask a specific crew member a question, and the master of ceremonies then did the necessary. As a hitherto near-silent member of the cast, nobody was interested in asking Ruby a question, though someone who had also been in her lifeboat mentioned it had been the last one launched. Eventually, a young man with a good short-term memory and an eye for the ladies cheekily asked Ruby how a pretty young thing like her had come to be in the last lifeboat launched. Ruby felt too demeaned and too tired to reply with anything other than a desultory, accurate course of events.

She gave the audience a truncated version of how she had ended up trapped in the bowels of the ship with water above her, and how when she was refusing to get in the lifeboat, a man had picked her up and thrown her in. And it turned out to be the one lifeboat that went back to try to save people.

She was the star of the show after that but fortunately the time restraints of the theatre meant she was soon free, along with the rest of the cast, to scrabble on the floor for the coins that had been tossed on stage by the audience in appreciation at the end of the performance. One of the crew was struck in the face by an over zealously thrown nickel but Ruby didn't notice. She was on her hands and knees with everyone else grabbing her fair share of the tips. She could not feel any more humiliated so just needed to get on with supplementing her stage appearance fee, and put it towards the cost of her rail ticket out of there.

Ruby arrived back at her lodgings so tired that she feared she would sleep too late the following morning. She needed to arrive at Woolworth's early to ensure she would secure what would surely be a sought after job, so rather than go to bed she sat on a hard wooden chair and closed her eyes. No matter how tired, she knew she would only sleep fitfully if sitting up and uncomfortable. It had the desired effect. She dozed in and out of a shallow sleep through the night, nodding and almost falling to the floor on one occasion, and left at dawn to make her way to the shop.

Woolworth's were offering Titanic crew-members one-day jobs at their new shop's grand opening. In a fine symbiosis of philanthropy, shop promotion and wage-saving, the temps were to be allowed to pocket whatever money they collected behind the counters. Ruby's early arrival was rewarded by the shop manager. She had anticipated that she would be able to replace her increasingly filthy Titanic uniform with a nice clean Woolworth's one for the day, but it turned out to be a naïve hope. She and her uniform were to be on show every bit as much as the special offer chocolate bars. But anything was better than that theatre. She already had a matinee performance lined up there, but the show would now have to go on without her.

The Woolworth's counter proved lucrative so the following day Ruby, confident she had enough in her coffers to pay for her fare to, and lodgings in Halifax, made her way to Penn Station. The exodus to Halifax had slowed and she was able to get on a train without delay.

Chapter 7

"This traditional custom (of women first) is now carried out without the direct consent of the individual men who are thereby doomed to die, or of any wish expressed by women who no doubt are almost equally deprived of choice."

Lady Aberconway, Liberal Women's Suffrage Union

Nash's resolution to abandon his attempt at a new life had come about as suddenly as the original decision to leave the old one. He had left England on a whim. His old uncle Stan, at the end of his last day in the job after fifty years as a worker in the Surrey Docks, had been stopped and searched, much to everyone's amazement, as he walked out of the dock gates into retirement. There, in his tatty little leather bag which carried his tobacco tin, cigarette papers, box of matches and lunchtime sandwich, was a tin of corned beef, supposedly pilfered, planted there by the management. Old Stan had been due to receive a pension. Not much of one but having been a stevedore, the most highly skilled and best paid of the dockers it would have been enough to keep him out of the workhouse for the rest of his life. But there was no pension for a man caught stealing of course, and stevedores, unlike other dockers had no union. The dock management had been well aware that their target had no one to whom to turn. And as a recorded thief, the old man would fail his 'good character' test so would not even be eligible to receive the paltry five shillings a week state old age pension when he reached seventy on his next birthday.

Nash had tried to make enquiries about who had perpetrated the planting of the corned beef, but he didn't know anyone who worked in the Surrey Docks so it was an impossible task. He had long held his nation in contempt, particularly due to the way it treated its poor, going back to the death of his parents in the workhouse. And his uncle was following their path.

It was at this time that Nash had happened to spot a poster advertising the Titanic's maiden voyage to the land of opportunity, and without really thinking it through, had purchased his ticket. But now he just wanted to get back to England; not to his ex-home of Whitechapel, because he was not prepared to return there with his tail between his legs, but to East London at least. The only legitimate work that he knew was dock-related, so settling back in East London's dock area beckoned, but he had vowed never to go back to work directly in the docks after what had happened to his uncle. And the frostbite in his feet suggested that his little swim in the ocean might have left a lasting weakness, and if it had, the docks were no place for any man who was not entirely fit. He had family in Bow, cousins who had their own little business as wood cutters, and they had always said there was a job for him anytime he wanted, so he would take them up on their offer.

The White Star Line's offices were still besieged though Nash did not have to queue for quite as long as Ruby. Once inside he began by explaining to someone behind the enquiries desk that he had been a passenger in third class on the Titanic. The clerk went immediately on the defensive, stating that there were charitable agencies dealing with the requirements of steerage passengers and he suggested Nash should avail himself of their services. Nash reassured him that he did not need any assistance other than help in tracking down a surviving crew member with whom he had become friends. The clerk took this as his cue to take a haughty tone. The White Star Line was not at liberty to give out details about the whereabouts of their staff. They were being provided for and would be returned to England at the White Star Line's expense. This would be at the earliest opportunity but he could not say precisely when or on what ship. Nash was relieved that Ruby was being looked after and was going to leave it at that. It was time he made his way home back to England.

He was about to turn to leave when on impulse he decided to try something. He looked at the unhelpful pipsqueak in front of him, winked and lowered his voice.

"Got any ideas where I can sell this 'ere Titanic clobber?" he asked, motioning to the bag he was carrying which held nothing but a box and a tin of shoe-polish. "This lot should fetch a pretty penny from souvenir 'unters from what I 'ear."

Had the man answered in the negative, Nash would have shrugged and made his way straight to a shipping company to buy his ticket home. But, despite only understanding one word in two of the Londoner's offering, the clerk got the gist and fell for it; hook, line and Titanic. He leaned forward and seemingly turned into Uriah Heep, hunching his shoulders though thankfully stopping short of clasping his hands together.

"I could be interested. What do you have?" he smarmed.

Nash answered with whatever came into his head that could be small enough to be in the bag, trying to speak with as little accent as possible so he could be understood without having to repeat himself, which he had hitherto needed to do several times.

"Torch, pennant and flare I got from my lifeboat; and some little towels I swiped from the swimming pool when I was what they call amidships just before the ship went down. They've all got Titanic on 'em. I've even got some of the ship's biscuits with T on 'em. T for Titanic and the drinking type of tea as well. A joke see."

"How about a look at the merchandise?" asked Uriah.

"Not 'ere!" implored Nash looking round nervously like a bookie's runner.

Five minutes later the dishevelled young clerk was making his way back to his office from a nearby alley, rubbing a little brick mortar off his face and grimacing a little as he flexed his right shoulder. The violent son-of-a-bitch Limey had recommended that he should be a little more helpful. And sure enough he had suddenly remembered the young woman the man was asking after. She had been in the office a couple of days ago asking about her dead father. They had told her about the ships taking the bodies back to Halifax, Canada. And she had seemed interested when one of his colleagues had told her about the work that was on offer at the Imperial Theatre and Woolworth's. And as Nash had shoved Uriah's right arm another inch up his shoulder blade just to ensure that all available information had been imparted, the New Yorker had volunteered that the young woman had stopped being paid from the moment the ship sank.

A long walk later Nash was being told by a frustrated theatre impresario that his star act of two nights ago had not turned up for work yesterday afternoon and he had not seen her since. The man suspected the rough old Scandinavian, or whatever he was, in front of him might have been a crewman off the Titanic, but a sixth sense told him not to offer him a job on his stage.

At Nash's next port of call, the Woolworth store manager took one look at the scary looking, unshaven man with ill-fitting clothes standing before him and decided he wanted this fellow out of his shop as quickly as possible. Thus he was particularly helpful, telling Nash whilst walking him towards the exit that Ruby had done a fine day's work and made herself a tidy sum. He believed she was going to use the money for a trip to Canada. Nash asked the manager for the distance to Halifax and was quickly given the answer which left him both perplexed and standing alone, save for a few tethered horses and their respective burdens, in front of the shop's entrance.

A thousand miles! Further by the time you changed trains in Montreal. Nash was staggered. He accepted that despite his best efforts, he was not going to be able to assist Ruby. He was a lot more disappointed than when he had failed to help the Irish woman, but Ruby had reached whatever age she was without his help, and she had shown on board ship that she was as tough as old boots. She could fend for herself well enough.

He made his way to the nearest shipping agency to make enquiries about getting home. It transpired that there was presently a shortage of availability on ships bound for England. The Titanic's return journey had been sold out and those on its passenger list had to be found alternative arrangements. Some of the Carpathia's Gibraltar and Italy-bound passengers were now sailing to Southampton and changing ships there. Many of the Titanic's European first and second class survivors had cancelled whatever their reason had been for travelling to America and just wanted to get home. The White Star Line had block-booked a lot of steerage accommodation for Titanic's surviving crew. And ocean-going liners were also being delayed by a sudden desire by their owners, responding to a far greater desire by their passengers, to upgrade their lifeboat quota.

Nash was informed that he would have to wait weeks for a third class passage, somewhat shorter for a second class one. He had enough money, thanks to Mr Littlejohn's donation, to book second class, and it would have actually worked out cheaper overall because of the saving made in board and lodging in New York, but Nash did not consider it. He was not going to have second class passengers looking down their noses at him.

The agency clerk asked him if he wished to go ahead and make a booking. Nash hesitated. He asked the clerk if he knew on which ships the Titanic's surviving crew were booked and when they were sailing. The clerk gave him a knowing look.

"After some Titanic souvenirs are we?" he asked conspiratorially.

"Son, I was on the bastard, I don't need no souvenirs of it," said Nash flatly. "Just got some friends in the crew thas all; fought I might sail back to England wiv 'em."

He got out his entire stash of money in full view of the clerk before continuing in a friendlier tone.

"Don't spose they'll be room in steerage on their ship. I'll 'ave to book second class I shouldn't wonder? On commission are yer boy?"

A few minutes later a ticketless Nash left the agency office with some of the information he had required, the clerk looking daggers at the back of the departing Limey time-waster. Nash didn't know on which specific ship Ruby would be travelling, but he knew which day it would be leaving. He doubted Ruby could get all the way to Halifax, attend to her business there and get back to New York in time for her ship home. And given Ruby's pay had been stopped from the moment the ship had gone down, her ex-employers were clearly not the sort of people who would be prepared to pay for Ruby's passage again on a later ship.

As for Nash's attacks on two members of White Star Line staff, he felt fairly confident that Uriah would not report being assaulted in the alley, but if he did, the description of his assailant would match that given by Littlejohn. And given Uriah's attacker was asking after Ruby Martin, their ex-crewwoman would certainly not be receiving any favours from the Titanic's owners.

There was also the matter of a passport. Nash had not required one but had not thought to ask in the shipping office whether that was also the case for crew. If Ruby had needed to have one, she would surely not have it now. Even if she had thought to slip it into a pocket before he had first met her amidships, which he doubted, the single sheet of paper certainly would have disintegrated when she slumped down into the water when all had seemed lost.

Nash did not like the idea of Ruby arriving back in New York, probably penniless, without any means of support or getting home. Charities had helped destitute steerage passengers reach their onward destination in the aftermath of the disaster but he was not sure whether they would now necessarily assist a crew member who had missed her ship home. Nash had never heard of Halifax. It could not be a very big place, and it might be a cheaper spot to stay for a while than New York. And perhaps he could get a ship home easier from there too. Thus he made the decision to track down Ruby to warn the young woman that her ship was sailing soon and to pass on the money he had kept for her. At least they were the reasons he gave himself for his quest.

A more profound thought then entered his head. It would also be good to pay his last respects in Halifax to those less fortunate than himself. The kindly gent who had simply accepted his fate and disappeared beneath the waves flashed into his thoughts. It had been the survival of the fittest in its original sense. Not physical fitness, rather those who fitted best the situation. Nash thought he and men like him survived when men like the kindly gent did not. Had the roles been reversed with the gent on the boat and him in the water, he believed he would still have survived, even if clambering on to the boat would have endangered the gent. Ever one to reduce the big questions of life to their simplest forms, Nash considered that there were three types of male Titanic survivor. Bastards, cowards and the lucky; and most, himself and that officer he rescued included, were two of the three. The kindly gent was none of those things. Nash decided that if the body of the gent found its way back to Halifax and there were relations there to claim it, he would introduce himself to them and tell of how their father, brother or whoever had died and they should be very proud of him.

The slow thousand mile train journey, much of it through attractive Upper New York State wilderness which was lost on Nash, left him plenty of time to ponder his decision to go to Halifax. There was the question of whether, if he managed to track down Ruby, she might think it rather odd that he had made such an effort, especially when he started to offer her money. Might she think he was up to some funny business? Blimey he was old enough to be her father.

Thoughts turned back to the dark days in Whitechapel. He remembered the number of child prostitutes who found themselves pregnant until 'the woman' sorted them out in a backstreet with a knitting needle or some such implement. Using that as a yardstick he was not far short of being old enough to be Ruby's grandfather.

He was not one for self-analysis but he started to question his own motives. Had he gone through the same experiences on board the Titanic with a young man rather than Ruby, would he now be making his way to Halifax to meet him there? He had to admit the answer was no. A man could look after himself. But what if the woman had been less good looking, less interesting or simply much older? He cheered himself by concluding that yes he would be making his way to Halifax to find such a woman. This self-delusion lasted a few seconds before he accepted that chivalry was not normally one of his strong points, but there was nothing wrong in putting yourself out to help a pretty young thing.

During his time in a hospital bed he had tried to block out the events of the previous few days and since leaving St Vincent's he had hardly had time to catch his breath. Now, for the first time since the sinking, he allowed the memories to course through him. He and Ruby had shared an hour together more intense than many people ever share with anyone in their whole life. He suspected seeing your old woman with your first born in her arms for the first time must beat it; being with her when the nipper died was another. But other than births and deaths he could not think of many other such occasions. And he had saved Ruby's life, and she had probably saved his too. He doubted he would have found his way out of amidships without her. That was some sort of bond between them wasn't it? Or would she think that he believed he had some sort of claim on her because he had saved her? There was also the probability that she just wanted to put the whole thing behind her and the last thing she wanted was reminders of it like him turning up. Blimey, this is all too complicated for me, he thought. That was enough of thinking about this sort of thing for one train journey.

He concluded that if he was successful in tracking down Ruby in Halifax he would simply lie about the main reason why he was there, but he could be truthful about everything else that had happened since he last saw her. He robbed the White Star Line official as retribution for the young woman in the next bed in the hospital; she had already left so he couldn't give her the money; he couldn't get a ship home from New York for some time so thought he would pay his respects to the dead in Halifax and maybe get a ship home from there; a shipping agent told him in passing that the White Star Line were shipping Titanic crew back home next week. Yes, that would be alright.

Chapter 8

"A Suffragist would have preferred to meet her fate alongside her husband. I would a thousand times rather go down with the ship under similar circumstances."

Mrs Cecil Chapman, New Constitutional Society for Woman Suffrage

Before she left, Ruby had bought a Hershey's chocolate bar from Woolworth's, the cost of which had gone into the coffers of one of her fellow crew members. It was the most disgusting thing she had ever tasted. She fantasised that if she got back to New York to find herself marooned there without any means of getting home, a job in the confectionery department of a big store beckoned. She would then persuade the manager to start importing Cadbury's or Fry's from England.

The chocolate was the only thing she had eaten on her tiring twenty four hour journey to Halifax. She was keeping the theatre and shop earnings she had left over after buying her train ticket for accommodation costs in Halifax and, more importantly, in case she needed it for her father's repatriation expenses.

As she stepped off the train on to the platform at Halifax station, it became immediately apparent that the local populace were well aware that the latest train from New York had just

94

arrived. It was mayhem. A number of reporters with their photographers in close pursuit dashed towards the latest VIPs with a Titanic connection to alight from the first class carriages. A sea of tour guides offered their services. No one realised Ruby was wearing a Titanic uniform. Most just saw an unkempt young woman who clearly did not have any money, so she only had to politely refuse the half-hearted offers of about one guide in three. But she made a point of wandering into earshot so as to pick up many a useful snippet of information from guides as they entered into negotiations with her fellow train passengers. The guides advised that all hotel rooms were full but they could find their customers a room for the night. Most had some family member or another who was kindly offering a room in their home, on payment of a fee that Ruby suspected would be more in line with that normally charged by a luxury hotel than the guest house it no doubt more closely resembled. The guides then ascertained whether they had caught people in their net whom were there to mourn or were among the first group of tourists in history to arrive in Halifax in April. If they were the former the guides would take a respectful tone offering to take them, when the time came, to the ice rink where the deceased would be lain out for identification and claiming by relatives. If they were the latter, the guide would enthusiastically offer them an excursion to the Naval Dockyards wharf where the 'death ships' would soon be returning with the bodies.

Ruby spotted a Titanic information sign. A temporary help desk had been set up in the station, from where she gleaned as much intelligence as was available from the helpful kiosk worker. This included a warning that all three thousand hotel rooms in the City were indeed full. The arrival of the body-recovery ships was imminent so Ruby decided to walk down to the dockyard. She would have to worry about a room for the night when the time came.

A couple of hours later, the time spent walking and standing being jostled in a large crowd had left Ruby so exhausted she barely registered the tolling of the church bells which was the cue the bodies were arriving at the quayside. The crowd pushed forwards as the ships docked. A line of twenty sailors kept the crowd and a bevy of photographers from interfering with the off-loading of the bodies.

The crowd as one removed their headgear as the first body appeared. It was a crew member, uncovered, the ghastly non-embalmed body in full view. The crowd gawped and gasped in equal measure while Ruby looked down at her feet, not bearing to look. Then she had to look. What was she expecting to see? Did she want to see her father? Not want to see him? All the time she did not see him she could deny his death. Somehow, somewhere he could have been saved. But she knew that to be a false hope and seeing him, terrible image though it would be, would at least enable her to start the grieving process fully. And it would mean she would hopefully be able to repatriate his body home to her mother.

The body was not that of her father's or anyone else she recognised. A series of grisly sights followed, none of whom she knew, before a number of canvas bags started to be unloaded. A pile of coffins waited their turn patiently at the end of the queue. Ruby displayed the grimmest of ironic, cynical smiles as it became clear to her that the bodies were being unloaded in reverse class order. First the uncovered crew followed by third and second class passengers lying in the relative splendour of canvas bags, then top of the bill the coffins of those who had travelled first class. There was logic to it, conceded Ruby. They were separated by class in life so why not in death?

It was at this point that Ruby's Hershey bar made a sudden reappearance, much to the momentary disgust of the man standing in front of her. But he was too engrossed in the macabre proceedings to worry too much about his impending laundry bill and Ruby got away with nothing more than receiving some blasphemous advice on the evils of drink.

As the ships unloaded the last of their cargo, everybody in the crowd bar one continued to look on in grim wonder. Ruby viewed the proceedings with growing bemusement. There were way too few bodies. The newspapers back in New York had confirmed that seven hundred had survived; over fifteen hundred had perished. Where were most of the latter?

The entertainment over, the crowd dispersed, small pockets of friends discussing which body had been the most gruesome with the macabre mix of fascination, humour and horror that their grandfathers would have portrayed at a mass public hanging. Ruby was so tired she could barely put one foot in front of another, but she did so, following the procession of horse-drawn hearses travelling between the dock and the ice curling rink.

On arrival at the ice rink Ruby found a room which had been set aside for grieving friends and relatives. She slumped down on a chair and wondered if she would be allowed to sleep there for the night. The room started to fill up and in due course four men came in and introduced themselves as respectively the Coroner, Medical Examiner, Deputy

Registrar of Deaths and a City of Halifax official. The four men wandered around the room talking to everyone in turn, like the star guests at a ball.

The first question Ruby had wanted answering was why so few bodies had been recovered. The Deputy Registrar of Deaths explained that only three hundred and twenty five bodies had thus far been found and when the embalming fluid had run out on board the recovery ships, bodies were buried at sea. Only two hundred and nine bodies were embalmed and returned to Halifax. Ruby had already guessed the answer to her next question but she asked it in any case.

"But why were there so few crew members amongst them?"

The Registrar did not have the decency to look embarrassed or even a little awkward.

"All first class passenger bodies recovered were embalmed and returned here. Most second class too. Most of the one hundred and sixteen buried at sea were crew and steerage. It's a decent Christian burial you understand. They were laid in ice beforehand and weights were used," he said matter-of-factly.

One aspect of being so exhausted was that Ruby did not have the energy to lose her temper, or even show any emotion.

"And personal effects?"

"I came up with an identification system. As each body was brought aboard, a square of canvas with a stencilled number on it was attached. Personal effects were put in canvas bags with the corresponding numbers. So if your relative was amongst those recovered, you will be able to reclaim their effects."

"If they are not on the ice rink and did not have any personal effects I suppose I will not know if they were amongst those buried at sea?" asked Ruby.

The Registrar allowed a trace of inappropriate personal pride seep into his voice.

"There's a full description of hair colour, height, weight, age, birthmarks, scars, tattoos put in a ledger against the number of each body recovered from the sea."

"You have thought of everything. Just like the men who built the unsinkable Titanic," said Ruby flatly, before she moved away to speak with one of the other men doing the rounds.

Between them the four men told Ruby everything they thought a grieving relative should know. The bodies would be laid in rows and kept at the ice rink for two weeks. They warned that some faces were indistinguishable because they had been struck by pieces of ice or wreckage, were black from exposure or injuries, or had been disfigured by sea creatures. The usual red tape regarding the transportation of bodies and the strict law of hermetically sealed caskets would be waived. A body would be transported to anywhere in America for the cost of the first class rail fare. Once a body was claimed it would be sent to the railway depot and placed on a train to Bangor Maine for onward travel. Those who could not afford to ship bodies home would see them buried in Halifax at the City's expense.

Ruby was not surprised to find that the transportation of bodies would not be free. Transportation companies were only interested in making money. She made a point of thanking the Halifax official for his city's kindness. They chatted for a while and when he realised she had nowhere to stay, offered her a bed for the night in he and his wife's home, which Ruby was only too pleased to accept.

The following morning, after a fitful but thankfully comfortable night's sleep, Ruby arrived at the curling rink on the dot of the start time for body-identification. She was surprised to find a body had already been claimed, removed and its hearse leaving just as she arrived. She asked the official if she had got the start time wrong. No she had not. It transpired that the richest man on the Titanic, John Jacob Astor, had died, and his undertaker had circumvented the procedure which had been set up. He had a letter of introduction to the medical examiner which allowed him to claim the body before the process was open to everyone else. Ruby thought that it had the same logic as the bodies coming off the recovery ship in class order. The usual rules did not apply to the very highest ranks in life, so of course did not in death. It crossed her mind fleetingly that it was surprising such an aristocrat did not survive as she had seen many first class male passengers get away in the lifeboats early. But then the ice rink was before her and all previous thoughts drained away in an instant.

She made her way along the coarse matting that had been laid alongside the rows of bodies. Ruby did not expect to see her father or anyone else known to her other than perhaps some first class passengers she had served on board. So it was with some surprise that she soon recognised someone; Lucy, an assistant source cook in the a la carte Ritz restaurant in which Ruby had worked. It was very distressing but Ruby could not help but give a sad wry smile as she saw why her colleague had made it as far as the curling rink. She was wearing a blouse with stand collar, silk dress, pleated bodice and sleeves, and a skirt with train, with the whole lot topped off by a fur stole knotted around her neck. She had clearly raided a first class cabin for warm clothing before the stewards had closed off the area, and once in there had decided to quickly don as many first class clothes, warm or otherwise, as she could manage. Thus on finding her body it had been assumed Lucy was a first class passenger, so she had got herself a coffin ride on the recovery ship rather than being tied to a weight and dumped in a watery unmarked grave.

Ruby thought back to her being below decks with Nashey. She had assumed the cabins had been locked purely as a precaution against their incumbents unwisely returning to save their things. She now realised that had been naïve. The slapdash officers of the Titanic who were unable to think of anything that might keep their ship and passengers safe had been right on the ball when it came to keeping valuables under lock and key. What was the first thing of which they thought when the ship was sinking? Lock the cabins in case somebody tries to steal her ladyship's furs. Better the furs go down with the ship than keep someone warm. She remembered her obnoxious little witticism at Nashey's expense about a 'fur steal'. My, she had been well trained by the White Star Line. And now their officers were as dead as her ladyship's expensive scalps. All except Lowe and a few others that is.

"God bless you Lucy, you were too quick for the buggers," said Ruby with a rueful smile. "But not as quick off the ship as a lot of the first class men."

But even the saddest of smiles was wiped off Ruby's face when she saw that there had been a price to be paid, even in death, for first class service. Lucy's frozen limbs had been forcibly broken to fit her into a coffin.

Ruby carried on along the rows of bodies and eventually recognised a good looking young first class male passenger whom she particularly remembered because he had actually looked her in the eyes and engaged her in conversation. It was only small talk, and she got the impression that it was her looks in which he was primarily interested, but at least he did it. Most did not. To the majority of her clientele she was invisible. A memory came to her of being taken to task by one of her workmates, who had eavesdropped on her conversation with the young man, for not responding more readily to his flattery and charm. She had been reminded that there was many an attractive working class girl travelling in first class. Particularly good looking women like her could marry up in class if they played their cards right. Look how well some gaiety girls had done. Her response to her colleague had been to query what she could possibly have in common with such a man. There had to be more to life than marrying well. But she had grudgingly agreed that if the young man spoke to her again, she would be more responsive. The iceberg hit that same night. Many a first class male passenger had saved themselves in a lifeboat whilst several hundred women and children were still on board. Perhaps this young man had that opportunity too but chose to do the right thing. Maybe she would have had things in common with him after all.

Ruby pondered her own aloofness. The Ritz restaurant had the most cosmopolitan crew of any section of the whole ship. Lucy had been one of Ruby's few English colleagues amongst the restaurant's complement of sixty crew members. Most had been Italian or French, with a smattering of Swiss and other nationalities. Ruby had found her foreign colleagues to be a friendly bunch, far more joyous and charming than the downtrodden British servants and crew she had worked with over the years. She had shared many a silly laugh with them, often prompted by kitchen mishaps and the ensuing mayhem. But because their English was slightly faltering, and they did not always fully understand her little quips, she had never attempted to have deeper, more meaningful conversations with them. She could not say she knew any of them well, or even much about them. Claudio had been a nice young man. Lovely dark eyes too. He was from Bologna and had been eager to return home there come Christmas. It had seemed a long way off to him. Mario had also been quite a character. Where was it he was from? Somewhere near a big volcano. It was interesting to hear why people lived close to such terrible things. He had been looking forward to seeing relatives living in New York's Little Italy when they docked. And now these fine young people and many others like them were gone.

Ruby continued to gaze at the grotesque scene in front of her for some time after she had looked at the final body. As she had expected, neither the ice rink nor the effects and descriptions of those buried at sea had thrown up any evidence of her father. He had gone down with the ship. She would not have been able to afford to ship his body home but part of her would have liked him to have a place of rest in a Halifax grave, albeit in a mass one for the poor. That said another part of her continued to conjure up images of bodies, canvas bags and broken frozen limbs. She concluded that on reflection going down with the ship had been the most honourable, dignified way to go, so she was relieved that her friendly foreign acquaintances had gone that way too. Nashey had been right. He always was going down with the ship.

Chapter 9

"Each boatload of persons taken off a sinking ship would consist of half men and half women."
Flora Drummond, WSPU

On arrival at Halifax railway station, Nash availed himself of similar information from the kiosk to that previously gleaned by Ruby, and then made his way directly to the curling rink. The face of the kindly gent was seared into his memory and Nash knew the image would never leave him. He walked along the rows of bodies and saw nobody he knew. He felt both disappointment and relief at not seeing the gent. At one point there were a handful of women in a row. These bodies had been battered by the elements, their frozen faces looking like those of poor women from a bye-gone era. One had clearly had a lump taken out of her by a shark. Nash remembered the weather-beaten women left dead by Whitechapel's 'shark'.

He found himself spending a little time studying each body on the ice rink, looking at their faces, their clothes, imagining who they had been and would never be again. He was on the ice rink some time before he bid his dead shipmates farewell with a grim nod.

It was clear that he had been unrealistically hopeful in thinking he could find Ruby in Halifax. It was a much bigger town than he had expected, and the place seemed to be full to bursting. The information desk had warned him all hotels were full and had been for some time, so it was unlikely Ruby would be staying in any of them. But he was glad he had come to pay his respects. He felt guilty that had it not been for Ruby he would not have journeyed to Halifax. And he suspected that few of his fellow survivors would make it up there. He couldn't blame them. The disaster was something to forget about and home beckoned. But it was their loss.

Nash took one last look at the ice rink and a number of questions poked their heads up. Was there to be a mass funeral and burial for any unclaimed people? Was there to be a memorial; with people's names on? Were donations needed? Why were there so few bodies? He noticed a sign introducing itself as the entrance to a room for friends and relatives of the deceased. They might have the answers in there. He walked in and immediately experienced a moment of sharp inhalation as he saw Ruby.

She had her back to him, talking to someone who looked as though they were an official of some sort. They were talking about the disaster. One of Nash's questions was immediately answered. There was to be a mass burial in the Baron Von Hirsch Cemetery there in Halifax. He stood there for a minute or two eavesdropping, until something was mentioned that gave him a perfect introduction into the conversation.

"… I hear say that Officer Lowe is a fine fellow, did the two of you hit it off?" asked the man lightly.

"He is most certainly not a fine fellow!" countered Ruby. "And we most assuredly did not hit it off as you put it!"

"I'm not surprised after the way you landed on 'im!" commented Nash loudly.

There was no feeling faint or fly-trap mouth. Ruby just walked quietly over to him, put her arms round his waist and snuggled her head into the side of his chest. There was a brief pause before her sobbing started.

The ice rink was clearly not an appropriate place to talk, so once she had gathered herself together Ruby made her excuses to the official without introducing him to the man whose arm she was clutching as she hurriedly took her leave. Once outside, neither of them suggested finding somewhere in which to talk. They simply started walking, quickly and excitedly at first whilst Nash gave Ruby a heavily edited version of how he came to be alive. As the conversation lengthened, widened and became more profound, the march through the streets slowed to a stroll. Nash need not have concerned himself with the reaction to his turning up in Canada. Ruby had been delighted to see him. And whilst he stuck to the story that he had not journeyed to Halifax in search of her, he felt comfortable enough to admit that he had hoped he might run into her if, as seemed likely, her father had perished and she had journeyed there to claim his body. And Ruby accepted the offer of a share of Littlejohn's White Star money in the spirit in which it was proposed.

They walked until Nash's frostbitten feet told him it was time to stop. They were completely lost by this time, so found a café where Nash slipped off his new shoes whilst he had Ruby giggling with the tale of wandering bandage-footed into a New York shoe shop. The café was unlike any that either of them had ever frequented. It was a far cry from the Lyons' tea shop Ruby used in Southampton or Nash's café of choice in Whitechapel's Toynbee Hall. Their initial request for tea was met with an apology from the waiter. Having scanned the other customers in the place and been unimpressed by the tiny measures being given for coffee, they fell back on the tactic in exotic climes of ordering what the people on the next table were enjoying. Two hot wines were duly delivered to them with a 'voila'. This led Ruby to mention that there had been plenty of French people working in her restaurant aboard the Titanic. She was thinking of her dead foreign colleagues when she was brought out of her sadness by Nash's face, which she thought looked a picture as he tried his first sip of what he clearly considered to be a dubious liquid. They obviously did not serve hot wine in that Toynbee Hall place he had just mentioned. Having finished their drinks, which had been damned by faint 'wet and warm' praise by Nash, they asked their waiter for directions to the railway station.

They would have liked to have stayed in Halifax for the mass funeral but the lack of anywhere to stay and the need to get Ruby back in time to catch her ship, meant that the two of them dashed back to New York via the next train to Montreal. The long journey flew by as they regaled each other with their respective stories since they had last seen each other. They also discussed their feelings about the disaster and Nash found that he had been correct about there being a bond between them. He would not want to talk about the tragedy to anyone else, but he found he positively wanted to discuss the topic with Ruby. And she made it clear to him that she was of the same persuasion.

He then gave her a potted history of his life to date, and concluded that whilst he had taken the catastrophe as being a sign that America was not for him, neither would he be returning to his old Whitechapel life. He would probably 'kip down' at a cousin's place temporarily while he found his feet. At this point he started to feel a little awkward at the depth and intensity of the conversation. Such discussions did not come easily to him. So he followed up mention of finding his feet by making a joke about the state of his 'plates of meat' thanks to his recent little dip in the ocean.

Ruby spotted the attempt at changing the dynamic but she wanted to hear more about the man who had saved her life. She decided to ask him a serious question which he could easily bat away with a frivolous remark if he so wished, and if that happened, she would accept it and allow the conversation to drift on to more light-hearted matters.

"You haven't mentioned any sweethearts Nashey," she said with a smile which gave him the option to come back with a wink and a joke. "A big, good looking feller like you?"

She was pleased to hear him take the question seriously. He told her that there had been a woman once. She had been a middle class slummer of all things. It had been a matter of opposites attracting he supposed.

"Soppy as a box of lights she were," he said with the brightness of fond reminiscence. "But educa'ed an' all. Funny to be daft and clever at the same time ain' it? But she taught me a lot and me 'er I wager. I gave up me villainy for 'er and we always got on in our way but the life was 'ard and it got to 'er in the end. The slums of Whitechapel ain' no place for no lady. She come down wiv dipferia. Got it from one of the nippers she tended I spose. She were our streets' nurse see, cos she knew fings about tendin' people from 'er education. Most adults who 'ad it got better but she never. She passed away."

He fell silent for a moment, looking out the window at

the surrounding wilderness, before looking back at Ruby with a smile and a wink to change the mood.

"'ow about you then? They must 'ave been round you like bees round an 'oneypot. All them young stewards. I reckon you could 'ave even bagged yerself an officer if yer'd played yer cards right."

"Like Officer Lowe you mean?" she sneered, before giving Nash a reassuring little smile. "No, I married the first man who made me laugh and didn't have his arse out his trousers. His name was Walter. He was a nice boy. We were both desperate to get out of the house away from our families. We found ourselves a nice room in a respectable place. He had a job in the Southampton docks; he was a clever boy; would have worked his way up to a decent paid job there one day. I had a job in the docks office doing the wages. That's how we met. But he fell into the hold of a ship and that was that. I was a widow woman before my nineteenth birthday. Sounds strange saying it, but there are plenty of young widows about; more now thanks to Smith, Lightoller and Lowe."

It was her turn to stare out the window.

"Smith, Lightoller and Lowe. Sound like a firm of undertakers dunt they?" sneered Nash.

"They were," confirmed Ruby still looking at but not seeing the countryside.

There was a silence before Ruby broke it, smiling at Nash.

"I was top of the class at sums when I was at school. The only good thing about being the youngest in a family is that you get some schooling. Mother had my sisters to help her with the jobs around the house so I was able to go to school. After Walter died I wanted to get out of the docks. I would have liked to stay in clerking by rights but other than in the docks, pen driver's jobs with sums, money and the like always seemed to be done by men. I did not want to be a typewriter or a telephone operator or anything like that so when a job in service presented itself I took it. A nice big house seemed better than a musty old office full of musty old men. But there was always some young footman who fancied his chances. Finding out I was a widow put some off. Others were still keen. But I was a bit of a madam if the truth be told. Working sixteen hours a day for the bone idle put me in a permanently bad mood. I thought there should be more to her ladyship's life than ordering the likes of me about and there should be more to a working girl's life than being ordered about. So there was nothing about me for a man to be interested in except the obvious. And how dare a man make up to me just because I am good looking."

"Swank dunt yer!" commented Nash, trying but failing to keep a straight face.

"Are you listening or not?" scolded Ruby, before continuing, her question not being one that had been asked to elicit a reply. "Some even thought I was just playing hard to catch. But I was no prize to be won or rose to be plucked. Many a randy young man who cornered me in the scullery got a knee where it hurts I can tell you. I changed houses a lot."

"So you were a surly little cow wot caused trouble everywhere you went. Them old butlers of yourn must 'ave put their 'ands togevver every time you 'anded in yer notice," said Nash with a smirk.

Ruby smirked back.

"Yes they did that alright, when they had not given me notice first that is. Always got a good reference mind; I was a good worker and carryings on in the scullery was no subject for an employer's letter. But I can't talk when it comes to men. I was a wrong un. I didn't mind using my looks to get a job on the ships when it suited me. I put on a bit of rouge and then laughed at some little man's not funny joke in the interview and the job was mine. As for stewards, they might have been my age but they were just boys. 'ark at me. I'm only thirty; must have got old before my time. And officers; I have never known a group of men who held themselves in such high regard with so little reason. And now there are fifteen hundred dead that says I'm right."

"You ain' no wrong un gell. Just a woman trying to make 'er way in a man's world. It'll change one day, you mark my words," said Nash with a confidence borne more from hope than conviction.

With the second train running to schedule and due to arrive in time for her ship home, Ruby offered to return Nash's money to him now she had no need of it in New York. But he insisted she keep it for her widowed mother. Ruby assumed that she would resettle somewhere in Southampton, and Nash had no fixed abode, so they swopped the addresses at which they could be traced, Ruby giving her mother's home and Nash his cousin's place in Bow.

The two of them conversed for a little longer agreeing that if either ever travelled to each other's city they would be the first person with whom they would arrange to meet. Then the events of the past few days suddenly caught up with both of them. They slept for hours until they pulled into Penn Station.

On arrival back in New York, Ruby bought some tatty second hand clothes from a market stall. Nash had offered to buy her new things from a shop but she had insisted the two of them needed every penny for the uncertain future that awaited them both back in England. She then waited for Nash to disappear into a shipping office to buy his ticket home before slipping off to discreetly treat herself to some new combinations and other personal items from shops nearby. And a quick trip into a public lavatory to change allowed her to finally escape from her salt-stained sailor-boy look.

The two of them then made their way to the White Star Line office, where Nash kept a low profile just in case Michael Littlejohn or Uriah Heep was about, as he didn't want Ruby's passage home complicated by his misdemeanours. Ruby had not needed a passport, but there was a minor complication to her passage home. She was exasperated to find that she had been booked on to the SS Lapland bound for Plymouth. Most of the Titanic crew were from her home city so there was no doubt a shortage of availability on ships heading to Southampton, so whoever was booking the passages may have thought they were doing her a favour by getting her home as soon as possible. But that would have taken initiative and common sense; commodities which Ruby considered were in short supply when it came to the White Star Line. So although it was going to be no hardship for her to get on a train from Plymouth to Southampton, she was in no mood to feel thankful.

Nash had booked himself onto a liner which would get him into Southampton only a few days after Ruby would get home, but they agreed they would not meet up again that soon. They told each other that they needed to get themselves sorted out and back in the routine of normal life.

But secretly they both wondered whether they would meet again. It might be awkward. They had become strangely attached; their usual barriers, which in both of them were bigger than most people's, had been let down to each other. They had discussed things which they would not normally have done with another human being, yet they were effectively strangers, twenty years apart in age and from different worlds. The reality of their normal lives beckoned and the Titanic and its emotions had no place there. If they ever met again, they would most likely be tongue-tied, unsure of how to relate to one another. Pleased to see their fellow survivor initially but once the obvious hearty greetings and small talk had waned, they might be relieved when they parted. Perhaps swopping a letter or two would be best, just to let each other know how they were getting on in their new lives, before easing back to the safety of merely sending a card at Christmas. And Ruby doubted Nash would even do that. She could not imagine he had ever sent such an item in his life, and would not be about to start now.

Chapter 10

"Titanic, name and thing, will stand as a monument and warning to human presumption."
Bishop of Winchester

Ruby had four sisters; Flo, Nell, Lil and June, all of whom were older than her. They were all married but still lived within a stone's throw of their mother's home. Ruby's four siblings formed a classic close-knit working class affair, always in and out of each other's places, and they enjoyed a collective, mutual disregard for their youngest sister. As far as they were concerned, Ruby was not just the baby of the family, but the good-looking, intelligent, outgoing, spoilt one who'd had the luck to be born just as the worst horrors of Victorian slum life were starting to ease. Their nickname for her was 'Miss', which to the uninitiated sounded perfectly respectful but in reality was a spiteful abbreviation of 'mistake'.

Their parents had been plunged into poverty by starting their young married life having four daughters in four years. They gave up on ever having a son and started taking precautions. Half a dozen childless years duly followed which enabled them to improve their economic situation before, still barely into their thirties, they had Ruby come along.

But right from the start she had been different. She seemed naturally well-spoken and unlike her sisters, she had refused to have her whole life mapped out for her. As she grew up she saved every penny she laid her hands on for a rainy day, and they all knew what that meant. The day she could afford to escape from that life. It was not good enough for 'Miss'.

Ruby was always surrounded by this bitterness yet she never fully understood why. In her younger years she had always attempted to be a good sister to each of her siblings but got nothing in return save for the mouthing of silent speech behind her back, and exchanged glances in front of it. The worst of it was that nothing was ever said. There was no rough and tumble sibling rivalry where insults were traded, blows exchanged, hair pulled, only to be forgotten about with a hug of reconciliation. There were no rows, no shouts, just cold back-stabbing disdain. Ruby knew that if she was ever in trouble of any kind, she knew exactly where not to go. It had hurt her throughout her childhood. And even once she moved out of the family home to get married, she allowed the foursome to upset her. Every week, her Saturday afternoon off work spent visiting her mother had ended with Ruby returning home fighting back tears after the ugly sisters had ensured she would not go to the ball, or to be more precise spend some quality time alone with her mother, whom she loved dearly. The sisters were always already ensconced when she arrived, sitting around the fire in the back room like witches at a cauldron, drinking their disgusting sterilised milked tea. And they were still there when she could not stand it any longer and bid her mother a fond farewell.

But the upset had faded over the years. As the isolation of home had been replaced by the desolation of widowhood and indifference of servitude, it had left her with a tough inner core. Not that she reciprocated her sisters' contempt, for that would have been to feel something. She felt nothing for them.

Whilst on board the SS Lapland she could not help but imagine her sisters on the Titanic. She was convinced that they would either have died on board, clinging to each other in the bowels of steerage as the water rushed in, or if rescued by a steward, would have been looking down at their feet in the bottom of a lifeboat as hundreds were left to needlessly lose their lives.

But Ruby had to admit that there had been a little of her sisters in her. She remembered giving up below decks. She would have died in that flooding corridor had it not been for Nashey. This caused her to wonder, if they should ever meet, what the gnarly East Ender would think of her sisters. A wry smile crossed her face because she immediately knew the answer.

Her thoughts then drifted back to the sinking as she recalled holding back as the last lifeboat was about to be launched, a caricature of a poor working class girl who thought she was not good enough to be saved, allowing men to make decisions over whether she lived or died. It would not happen again. She was as good, though no better than, anyone else; any upper or middle class woman or any man.

★★★★★★

The long journey from New York had given Ruby plenty of time to take stock. She had stepped back on to English soil having decided to make a fresh start, away from Southampton and its memories. Servitude had seen her lose touch with her childhood friends over the years, and the local acquaintances she had made during her time on the ships had mostly been lost in the disaster. Other than her mother, there was nothing keeping her on the south coast, so the obvious thing was to head for the great magnet only a few hours away. London beckoned.

Ruby felt a strange mix of joy, relief and depressing anti-climax as she arrived unannounced at Southampton railway station. Rather than immediately get a bus direct to Northam, one of the poorest neighbourhoods of the city where the family home was situated, Ruby enquired at the station's ticket office about train fares and times to London. She followed this by going for a stroll round the city centre, partly to look for a room for the night and partly to get her emotions together. This was all done at a leisurely pace because she needed to kill some time; she planned to arrive at her mother's place when none of her siblings would be in situ.

This achieved, there was an emotional hour with her mother that included being told of the church service for her father and the rest of the city's dead which she had missed. Ruby kept the details of the reality of the sinking and that of New York and Halifax to a minimum, but was more verbose when she relayed how her father had gone down with the ship. He had died a hero's death, still baking as the boat was sinking, so that women and children in the lifeboats had food to sustain them. This seemed to give a little comfort to his widow.

Ruby had just told her mother about a Titanic widows' fund which had been set up when the sound of a key in the lock told her that their precious time alone together was at an end. She quickly hugged and kissed her mother for the umpteenth time that hour, and informed her that first thing in the morning she would be on her way to go to live in London. But she would return when the time came to accompany her mother to see the Titanic widows' pension people.

The entrant turned out to be the eldest sibling, Flo, who was nonplussed, not so much at unexpectedly seeing her little sister, but at the change she could see at a glance had taken place in her. There was not the slightest pretence of recognition let alone welcome from Ruby.

"Miss," acknowledged Flo.

"Don't you *ever* call me that again Flo," said Ruby with a voice and expression as cold as North Atlantic ice. "I'm moving to London. You'll 'ave my address soon enough. See to it I'm told when mother's Relief Fund interview is. I'll be coming back 'ere to take 'er to it. None of you would 'ave a clue what to say there so if I'm not told there'll be trouble, d'you 'ear me?!"

The outburst had been delivered wide-eyed from no more than a couple of inches from the older sister's flinching face. Unlike the rest of the family, Ruby did not usually speak with a strong accent or drop her aitches, but it had added a certain something; a harshness. An amazing amount had been crammed into those few sentences. I've survived the Titanic so I will damn well survive you and your sisters. I was there with father when he died. That puts me in a position of power. I am no longer the little sister. I am in charge when it comes to mother's Titanic widows' pension. In fact I will be in charge when it comes to anything to do with mother from now on.

Flo nodded meekly but Ruby did not see the gesture. She had already brushed past her sister, her eyes staring ahead as she disappeared down the passage towards the front door.

******

The public outcry from the Titanic disaster had led to a huge number of donations being paid into the Lord Mayor of the City of London's Mansion House Fund, set up for poor dependants, mostly widows and children, of those who died. 85% of the donations were to be for crew dependants. £414,000 had been collected when Mansion House appointed local committees in the cities which had incurred the most deaths, Southampton, which had supplied 535 of the 673 crew killed, amongst them. Committees were drawn from the social elite. Southampton's Lord Mayor appointed himself, his wife, senior church and business people. The manager of the White Star Line in Southampton and Mrs Lightoller, the wife of the Second Officer, were also appointed. Thus, those who had done so much to ensure Southampton's loss was so great were well represented. Trade Unions requested that they have a member on the committee because they were acquainted with the personal circumstances of those who were to be within the purview of the fund. They were also concerned that other committee members had little or no experience of working class conditions. Their request was politely declined.

Ruby had sent a letter to her mother's home with her new address. Knowing her sisters would get to know of the contents, she kept it short and to the point. She had settled in to a nice room in South London and got herself a job in a factory where she had arranged to have a day off for mother's interview. Ruby's mother was illiterate and her three eldest daughters were too. The fourth, June, had received a little schooling and had thus been the one to read the letter to the rest of the family as well as pen a one-line reply informing Ruby that mother's interview was next Thursday afternoon.

It had been necessary for Ruby to tell a little white lie about being allowed a day off for the interview. There was no possibility of such dispensation for someone who had worked in a factory for only a couple of weeks, so her first position in London came to an end. The pittance in her pay packet just about covered her rent, funeral insurance and a return rail fare to Southampton. To afford little luxuries such as food, she had visited a pawnbroker. Her claim that the wrinkled, stained, old sailor boy-style dress she was offering up was a uniform from the Titanic was met with an old fashioned look from the canny old Deptford High Street shop owner. She had received the going rate for one dress in poor condition, and not a penny more. It meant she would be on a strict bread and water diet until she found herself another job and had done a week's work in lieu of her next pay packet.

Ruby arrived at the family home at a time that at least a sister or two would normally have been there, but they were all conspicuous by their absence. She could see that her mother, who was in her Sunday best clothing because she too had visited her local pawnbroker recently, was distraught. Ruby reassured her that it would not be like the workhouse test. It was just an interview to find out what her needs were. It was a charity; charitable people. It would be fine.

They arrived at the Mayor's offices and were shown into

a waiting room. Ruby's mother sat there, head down, hands meekly in her lap, with the world apparently on her shoulders. Ruby had the sobering experience that most children have to go through with their parents; that first moment of role reversal, after which the world is never the same again. Mother, so long the tough working class matriarch, whom Ruby had unconditionally loved, trusted, respected and feared all her life, was now reduced to relying on her youngest daughter for guidance, support and assistance. Ruby now saw how old, fragile and, despite her own presence there, alone her mother suddenly appeared.

Her mother's fear of being late had got them there an hour early, but it was not until the time prescribed for the meeting that Mrs Turner's presence was required by the committee. Ruby had assumed that she would be able to accompany her mother in to see the committee but on rising from her chair was told by a rather sniffy young secretary that owing to the personal nature of the interview, it would not be possible for her to be present.

"Come on Ruby, let's go home, I'm not going in on my own," said Mrs Turner with a confection of fear and high-horse affront.

"My dear there really is…" began the secretary.

"I think you'll find she isn't your dear and she isn't going in there if she doesn't want to," said Ruby at least equalling the secretary in haughtiness, a protective arm going round her mother as they turned away.

Ruby was immediately irritated by her own comments, her thoughts turning to self-scolding. 'I think you'll find' indeed. Anyone who ever starts a sentence with 'I think you'll find' should have the rest of whatever they say ignored as a matter of course. Why do these places make you feel like you have to put on airs and graces; try to be someone you're not?

They were half way out the door when Ruby reconsidered. She should not have allowed her annoyance with both the secretary and herself to affect her behaviour. Pride came before a fall. Her mother was destitute. They could not afford to look in the mouth of whatever gift-horse had a stable in the Mayor's office. The two of them would have to play the game. Ruby did not know how many dependents were to be supported by the fund but her cashier's numeracy skills had calculated that £414,000 multiplied by 85% divided by 673, and for the sake of estimation say there were 2 dependents per dead crew member, meant that her mother stood to receive a tidy sum somewhere in the region of £250. She would live out the rest of her days in comfort on that and the interest it would accrue. And Ruby would see to it that her sisters never got their hands on a penny of it.

The secretary had retreated back in to her office. Ruby walked through the door to find the woman was in mid-sentence talking to her assistant, advising her to pay each of the committee members their first class rail fares as expenses out of the fund. The secretary cut her conversation short as Mrs Turner's daughter entered the room. Ruby beamed the most apparently earnest of false smiles at the woman and produced her best, mock middle class, talking to first class passengers, voice.

"I do apologise. It's been rather a fraught time as you can imagine. I was on the Titanic too actually, with my father. Ghastly business. Perhaps you could tell the committee that and ask them if they would be kind enough to let me sit in, at least to start with; moral support and all that. Mother's a little fragile you see. I'm sure you understand."

A minute later a second small uncomfortable chair had been found in front of the committee and Ruby was sitting on it. The committee, with the Lord Mayor in the middle, were sitting next to each other in a long line of large chairs that were higher than those of their interviewees, whom they peered down at across a table that was almost as large a barrier as the class one that divided them.

The Mayor introduced his committee and then after the briefest of niceties allied with the most condescending of smiles towards the two women in front of him, handed over to his wife to do most of the talking. Ruby did not hear Mrs Mayor's opening salvo. Her mind had wandered as soon as Mrs Lightoller had been introduced. Ruby stared at her. The woman was wearing a spotted cotton dress, the wide collar edged with embroidered braid to match sleeve cuffs, fashionable ankle length skirt with side split and leather high heeled shoes.

Very nice too I'm sure, thought Ruby sarcastically. This woman did not look like she needed a widow's pension but she would have received one had it not been for Nashey. But thanks to him one of the men so complicit in transforming so many wives into widows by launching lifeboats half full, was still alive.

Ruby returned to the present, focusing on Mrs Mayor who was still speaking. But Ruby continued to look rather than listen. She now observed a woman who knew she would be speaking to poor working class women all day, yet her ensemble would not have looked out of place at Royal Ascot. Amongst the finery on display was a hat with wide brim and feather trim, short-sleeved silk dress with infill of lace trimmed with embroidered and beaded braid, long lace mittens and velvet handbag. Mrs Lightoller looked like a veritable ragamuffin in comparison.

Ruby forced herself to listen to the woman. She was explaining that the fund was to be maintained along frugal lines. The weekly pension to be paid was half the wage that had been previously earned by the deceased, which was for the maintenance of the widow, plus a separate allowance for each dependent child. The local manager of the White Star Line scanned a ledger and told Mrs Turner what she already knew to her cost that her husband had been on the lowest of the seven pay scales for crewmen on board so she would receive half of his twenty five shillings per week wage.

Twelve and six a week. Ruby considered the amount. That will be barely enough to keep mother out of the poorhouse, on the breadline in a slum.

"Why is mother being paid according to what father earned; only twelve and six when the widow of an engineer gets two pounds? They've both lost husbands the same haven't they? They've both got to feed and clothe themselves and pay their rent and funeral insurance?" asked Ruby, directing her gaze and therefore her question at the still married Mrs Lightoller.

The wife of the second officer was only there as window dressing. She had not expected to take an active role. She looked along the line for reassurance. A wealthy local businessman, William Richards, took this as his cue to make his contribution to affairs.

"The fund is to maintain but not improve existing living standards," he said bluntly.

Ruby took a breath. She knew it was important to keep the growing anger she felt out of her voice.

"But when father was away on the ships, he didn't cost mother anything for food, and the rent and keeping warm in winter stays the same whether two people are in the house or one. Mother needs almost as much now as she did when father was alive. But in any case, why cannot mother have her money now, in one go? I worked it out she must be due a tidy sum that she could live very well on for the rest of her days; perhaps two hundred and fifty pounds or thereabouts."

The businessman didn't have an answer about the food, warmth or rent, so concentrated on Ruby's query about a lump sum payment.

"Poor widows cannot be expected to manage money responsibly."

Out of the mouths of bastards, thought Ruby.

"I am a widow," said Ruby. "I have been one since I was eighteen. I was a cashier on the Titanic. I made my balance every night."

Richards was not used to being talked to like this by a woman. He grunted his disapproval before glaring towards Mrs Mayor for support. She duly obliged by aiming a puzzled frown and pursed lips at the young woman. She found this arguing over money to be all very tiresome. As far as she was concerned these people should be grateful the committee were being kind enough to take the time to deal with such affairs on their behalf. She rustled amongst her papers and found the letter she was looking for, and held it up for the two women in front of her to see.

"If mother wishes to increase her income, we have been contacted by someone who has asked us to supply her with a woman to act as her servant," said Mrs Mayor, smiling condescendingly at the woman whom she had just called 'mother'. "She does state that she requires someone under forty as the work will be hard, but we could contact her to enquire if she would consider…"

"Does mother still keep her pension if she finds work?" queried Ruby.

"Under normal circumstances, no. She would lose her pension if she found other means of support. As my colleague Mr Richards has quite rightly pointed out, the fund is there to maintain not increase levels of income. But with regard to this position I am sure we could …" at this point she looked along the line for nods of agreement which she duly received, "make an exception."

Ruby smelt a large aggressive rodent but she was not going to make it easy for this woman. She did not ask the obvious question. She simply sat there looking back at the committee, as did her mother. Thus Mrs Mayor felt the need to fill the void.

"The remuneration is you see, just two shillings and sixpence per week," she said with a remarkable lack of embarrassment.

Disgust and sarcasm fought each other for attention in Ruby's thoughts. Remuneration indeed; are you sure it's not a stipend?

It was clear to Ruby that Titanic widows were now considered fair game by the sweated labour market. And these so called do-gooders in front of her were quite happy to act as brokers.

At this point Mabel Turner spoke for the first time. She knew her daughter's temper well enough to know that she might be about to tell the Mayor's wife exactly where she could tell that chancer to stick her job.

"That's all right your ladyship I'm sure I can manage on what you people kindly give me. I wouldn't want to deprive some poor younger widow the chance to earn a crust."

Being called 'your ladyship' succeeded where offering a poverty stricken old woman a job for a fraction of the going rate had failed. A suitably uncomfortable Mrs Mayor moved the meeting along, being sure to conduct what she was saying to the hitherto virtually ignored widow, who was advised that she would be visited regularly by one of the committee's lady visitors to see how she was getting along.

Ruby guessed what this would entail. A middle class woman would be checking up and reporting back to the trustees on whether the money being handed out was being spent in a right and proper manner. They could not have a widow spending it on what the benefactors might consider frivolous. Only the deserving poor were to be eligible for this charity. And this visitor would also no doubt be checking that the widow's standard of living had not gone up, which would suggest she had found other sources of income. These widows were not to use charity to rise above their station.

Ruby was incandescent. This committee was so full of prejudice against working class women that they consigned widows and their families to poverty despite the great fund collected in their names. Women sat on the committee, but they were only there as assistants, selected by men, for men. Mrs Lightoller was nothing other than a man's wife, and an inferior man at that. Mrs Mayor was tarred with the same brush. Did she have a name of her own? No doubt she did but it was about all she did possess.

But Ruby said none of this to the committee members who were looking down on her and her mother in more ways than one. It was impossible to fight such a system individually. Making a fuss would do nothing but possibly count against her mother. Such people could make a moral judgement to write a poor widow off as undeserving of her pittance of a pension with a stroke of the pen. Nashey telling her about London's docks officials robbing his old uncle of the pension he was due sprang into her head. She thought moral and immoral judgements were sometimes not so far apart.

The meeting came to a close and Ruby got up to leave, but buoyed by the success of her previous entry into the conversation, her mother suddenly spoke up.

"What about my girl here? She's a widder-woman same as me and she was on that ship of yours when her father died. Doesn't she get any pension?"

Ruby knew that pensions were only for women widowed by the disaster but she had not thought to inform her mother of this. But Mrs Mayor was quick to do so.

The two women sloped off home, the old one relieved to have escaped from her betters and thankful for small mercies, the other wondering if there were any latter day Annie Besant's to take up the cudgels on poor women's behalf.

Part Two

Preface

Sylvia Pankhurst had come to believe that her mother and sister's new campaign, increasing the level of violence perpetrated by their Suffragette movement, was becoming counter-productive. The recent attacks on the West End of London which had culminated in two hundred and forty women smashing almost every ground floor Oxford Street shop window had proven a tipping point. There was a level of civil disobedience that the public would tolerate, even perhaps appreciate and support on occasion, but these latest attacks had gone too far. Press and public opinion, which the Suffragettes had worked so hard and so successfully to change and cultivate over the past nine years, had returned to its earlier hostility towards them.

The efforts of middle class women were all very well, but Sylvia believed the movement needed to return to the beliefs and direction she and her mother had originally envisaged for it before what she considered the unrealistic principles and snobbery of her sister Christabel changed its course. The fight for the vote needed to be for, and by, all women including those of the working classes. But she appreciated that working women had more pressing duties to hand than mere politics. She needed to get working class men on board because only through their good graces could progress be made.

Sylvia thus decided to decamp down to the East End, to

set up her own semi-autonomous branch of her mother and sister's organisation. This particularly poverty stricken part of London would be Sylvia's headquarters from which she would attempt to galvanise working men and women to the suffrage cause. She chose to settle in Bow so she could offer her support to George Lansbury, who had just resigned his safe Labour seat in the House of Commons to fight the resultant Bow and Bromley bye-election as a Women's Suffrage and Socialist candidate.

She thought Lansbury had been naïve to allow himself to be used as a tool of the WSPU. In resigning he had alarmed the establishment that other MP's might do the same on their issue of choice such as Ireland and industrial relations, which were the dominant subjects of the day. Consequently the strongest possible challenge would be mounted in the East End against women's suffrage. Votes for Women in Bow would need all the support that Sylvia could muster.

Chapter 11

"We are here, not because we are law-breakers;
we are here in our efforts to become law-makers."

Emmeline Pankhurst, leader of the Women's
Social and Political Union

October 1912:

Sylvia Pankhurst and a young American woman, her friend
and assistant Zelie Emerson, had ventured down to Bow
looking for suitable premises for their new organisation. It
was barely evening but autumn was already bringing down
its curtain of early darkness. The two women were walking
along Bow High Street passing the area's central focus,
Bow Church, when they noticed a huge man standing on
a costermonger's barrow outside the church. He was
reaching up to paint a large statue of the old Liberal Prime
Minister, William Gladstone. He had only painted the
hands so far. The man spotted the women and appeared
less than enthralled with having an audience for his
handiwork.

"Wot you two gawpin' at?" he barked.

"Beg pardon I'm sure. Curiosity did kill the cat did it not?
I will leave you to your work sir. A long job ahead I see,"
replied Sylvia courteously.

The man had painted the hands red. Sylvia assumed this must be the start of an undercoat.

"Finished," said the man with a hint of triumph in his voice.

And with that he jumped down off the cart and stood next to them, looking up at his handiwork with the grimmest of smiles on his face. His initial grumpiness appeared to have disappeared. Sylvia detected the man wanted to tell them more.

"Red hands, a mystery to be sure. Can I ask its significance?"

"There you are bein' that cat again," said the man gruffly as he wiped his hands with a rag.

But just as Sylvia had wondered whether she had misread the situation, the man winked to reassure her that she had not. The man launched into a short history lesson, telling the two women that the statue had been paid for by one of the owners of the Bryant & May matchbox factory, which had once been the largest factory in Britain. He nodded towards a street corner, a short distance up the high street, telling the two women the factory was still there, just down that road.

Sylvia was well aware of the infamous factory. At an early age her staunch socialist father had told her of the evils of the place. The appalling conditions, the terrible wages, the inhuman treatment of its workers, the famous strike where thanks to Annie Besant, one of Sylvia's heroines, the first ever victory of a woman's trade union had taken place.

There was a presence about this huge man that made Sylvia want to make a connection with him. Thus she interjected into his little speech.

"I know of it," she said portentously, nodding. "The

women worked with phosphorous. They suffered Phossy Jaw. Pea-sized pieces of bone falling off as women's jaws crumbled. Vomiting at the factory gates after a shift finished. Sweated wages paid, less fines just for talking or even having dirty feet. And all so the factory could pay its shareholders a fine return. Such things are why I am in politics I assure you."

The man was impressed.

"You know some of it. You don't know all," he stated, careful to keep his tone gentle and without scorn.

He proceeded to tell the two women the story of how the government had once been about to place a tax on matches. The factory owners, concerned higher prices would affect their sales, threatened to deduct the cost of any tax from their workers' wages, and thus matches would not increase in price. The government, well aware the women were already barely keeping out of the workhouse on the wages they were being paid, backed down and to celebrate their victory, Bryant & May had a commemorative fountain built. And they docked money out of the workforce's wages to pay for it. Some of the women had cut themselves in protest. At this point the man nodded along the street again and told Sylvia and Zelie that the fountain was a short distance away.

"So the bastards 'ad blood on their 'ands; Bryant & May and Gladstone cos 'e were in power for donkeys years and never did nuffin' to 'elp those poor little cows or any other poor women round 'ere. I only moved to Bow recent. I saw the fountain so I were gonna smash it up but when I sees this statue I 'ad a better idea. More clever see."

He nodded up at the blood now on Gladstone's hands.

"A fine art work if I may say so Mr er…" smiled Sylvia.

"Nash. But everyone calls me Nashey."

"But I fear the LCC will be along sharply enough to remove your handiwork Nashey."

"If they do, it'll be back the next day. They'll soon get the picture." This confident tone was then replaced by one of ominous menace. "And sharp if I catch one of 'em doin' it."

Sylvia didn't doubt it. She feared for the poor council worker who ended up on the wrong side of this man. Before she had a chance to reply, Nash changed the subject.

"Any'ow, what you ladies down 'ere for this time a day? It's gettin' dark, time yer got yerselves off 'ome."

"Oh, we're looking for shop premises for rent," said Zelie. "I guess you don't know of any round these parts? We want plenty of window space in front and office space out back, but can't find what we want."

"There appear to be no bow windows in Bow," joked Sylvia.

Nash thought the quip quite funny but kept a straight face. He nodded over the two women's shoulders.

"Woss that, Scotch mist?" he said sarcastically.

Neither woman understood his question but both followed his nod, spinning round to see a large empty double bay windowed shop, just yards along the main street, opposite Bow Church. Anything that large was sure to have space at the back too. It looked perfect.

Sylvia's reference to politics had registered with Nash. And there were no members of society of whom he had a lower opinion than politicians. He had never forgiven them for their inaction in the East End after the Whitechapel Murders. They had been all indignation and bluster whilst the killer had been on the loose, with every newspaper, liberal intellectual, philanthropist and women's group querying how a society could allow so much poverty, prostitution and degradation to exist. But once the Nemesis of Neglect had disappeared back into the shadows from whence he came and the killing spree stopped, politicians inhaled a huge breath of relief and carried on as before, namely doing little or nothing to solve the East End's ills. The very reason Nash had not killed the maniac when he had had the chance, before the monster committed his final most appalling murder, was the belief that social improvements would come out of the publicity surrounding the crimes. But Nash had been taught a terrible lesson, that whatever the end, it can never justify the most terrible of means.

Nash's inclination was thus to become less sociable to this pair, but now he was the inquisitive feline. He wanted to find out what these two were up to, and the best way to do that was to appear friendly.

"Wot you ladies wanna rent a shop round 'ere for? Wot yer sellin'?" he enquired in a light tone.

"Votes for women!" said the two of them in unison as if they had rehearsed it.

Nash had never thought about the vote one way or the other. What was so important about putting a cross in a box every few years? The wealthy men who collected their dividends from Bryant & May were members of the politicians' brotherhood. Liberals, Conservatives, they were all the same. The small victory of the women at the factory had shown it was trade unions, not politicians that could make a difference. And they had made good gains over the past twenty odd years. But Nash was not interested in talking politics with these women. He kept the tone frivolous.

"All very good I'm sure ladies but that won't pay the rent will it?"

"Oh, we will be selling things too. But at a price people can afford, so as to attract them in to see us. Perhaps you can advise what would be a good stock Nashey?"

Sylvia had asked this with just the slightest coquettish gleam in her eye. Her intuition told her that this man could be useful to them. He was clearly a man of principle, determination and fearlessness, with an appreciation of and respect for women and an understanding of unfairness. She would need men like this on her side if this branch of the WSPU was to survive in Bow.

"Tea, thas yer best bet gells, you mark my words. Thas what people live on round 'ere. Tea and fresh air only the air ain' so fresh is it? The chandler's shop on the corner charge summin' criminal for tea."

"But aren't there bigger, less expensive shops for such staples heh?" queried Zelie.

Sylvia cut in quickly, beating Nash to the chance of correcting her friend.

"People are not disposed to use such establishments Zelie because they have to buy in larger quantities they can ill afford. The corner shop will sell in small affordable quantities, though expensive in the long run. And I daresay the shop may offer them credit too, to see them through to pay day. Is that not correct Nashey?"

Nash was impressed. This plump middle class woman knew her poor working class onions. She seemed unlike any politician or lady slummer he had ever come across. His initial disdain for the two women started to evaporate as quickly as it had appeared. He nodded his assent and there followed a good deal of talk, too vital to be considered small. Nash advised the women on whom to contact regarding the rental of the shop and, once it became apparent the women intended to live in the area too, did likewise about lodgings, and how much they should pay for both. If the owner of the shop would not budge on what was bound to be an inflated price to a couple of perceived slummers, they were to mention they were friends of Nashey. He felt sure that would speed the negotiations to a satisfactory conclusion. Nash also educated the women in elements of life in Bow that might be of use to them, whilst the women reciprocated by imparting information about what their plans were in the area. Nash thought they were wasting their time but kept this to himself. He wished them good luck and told them where they could find him if they ever needed any help, but it was just something to say in parting. He didn't expect to see them again.

******

The negotiations for the rental of the shop had gone pretty much as Nash had predicted. The owner had taken one look at what he thought to be a couple of slummers with more money than sense and immediately doubled the price he had in mind for the shop. And great political debater though she was, Sylvia was no match for arguing money with a savvy, avaricious East End slum landlord, till Zelie casually threw the name of Nashey into the conversation. Ten minutes later the man had a month's fair rent in his back pocket as he handed over the keys of the shop.

It had been a baker's premises, and still retained a doughy aroma, which was perfume to the women's noses compared to the disgusting bouquet of death that assaulted their senses on the streets from the neighbouring soap-works and tanneries. The next few days saw the inside of the shop swept, cleaned and fitted out, before the two women then set about advertising their wares. George Lansbury's son Willie had arranged for material from the family's wood factory to be used to build a speaker's platform from which Sylvia and her supporters could hold meetings. This now stood outside the shop, but for the time being it had another purpose. Sylvia stood atop the platform so she could paint Votes for Women neatly on the shop's fascia, using her artistic skills to gild it with gold leaf. Meanwhile Zelie busied herself by adorning the brickwork either side of the shop window with posters. One promoted a talk by a friend of Sylvia's, the ex-financial secretary of the WSPU Fred Pethick-Lawrence, entitled Government Burglars. Another was an advertisement for the Votes for Women newspaper. But pride of place went to advertising a forthcoming public meeting at Bow Baths where George Lansbury was to speak. Further posters were hung up inside the shop window and almost as an afterthought some stock for sale was also placed in the display.

They had taken Nash's advice and were offering tea. The WSPU's impressive merchandising department had been set to work on procuring, packaging and labelling the stuff. Within days Votes for Women tea had been brought to market, at a price that was sure to attract customers.

The two women and their shop brought astonished looks from the passing populace. And that most enquiring of minds, of the street urchin, ensured the shop soon became a congregating point for children. The two women were quick to make friends with their new found fan club and, along with sweets, plied them with Votes for Women leaflets to take home to their parents.

Zelie was a big hit with the older boys in particular, not just for what they thought was her highly amusing accent, but because when she had been handing out sweets to one of them he had spotted the scars across her wrists. He was old enough to appreciate what they represented.

"Cor, what you been doin' to yerself lady?" he asked in hushed, awed tones.

"Never you mind about that my lad," interjected Sylvia with a playful tap to the boy's head, and sent him on his way.

He left whispering to his little gang of mates, each of them looking back over their shoulder to take another look at the woman with the funny voice who at some point in her life had tried to commit suicide. Sylvia swopped a meaningful glance with Zelie as they both remembered that awful time when the force-feeding in prison and the feelings of despair and hopelessness that it engendered had got too much for the young American to cope with any longer.

The moment was broken when a man rushed out of their shop head down, shoulders hunched and carrying something as if he was walking into a strong piercing wind holding a baby in his arms. There was a case for less haste more speed as he barged into one of the boys. A small package fell to the ground.

"'ere! 'e's nicked a load of your tea lady!" observed one of the boys to Zelie. "Get 'im lads!"

The chase was on and a foot race began, by a group of older boys and a stream of younger children eager to join in the fun whose shorter legs and lesser determination rendered each of them backmarkers well behind the criminal pied piper.

The women were later in the process of closing up shop for the day when they saw a policeman making his way purposefully towards them. Their hearts sank. They had been careful not to break any laws as far as they knew. Sylvia suspected there must be a local council rule about fly-posting they were unaware of and the police were going to use that against them. The policeman, carrying a small plywood open crate under his arm, walked into the shop and set the container down before taking off his helmet. Unused to having to deal with middle class women in darkest Bow there was an uncomfortable look to the policeman as he addressed the women with a nod for each of them accompanied by a tautology.

"Beg pardon marm, marm beg pardon."

"What can I do for you officer?" enquired Sylvia, adopting a haughty tone to maintain her apparent superiority over this nervous man.

"Are you able to identify these goods marm?" he enquired, Adam's apple bobbing.

The two women glanced down at several packets of Votes for Women tea. Having had it confirmed that the tea was their property, the policeman told them the story of how a man had been arrested in connection with the stealing of said property, and that they will shortly be receiving a summons to appear before the magistrate to give evidence in the case. As he donned his helmet to leave he also advised them that they should take a little more care to ensure more stock was not stolen in the future. This was Bow after all. The two Suffragettes thanked the policeman and offered him one of their Votes for Women handbills as a passing gift which they hoped he would pass on to his wife or sweetheart. They had only been teasing him but much to their surprise he accepted the leaflet and promised with such seriousness he would indeed pass it on, that they did not doubt it.

As the policeman thankfully escaped their clutches, the two women shared a smile at the irony of them receiving a summons to appear before a magistrate. It would be the first time they had done so and not ended up in prison, after which their next meal arrived in their stomach compliments of a steel gag, funnel and feeding tube.

The following morning Sylvia and Zelie arrived to open up the shop, discussing how they might take the policeman's advice of the previous day to make their stock a little more secure. A heavily pregnant young woman was waiting for them at the shop door. Good mornings duly swopped, the three women entered the premises. The woman quickly introduced herself as the wife of the man who had been arrested for stealing the tea. She and her husband had several small children and were suffering hard times due to the husband having no work. He was a coalman by trade so things were always tough in the summer but they usually saved a bit the previous winter, and this, trips to the pawnbroker and getting credit from the local shops, usually saw them through. But the previous summer having been the longest hottest one in living memory had meant they had struggled even more than usual this past twelve-month, and now the following autumn having been so mild to date, there was still not enough work about. The tattered rags in which the woman was dressed bore evidence that there was genuine sob in this story. Her husband had been passing their shop and had not the slightest intention of committing any larceny, but when he had seen the two shopkeepers outside playing with the children, having left the tea unprotected, on the most terrible of impulses he had dashed in and grabbed as many packages as he could hold. He was a good man, only drank when he could afford to, didn't knock her about and was normally law-abiding. It was just a moment of madness brought on by desperation.

It was not long before Sylvia was standing before the local magistrate. She wondered how long it would be before she was standing before him again, only this time with her in the dock. Sylvia claimed that the whole tea-stealing incident was a joke; a simple piece of mischief as many such acts were against Suffragettes. She continued that whether one believed in their cause or not, one had to admit that Suffragettes could bear a joke at their expense better than anyone. And she felt sure that if released the man would be kept out of any future trouble by his fine upstanding wife. At this, Sylvia shifted the attention of the magistrate with a casual wave of the arm towards the heavily pregnant woman sitting in the front row of the viewer's section, perched high on a large cushion so that her large bump could be seen by the official on the bench. The magistrate let the husband off with the sternest of warnings about his future conduct, delivered with a stare from above dipped spectacles as only a magistrate or perhaps a headmaster could.

Chapter 12

"Men make the moral code and they expect women to accept it. They have decided that it is entirely right and proper for men to fight for their liberties and their rights, but that it is not proper for women to fight for theirs."

Emmeline Pankhurst, WSPU

Stone-throwing to break windows, which had become the Suffragettes' stock-in-trade act of violent protest was accepted by the majority of the poor working class as a reasonable piece of municipal insubordination. The previous month's attacks on golf courses, when the words 'Votes for Women' were burnt into greens with acid had been met with amusement amongst a populace who wouldn't know a pitch from a putt. And they considered it fair play for telephone and telegraph wires to have been cut. The poor did not have the means for a telephone and the only telegrams they ever received informed women they had been widowed or lost a son fighting for the country that did not allow them a vote. But recent Suffragette arson attacks such as the one in Regent's Park last week were edging up close to the line in the sand across which the poor working class would not tread.

Sylvia needed to rouse East Enders to the cause of Votes for Women before she was tarred with her mother's increasingly violent Suffragette brush. Her first speech on her new home soil of Bow was to be delivered from atop her wooden purpose-built speakers' platform. She had only expected a small crowd to gather so thought she would keep it short, essentially just introducing herself and her organisation, and telling of her support for George Lansbury at the forthcoming bye-election. But she was pleasantly surprised to see a sizeable audience.

The name Pankhurst had had the desired effect of attracting a large crowd. Not that there were many women to be seen. Most heads had caps on them. A good collection of working class husbands, fathers, brothers and sons had come to hear her speak more out of a sense of curiosity and celebrity-spotting than any desire to hear political doctrine. The chance of seeing one of the infamous Pankhursts was too good an opportunity to miss. Another fair number had come purely to heckle and laugh, to have a bit of fun at the expense of women in general and this woman in particular. A few inverted snobs were also there to show their displeasure at this woman trying to impose her middle class views on the poor. And there were a few more serious politicos, men fervently opposed to women getting the vote, who were there on a reconnaissance mission to appraise the opposition and, if the occasion presented itself, test it too.

But for Zelie and George Lansbury's young daughter-in-law, Daisy, who had come along to add her support stocked with banners and handbills, Sylvia believed there to be no supporters of women's rights there. She thought she was entering the bear pit alone.

******

Nash had heard the story of how those two women at the old baker's shop had saved a mate of his nephew's, young Jimmy Pearson, from getting a stretch in prison. He had been impressed when he had first met them, but now they had really gone up in his estimation. And Jimmy was so thankful he had become a dedicated supporter of their cause.

On answering a knock on his door, Nash had been amazed to find Jimmy standing there with a bundle of Votes for Women handbills in his hand. Nash had accepted one and then had to stand there and hear all about how East End men had to become part of the women's movement. Nash had only got rid of him by promising to go along to hear Sylvia Pankhurst speak later that day. Jimmy was astute enough to know that being fobbed off with a promise was only so much talk. He told Nash he would call for him and they could go along together. Jimmy had refused Nash's invitation to come in, so Nash had been standing at his door so long his frostbite-ravaged feet had started to ache. He agreed to Jimmy collecting him just so he could shut the door and go for a nice sit down.

When the knock on the door came, Nash opened up to find a sea of men's faces in front of him. He was far from being the only one Jimmy had cajoled into going along. Nash took his place in the sizeable group and they made their way towards Sylvia's meeting.

They arrived just in time to see Sylvia climb up on her platform. She started her speech by telling the crowd that she had moved to Bow to create a rallying cry to working class women around the country. She was also anxious to fortify the position of working women when the vote was, as it would inevitably be, won. The existence of a self-reliant movement amongst working women was the greatest aid in guarding their rights. She wanted to rouse women to fight on their own account, to revolt against terrible working and living conditions and demand a share of the benefits of civilisation and progress.

Some of the audience, despite their antipathy towards Suffragettes, found themselves warming to this sparkling young woman. Men nodded to each other, grudging smiles silently saying to each other, 'she's a bit of a gell ain't she?' There were shouts of approval, albeit with a level of condescension in them.

But the likely lads who had come to have some fun thought it was time to have their say. There was some light-hearted heckling and banter which Sylvia handled in her usual witty and charming way, but then something potentially a little more serious was shouted from the crowd.

"Votes for Ladies!" heckled a young wag, raising a few laughs.

The simple slur cut directly to the Achilles heel of any Suffragette speech. Mrs Pankhurst's organisation was only fighting for the vote for propertied women. But the only women of property in Bow were a few madams who owned houses of ill repute. The WSPU's rallying cry was essentially 'votes for women… of the middle class'. And even if they did flock to become active militant members of Sylvia's more local-interest branch of the organisation, how could working women afford the loss of earnings or have their children cared for, whilst they protested or worst still went to prison for their beliefs. It was only 'ladies' who had the luxury of a private allowance and nursemaids.

Sylvia had been expecting such a taunt and had her

riposte ready, but before she had a chance to deliver it, several men started shouting in unison as if it were part of a prearranged plan, in a far more aggressive tone, completely drowning her out. It was now apparent that the crowd was larger than expected because members of the Men's League for Opposing Women's Suffrage had turned out in force.

"Boats for women! Titanic! Titanic! Titanic!"

The chant was repeated again and again, ad nauseam. And with each shout, it got louder as men, who had been listening to Sylvia's arguments with interest, were swept away in the moment. The implication was clear. It was not merely a matter of men dying on a sinking ship whilst women were saved. Men fought wars; saved the nation; women didn't. Why should women be allowed to vote on such matters when they didn't fight themselves? Women were natural pacifists. With women voting we might not have fought the Crimean, China, Zulu or Boer wars. And then where would we be?

Nash did not like bullies but the 'Votes for Ladies' taunt had been light hearted enough and from what he knew of Sylvia Pankhurst from their meeting and from what he had heard about her from Jimmy, he had been confident she could look after herself. A smile had been on his face as he awaited her response, but it was soon wiped off by 'Titanic!'

Nash had only taken a couple of steps towards the hecklers when Jimmy waved the back of his hand somewhere in the general direction of Nash's chest, without having the temerity to actually touch it.

"My boys'll do it; this ain't your fight Nashey."

Jimmy nodded to some hard cases amongst his gang and they pushed their way towards the hecklers who had started the chant. Straw boater-wearing Men's League bully boys were no match for Jimmy's East End lads, who dragged the trouble-makers away as quietly as possible. There were some blows thrown, oaths sworn and threats made, but there was little in the way of real violence, at least within sight and sound of the meeting.

Nash pushed through the crowd towards the front and climbed up on Sylvia's platform. The momentum of the chant meant that some in the crowd were still shouting it even though its original perpetrators were now around the corner in an alley receiving the roughest of facials.

A few of the younger wags started to shout things at the man on the platform who was spoiling their fun, but others spotted who it was and fell quiet. Those who only liked to shout on the bandwagon of others also went silent, and the pandemonium stopped as quickly as it had started. Nash stared at the men.

"Some of you know me. Boats for women. Fink that's funny da yer?! I 'ear the word Titanic again and there'll be trouble for thems that says it! D'you 'ear?! A lad just told me this weren't my fight. Well now I'm tellin' yer it is. This brave little cow's worth ten of any of yer. Now 'ear what she's got to say or fuck orf oud of it!"

And with that he got down from the platform, walked to the side of Zelie and Daisy, and stood there, huge forearms folded across his chest, looking with a face like thunder out at the crowd. The two women, feeling not a little uneasy standing next to their new recruit suddenly found their shoes had become rather interesting. Those men who didn't know him, and therefore would have been happy to pour scorn on a man acting tough who was old enough to be many of their fathers, cast sly glances round the crowd to see who would be the first to have a go. The faces of those who did know the man, gave them their answer.

"Bravo!" shouted an enthusiastic male voice to end the momentary silence.

The young man standing next to him repeated the cry. The phrase suggested they were a brace of well-educated young men from the Lansbury family. And then the two of them shouted in unison.

"Votes for Women!"

This changed the atmosphere again, back to a friendlier more positive one, clearing the way for Sylvia to continue her speech. She spoke about enfranchisement of not just women but working class men. Her audience cheered, the crowd now displaying a heartfelt honesty in their appreciation, the condescension gone from their voices.

Sylvia kept the speech short, knowing when to quit while she was ahead. Realising she needed to make the most of the positive atmosphere she jumped down from her platform and urged everyone to follow her on a procession around the district. Rapturous cheers of assent rang out as the crowd started to follow her. This was going better than she could possibly have imagined thanks to Jimmy and that man whom she had met by Gladstone's statue.

She marched down Fairfield Road past the infamous Bryant & May factory, shouting criticisms as she passed, before turning and heading east shouting Votes for Women slogans. Heads started to pop out of windows. The size of the crowd following her swelled with women as well as men. And when the River Lea blocked her way, she led the crowd back to central Bow where, on the street corner opposite her own shop stood a brightly lit undertaker's premises. It was too good a target to ignore. Sylvia picked up a heavy flint and threw it at the window of the shop. She was not at risk of being recruited by the local cricket club, the window proving not literally too good to miss as the unsuccessful spent projectile clattered on the cobbles. But someone in the crowd with a better throwing arm got the idea and did the job for her, a large cheer accompanying the sound of breaking glass. Other local men joined in the fun so the undertaker's was soon lying open to the elements, though its main stock in trade was unlikely to be pilfered.

A couple of constables had joined the crowd by this time and crunched over the glistening pavement to arrest Sylvia on the spot. Daisy Lansbury grabbed hold of a policeman, and Zelie, who having brought up the rear of the growing procession had missed out on the carnage at the undertaker's, found a nice juicy Liberal Club window to her liking. The two of them were soon bundled into the police station to join their leader. Sylvia did not want the incident to escalate so made it clear to her new supporters that she wanted to be arrested to gain publicity for the cause and that they should simply go home and tell their wives, mothers, sisters and daughters what had occurred.

In the chaos the male stone throwers were ushered away in the crowd. Having got to safety away from the risk of arrest, Nash surveyed the scene in reflective mood. Why had he not only joined Sylvia Pankhurst's procession but been right up the front of it almost by her side? And why had he risked arrest by being the first to throw that stone through the undertaker's window? Telling the crowd that the women's fight was now his had been just something to say in the heat of the moment; for effect; to play the tough man; but now he was glad he had said it. He had never thought the vote important, for working men, or women, but he now saw how this young slip of a woman could hold a crowd in the palm of her hands. And an East End crowd at that; there wasn't any tougher. That was real power. That was what could change things for the poor. Make the changes that politicians should have brought about twenty five years ago. This woman was different; she understood what was needed. And rather than just shout the odds in a place full of her own supporters guaranteed to provide a rousing ovation, like male politicians did, this woman had the bravery and determination to not only make speeches in Bow but have the courage of her convictions and live there too. That was more than any male politician would ever do who wasn't from around these parts. And someone in the crowd had informed him that this woman had a mother and a couple of sisters at home who had that same power.

He had sold his soul that terrible night a quarter of a century ago when he had thought he had the power of life and death. He had been morally wrong from the start, but it was the politicians who did nothing to improve the lot of the poor who proved he was also quite actually wrong, and not a day had gone by since when he had not wondered how he could fight back against them. And now for the first time he was convinced that he knew.

★★★★★★

Sylvia, Zelie and Daisy were marched off to Bow's police station where, once inside, the dynamic between the warring parties changed to a friendlier one. The young policemen, unused to having to manhandle ladies, were relieved to have finished performing an awkward duty and were also thankful that the women had deflected the crowd from what could have become an ugly incident. For their part the women were full of the excited energy that the freedom of the cause, away from the normal stultifying life of a middle class woman, afforded all Suffragettes. The great middle class female pastime of keeping up appearances was still followed with alacrity, but it was the appearance and reality of being a serious politician. It had been like a game of rugby with the police; war for the duration of the match, then shake hands and become friendly afterwards. The women and constables bounced witticisms off one another before a few sharp words from the latter's sergeant reminded the young men of their duty.

Daisy was dismissed by the court but Sylvia and Zelie, who looked familiar to the old magistrate, though he couldn't quite place where from, were found guilty of criminal damage, given a fine and bound over for six months under their own recognizances. The two women did the usual Suffragette protest of refusing to pay their fines or be bound over. For the more serious offence of contempt of court, they were sent to prison.

Mrs Pankhurst no longer approved of her daughter's more democratic desire for the struggle to be broadened to include the vote for the working classes. On hearing of her daughter's incarceration she immediately paid Sylvia and Zelie's fines anonymously so they were released from prison the following day.

Daisy had opened the shop in their absence. They arrived back there to find it crowded with new followers scrubbing tables and doing further cleaning and tidying, whilst others had been arranging to march on Holloway to cheer them. Mrs Watkins, a widow struggling to maintain herself by sweated sewing-machine work and a feisty young woman called Mrs Moore, seemed to be in charge of affairs. It transpired that they lived on the route Sylvia had taken on her procession, and were swept along in the crowd. They had turned up at the shop the next day and signed on as WSPU delegates, and these two leading matriarchs of the area had soon got others on board too.

Chapter 13

"I do not agree recent violence is by a few excitable members getting out of hand. It is obviously premeditated and arranged and will get more violent then it will lose support."

Millie Garrett-Fawcett, president of the National Union of Women's Suffrage Societies

Ruby's best pal on the Titanic, an assistant fish cook in the Ritz restaurant, was a South Londoner who was now lying at the bottom of the ocean, the fish having their revenge. She had once advised Ruby that she could do worse than settle in her own neck of the woods, in a place called St Johns. It was a good spot in which to find work, a poor but respectable working class area wedged between the more affluent Lewisham and the poverty of Deptford and Bermondsey. There was shop work in Lewisham, lots of factory work in Bermondsey and a good market in Deptford at which to buy cheap food and clothes. It also had a railway station only a few short stops from Waterloo, London's railway terminus coming from Southampton, so it could not be a much easier journey, and not being that far away she should be able to save up the rail fare home to see her mother a few times a year.

Ruby was determined never to go back to domestic servitude and as far as she was concerned returning to ship-work was out of the question. With her natural aptitude for figures, she had considered training as a typewriter with a view to working her way up to being a clerk, but from what she had heard of such positions, they were still the exclusive domain of men, and the idea of employment in an office with no chance of advancement to figure work horrified her. She had thus settled in St Johns with a view to getting work in Lewisham High Street, which was developing into a major shopping thoroughfare.

Shop work had also traditionally been the domain of men, with an apprenticeship given, but stores were becoming larger, taking on more staff, and employment law now made hours of work less arduous. And the most important aspect of the job had become to attract customers. Shop owners were thus now employing more and more women, especially young and attractive ones.

Ruby was just the type that shops were looking for, but she had arrived in London destitute, still wearing the cheap second-hand clothes she had acquired in New York. And tending to have to wash her hair in cold water meant that she struggled to achieve the prim and proper, pinned up lady-like hairstyle which was required. So despite putting on her best pseudo middle class accent, she simply did not look smart enough when she called in at Chiesman's, Lewisham's big flagship department store, looking for work. She didn't even make it as far as the offices where she might have been able to win over someone in recruitment with her charms. An old male floorwalker was asked to see her out. He appeared snootily full of his own importance as he escorted her through the store but at the front door was kind enough to wish her good luck in her search for a position and mentioned the new Woolworth's that was opening soon in Lewisham. Apparently they had already opened a store in nearby Peckham and had others planned throughout London. He left it unsaid that opening up so many stores meant they were likely to be less discerning about the quality of the staff they employed.

"You might say they are opening up all over the shop," said the old man smiling at his own pun. "I suggest you make application to them."

"Thank you. I will," said Ruby with an enthusiastic but false smile.

She tried every other shop in Lewisham except Woolworth's. But stores were tending to lay off staff rather than take them on in the present economic malaise. Bermondsey factories were far less discriminating as their wages had not risen since the turn of the century despite over a decade of high inflation, so jobs in them were easy to find.

Ruby worked short spells at Cross & Blackwell, Pearce Duff and Hartley but she found the highly repetitive nature of the work boring and demeaning.

The poor rates of pay in these factories meant Ruby had been unable to save a penny since her previous trip to Southampton to take her mother to see the Titanic Relief Fund Committee, so visiting her on the day of the Relief Fund lady visitor's first appearance was out of the question. A letter, written by her sister June on behalf of their mother, soon informed Ruby that the lady had been every bit as haughty as the members of the committee. Ruby felt guilty that she had not been there to assist her mother.

How her sisters would have enjoyed her absence, she thought. The little sister who they believed considered herself too good for the sort of menial work they did for a living, now reduced to working for a pittance in a factory. But they were wrong. She considered factory work to be no worse than domestic service or working on a ship. After all, it had been her choice. It was dirtier and smellier of course but you soon got used to that. It was the lack of any chance of betterment, any light at the end of the tunnel that was so depressing. The women worked, the men oversaw. And judging by the low morale of the workforce, her fellow workers felt the same.

She considered that trade unions were all very well but they were mostly concerned with getting better pay and conditions for male workers, and within an existing status quo that said of women, give them a regular weekly wage packet to keep themselves and their families out of the workhouse and they'll be content. Not happy or fulfilled, nor treated or paid the same as men, but thankful for small mercies. Ruby was far from content in any of her jobs and always moved on, searching for something different. She didn't know what she wanted, but she knew that this was not it. She was a square peg in a round hole who believed that there had to be more to a working class woman's life than servitude of one form or another.

★★★★★★

Ruby was on her way to start a new job at the Peek Frean's factory in Bermondsey. The biscuit company's success in rebranding the Creola as the Bourbon, and also introducing the Cream Sandwich, its most successful new line since the Garibaldi, gave Ruby hope that this would be a more uplifting place to work. At least this factory was a success and must be well run. And such success must mean that the figure work needed would be increasing all the time. Perhaps once she got her feet under the table she might hear of a position going as a clerk, for which she could apply.

Not being able to afford to take the bus, she would walk the two miles to the factory. Her initial route took her close to the train tracks. She was close to St Johns railway station when she saw a woman wheeling herself along in a strange looking contraption. It was a wheelchair of sorts. Ruby had only ever seen such a thing on board ocean liners, where a few of their older first class passengers had them. She had never seen one in the poor areas of Southampton or South London, where the paralysed and limbless were left to crawl around the best they could, often hidden away from public gaze in the workhouse. And this woman was incongruously smartly dressed for St Johns. She wore a felt hat with small brim trimmed with three-coloured ribbon band; coat with fur collar and cuffs and leather button boots. And even her practical heavy duty leather gloves looked expensive. She was surely middle class.

The woman pivoted the chair and was now trying to bash her way through the a-jar front door of the corner shop. Ruby usually avoided the shop because on her first and only sortie into it she had seen a huge advertisement on its back wall for Hacks cold lozenges, complete with a horrible looking old man sneezing into a handkerchief. The man reminded Ruby of one of the men known locally as 'Carrington House wallahs' who lived in the huge nearby men's hostel of that name. She thought it was surely the most disgusting advertisement ever devised.

There was clearly something inside the shop that was stopping the door from fully opening, so despite an enthusiastic impersonation of a battering ram, the woman could not quite get through. Ruby could not afford to be late for her first day at a new job. They would probably tell her that if being late was the best she could do on her first day, she need not have bothered, and send her on her way. So she crossed the road to avoid passing the woman and quickened her step. She got ten yards before she craned her neck to see the disabled woman still struggling to get in. Ruby could see through the glass shop-front that the shopkeeper was busy with a customer and was ignoring the woman's efforts. Ruby cursed under her breath and ran back across the road to assist the woman.

On closer inspection the wheelchair was a tricycle with hand-control modifications. Crutches were lodged on either side of the self-propelling makeshift invalid chair.

"Have a mind! You'll have the paint off the door," scolded Ruby.

She was annoyed this distraction would have her running part of the way to the factory to arrive on time for work. And running tended to inflame one of her feet. She had been lucky that the freezing water in the bowels of the Titanic followed by a night in an open boat had left her with nothing more than frostnip, a minor form of frostbite. But all the walking she had done in New York and Halifax on damaged feet had contributed to her being left with a slight weakness in one foot. Her new job would no doubt involve standing all day; it always did, so her weak foot would now be 'killing her' by the end of the day.

"Let me have a go at it," she said with obvious impatience in her voice, easing herself past the tricycle.

She slid sideways through the narrow space in the doorway and saw that the shop had just had a delivery. There were dozens of jars of sweets and several open wooden crates full of cartons of confectionery on the shop floor. There was also a large tin on the outer fringes of the huddle, which if removed would free up enough floor space to allow the door to swing fully open. Ruby tried to move it with her foot at first but it wouldn't budge, so she bent down, grabbed it between her hands and dragged it across the floor. Mission completed she gazed down at her adversary. It was a huge tin of Hacks, complete with handkerchief-man sneezing at her.

The woman wheeled herself in to the shop and thanked Ruby with warm eyes and middle class voice. But no sooner had the woman smiled and her countenance suddenly changed to one of alarm.

"Goodness, look at the clock, I must take my leave," she said.

And with that she spun the chair around in the tight space, knocking over a few thankfully sturdy glass sweet jars as she did so, and was out the door a good deal quicker than she had entered through it. Ruby raised her eyebrows in a look of apology to the shopkeeper, who had glanced upwards for a moment whilst still dealing with his customer, before she followed after the fleeing woman.

"Excuse me missus, but what was all that to do?" she enquired as she jogged alongside the frantically wheeling woman.

"It is 'miss' actually. Which is rather appropriate don't you think, as I *missed* getting into that shop and am about to *miss* my train unless, as my friends in the East End say, I get my skates on. Thanks to you I saw the clock behind the gentleman's shop counter d'you see."

"Train? You're a cripple you can't get on a train!"

"You would be surprised what I can do young lady, and getting on a train is very low on my list of achievements, I can assure you. Now if you will excuse me, needs must don't you know."

The woman having reached a downhill section of street then increased her work rate on the wheels and left Ruby trailing in her wake. Astonishment and curiosity replaced all thoughts of Ruby getting to work on time, her jog accelerating into the fastest pace at which her embattled feet could take her. It was pretty much a dead heat as the two women raced into the ticket hall of St Johns station.

"Good day to you Miss Billingshurst," said a railway porter jovially, touching thumb and index finger to his uniform cap in the usual mark of respect.

The woman exchanged pleasantries with both the porter and ticket booth clerk before asking if the special London fare she had paid last time she had travelled was still available. An apologetic ticket clerk explained that the previous fare, which was a return ticket for less than the cost of a normal single, had been a Lord Mayor's Show special. It was no longer available. But seeing his customer's disappointment he was quick to tell her of a new offer which was two return tickets to London for the price of one. It was, however, only available to passengers departing before half past seven, and the 7.21, the last train before the deadline, was due to arrive imminently.

Ruby had looked on a little out of breath. The middle class woman turned to her panting Good Samaritan, eyed her up and down for a second and then asked if she would like to accompany her to London. There was a second ticket going free after all, so she was very welcome, and she would be useful help getting on and off the train.

A startled Ruby had begun to hesitate when the porter cried out that the 7.21 to Cannon Street was about to pull in. As she paid her fare the woman said that she would take the second return in any case, so the ticket clerk readily passed the little bits of card to her. The porter clipped the tickets but made no attempt to assist his passenger. He knew not to push the fiercely independent woman. She wheeled herself on to the platform as smoke billowed down from the incoming train like a brunette's cascading locks. The column of air the train pushed along in front of itself ruffled the purple, white and green ribbon on the woman's hat as she wheeled herself along, heading in the opposite direction to the arriving steamer.

Ruby saw the woman heading for the very end of the platform, and on a whim found herself running to join her. She could work in a factory any time but it was not every day of the week you were offered a free trip to London, and by a mystery invalid woman at that.

Crowded carriages flashed by them before the train came to rest with the final, far emptier carriage next to them. It was now clear to Ruby why they had come to the end of the platform. She grabbed the handle of the slam-door in front of her, pulled and looked around for guidance as to what to do next. All she saw was the back of a wheelchair as her ticket benefactor headed for the guards van at the back of the train. The guard opened his door and stepped onto the platform, ignoring the woman as he went about his duties, waving a flag and blowing his whistle. Ruby hesitated, feeling the awkwardness of the uninitiated able-bodied in the presence of the disabled. The mystery woman grabbed her crutches, pulled herself upright and held a precarious tottering balance as, with great difficulty, she managed to pull the stronger of her two polio-ravaged legs up the step into the guard's van, dragging the other one up behind her. The guard matter-of-factly picked up the tricycle and placed it in the van, immediately behind the woman.

"All safely aboard mother," he said brightly.

The woman allowed gravity to dump her back into her contraption then rehoused her crutches on the side of it, before words of appreciation and recognition were passed to the cheery young guard. Ruby then rather sheepishly stepped aboard, which had her companion apologising to both her and the guard for not knowing their respective names as an attempt was made to introduce the two of them. Formal pleasantries were duly exchanged between the three new acquaintances.

The guard was quick to apologise to Ruby for not offering a lady his seat. Unfortunately it was company regulations that passengers were not allowed to sit in the guard's designated place. Ruby was quick to tell him that he need not concern himself.

"I would not have taken it had you done so. We are equal, you and I. I have no more right to your seat than you have to mine. There is no such thing as women and children first, that I do know I assure you."

The woman in the wheelchair was studying Ruby intently and had spotted a strange expression flit across the young woman's countenance as she had delivered the last few words of her little speech.

The journey took only twenty minutes from St Johns to Cannon Street. The time was filled easily with small talk initiated by the young man about Deptford's Douglas Way market being known locally as Douglas Street, and London Bridge being the oldest railway station in the world. As the train crossed over the Thames and the guard readied himself to go about his duties at the end of the line, Ruby flummoxed him by propounding that London Bridge could not be the only station of the same age, for surely the first train from it had to run to a destination, and whatever station that was must share the accolade of being the oldest station in the world.

The woman in the wheelchair smiled inwardly. That could have been Christabel Pankhurst herself talking. It was the same unbeatable logic; same type of penetrating mind that had destroyed Lloyd-George's arguments in court; had turned Churchill puce with rage and embarrassment. And though eloquent and quite well spoken, Ruby was clearly working class. She would be a particularly useful recruit.

Ruby helped her new acquaintance from the train and out of the terminus before asking a question that had been on her mind for a few minutes.

"Miss Billingshurst, why did that guard call you mother? You clearly are not his mother. I thought it a most rude way indeed for a young man to speak to a much… a lady."

The hesitation had been spotted for what it was. Ruby had been about to say 'much older lady' but had thought better of it. The older woman was used to such hesitations, but they usually related to something other than her age. She explained to Ruby that it was just the patronising way that many men spoke to her because of her condition.

"But all women, disabled or not, are patronised by men in ways far more unacceptable," she said. "It is a matter of no import today. Let us not speak of it. There are more far more important fish to fry as my friends in the East End would say. Such as, would you like to climb to the top of The Monument Mrs Martin? I am on my way there. And afterwards I will be journeying to Bow and Bromley, where I have some further business matters to which to attend. But before I do, remind me to give you your return ticket home."

Ruby was well aware that climbing to the top of the Monument was impossible for her companion, but the older woman read her thoughts so continued.

"You see I particularly wish to go to the area close to The Monument. I have some business to do in the vicinity. You would be doing me a most awfully good service if you could accompany me. While I take my leave, you could take the steps to the top. I would pay your entrance fee. It is the least I could do in return for all your kindnesses towards me this morning. I am informed it is a most arduous climb to be sure but worth it, for the view is splendid."

Ruby was thrilled and said so. She never thought she would ever get to climb to the top of one of London's greatest sights. The ice, well and truly broken, the older woman thought it was time to be less formal.

"Please call me May, Mrs Martin. And if I might be so bold as to correct you, I am May Billinghurst. The porter chap at St Johns and the guard always call me Billingshurst with an 's' but I don't correct them. They're only men after all. Can't be expected to get things right can they now eh what!?"

The two women shared a chortle at men's expense before Ruby made the obvious reciprocal gesture of informality as they made their way along Cannon Street to The Monument. The ticket booth attendant was just opening up as they arrived. May pulled a purple, white and green scarf out of her pocket as she slipped the man the penny admission fee for Ruby.

"You will be the very first person to the top today Ruby. Take this scarf and dangle it out when you are there to mark the occasion and I can better see you."

Ruby obliged and disappeared into the edifice. Once Ruby had started her climb and was out of sight, May turned back to the attendant.

"And another ticket for me please," she said with the straightest of faces, unclipping her purse.

May liked her little jokes. The attendant's face was a picture as he made no attempt to hide his dismay at the problem which was confronting him.

"You can't…" started the man before May cut him off.

"No my good fellow, of course not, I just want to look up at the steps. It would be such a treat. Might I take the liberty?"

"Well, be quick about it," said the man gruffly trying to hide his awkwardness, "then I won't have to charge you nothing."

The offer was appreciated. It was the sort of tough take-it-or-leave-it charity that May was happy to accept. She put her penny back in her purse and wheeled herself to the foot of the steps. The spiral staircase disappeared out of sight almost immediately. May nodded her satisfaction and headed back out into the surrounding square, bumping across the cobbles towards Pudding Lane before craning her neck to see if she could see her scarf. A few seconds later a breathless Ruby began waving it from the top.

"Yes, that will do very nicely," muttered a self-satisfied May quietly to herself.

A quarter of an hour later an excited and thankful Ruby had re-joined her new friend. She spent the next few minutes regaling May with details of what she had seen. It was only when she started to calm down a little that she thought it might not be appropriate to tell someone in a wheelchair about the views that only someone able-bodied could see. It was time to change the subject.

"Earlier you spoke of Bow and Bromley. Is that near the Bow in the East End? I have a friend who lives there to whom I have been meaning to pay a visit."

"Bromley by Bow and Bow are both in the East End my dear," confirmed May. "They make up the constituency of Bow and Bromley. They are really the same place. Same dinner only different gravy as my friends in the East End say," she chuckled.

Ruby wondered whether she could accompany May to Bow. Perhaps while May was going about her business there, Ruby might have time to look up Nashey. But May had not mentioned her going along so perhaps it was not convenient.

"You have friends in the East End May?" she asked.

"Indeed. I have made many a friendly acquaintance there, just while I have been fighting bye-elections these past few years you understand. Simple people of course but they treat me as they find me, which is to my taste."

"A bye-election?"

Ruby knew what a bye-election was, but was wondering what May could have to do with one.

May took them into an Aerated Bread Co. café as she informed Ruby that she was a Suffragette. Over breakfast

May held court on women's fight for the vote in general, and the Suffragette movement in particular. She was aware that politics could seem rather dry and uninteresting to working class people, so she spiced up the conversation with enthralling tales of Suffragette derring-do. Her pièce de resistance was the story of Black Friday two years earlier.

"Winston Churchill was the new Home Secretary at the time. He had given the police new orders on how to deal with hordes of marching women. They were not to be arrested; they were to be held back and no more. At least that was the official explanation, given after the event for what happened, though I suspect more sinister directions were afoot. We had attempted to march from our open air meeting in Trafalgar Square to rush the House in protest against Prime Minister Asquith's blocking of the Conciliation Bill which would have met our demand that propertied women be given the vote. We were met in Whitehall by a huge cordon of police, and there followed six hours of most horrid and cowardly brutality. Women were hauled off into side streets where bully boys lay in wait to do the police's dirtiest work for them."

May paused for a moment to take a sip of her tea whilst glancing about to check she was not being overheard from neighbouring tables. She leaned forward and lowered her voice somewhat.

"The police were most dishonourable. They used deliberate cruelty and handled our person in a most base way, the details of which one lady cannot relay to another. They also rubbed faces against railings; our oldest lady was punched in the face and hit her head on falling to the ground; one woman was marched to the police station with her skirt over her head."

"And what of you May?" interjected a horrified Ruby.

"Oh, I was thrown out of my tricycle and arrested. We eventually defeated the no-arrest policy I am pleased to say," replied May matter-of-factly.

Ruby was aghast.

"But your…" Ruby felt too perplexed, not to say too awkward, to do any more than leave most of the obvious question unsaid.

"Invalidity? It was of no account. I was cast to the ground of course."

At this point May's matter-of-fact tone changed somewhat to one of pride, seasoned with just a dash of humour for flavour.

"And then no less than three burly young policemen had the onerous task of transporting me to Cannon Row, carrying me above their heads like Billingsgate porters with tubs of fish."

"Cannon Row?"

Two word questions were about as much as the shocked Ruby could muster.

"It's the police station adjacent to Whitehall. It has no cells mind you, but one is taken there to have one's name taken, be charged, and so on. Then it was a ride in a Black Maria for my fellow protesters to Bow Street where there are cells. Sadly I was unable to join them on their journey because the tiny individual cages one is thrust into within the vehicle are only suitable for the able-bodied. One has to bring the knees up under ones chin d'you see such are the limitations of space available. Thus I had the veritable luxury of a motor taxi ride to the same destination, with a policeman guarding me. He told me off for wasting police resources but

I saw him looking excitedly out of the window. His first ride in a motor I'll be bound."

Ruby's thoughts changed in an instant as she remembered her own first motor ride. The change of expression was quite apparent so May attempted to reassure her.

"Do not distress yourself my dear it was a victory I can assure you. We had discredited Mr Churchill just as we had his predecessor Herbert Gladstone, who had been deposed from his office by a previous shocking Suffragette story. And what is more, we even displaced that dastardly Dr Crippen off the front page of all the newspapers!"

Ruby was relieved that her companion had mistaken her dark thoughts for something else. She cast New York back into the little box in the back of her mind where she tried to keep all matters Titanic under lock and key. She re-entered the conversation at hand.

"But that is not a way to treat a cripple lady," she said.

"Oh, it was what I deserved my dear." At this May threw a saucy little smile across the café table before continuing in a matter-of-fact tone. "I had, after all, been using my tricycle as a battering ram. There were not a few policemen and bully boys nurturing bruised shins from my attentions."

Ruby's eyebrows headed north in amazement but she stuck to her argument.

"But a lady should not be treated so."

"You are quite right my dear, she should not. Because she should not be forced to such acts by the unequal laws which make women inferior to men. But when she does, it is only right she be dealt with the same as men. She asks no quarter. She asks simply to be equal."

Ruby agreed with the sentiments entirely but nevertheless

172

she felt her little Titanic box creak a-jar. And before she knew it, the lid was up and the hinges had given way.

"But what of 'woman and children first' and all that?" she queried.

A spontaneous laugh escaped May, her gloved hand immediately shooting up to cover her mouth.

"You see, I am a lady; too well brought up to laugh in a café as I may in my own home," she said before taking a less frivolous tone. "Forgive me my dear. I did not wish to mock I assure you. But did you notice that when we arrived here I replaced my leather wheeling gloves with these fine embroidered lace ones? It is what a lady wears in a café. You see, one can be different from, but still equal to men. But bully boys I will no doubt be locking horns with shortly in Bow will shout 'Titanic' at speakers supporting women's suffrage. 'You want to be the first off a sinking ship *and* have the vote'!"

Ruby laughed on cue at the stupidity of the male argument but inwardly felt annoyed with herself for steering the conversation as badly as Captain Smith had his ship. She threw the hapless captain and his boat back in its box.

Chapter 14

"That was a disgraceful thing for you to say sir. You will go down in history as the man who tortured innocent women. You ought to be driven from public life. The women are fighting for principle. Members would be better employed in doing same."

George Lansbury MP, to Prime Minister Asquith in a House of Commons debate on force-feeding

Though following the principles of her idolised WSPU leaders without question, May secretly disagreed with their belief that the Suffragettes should be an exclusively middle class organisation fighting purely for the vote for propertied women. She thought they should recruit working women because victory might only come about if the movement became a mass one. Thousands of middle class women might irritate the government like so many wasps at a picnic but there was not enough of a sting in their tails. They needed a million hornets to turn up. After all, the Irish were starting to make progress with the government on Home Rule, and she felt certain it was the threat of a great sting in their tail that brought the British government to the negotiation table.

So it was with some Machiavellian pleasure May had noted Ruby hint that she might be interested in a trip to Bow, albeit just to see a friend. And it was clear that she had been enthralled by the Suffragette stories. May thought it was not beyond the realms of possibility that she might be signing up a new recruit to the cause before the day was out. She was confident Christabel, her commander-in-chief, would find it acceptable. After all Ruby, though working class, was clearly intelligent.

It was time for mid-morning coffee. A pot was ordered and during its consumption May filled in some details about her work within the women's movement. She had joined Mrs Pankhurst's Women's Social and Political Union five years ago, and became secretary of the Greenwich branch of the WSPU three years later. She had two important roles. The first was one which any Suffragette might be required to fulfil. She was a day to day organiser of bazaars and demonstrations, worked in a WSPU shop and had a role in the civil disobedience campaign. She was the chief organiser of attacks on pillar boxes by pouring various noxious substances down them to ruin the letters inside. The second role was unique to her. She and the leadership were aware of the importance of the 'Cripple Suffragette', as May was called by the press, in the propaganda campaign. She was thus always to the fore in demonstrations to underline both the brutal tactics employed by the police and the vulnerability of women.

May attempted to emphasise to Ruby the lengths to which women had to go to get the vote, and the depths to which the government were prepared to descend to stop them. The zenith of police brutality, Black Friday, had been just one of several occasions on which she had been arrested. She had always refused to pay her fine, so her original charges of disturbing the peace, assault or criminal damage had been upgraded to contempt of court. She had gone to prison.

175

Having been incarcerated in Holloway as a common criminal she had gone on hunger-strike for political prisoner status and as a result was force-fed.

If the Black Friday tale had shocked Ruby, finding herself in the company of someone who had done several sentences at his majesty's pleasure and been force-fed into the bargain, had left her quite dazed.

May noticed that her new friend had gone rather quiet, there being none of the excited questions issuing forth from her that had been the case earlier in the conversation. May was cognisant of the fact that the respectable working class held adherence to the more serious laws of the land very highly. Minor infractions that got one the sack from a job, a cuff round the ear from a constable or an admonishment by a magistrate were one thing, but someone who went to prison would lose all respect; lose caste, in a respectable working class community. May realised that she had overstepped the mark, at this early stage of what she hoped would be the start of a Suffragette friendship. The mistake made, May was concerned that she would not after all get her shocked young companion to the bye-election.

She changed tack by asking Ruby about herself, but the young woman had not been terribly forthcoming by the time the coffee cups had been drained. They had been in the café an awfully long time. It was time to leave.

"I suppose you are wondering my dear how it came to this for a thirty seven year old invalid woman from Lewisham?"

May was well aware that she looked older than thirty seven. She hoped this would surprise her friend out of her present mood. It did the trick. Ruby was relieved at the change of subject, but was also keen to avoid having to comment on May's age, so was only too pleased to pick up on the fact that the woman in front of her had mentioned a part of South London she had come to know.

"Oh, you are from Lewisham? I wondered why a lady such as yourself was in St Johns. But why did you not board the train from Lewisham?"

May beamed. The ice, if not re-broken, at least had a crack in it.

"The approach to Lewisham station is a little steep for me and I live in Granville Park, on the far side of the town, so I would have to take my life in my hands crossing the High Street. It is easier for me to cut along the river and through the recreation ground to St Johns. Bumpy and not some little distance but I prefer a smaller station. It is lucky indeed my work in the East End and at the WSPU HQ in Kingsway means I use terminus stations at Cannon Street and Charing Cross which are quite favourable to me."

Ruby felt ashamed that she had never really thought about a person in a wheelchair before. The simplest journey had such complications. She tried to imagine May attempting to run the gauntlet of Lewisham High Street, with its busy crossroads, shops and market, chock full of buses, lorries, carts and costermonger's wagons, with the odd motor car thrown in to the mix to cause havoc amongst the horses. And that hill up to the station had no pavement. It was just one mass of bumpy cobbles and horse dung. And once there one had to negotiate steps to some platforms, which would be impossible for May. The Titanic's stairwells jumped out of their box. Ruby saw the steps leading down to steerage consumed by water.

May mistook the gamut of expressions in the face across the café table.

"It really isn't too tiresome my dear. I have this tricycle, complete with hand controls, which is far better than any conventional wheelchair."

Ruby's gaze shifted from the empty coffee cup she had been staring into, and transformed into a weak smile. She refocused on wheelchair journeys.

"May, is the East End far? It is some way off I wager. How do you get there?"

"The beginning of the East End is a mere stone's throw away from here. Further than the usual Suffragette throw of a stone perhaps, but close enough. It is at the *east end* of the City of London d'you see? But Bow is at the furthest point of the East End, quite some miles away, though it has been a most interesting route for me to wheel myself through on my previous sojourns. One passes through Aldgate, Whitechapel, Stepney and Mile End. On one occasion a few years ago when we were fighting a bye-election in Haggerston, which is also in the East End, I had a bobby wheel me back to Cannon Street station. I think it was to ensure I did not get into any more mischief!"

"Wheel yourself miles? *Some* miles!" said an incredulous Ruby. "You will not need any bobbies today. I am wheeling you both ways."

There was a determination in that voice May liked.

"That is very kind of you my dear. I readily accept your kind offer. So, let us be orf there."

'Orf'. May had said it with a middle class accent, but it reminded Ruby of her friend in Bow. He said 'orf' too, though in a very different way. She was quite a woman, this new friend of hers. Getting on and off trains balancing on two sticks and now she's 'orf' to the East End. She would not be beaten. Just like Nashey would not be beaten by the little matter of a sinking liner and the Atlantic Ocean.

Ruby was thrilled that she would at last be seeing the infamous East End of London. Momentarily she considered showing May her Marie Lloyd impersonation. 'I'm one of the ruins that Cromwell knocked aboud a bit'. But she thought better of it. She was still concerned about her insensitivity regarding the views from The Monument. And May had friends in the East End. A young Hampshire woman attempting the broad Cockney accent of 'Hoxton's Very Own' might be seen as a little disrespectful.

En-route to Bow, May had planned to act as a Thomas Cook tour guide, pointing out landmarks and places of interest such as the Aldgate Pump, the London Hospital and the Sidney Street of the recent siege. But whilst they were still within the confines of The City, she was constantly interrupted by people coming up to introduce themselves to the two women. Most of them either spoke to Ruby about the woman in the wheelchair as if she wasn't there, or to May as if at best she was a four year old, at worst an imbecile.

Ruby was becoming increasingly exasperated with such people when a middle aged man approached them. Judging by his round collar shirt, necktie, striped wool suit and leather shoes, he was a wealthy businessman. He had peeled off from a couple of similarly attired gentleman to join them. He doffed his bowler, smiled benignly down at the woman in the wheelchair and was immediately hit by a volley of abuse by her assistant. The City man had never been so insulted, and made a speedy exit, a "well I…" and further exhortations of the affronted fading from earshot as he turned and marched away. An overused walking cane and wrist worked in perfect cocked harmony as he overacted his way back to his friends. Ruby, arms akimbo, looked at the back of the retreating figure like a goose that had just seen off an egg-hungry rat.

"I do wish you had not spoken to the Prime Minister in that manner my dear," admonished May in a voice more tired than upset. "I am sure Mr Asquith was only coming over to convey his best wishes. We will never get the vote like that, will we?"

Ruby stared back at her, crestfallen, for a couple of seconds before May continued in the same tired voice.

"And when you are among Suffragettes, you really must learn to know when someone is having a joke at your expense."

May looked for a sign of recognition from the young woman but nothing was forthcoming from the still concerned face above her, so she allowed a smirk to first enter her eyes then move down through the cheeks to her mouth. It was at this point Ruby realised she had been fooled.

"You've been pulling my leg!" she said wide-eyed, before adding an after-thought. "As your friends, in the East End would say!"

"Quite so my dear, quite so!" laughed May.

The two women shared more jollity as they set off again, before the conversation duly turned to weightier matters. May explained that being patronised in the way she was on a daily basis had led her in to the fight for the vote from an early age. Women were patronised by men just as the disabled were by all. It was all part of the same process. Fighting back the way Ruby had done to the gentleman made one feel better for a brief moment in time, but it did nothing to alter anything. It was only by changing laws and by education that the dilemmas of the day could be solved, be they women's rights, poverty or invalidity.

May left it that. Words only took someone so far along the line of indoctrination. Ruby would either become a Suffragette or she would not, dependent on how she reacted to what she saw at the bye-election that afternoon.

A combination of her own curiosity as to what would occur at an East End bye-election and concern for her new friend, as she had heard such events could get quite boisterous, led Ruby to offer to stay at May's side throughout the process.

"What of your friend in Bow my dear? Do you not wish to visit her?" asked May a little disingenuously.

"It's a gentleman actually," corrected Ruby, smiling inwardly to herself about calling Nashey by such an epithet. "Oh, perhaps I can meet him later?"

May was quick to agree and then thought that she should tell Ruby what to expect. She explained that it was WSPU policy at bye-elections to always support the party which was opposing the Liberal government, because it was Prime Minister Asquith's Cabinet who were blocking the vote for women. This meant that the WSPU invariably supported the Conservatives at bye-elections, but unusually there was no Liberal or for that matter Labour candidate fighting the Bow seat. It was to be a straight fight between the Conservatives and George Lansbury who was standing as a Women's Suffrage candidate. Thus she was going along to lend her support to Lansbury against the Tories.

Ruby was puzzled. No wonder she, and every other

working class person she knew, didn't tend to be too interested in politics.

"But that means you are for people one day and against them the next?"

"That my dear is the political game."

"And from what little I know of it I thought Liberals were more in favour of women getting the vote than Conservatives?"

"Well, it is true that at some bye-elections we support a Tory candidate who does not believe women should get the vote, against a Liberal who is in favour of women gaining the franchise, but that is a necessary evil I am afraid. We cannot assist a government to retain or increase its majority when it is blocking us."

This made no sense at all to Ruby.

"What of the other women's suffrage societies? There are lots of them aren't there, many with a good few more members than you?"

"They support whichever candidate is most in favour of women's suffrage."

"So at the same bye-election, you can be shouting the odds for one candidate and the Women's Freedom League can be supporting the other?"

"Yes my dear. It is not ideal of course, but this is what this undemocratic Cabinet, which ignores the views of its own backbenchers, has brought us to. Even within the Cabinet there is only a handful of the nineteen who oppose us directly. Mr Asquith is one of four who openly oppose, and there is the wobbler Mr Churchill, who one is never sure of one way or the other. But unfortunately they are the strongest and our friends there such as Sir Edward Grey, the Secretary of Foreign Affairs, are the weakest."

Ruby doubted that just four or five men, even if one of them was the Prime Minister, could control the whole country. But she had to admit that it was the Suffragette leaders, the Pankhursts, who were the reason that she had at least a slight interest in current affairs. They were active decision makers who were certainly getting things done, and Ruby liked that about them. The Titanic would not have gone down with the Pankhursts at the helm. Of that she was certain.

"Might there be some trouble?" she asked, with concern in her voice.

May explained that the National League for Opposing Woman Suffrage would no doubt be sending some bully boys along to try to sabotage proceedings. They might on this occasion get some help from the pro-Conservative Primrose League. Votes for Women supporters will enter the fray to stop them and a scuffle might ensue. Violence was abhorrent of course but breaking the law in a just cause was acceptable.

The two women eventually arrived in Bow and made their way to the town hall, outside which Ruby was introduced to a flock of politicos. This included a short stilted conversation with Millie Garrett Fawcett, the leader of the largest of the women's suffrage organisations, the NUWSS. She was there to lend her support to the Votes for Women candidate, but she was careful to distance herself from WSPU members as she and her society did not agree with the violent tactics of the Pankhursts.

There was much shaking of hands and jolly small talk with all and sundry, as if they had just arrived at a village fete, with senior grass roots members of the Constituency Labour Party, there to support George Lansbury, replacing the vicar and his wife as the people holding court. It transpired that the town hall was merely a gathering point. The Labour people stayed put, whilst the Suffragette element decamped to a busy shopping square nearby

May soon got to work distributing handbills and talking to anyone who strayed into her path. For once her being in a wheelchair was an advantage. She would stop anyone who came near, and successfully engage them in conversation whilst she slipped them a handbill, whereas Ruby noticed that the other Suffragettes were getting rather shorter shrift from their attempts to woo the local populace. Ruby marvelled at the tricycle's turn of foot and manoeuvrability when May spotted likely quarry. Few passer-by flies would evade this spider's grasp. And the conversations had a very different dynamic to those endured by May when people had come up to patronise her en-route through the City. The people might initially flash her a condescending smile as they took a handbill, but duly reeled in they were then forced to nod in agreement, as May posed opening questions which were difficult not to answer in the affirmative.

"Would you agree sir that there is too much poverty in East London?" was a favourite opening gambit.

Half a dozen more questions, all asked with a level of enthusiasm that was only surpassed by the charm that accompanied it, were couched in such a way that even the most ardent of government supporters found themselves agreeing to things straight out of the Suffragette manifesto. Each person eventually made their escape but not before they had promised to return to the square at the top of the hour to hear a speech from a Suffragette colleague of May's.

It became clear to Ruby that she was not expected to help

out. After all she was only really there as a bystander. She felt rather at a loose end so looked about at the hive of industry around her. All the people she had been introduced to, whilst friendly enough, were towards the upper end of middle class, so she felt a little uneasy in their presence and had always been relieved when May had moved them on to the next person to meet. But one woman was very young and spoke in such an odd, clipped manner that Ruby couldn't help but take a shine to her. And now Ruby saw her kneeling on the pavement. Ruby wandered over to see what she was doing. The young woman looked up as Ruby approached.

"Keep an eye out would you? Bobbies. Defacement of the highway d'you see. Don't want to be nabbed. Not for this. Other fish and all that."

The young woman was chalking 'Votes for Women' on the pavement in the three colours of the Suffragettes, using purple, white and green chalks alternately from letter to letter. It looked good but continually changing chalks meant that progress was quite slow. Ruby did as she was asked. Without realising it, she had taken her first orders and committed her first offence for the Suffragette movement.

This job complete, the young woman now needed help hauling an empty costermonger's cart from a nearby road into the square, and Ruby was only too pleased to assist. The cart was no sooner in position and a woman with a chubby face, wearing a heavy full length coat and a simple woollen hat, was clambering up on to it. She looked quite different from all the Suffragettes Ruby had just come across. She assumed the women must be a local working woman. Ruby was relieved that she was not the only working class woman there. May appeared at Ruby's side and nodded towards the woman.

"Sylvia Pankhurst," said May with pride and awe in her voice.

"Oh, I thought… Is she related to Mrs…"

"Her daughter dear; Sylvia's hear to speak."

And no sooner had May said this and Sylvia, hands clasped together behind her back, started yelling at the top of her voice about the man she was there to support, George Lansbury. The young woman whom Ruby had helped with the chalking and fetching of the cart and several other Suffragettes gathered behind Sylvia's platform. Several passing men were immediately stopped in their tracks by Sylvia's shouting, and wandered over to see what all the fuss was about, swopping amused expressions and winks with each other before settling next to the cart to listen.

May motioned to Ruby that they should join the rest of the WSPU women.

"You will enjoy it. Audiences are strange things to handle. We are taught never to lose our tempers; to always get the best of a joke, and to join in the laughter with the audience even if the joke is against us. This training makes most Suffragettes quick-witted, good at repartee. And speakers that an audience take a delight in listening to, even though they do not agree with them, are paid attention to, and that's all we crave. If they listen the argument is undeniable."

Over the next few minutes the square filled quickly with people, almost every one of them wearing a short back and sides.

"Every member of the audience is a man! Where are the women?" asked a puzzled Ruby.

"They are looking to their homes, their children or keeping penury from the door by working in a factory or sweatshop," replied May. "We are here for them, but not necessarily to speak *to* them. We are here to speak to their husbands, brothers and sons."

Just as May had finished speaking a large fish came sailing through the air towards them, thrown by some woman's son at the back of the crowd. It landed on the costermonger's cart, but its momentum carried it on, almost hitting Ruby before bouncing off the wall at her back and coming to rest at her feet. A huge wave of laughter that Little Tich himself would have been pleased to solicit from a sell-out theatre crowd, burst forth, followed by several attempts by young wags to out-do each other with the crudity of their double entendre. More laughter ensued.

"Oh, how ghast…" was as far as Ruby's exclamation got at her close encounter with one of the River Lea's finest, before it was cut off by May.

"Keep quiet dear. Ignore it. Look, listen and learn."

Sylvia had not missed a beat, her arms still held behind her back, showing no fear, her smile still broad, as if she was out for a pleasant Sunday afternoon stroll in the park. She finished the opening salvo of her speech and turned her attention to the missile which had been launched her way. She turned theatrically and peered back at the fish, catching Ruby's eye and winking at her, before turning back to her audience.

"I see we have a Billingsgate man here!" shouted Sylvia. "I thank you for your fish sir! All contributions to the fight for the vote for women gratefully received I assure you! That will go in some poor woman's pot tonight, and her husband will thank us for it! You sir may have provided us with a convert! God bless you! But I must ask you most seriously sir, where are the chips?"

Laughter burst forth again, and individual wags were again quickly to the fore with brutal shafts of East End wit, this time aimed at the fish-launcher to whom the crowd had turned to denigrate. The wretch made the mistake of trying to bat Sylvia's volley back at her.

"That weren't no Billin'sgate fish. It were out the…"

"Oh fuck orf oud of it!" and a thesaurus entry of similar oaths that implied sex and travel were showered upon the man, followed by the ubiquitous quips of the wags.

"Play the white man!" "Take yer medicine!" "Play the game!" was the gist before one wag brought the house down with a play on words using an old cockney term for the word 'joking'. "She were only codding with yer!"

One man in the crowd had been holding a dead cat ready for launch, and a bunch of likely lads on seeing the Suffragette get up on the cart had quickly availed themselves of rotten carrots and potatoes from the gutter of the nearby market. But there were to be no more projectiles this day. The meat and two veg were unobtrusively dropped to the cobbles.

The crowd settled down and listened to what Sylvia had to say. She informed them that the vote had to be won as part of the fight against inequality, which was the only way to deal with the country's ills; unemployment, low wages, poor housing, lack of sanitation, poor health, disease and squalor.

She was about to move on to the need for better education, when a mob organised by a couple of staunchly Conservative pub landlords, came in from the side of the crowd and started shouting her down. The East End audience were great believers in fair play, so didn't appreciate the likeable young woman before them being bullied by her opponents. The earlier good natured ribaldry was replaced with a more heated atmosphere as shouts of abuse were aimed at the disruptors, before Lansbury supporters, Labour and Suffragette waded into them. This acted as a prompt for hitherto unnoticed bully boys working for the National League for Opposing Woman Suffrage to join the fray. Their goal was to pull Sylvia's costermonger's cart away to destroy the meeting, and if she stayed on it, all well and good, they would deal with her down the nearest alley. East End men, who had no real interest in politics and had originally only been stopped from going about their business by the thought of having a bit of fun at a woman's expense, found themselves literally in their first political fight, and without even realising it, were fighting for the vote, for themselves as well as women.

The Bow police had underestimated the level of manpower they were to need at Suffragette meetings now that such a big political beast as Sylvia Pankhurst was living and working in their jurisdiction. Just two policemen had been dispatched to oversee what was assumed would be a fairly minor event.

Once the trouble started, one of the policemen's helmets was a trampled thing of the past within seconds, whilst his mate got some blasts of his whistle off before said instrument, complete with chain, was ripped from his uniform. The whistle blasts did the trick, a number of burly policemen, most of them several inches taller and a couple of stone heavier than the stunted poverty stricken populace, arriving to restore order. It was clear that a couple of them had been given more specific orders. They made a beeline for Sylvia, who was trying to keep her balance on the cart which was now essentially the rope in a tug of war between the two warring factions. She saw the policemen coming to put a stop to her balancing act so jumped off the cart just as one of them made a grab for her ankles. A uniformed arm made enough contact with one of her legs to knock her off balance, causing her to land heavily on hands and knees.

One of the policemen was about to grab Sylvia when a large fish smacked him in the face with some velocity. Ruby stood holding with both hands the wettest of coshes, battered by its collision with the officer's nose rather than in the usual way fish was battered in those parts. This gave Sylvia enough time to get up and hobble away, around the corner and down a side street, but the other policeman was about to catch up with her when a large fist plummeted into his jaw. He went down like a sack of potatoes, just as his mate recovered from his fish-coshing and grabbed Ruby by the wrist.

"I'll pay you!" he warned as he squeezed his attacker's wrist viciously before releasing it to set off in pursuit of his quarry.

He ran round the corner into the side street and saw his prostrate colleague a split second before a large fist had him join his fellow officer kissing the cobbles.

The two women made their getaway at a rate of knots, May wheeling herself at full speed with Ruby pushing from behind like the anchor man on a St Moritz bobsleigh team. May was attempting to impart reassurances loudly over her shoulder.

"It is all very tiresome of course but one gets used to this sort of thing. It is the world of politics I am afraid. But all good publicity for the cause; publicity is the oxygen of our movement d'you see."

"But why did we not take off after Miss Pankhurst?"

queried the perplexed potential recruit. "Even if she evaded those two policemen she may have been hauled into an alley by some bully boys."

"Oh, I should not worry about Sylvia my dear," came the matter-of-fact reply. "She has a guardian angel looking after her."

Ruby was not sure she liked this new found, uncaring side to May's nature. If leaving your friends when they were in trouble was politics she would have none of it. Women sitting in lifeboats looking down at their feet sprang in to her mind for a moment, before the link between the past and present entered her thoughts. Dashing off had meant she had missed going to see Nashey.

During the return journey back through the East End, May became aware that Ruby had fallen silent and was concerned that the confidence she had portrayed in Sylvia's safety may have been misconstrued as indifference. On arrival back at Cannon Street station she was therefore somewhat relieved to find that they had just missed a train and it being a quiet period for commuters there was a long wait for the next one. This gave her ample opportunity to speak at length to Ruby. They sat in the station and discussed the events of the day.

When May dropped the bombshell that a certain rough diamond by the name of Nashey was Sylvia's protector, Ruby sucked in her breath almost as hard as when the freezing cold ocean had hit her in that Titanic passageway. She thought it was as well she had not been eating anything at that moment; she would have choked. The man she had last seen on the other side of the Atlantic had just been in the very next street and she had not even known.

For her part, May was delighted that Ruby knew Sylvia's bodyguard. She considered the friendship to be a link, albeit perhaps only a tenuous one, between Ruby and the Suffragette cause.

"Of course if Nashey were required to censure a constable, he would no doubt have used a rather more solid instrument on him than your fish my dear," said May knowingly. "But he is under strict instructions from Sylvia, who is a pacifist, never to use any more violence than is absolutely necessary for her protection, so I am sure any injured policemen will already be on the mend."

Ruby would have liked to talk about Nash at some length but knew this would inevitably mean telling of how she had come to meet him, which she was not prepared to do. Consequently she kept the conversation on Votes for Women. She made the point that whilst the Bow incident had certainly taught her that there were occasions when self-defence was necessary, she felt uneasy about the violence that seemed to follow the Suffragettes around. May countered that actually the policeman Ruby had struck with the fish was not in any way attacking her. He was merely attempting to carry out his duty, which appeared to be to arrest Sylvia. It had been the camaraderie of a shared cause that had driven Ruby to defend a woman to whom she had never even been introduced. The shared cause in her case was perhaps merely that of womanhood rather than the suffrage movement, but the two became interwoven very easily.

Ruby pondered this for a few seconds before moving the conversation back towards her mentor.

"You have told me all about your Suffragette history and

experiences May, but how did you become a supporter in the first place?"

"When I was young there was no paid position open to me. A woman of my rank, should she need to take paid employment, had a choice of governess or primary school teacher. Neither of those positions was possible for an invalid of course but I was indeed fortunate to be free of any concerns over remuneration. I chose to do voluntary work at the Greenwich and Deptford workhouse. My heart ached. I thought surely if women were consulted in the management of the state, happier and better conditions must exist for hard working sweated lives such as these. It was gradually unfolded to me that the unequal laws which made women appear inferior to men were the main cause of these evils. I found that the man-made laws of marriage, parentage and divorce placed women in every way in a condition of slavery, and were harmful to men by giving them power to be tyrants."

"That sounds just like the reasons an American lady, Mrs Margaret Brown gave me for her fighting for the vote in her country."

"Is that *the* Margaret Brown? Of Colorado?" asked May, intrigued.

"I suppose so. She was from Colorado and knew all about Mrs Pankhurst and the Suffragette movement. And she knew a lot of the most important women suffragists in America. She was also involved in starting up a woman's club to improve women's lives. And she had divorced, and as part of a settlement had ownership of her own house. And she had a huge monthly allowance from her husband as was!"

The 'hads' had been relayed with increasingly emphatic enthusiasm; it was clear the monthly allowance was Mrs

Brown's greatest achievement as far as Ruby was concerned.

"But how do you know the Unsinkable Margaret Brown?" asked an ever more intrigued May.

Ruby's fervour drained from her in a millisecond.

"Oh, she was sinkable all right. We all were."

May understood immediately and further appreciated that it was not a subject to be discussed further, not today in any case. She just gave the briefest of nods then waved towards the recently arrived train that was billowing smoke in their direction.

"Come my dear our chariot awaits," she said lightly.

Ruby was staring in to space.

"If someone were to ask of me when I became a Suffragette, I would not say it was today because it was not. I would tell them it was in a lifeboat. It just took me till now to understand that."

The two Suffragettes exchanged the saddest of smiles as they started for their train.

Chapter 15

"(Mrs Pankhurst) threw scruple, affection, human loyalty and her own principles to the winds. The movement developed all her powers for good and for evil. Cruelty, ruthlessness, betrayal, courage, resourcefulness, diplomacy… beautiful tenderness and a magnificent sense of justice."

Emmeline Pethick-Lawrence, Women's Freedom League (and ex-WSPU)

May had been quick to write to Christabel Pankhurst, who was in exile in Paris since escaping the country to avoid being arrested for conspiracy the previous year. May enquired about signing up her new convert as a paid employee of the WSPU. Cognisant of Christabel's snobbery, May conveniently omitted the first name of her new recruit, given that 'Ruby' tended to be popular with working class parents. She wrote that Mrs Martin had just returned to the country from America, and was intelligent and practical, but having no private means of support she had in the past used her numeracy skills in paid employment, and was about to start her first London position. This would mean she would be of limited use to them; a great recruitment opportunity missed.

Strictly speaking this was all true, though the reality was that Ruby had turned up at Peek Frean's a day late and managed to charm her way into being given a second chance at becoming factory fodder.

Christabel had replied that she did not like the idea of someone coming straight into the organisation as an employee. That was not how it usually worked. One had to earn one's spurs as a volunteer before being given the lofty status of a paid worker.

Undeterred, May had written again conveying that Mrs Martin happened to be a friend of the famous American suffragist Margaret Brown, which would surely be a useful contact. This new recruit had also been very resourceful at the Bow bye-election. And it was the relaying of the tale of the fish and the policeman, which amused Christabel no end, that finally secured Ruby the £2 a week job on the WSPU payroll.

As well as not having to worry about earning a living, being a paid worker effectively fast-tracked Ruby into what the Suffragettes called 'danger work'. There were plenty of unpaid volunteers to complete the more mundane duties of office work, hawking newspapers, selling advertising space, distributing handbills, chalking pavements and the like. Paid workers were expected to be at the sharp end.

******

Despite her notoriety as the 'Cripple Suffragette' and chief organiser of the pillar box sabotage campaign, May was not particularly high up the pecking order of the WSPU leadership. A few weeks after Ruby's enrolment, May was therefore surprised to be summoned to a meeting chaired by Mrs Pankhurst herself. With Christabel in exile, Mrs

Pankhurst had to take time off from her role as the evangelist of the movement, travelling around the country spreading the word with her great charisma and gift of oratory, to become more involved with day to day affairs. Other leading lights of the Suffragette movement, Annie Kenny, Grace Roe and Flora Drummond were also present. Such meetings were not an open forum for discussion. The women were there primarily to hear from Mrs Pankhurst how the latest two big developments, namely the passing through Parliament of the Prisoners' Temporary Discharge Act, and her own imminent sentencing at the Old Bailey, were going to affect the campaign. This would be followed by them receiving their orders from the autocratic leadership.

Christabel, who had a degree in law, was the WSPU's legal expert. She reported to the meeting via Annie, who visited her in France each weekend to receive instructions. Annie relayed that once the government had introduced the new Act, when a hunger-striking Suffragette had to be released from prison on health grounds, it would no longer spell the end of her sentence. She would now be released on licence, with the condition that as soon as her health had recovered, she would be re-incarcerated to proceed with the remainder of her sentence. This process would be repeated as many times as was necessary to complete the prison term. The Act did not allow the authorities to enter anyone's home to ascertain whether or not the required improvement in health had taken place, but anyone attempting to leave their home would be deemed, de facto, fit enough to return to prison and summarily re-arrested. Policemen would, it could be assumed, be encamped outside released Suffragette's homes waiting for the women to set foot outside.

"Fred, ever the wit, has thus nicknamed the whole business the Cat and Mouse Act," finished Annie.

Mentioning Fred Pethick-Lawrence was not the most tactful thing she could have said. He had, until a few months earlier, been the financial secretary of the WSPU until he and his wife, the Suffragettes' chief fund-raiser, were both summarily expelled from the organisation. Their crime had been to dare challenge Christabel's decision to start an arson campaign and increase the levels of violence already being perpetrated. Everyone at the meeting bar Mrs Pankhurst knew the expulsion had been a huge error so Flora was quick to speak to ensure there was not an awkward silence.

"But surely it will take a large number of police away from their other duties, and for what, to stand about for days on end waiting for women to stick their heads out?"

"Yes, just as Black Friday took them away from their duties Flora," said Mrs Pankhurst drily. "There are always more police, and they are a simple race are they not? Doing no more than waiting about is what they do best."

"Art. We must have art for this Cat and Mouse business. Is Sylvia available?" asked Grace.

In her student days Sylvia had taken the Royal College of Art's national scholarship examination and finished first in the whole country. She had used her gift on numerous projects throughout the Suffragette campaign.

"Sylvia? What is she to do with this?" asked May.

"Ah, yes May, you no doubt are wondering what you are doing here?" replied Grace.

She had simply meant to be business-like but it had come out as rather matter-of-factly abrupt, but May was not in any way upset by the apparent slight. May respected immensely all the leading lights of the Suffragette movement for their penetrating minds and inspirational leadership, but her feelings for them went beyond that of a mere loyal political servant. Emmeline and Christabel Pankhurst, in particular, were two of the few people outside of May's own family who treated her exactly the same way as anyone else. They did not see her wheelchair save for using it to their political purpose; rather they saw a woman from whom they demanded unquestioning loyalty and commitment to the cause, just as they expected it from all their supporters.

Mrs Pankhurst was quick to use her charm to reassure May, smiling kindly without a hint of the condescension that accompanied many such expressions aimed at her by others.

"I cannot tell you how deeply I feel your splendid courage and endurance May. And I wanted to ask you how your Monument idea was coming along. But all in good time."

Grace mentioning Sylvia had taken the meeting away from its running order, to which Mrs Pankhurst was keen to keep, so the great leader continued by returning to the Cat and Mouse matter at hand.

"Grace, excellent idea; a large menacing cat holding in its jaws a much smaller helpless woman I think; something along those lines. Who drew the Modern Inquisition piece about force-feeding? That woman from the Artists' Suffrage League wasn't it? Get her on it. I am afraid my daughter is far too busy with her East End chums to have time to spare us her artistic genius."

May had heard Sylvia make subtly barbed comments about her mother and particularly her sister Christabel, and now she could see the antipathy within the family was certainly mutual. In fact the leadership's side of the family appeared the more openly hostile.

The meeting carried on with Mrs Pankhurst issuing orders to set up safe houses for members released from prison under the Cat and Mouse Act, and for the most active militants to become a clandestine, underground collection of small cells to avoid recapture. They would now, rather than welcome arrest after committing an offence, endeavour to make their escape.

The great leader suddenly returned her attention to May with another smile.

"May, my dear, I must apologise. This whole business leads us sometimes to forget our manners. Please can you supply us with a progress report on your Monument project?"

May told the meeting what she had planned. Mrs Pankhurst was delighted.

"Good work May. My heart will be with you during the ordeal that lies before you. You are an inspiration to us all," she said warmly before changing tone to a more business-like one. "And that new recruit of yours, how's she coming along? Is she ready?"

"She has taken to things like a duck to water," said May with enthusiasm. "She has assisted at meetings throughout London on a daily basis over the past few weeks, but has been under orders not to get arrested so that she may be available for the Monument. She has been well trained in all active matters, and will add valuable support to those two experienced WSPU stalwarts Miss Spark and Mrs Shaw. We are ready primed for Monday next."

This prompted May's leader to change tack.

"Ah, this brings me to the second item on the agenda, Mrs Pankhurst's prison sentence."

This was the first time May had heard her leader refer to herself in the third person.

Mrs Pankhurst went on to announce that tomorrow she expected to receive an outrageously draconian sentence. Christabel had predicted that it could be as much as three years' penal servitude. She herself doubted it could be quite that extreme, but whatever it was she and Christabel had decided that the WSPU would respond by increasing the scale and frequency of their arson, bombing and generally destructive civil disobedience campaign. She was also pleased to confirm that imminent major attacks were planned at Hampstead Garden Suburb, Manchester Art Gallery, Stockport, Chorley Wood, Oxted, Norwich, Aberdeen, Nottingham, Ayr and Kelso. Women around the country were investigating possible future sites to be attacked. Anything large that was left empty and unattended for periods such as racecourse grandstands, cricket pavilions and wealthy people's second homes were being considered. Kew Gardens was one of several well-known beauty spots that looked vulnerable and Lloyd-George was having a large second home built in Surrey which would be an obvious target.

"It will take some little while for the Cat and Mouse Act to come into effect. And due to my poor health and the government's fear of force-feeding me and perhaps having me die in prison a martyr, I estimate that I will be released under the existing regulations quite readily, sometime next week. This will enable me to go freely from prison to attend meetings and we will make Mrs Pankhurst's release as big a news event as possible. The Monument, being in the heart of The City of London, will be something of a flagship event, gaining far greater publicity than any of the afore-mentioned attacks so it will be delayed to coincide as closely as possible with Mrs Pankhurst's release."

For a moment May thought the mixing of the first and third person odd not to mention a little confusing, but then it dawned on her. 'Mrs Pankhurst' was not the leader, or a woman, or even a human per se. She was the figurehead; the movement. She was all women, and men too if they only knew it. She was humanity.

Having been addressing the meeting as a whole, Mrs Pankhurst then looked directly at May.

"Christabel believes that the Monument demonstration may not lead to the arrest of your women. She forecasts that the police will be under orders not to give the incident even more publicity than it will have already generated by making arrests. So given that we no longer want our women arrested if it can be helped, we wish to treat this as a veritable quid pro quo. So given the nature of the demonstration must inevitably see your women initially captured by the police, you are to instruct them not to resist or become involved in any form of affray. And unless otherwise entreated by me, the Monument event shall be Friday April the 18th."

Chapter 16

"Mr John Burns treats our women with ridicule and contempt, and talks of restricting women's work, forgetful of the fact that his own mother worked to support him."

Sylvia Pankhurst on the working class President of the Local Government Board (a Cabinet post)

When George Lansbury had narrowly lost the Bow bye-election, primarily due to members of the mainstream WSPU alienating East Enders with their high-handed, haughty approach, it had been assumed by many that Sylvia Pankhurst's work in the East End was doomed to failure.

But in setting up her own East London Federation of Suffragettes, albeit as ostensibly a branch of the WSPU, Sylvia had successfully distanced herself from her mother and sister's actions. And it was Sylvia's remarkable ability to understand the poor and appreciate what was needed to help them that had made her such an instant and huge success both with the East End in general and Nash in particular. She had just blended in and been accepted into Bow life at the very time when Suffragettes had become so unpopular, countrywide.

Nash had seen how within weeks of her arriving in Bow, Sylvia had been asked by occupants of hideous tenement slums to visit and expose them. This she had done, before going on to set up, amongst other things, a mother and infant welfare clinic staffed by a doctor who treated patients free, and a milk distribution centre for babies, many of whom were too weak to digest food.

Women had soon started to flock to her meetings, at which Sylvia gave tuition in public speaking and urged her new recruits to start making speeches at indoor meetings. And it was not long before she was encouraging them to stand in for her at small outdoor meetings carried out from market stalls or in side streets. Married East End women, already working their fingers to the bone, started to rise earlier and work later to make time for Sylvia's and now their cause. Young factory women, working twelve hours a day for a pittance, dragged their exhausted bodies around the streets knocking on doors to distribute East London Federation of Suffragettes literature.

And the authorities were becoming increasingly concerned about the success Sylvia was achieving in the East End. A police detective had recently knocked on the door of the poverty stricken widow living opposite Sylvia and offered a considerable sum of money to rent her front room so that the police could use it as a base from which to spy on their prey.

"Money wouldn't do me any good if I was to hurt that young woman," replied the widow.

Much shoe leather was then wasted as the detective visited each house in Sylvia's street, making the same offer. The poor inhabitants rejected the proposal one by one, most of their rebuffs being rather less polite than that of the widow.

Sylvia's landlady, Jessie Payne, was the alpha female of

the street. Amongst other fine deeds she lent money to neighbours to keep them out of the clutches of money lenders, and was often not paid back. Thus the refusals were to an extent out of respect for Mrs Payne, but local admiration for Sylvia was profound. Had the detective been more successful he would have seen from his front window an old age pensioner, who had walked all the way from Poplar, deliver to a Sylvia weak from prison hunger-strikes, two fresh eggs laid by her hens. Other women brought fruit and flowers.

******

Nash had spent his formative years in the Whitechapel of the 1880's as a night predator who followed gentleman from the St Botolph's Without church area, where they had availed themselves of the pleasures of the youngest prostitutes the East End had to offer.

Twelve hundred prostitutes had roamed the streets of Whitechapel and surrounds at such time. Many of them middle aged women ravaged by years of the horrors of East End poverty and whoredom. These women serviced rough trade; men looking for a 'fourpenny kneetrembler' or a 'tuppenny upright'. The Metropolitan Police, like the rest of society, closed their eyes and let them get on with it. In contrast, the City Police kept a firm check on prostitution in their jurisdiction. They were under strict orders to arrest any woman seen to be soliciting. Thus it simply was not worth a prostitute attempting to advertise her wares where the gentlemen worked. But young girls were popular with City gents, not simply due to their youthful looks, but because they were far less likely to be diseased. So these youngsters stood on the steps of St Botolph's, a spot within view of, yet just outside the City, advertising themselves, free from concerns of arrest, and let the gentlemen come to them. A young woman could earn more from a minute or two of grotesqueness, than she could from a week in the horrors of sweated labour.

To return to the City after the men had finished gaining their sexual release, either to go back to work or get a taxi cab home, usually meant them walking down a narrow, high walled, pitch dark alley. And if they met Nash in such a spot, they were harmed grievously and relieved of their valuables. Nash had always used more violence than was necessary in the naïve belief that this was in some way getting some revenge on behalf of East End women. It took the Ripper murders to impress upon him that you could not seek vengeance against bad men, be they City gents or even the killer himself. Rather, you needed to eradicate the conditions that bred them.

This previous life of crime had left Nash with a deer's instinctive sense of danger. He could spot a uniformed or more importantly plain clothes policeman long before they noticed him. And he used these skills as Sylvia's primary bodyguard.

The two of them had become firm friends since Nash had committed himself to the cause. Nash was enamoured by Sylvia being part all-knowing intellectual who commanded respect from some of the greatest political minds in the country, and part woman of the people who would dirty her hands mucking in to do any job. It also amused him that she was such a poorly dressed, couldn't boil-an-egg young middle class woman who was not above taking a father-like scolding about the ways of the world from an old East Ender when the mood took him. But above all it was her mental toughness that amazed him. She was the toughest person he had ever met.

For Sylvia's part, Nash was her rock. Eager to know more about a man she felt had the potential to be a useful ally, she had made enquiries about him after the first time they had met next to Gladstone's statue. She quickly picked up on the almost reverent way men would talk of him. He was out of Whitechapel and had been infamous as the hardest man there in the 1880's. Given what she knew of Whitechapel back then, she had shuddered to think what he must have done to earn such a reputation. But more recently an old man had told her a rumour about Nashey that meant she no longer had to imagine anything. The story was that back in 1888 he had made it his personal mission in life to track down Jack the Ripper after the maniac had slaughtered a close friend of his. Then one day, he suddenly stopped looking, and no more murders were ever perpetrated. The assumption was clear. The sort of man who preyed upon poor defenceless women with a knife would have no chance if Nashey ever caught up with him, knife or no knife. The monster's body no doubt floated down to Limehouse to be picked clean by its resident toshers and mudlarks, then took a bit of pecking from seagulls and crows before the authorities dumped what was left of the carcass in a pit or incinerator somewhere; a suitable end.

It had been a chilling tale. And being a pacifist, Sylvia abhorred the violence in which Nash had been involved in his earlier life, and felt ill at ease with some of the things he had done in his present role as her bodyguard. But she was also well aware that whilst women would surely be winning political rights soon, and as a result inequalities in their lives would no doubt be addressed, women still needed to be wary of bullies, be they husbands, fathers, employers, policemen, politicians or attackers on the streets. The intellectual fight may be about to be won but it was only a battle within the war, and legislation would only do so much. Victory in the war against misogyny was still some way distant. Thus Sylvia found comfort from knowing the man with whom she had such natural rapport was such a protector against the misogynist foe. Nash only saw right and wrong. The fight for the vote for women was right, bullying of women wrong, and any man who thought otherwise would have him to deal with.

Chapter 17

"When you are tricked and deceived when Parliament betrays its sacred trust, you have a right to rebel. Let all of us stand shoulder to shoulder with the militant women."

George Lansbury, ex-MP for Bow and Bromley

The four women arrived at the base of The Monument at ten o'clock as arranged. Miss Spark, Mrs Shaw and Ruby paid for admission and waved a cheery goodbye to May. They appeared to be three young women full of the joys of spring waving to their less fortunate friend. The attack had originally been planned as a two-woman mission but May thought the addition of a third would further ensure its success.

Miss Spark was a pretty young thing resplendent in straw hat, dress with low neckline in-filled with lace to match three quarter length sleeves, plus elegant accessories. She reached the top of the three hundred and forty five steps well ahead of her companions, and engaged the two male attendants on duty in friendly banter that stopped tastefully just short of the flirtatious. She mentioned that her two friends would be arriving shortly. They were lagging behind because one of them felt faint from such an exhausting climb. A huffing, puffing Mrs Shaw, bending over as if in some distress, stopped half a dozen steps beneath them as Ruby, a further twenty steps below, collapsed to the floor.

"I say you chaps could you go to the rescue of a damsel in distress? My friend has fallen," gasped Mrs Shaw.

The two men were quick to dance down the steps, whilst Mrs Shaw surreptitiously joined her friend at the top, the two of them adeptly stepping through the small doorway that accessed the viewing gallery, and slamming the door shut behind them.

Mrs Shaw had initially stopped and bent over to help keep concealed her cargo. She produced two iron bars from beneath her heavy coat and used them to jam the door. A further rummage through her clothing produced a cornucopia of WSPU promotional material. Her comrade-in-arms took the latter and ran to the Monument's big flagpole, hauled down the City flag and replaced it with the purple, white and green WSPU equivalent, before hoisting the standard to the top of the mast. Mrs Shaw then unrolled a long banner bearing the slogan 'Death or Victory' and tied it neatly to the railings, from where, as the highest thing in the City east of St Pauls, it could be seen and read from far and wide. A three coloured streamer was unfurled to flutter in the strong breeze, and that just left a pile of Votes for Women handbills. The women would wait till a crowd gathered in the square below before allowing gravity to act as their postman.

The two attendants had reached Ruby just as the door slammed shut. The natural reaction to the noise had them looking back blankly at an equally blank door, before returning their gaze to a smug, smiling Ruby proffering them a couple of Votes for Women handbills. They dashed up to the jammed door doing a passable impersonation, Ruby thought, of a couple of bemused Titanic officers, before descending the stairs treacherously two at a time for the exit. One of them stared at Ruby as he passed her.

"I'll pay you!" was shouted over his shoulder as he carried on descending.

She had heard that before but preferred to convey something different as her retort.

"I do caution you to be careful. Those steps are slippery, what with all those Votes for Women handbills scattered over them!"

The frazzled men flung themselves out of the entrance door to find a woman was looking up and shouting at the top of her voice that Suffragettes had captured The Monument. The man who had threatened Ruby on the stairwell stopped to reassure her.

"Don't you worry mother, we'll soon have them out of there," he said confidently.

"Oh, I think not my dear fellow," said May, as she reached up from her tricycle to offer him yet another WSPU handbill. "Not till we've attracted a much bigger crowd."

The first policeman to arrive noticed the urgent shouts of a woman in a wheelchair. Having gone to the woman's assistance and asked her what all the commotion was about, he had his attention drawn to two Suffragettes draping a banner off the top of The Monument. He duly blew his police whistle, effectively doing May's job for her, attracting a large crowd in double quick time.

The little cobbled square surrounding The Monument was soon full to bursting. Had it had rafters it would have been packed to them. Every vantage point, including window sills, brewers' vans and fish carts were used by enthusiastic spectators. People trying to alight from the most popular exit of Monument underground station found a wall of backs blocking their way. On the other side of the square the crowd spilled back beyond Pudding Lane, aptly packed liked sardines towards Billingsgate fish-market. But despite the overcrowding there was none of the dangerous swaying of a football crowd eager to lean forward to see the latest goalmouth action. This gathering's skyward gaze kept them rooted to the spot.

Ruby had made her way back down the steps and slipped quietly out of the entrance to The Monument. She stood watching the scene unfurl as May kept to the outside edge of the crowd and orchestrated the whole thing beautifully, shouting and using her crutches to point up to the action for the benefit of new arrivals. Ruby was about to make her way around the throng to join her cohort when a shout came from a few feet away.

"The cripple's one of 'em! She's not helping. She's just bringing in the crowd! Look, she's handing out handbills now if you please!"

Ruby turned to see the ticket booth clerk pointing at May with two policemen looking on. May had told Ruby and her two associates that the leadership had decreed that they should not resist the police in any way because purely making a nuisance of themselves at a sightseeing landmark was not an act for which they were likely to be arrested. The authorities would want the stunt to receive as little publicity as possible. But Ruby felt certain that May must be committing an offence by attracting such a huge crowd. It would surely be considered a breach of the peace at the very least.

On seeing the police start towards her friend, Ruby made a brave attempt at a bit of wing three-quarter play, throwing herself down into the upper leg area of one of the men. Ruby, never having played rugby, did not manage the best timed of tackles, the crown of her head ploughing into a delicate part of her adversary's groin. The tackler was the first to get to her feet, partly because her opponent was writhing on the ground in agony, and partly because the other policeman had grabbed her by the scruff of the neck and hauled her upright.

"This is a red-handed catch if ever I had one," said the only policeman in a fit state to say anything.

He then turned his attention to his colleague.

"Get up yer big Mary Anne!" he said with a snort, trying but failing to remain professional; clearly finding his colleague's discomfort most amusing. "You keep hold of this one while I get the cripple."

"May! Police! Clear off!" shouted Ruby.

May looked across at Ruby and surveyed the situation for a moment, then simply sat there and started shouting to the crowd at large.

"Look at us! We are compromising our delicate physiques and ladylike demeanour for our cause! We are doing this because we have been left with no alternative! Recognise our desperation! Our vulnerability!"

Ruby giving out her name and then May doing her best Henry the Fifth tipped the policeman off as to who he might be arresting. He turned his back on May and spoke to his colleague who was still crouched over in pain.

"Christ almighty, you better count 'em!" he chortled before returning to the matter in hand. "I think the wheelchair woman could be the Cripple Suffragette we've been warned about. We're not to arrest her no matter what. It looks bad."

He turned his attention to his prisoner.

"You shouldn't have shouted that warning my girl. That's two offences you've committed now."

At this point Ruby realised that the leadership would be furious with her. Not only had she disobeyed orders and was thus about to get herself arrested but she had committed offences which, though they might only carry a fine for other lawbreakers, would nowadays certainly get a Suffragette imprisoned. On an occasion when she would have paid a fine, she was unlikely to be offered the opportunity.

A moment later it dawned on the policeman that if his report gave an accurate account of the events that had just taken place, his sergeant would haul him over the coals for alerting the woman in his custody to her fellow felon's predicament, and thus allowing her to shout the warning. Consequently he changed his tone to a friendlier if more pompous one.

"Seeing as you were only helping a poor cripple woman, I'll let you off the second charge this time. But you'll still have to go before the magistrate for assaulting a police officer."

"How dare you young man!" shouted May haughtily as she wheeled herself over to the policeman, who was quick to admonish her.

"You should look to yourself my good woman. If I was to arrest you now you'd be in prison and then hunger-striking and being force-fed soon enough I shouldn't wonder. What would your mother say if you were brought home a wreck or worse?"

This assumed that May lived with her parents, which though correct she took particular umbrage at because there was a clear presumption that a disabled women could not look after herself. The policeman was about to find out that was very far from the truth.

"My mother would sooner have me taken to her home a corpse than a coward," stated May indignantly as she trundled her tricycle into the policeman's shins at a fair rate of knots.

Orders or no orders, the cursing limping policeman arrested May on the spot.

Chapter 18

"If you take a woman and torture her, you torture me. These denials of fundamental human rights are really a violation of the soul. The Suffragettes have succeeded in driving the Cabinet mad. Mr McKenna (Home Secretary) should be examined at once by doctors. He apparently believes himself to be the Tsar of Russia."

George Bernard Shaw

The two women at the top of The Monument gazed down upon the sea of caps of their neck-craning audience. There was not a woman to be seen in this male bastion but the protest was seemingly attracting every working class man in the City, from Billingsgate porters to bank messengers. And City gentlemen were looking on from afar; inquisitive but unwilling to stand too close to the riff-raff.

When a wad of Votes for Women literature was thrown from the top of The Monument, it was met by a roar from the crowd. Within seconds men were reaching up to grab the fluttering pages like the keenest of wedding bouquet fielders eager to be the next bride. The crowd cheered and waved their handbills at the women. All were impressed with the temerity and ingenuity of these Suffragettes, and anything that made fools of the police and local officialdom was always popular. But there was more to the atmosphere than mere communal high spirits. Men who until very recently would have been preparing to pelt the women with whatever rotten fruit and veg that came to hand, were becoming converts. This part of the City was only a few minutes' walk from the start of the East End; Sylvia Pankhurst's East End.

Police and City Corporation employees, with the aid of a twelve pound sledge-hammer, eventually smashed down the barricaded door and pulled down the flags and banners amidst jeers from the thousands below. But as the triumphant women reappeared at the entrance to The Monument, so the cheers rang out again. Harassed constables then escorted Miss Spark and Mrs Shaw into the underground station and ushered them on to a train while a line of police held the crowds back for safety purposes.

May was packed off to Bishopsgate police station by taxi, whilst Ruby was locked into one of the tiny individual cells of a Black Maria. It was noisy and dark as the vehicle clattered over the cobbles. This rumble was added to by the caterwauling of a couple of young prostitutes angry both with the City police and the world at large which had led the poor wretches to such degradation. But soon enough the Suffragettes, who thanks to some window-breaking in the vicinity had a working majority in the coach, drowned out the swearing and screaming with their rendition of the Women's Marseillaise.

The process of being arrested was a rollercoaster of emotions. The claustrophobic scariness of the Black Maria ensured that the confection of excitement, elation and feeling of achievement initially engendered by the illegal action committed, was replaced via a big mood swing to a sense of fear and foreboding. The singing not only showed the usual Suffragette defiance, but dried out dampened spirits.

Justice was nothing if not summary. Ruby was quickly up before the local magistrate. Such law officials thought they had seen it all. They were used to dealing with the sullen silence of seasoned felons furious with themselves for being caught, or the ingratiatingly apologetic trying to fool 'the beak' into thinking they were full of remorse so they might get a lighter sentence. One thing magistrates had not seen, and were unaccustomed to was a well-trained, well-rehearsed eloquent young woman defending herself confidently and aggressively in a court of law, making speeches about political injustice. But this was what they had to deal with on this occasion, and such audacity and lack of respect for the court was dealt with by an affronted old man handing down a sentence which was more severe than the offence warranted.

"You belong to the class of hysterical women, many of whom are associated with this movement, who appear to be animated mainly or at any rate in some measure by a desire for notoriety. You will go to prison for three weeks. Under Rule 243a I am required to give you prisoner status in the one and a half class."

As she was led away Ruby decided not to shout what she thought of the court and its justice. She feared that would be adjudged as contempt which might add time to her already stiff sentence for a first offence. There was also the consideration that she could lose her one and a half class status. The 243a rule had been a hard won mini-victory by the WSPU in obtaining a compromise from the Home Office. Suffragettes were categorised as a special case; neither second class common nor first class political prisoners. The women received most though not all first class privileges and the government saved face by not recognising Suffragettes as political prisoners.

In contrast to prison-bound Ruby, the all too newsworthy 'Cripple Suffragette' was released. This was thanks to a sheepish, under orders policeman giving evidence in court to the effect that he might have been a little over zealous in arresting Miss Billinghurst. She could have collided with him accidentally whilst attempting to escape the overcrowding at The Monument. And like the two women she had directed to the top of the monument she had not hitherto that day committed an arrest-worthy offence. The judge appeared to be in on the act as he spoke in his most patronising voice to the wheelchair in front of him.

"No one could, I think, doubt for a moment, as mistaken as I think you to be, that you were animated by the highest and purest of motives in what you did. You are free to go."

May, who was under orders from her superiors not to get herself imprisoned for contempt of court, had glared stone-faced at the judge but left it at that.

Ruby's mood continued to fluctuate, the shame felt by being in a police station cell having rapidly been replaced by the thrill of making her Suffrage speech in court, before she plunged to new depths of despair when passing through the forbidding entry gate of HM Prison Holloway.

On decamping from the Black Maria, Ruby and the rest of the latest batch of Suffragette arrivals were left in a small yard and told they could 'stretch their legs' for a few minutes. The yard was empty save for a large enclosed van, which was taking up much of the space. It was illegal to take a photograph of someone without first receiving their permission to do so, but this mere detail was not stopping the authorities taking covert snaps of Suffragettes from within the van. Copies of the photographs would then be circulated to all major public places in order that stewards on the door may be able to recognise known troublemakers before they got up to whatever protest they were about to attempt. But once they had started hunger-striking and being force-fed the women would not look much like their normal selves, so it was best to take the photographs on arrival.

Prior to the attack on The Monument, a Suffragette who worked in the beauty section of Selfridges, had given Ruby the benefit of her expertise, which included applying make-up and brushing her hair up in the style of the fashionable young things of the day. Thus Ruby had looked suitably demure and damson-like when she had cried for help from the Monument steps. Photograph 13, was thus the illegal mug-shot of a woman attractive and well groomed enough to be a gaiety girl, who looked somewhat reminiscent of a Titanic restaurant cashier. But she held only a passing resemblance to Suffragette troublemaker Ruby Martin.

Each Suffragette in the prison yard, having in due course unknowingly peered towards the police camera lens, was then locked into dark holding cells, four or five women to each one. These were the blankest of canvasses, the only infrastructure being a lidless WC, which looked sufficiently insanitary to ensure that even the most tired, bilious or bladder-desperate would not avail themselves of the facilities.

After some hours standing in the black hole of Holloway, they were called in front of a wardress, who barked one-word questions at each of them in turn.

"Name?!" was snapped at Ruby.

"Votes for Women," came the somewhat less than accurate reply.

The wardress didn't miss a beat, her eyes remaining fixed on her clipboard as she wrote down what she had been told.

Questions as to age, occupation, religion and length of sentence received the same three-word answer before Ruby took her place in a line-up, breathing in the stench of disinfectant whilst waiting for the prison doctor.

"All of you unfasten your chests!" shouted another wardress.

The prison officer may not have had the greatest grasp of the English language, but it was obvious what was required. The doctor arrived and passed along the line of prisoners asking mechanically of each woman "are you right?" without waiting for an answer. He then touched them with a stethoscope without applying the other end to his ears. The Home Office regulation that each new prisoner be questioned about their health and examined by a doctor had been duly adhered to.

Ruby was separated from her fellow Suffragettes, marched to a large room which included other prisoners and told to undress. She refused, stating that under Rule 243a she was allowed to wear her own clothes. The wardress replied that no prisoner by the name of Votes for Women appeared on their register of those detained under that rule. Ruby suspected that this must be unofficial. They were just making a point, instilling discipline, showing her who was in charge. But they surely could not ignore her class one and a half status. She crossed her arms defiantly and continued to refuse to undress, which resulted in her being forcibly stripped by wardresses, which also served as the compulsory body-search.

Ruby had a bath in the filth of previous occupants and was then bedecked in arrowed clothing. This included scrambling on the floor with the other prisoners to grab dresses and skirts which had been piled in heaps on the floor. The Imperial Theatre New York flashed through her mind. Ruby's stockings flapped around her ankles so she queried if there was anything with which to hold them up.

"No garters here!" was the barked reply.

Ruby then grabbed ill-fitting odd shoes from a pile, before being handed two pieces of cotton. One of these was to be worn as a neckerchief, the other a handkerchief. The former had certain advantages over the usual middle class woman's neckwear which involved hooks, eyes, pins and brooches. Ruby saw one prisoner tie her cravat with gusto but as the woman picked up her hankie a frown spread across her face. There were no pockets in any of the clothing. A wardress spotted the expression and took her cue.

"Handkerchiefs to be hung from waistbands!" she bellowed to the room at large.

May had previously told Ruby about her own experiences as a second class prisoner. Ruby wondered how long the woman would be so pleased with her comfortable new cravat when she saw the laundry come back stained and not properly washed, and realised that her neckerchief this week had been someone else's hankie the week before.

The final part of the women's induction course was a march to the cells along claustrophobic, echoing, stone corridors. Ruby was taken to the wing which had been given over to the exclusive use of Suffragettes. All the earlier one-word questions were repeated by a different wardress. Ruby sighed and answered correctly this time. The wardress gave the Suffragette a smug knowing look to the effect of 'not so clever now are you' and returned the prisoner to retrieve and don her own clothes. Ruby was then brought back to the wing and handed a pair of sheets, bible, hymn book and cloth disk, and ushered into her cell. The wardress informed her that the disk should be attached to her outer clothing at the shoulder. This had her cell number on it, which was what she would be addressed by when spoken to by prison staff. 'Thirty two' was duly locked up.

Ruby surveyed her new fixed abode. It measured seven feet by five, and came complete with a stone floor, small barred window too high to see out of and which could not be opened for ventilation, and a flickering gas light set in the wall and covered by thick opaque glass. Under the light was a wooden shelf which was the closest thing to a table. Another corner shelf held the most basic of kitchen and bathroom bric-a-brac provided to keep body and cell together, some of which were second hand from the previous tenant. Items that the new occupant would certainly not be touching were the water can and prison rules cards. A wash basin, plank bed two inches above the concrete floor with a bone hard mattress and pillow, and a small wooden chair completed the grim scene.

The cell was airless, cold and most of all for someone who had just gone through such a dehumanising process, lonely. Yet its new incumbent did not feel her rollercoaster plunge down into another dip. She felt strangely upbeat. It was the first time in her life she had felt of use; part of something. To date her life had seen little sense of the kinship of labour or the camaraderie of a shared cause. Working as a servant from the instant she got up to the moment she flopped exhausted into her bed at night, had produced the indifference of mutual drudgery rather than any bond of service with her fellow servants. There had been no feeling that she was contributing to the maintenance of something worthwhile. And having been a sub-contracted employee of an ocean liner company meant that she had simply assisted not one but two uncaring businesses to turn a profit. The termination of her employment from the moment the Titanic sank had proved that. And as for the crew of the lost ship, whilst she had shared a terrible experience with them, she considered some of the survivors to be cowards, a couple even murderers. The only Titanic survivor with whom she had any affinity was Nashey.

But where once she had been a downtrodden hostage to fortune, she was now a free woman, free to follow her wonderful and just cause. Ruby remembered the two words of Morse code she had been taught as part of her Suffragette militant training course. Picking up her tin pint mug she tapped out 'no surrender' on a pipe. Within seconds a woman in a nearby cell was answering with the same message. And then another; and another.

******

Being awarded one and a half class status had not put an end to Suffragette hunger-striking. Such protests had originally been purely to demonstrate against not being awarded political prisoner status, but now they were made within the wider context of the women's fight for justice. Consequently, though Ruby had not deliberately got herself imprisoned, now she was there, she intended to hunger-strike. A thirst as well as hunger-strike would get her released quicker because it had such an immediate and detrimental effect on the body so she intended to decline all forms of nourishment.

But other than hunger and thirst-strike Ruby thought she would now follow the rules of the prison for a day. She wanted to get to know the procedures before ascertaining which ones she would endeavour to disrupt in protest.

Her first full day in prison began with the cell door being opened at six o'clock and the wardress telling her charges gruffly to 'slop out!'

Breakfast soon followed. May had once told Ruby tales of the earlier Suffragettes being offered no more than a pint of thin gruel and a wedge of bread for breakfast and supper, with tasteless porridge or something equally unpalatable for mid-day dinner. But nowadays, thanks to being awarded a higher classification of prisoner status, such poor quality food was a thing of the past. The irony was that the better meals being offered and the monthly food package Suffragettes could now receive from outside were a greater torment to those on hunger-strike.

Breakfast was duly declined, and this out of the way Ruby was set to work in her cell. There were sheets to hem, mail bags and shirts to sew. At 8.30 the prisoners were walked in single file to chapel, at which point wardresses clamped down on any potential threat to prison discipline.

"Who is that speaking?!" demanded one though Ruby had not heard anyone utter a word.

"Tie up your cap strings Twenty Three! You look like a cinder-picker! You must learn to dress decently here!"

"Hold up your head Twenty Nine! And don't shuffle your feet!"

Ruby looked to see who the cinder-picker and foot-shuffler were.

"Don't look about Thirty Two!"

Blimey, thought Ruby, her time in London having had her pick up the odd cockney term.

The chaplain spoke harshly to the sinners placed in front of him.

Back in her cell Ruby had plenty of visitors that morning, and each was announced with some pomp though little ceremony.

"Inspection!" "Doctor!" "Governor and matron!" "Visiting magistrate!"

Each passed with Ruby having to remain silent whilst she was discussed as if she was not there. To speak, a prisoner had to have made advance application.

Late morning turned out to be the highlight of the day – associated labour. Prisoners sat in rows knitting their stockings or sewing their underwear whilst discipline was relaxed, the women being allowed to speak freely to each other. The whole afternoon was given over to sewing in one's cell, though Suffragettes' one and a half class status meant their cell doors were left unlocked during the day. Ruby was thus able to wander into neighbouring cells for brief chats with allies, who returned the favour.

Supper was easily ignored though her grumbling stomach and dehydration headache put up an argument. After lock-up, the dim lighting was not sufficient to be able to read the bible. This was the only thing Ruby would have to read until she made her first visit to the prison library or she received her first letter. At 8pm a wardress raised the cell door's spyhole.

"Are you alright?"

It was lights out.

Ruby's second day started out pretty much the same as the first except from now on her one and a half class status allowed her to exercise twice daily in the yard. She was now feeling so weak that ordinarily such exertion would have been the last thing she would have wanted to do, but May had advised her to take exercise whenever possible because it helped maintain muscle strength, so when it was offered the opportunity was taken.

Prisoners were not allowed to speak whilst exercising and had to walk in single file. Mrs Pankhurst had once famously ignored the rules when in prison with daughter Christabel, the two of them walking arm in arm chatting whilst the wardresses' threats were disregarded with haughty disdain. Ruby thought of this when at one point she started to step around a puddle that was in her way only to be shouted at by a wardress to walk through it. Prison rules stipulated that the route of the walk had to be rigidly adhered to. The warning had caused Ruby to stop in her tracks, but she then fixed her gaze on the wardress and continued to walk around the puddle.

"Where's that Sir Walter Raleigh when your need him eh?" croaked Ruby defiantly.

It had meant to come out as a sneering shout, but the thirst-strike was increasing its effect on her. The inevitable warnings of dire retribution were bellowed into her ear from point blank range by the wide-eyed wardress, but the target of this verbal attack was already starving, slowly dying of thirst and no doubt soon to be tortured by force-feeding, so any threats were idle.

The exercise had left Ruby feeling even more light-headed and poorly so once back in her cell she decided to combine further disobedience with some much needed rest and recuperation. Prisoners were expected to roll up their mattress into a neat Swiss roll at the start of each day. And from the shouts of dismay at prisoners Ruby had heard that morning, there was clearly nothing more guaranteed to gain the wrath of a wardress than a slovenly tidied away mattress. Officer Lowe's neat stowing of the lifeboat's oars came to mind, though one aspect of a splitting headache was that it was now difficult to concentrate on anything for long so at least the Titanic departed from her thoughts as quickly as it arrived. She untied her Swiss roll and placed the mattress back on her plank bed. Another fundamental rule was that prisoners must not lie on their bed during the day. So Ruby did, clasping her hands behind her head and stretching out to give an appearance of optimum comfort and contempt for the rules, whilst she closed her eyes and allowed her mind to go for a swim.

When a wardress saw her laying there, the apoplexy Ruby had hoped it would induce duly occurred. The wardress had the bed and its bedding taken away, and told her charge that she would have to sleep on the cold cell floor from now on. The obstinate prisoner was then hauled before the governor and told in no uncertain terms that for such a flagrant disregard of prison rules she would be placed on bread and water.

"I am on hunger and thirst-strike," croaked Ruby literally dryly, trying but failing to avoid any hint of sarcasm.

But any underlying smirk was wiped off her face when the governor went on to say that due to her disgraceful behaviour since arriving at the prison she had forfeited her previous status, and would now be treated as a second class prisoner. This meant no open cell, no books from the prison library, no fortnightly letters, no monthly visits, no talking except in hushed tones at associated labour, and twice-weekly rather than twice-daily exercise. And she could think herself lucky that due to space constraints she was being allowed to stay within the Suffragette wing.

Ruby wasn't sure whether such a change to a court ruling could be legal, but the authorities seemed to make rules up as they went along when it came to Suffragettes. And to whom could she complain?

A few hours later, her heart sank when she was presented with a dinner of chicken, haricot beans and fruit. This was the sort of tasty meal that women being force-fed were offered to try to woo them away from their protest. It was clear the torture was about to start. To go through this was always the goal, but now it was here, she suddenly felt hawk moth-sized butterflies in her grumbling stomach as tears of self-pity welled up in her eyes. A few seconds later she flicked the warm tears off her cheek with her index fingers and thought of freezing cold water cascading down a corridor wall, of feeling complete hopelessness, of Nashey refusing to be beaten.

"No surrender," she said coldly, quietly.

She was not ready, no one in their right mind could be for such an ordeal, but Ruby was as ready as she was ever going to be.

******

A set of missiles had been lined up neatly along the shelf. When Ruby heard the wheels of what she knew to be the force-feeding trolley squeaking along the corridor, she picked up the first couple of pieces of her arsenal and waited. There was a jangle of keys and then the cell door opened. The first head through the doorway, that of matron, was hit by a flying prison mug; a wardress received similar treatment from a hurled plate and then the doctor had a shoe do a pirouette off his skull.

More wardresses dashed in under enemy fire and Ruby was eventually, not without some difficulty, overpowered by a hit-squad of six and shoved down onto her chair. The matron seized her by the head and pulled it back while the doctor thrust a sheet under her chin. Four wardresses worked to a well-rehearsed battle plan. Two each gripped an arm whilst another grabbed both feet before passing one to a colleague to quickly bind an ankle tightly to a chair leg. The other leg quickly followed into captivity. The women who had bound the legs then concentrated their efforts towards pressing down on the thighs. The doctor thrust his fingers harshly between Ruby's lips and forced his hand into her mouth to set about trying to find a gap between her gritted teeth. Ruby's fondness for all things sweet allied to an inability to pay for dentistry over the years had left some easy targets. A steel gag then clattered around inside her mouth, inflicting sharp pain as it was forced round the gums and into a gap in the teeth. Once in position the screw of the gag was turned and Ruby's jaws were slowly but surely forced apart to a point beyond their natural width.

A wardress, knowing she would have to resign so she never had to do this again, cried out urgently to the doctor.

"Don't hurt more than you can help!"

Ruby was summoning every ounce of energy out of her

stricken body to buck, twist and thrust like a yearling which refused to be broken. This resulted in the wardress holding her left arm having to move round towards the back of her prey to apply more pressure on the left shoulder, and the woman pushing down on the left thigh had to kneel down to grab a calf and knee which was still managing to find some freedom. The matron had planned to pour the food but such was Ruby's struggle that all five women were needed to keep hold of her, so the doctor said he would do it himself. The normal practice was for doctors to torture their victims from behind, but the only space now available was between the two struggling wardresses in front of the prisoner.

The doctor fed the feeding tube through the bruised mouth, past sore, bleeding gums, down Ruby's throat. She fought for breath as the thickness of the tube proved unbearable, and started to choke. She coughed up the tube three times. The fourth time the doctor thrust down harder, Ruby feeling the terrifying sensation of the tube in her stomach. Moments later, holding a jug in one hand and the funnel attached to the other end of the tube in the other, the doctor poured hot thick brown liquid into Ruby's stomach. The stench of cheap broth and medicine filled the cell.

There was very good reason why doctors usually stood behind their victims. Ruby was sick all over him.

"Do that again and I'll feed you twice!" warned her torturer.

She vomited over him again, so the doctor, more hypocrite than Hippocrat, slapped her hard across the face. She vomited again as the tube was taken out and brought up large quantities of bile. Just for a moment Ruby tried to think of something defiant to say, but she couldn't clear her head; she was in no condition to bandy words with the Inquisition.

231

After her colleagues had escaped from the scene of their crime, a lone wardress, the one whose entreaty to the doctor had been ignored, started to clear up the paraphernalia of pain. The torture had left sick all over the walls, throughout Ruby's hair, and her clothes were saturated.

"The office is closed for the day," said the wardress sheepishly. "You'll have to stay in those clothes till tomorrow."

Ruby was determined to answer, and do so defiantly, so she summoned up every bit of resolve she could find to speak.

"I've been wet all night before," she croaked. "I was on the Titanic. Men like that…"

It was as far as she managed to get before convulsing in a shivering fit, teeth chattering. Her shoulders were bruised and her head and back ached, but far worse than any pain was the sense of degradation and defilement.

She had been raped.

★★★★★★

Lying on her bed she remembered that May had given her a tip about pushing fingers down the throat to produce the retch reflex. Drained of all energy, head throbbing and throat painfully sore, she summoned up every bit of will power she could muster to get up. Moments later she was throwing up the remaining contents of her culinary experience into her slops pail. Her eyes were streaming and the flesh around them painful, but she felt, mentally at least, a little stronger for having ejected the purpose of the rape from her body. It was not a bath or shower, but it served the same purpose.

Ruby was placed in solitary confinement for the seemingly heinous crime of throwing the shoe. She was still to be allowed twice-weekly exercise but not at the same time as her Suffragette comrades so she told the prison authorities that she would not be partaking of their offer.

The second force-feeding followed similar lines to the first though Ruby had become so weak that she had not been able to put up anywhere near as strong a struggle, and had fainted at the end of the ordeal. When she had recovered consciousness and been returned to her cell, she decided to start a pacing vigil. She had been advised by May that constipation was one of the many unpleasant side-effects of the torture, and that exertion helped ease it. Sylvia Pankhurst had been the first to pace non-stop up and down in her cell, both as a protest and as exercise. And what was good enough for the great champion of the fight for the vote for working women, was good enough for a poor girl from Southampton. And doing anything, even self-torture, was better than just lying there shaking as she recounted the horror. The physical pain helped keep its mental equivalent at bay, a little at least. Ruby paced up and down in her cell non-stop for two hours. She had started to get chest pains when her weak foot gave way and she blacked out.

This meant an end to solitary confinement and a change of address; she was transferred to the prison hospital. Once consciousness returned, Ruby, still groggy, took a few moments to take in the fact that she had been moved. From her bed she craned her stiff aching neck around to survey her new surroundings. The hospital ward was quite an improvement on her solitary cell.

"Associated labour!" shouted a wardress.

Any woman who was able to, rose from her bed because this was the only chance she was going to get to speak to her fellow patients. The women sat in the usual rows knitting or sewing, speaking in hushed tones to their immediate neighbours either side of them.

Despite her head spinning far worse than any hangover she had ever suffered, Ruby was determined to get up. She dragged herself up and along to the benches, then sat down and waited for the room to stop imitating a fairground carousel. Once her ability to focus a little returned, her attention was drawn by someone sitting down next to her. Her neighbour was an attractive, tall, thin redhead with greying hair and striking green eyes. Rather than attempting the usual introductions she asked Ruby quietly the double question of how she was feeling and if she was a Suffragette.

Concerned that she could burst into tears at any moment, Ruby didn't answer immediately. Nashey telling her to take a deep breath leapt in to her mind. For once a Titanic memory was a good one. She did as she was told by the big East Ender before croaking out answers that were short and to the point.

"Bad. Yes."

The neighbour was only too aware of how this new hospital inmate was feeling. Deciding that she would do all the talking whilst her fellow Suffragette tried to recover her senses, she informed Ruby that she too was an active WSPU militant and spoke of her own ailments and how they had been received. Her attendance in the hospital had come care of throwing herself off the top of a prison stairwell and landing heavily on the bottom of its steps. She was in prison for arson; soaking rags with paraffin, setting them alight and posting the flaming packages into pillar boxes. After several successful incinerations, she had waited at a pillar box with a fuelled rag until a policeman had come along so she could claim responsibility for her previous efforts and get herself arrested. It was time for introductions. Her name was Miss Davison. Emily Davison.

Despite feeling terrible, Ruby felt a surge of excitement course through her body. This was the woman whom Christabel had sacked from being a WSPU paid worker for being *too* militant! She had become a free-agent Suffragette who had invented pillar box sabotage. She had also at least twice as far as Ruby could remember successfully stowed away in the House of Commons.

Ruby managed to croak out a question, again keeping her words to a minimum.

"Why hide in Commons census night?"

Emily didn't seem to mind the abruptness of the enquiry and answered animatedly.

"Many suffragists hid themselves away to boycott the census. I thought I should like to do likewise but hide in Parliament, so should I be found my address on census night would be the House of Commons. It is the address we are all fighting for is it not? I was found in the Commons crypt soon enough and my landlady erroneously recorded me as being present in my lodgings too, so perhaps rather than boycott the census I appear twice!"

Ruby managed the weakest of smiles. And she was keen to ask another question, this time about Emily's most famous escapade, in Manchester's Strangeways prison.

"Strangeways?" she muttered.

Emily smiled. She clearly enjoyed the limelight and

proceeded to hold court about the incident that had found her on the front pages of the national dailies, and which greatly embarrassed the government in general and the Home Office in particular. She told Ruby of how, after she had been force-fed a dozen times, her cell had been in such a state that the prison authorities decided to move her into another while they cleaned hers up. They moved her bed to the new cell, which already had its own bed. Spotting that two beds placed end to end could be wedged between the cell door and far cell wall, she barricaded herself in. They pumped freezing cold water on to her through a hose pipe fed through the cell window, but despite starting to shake and not be able to breathe properly she stayed put. With great difficulty the authorities eventually forced the cell door open.

Ruby knew a thing or two about freezing water. She nodded in appreciation but immediately wished she hadn't as her brain seemingly slid about inside her skull. Through the haze of head pain Ruby thought Miss Davison was clearly someone to admire. Yet she looked and sounded so unassuming, frankly so ordinary.

The room had slowed its revolving from fairground carousel to mere playground roundabout, and Ruby's infamous Suffragette neighbour had also made her feel a little better. She managed to hold herself together while she introduced herself. Both women having agreed to address each other by their first names, Ruby went on to tell her colleague how she had come to be in prison. Their respective exploits duly exchanged, Emily then admitted that it was not sheer chance that the two of them were sitting next to one another, she having made a beeline to sit next to Ruby. Emily explained that she had recently had a meeting with May

Billinghurst to pass on some tips about the various ways one could sabotage pillar boxes. She had asked May if she happened to know anyone who was an expert on horse-racing and Ruby's name had been mentioned. Emily's ears had thus pricked up when she had heard that Ruby had been admitted to the prison hospital.

Ruby was amazed by the Suffragette grapevine. She remembered how on a train journey with May she had once picked up a discarded newspaper and studied the racing page. This led to her telling May that she and her father had enjoyed going horse-racing together at Wincanton every Boxing Day, and they had also once saved up to go on a charabanc excursion to Newbury races on a big race day. And now that she was living in St Johns she would like to go to one of the big London tracks such as Sandown one day. May had explained that racecourse grandstands were now a target for the Suffragette arson campaign. Being large well known places that were left unattended for long periods, they were ideal. Razing one to the ground was spectacular and therefore newsworthy but also very importantly safe from any possibility of harming anyone. May had thought that Ruby's knowledge of racing might be useful once she had received arson training.

From this one casual conversation, it was now clear to Ruby that according to the WSPU grapevine she was considered the organisation's horse-racing ace. And as the grandstands at Ayr and Hurst Park racecourses had recently gone up in flames whilst a planned attack on Kelso's had been unsuccessful, Ruby suspected Emily was about to invite her along on a similar attack.

Given that prison walls had bigger ears than most, Emily

was very careful with her words, simply whispering that she too had an interest in the Sport of Kings and that it would be nice for the two of them to go racing together soon, especially now that the weather was improving. Both of them were due to be released forthwith on health grounds, and the Cat and Mouse Act had not yet become operational, so they would be free to go as they pleased.

Ruby agreed to go racing with Emily, winking as she did so to let it be known that she appreciated that there was more to the offer of the excursion than met the eye.

"It is a shame over the sticks is finishing," said Ruby. "We will have to make do with the flat."

From the vacant expression on Emily's face it was clear that she had never been horse-racing in her life.

Chapter 19

"After driving independence out of their ranks, after crystallising the forces of their enemies and splitting the forces of their friends, by their big words and small deeds they virtually lay militancy as a task upon the few – militancy which to make itself set has to be such as to stagger humanity."

Dora Marsden, editor of Freewoman (and ex-WSPU member)

Both women had needed time to recover from their debilitating prison ordeal. Emily had gone to stay with her mother in Morpeth in Northumberland whilst Ruby had checked herself into a cheap but respectable boarding house for a week in Southampton. Her mother had offered to put her up but Ruby had wished to have a bolt-hole to escape to, so she did not have to be in the company of her sisters for any length of time. Ruby did however ensconce herself in her mother's home for much of each day. Whenever there were just the two of them in the house, Ruby rested with her legs up on a chair whilst allowing herself to be pampered with regular cups of tea, biscuits and expensive food such as fruit which she knew her mother could ill afford. Ruby had lost 2lbs in weight per day whilst in prison, and was suffering from her skin becoming fiery red and having eczema-like dryness. She would also go hot and cold, had chronic headaches and her digestive system was suffering; she was constipated and had acute flatulence. She also found it difficult to sleep at night so much of the time in her mother's house was spent dozing. But when any of her sisters arrived, Ruby would bring her legs down, sit bolt upright and use every bit of will power she had to look alert and every inch the tough London Suffragette ex-convict. She impersonated traits she remembered from Nashey and the body language of scary non-Suffragette women prisoners she had come across in Holloway.

Ruby heard from her mother that the Titanic Relief Fund's lady visitor was an arrogant, snooty young woman whose visits were dreaded. This had surprised and upset Ruby as the impression she had got from June's letters was that the lady was haughty, as one would expect of such a visitor, but no worse than that. It turned out that her mother had simply not wished to worry her. Ruby would have liked to have stayed on to be there for the next visit but she was becoming increasingly concerned at the debt her mother must be running up at the corner shop to pay for the goodies with which it was insisted she be plied.

There were also the mental effects of Ruby's prison torture to be addressed. Soon after arriving she had poured her heart out to her mother about the appalling treatment she had received. Her mother had hugged and caressed her and said all the right things to give comfort and support, which had been reassuring. But as the week had gone by, Ruby had started to feel the urge to return to the Suffragette fold. She was starting to recover physically from her assault but felt that in order to begin what was clearly going to be a lengthy battle to overcome the mental effects, she needed to be with others who had gone through the same ordeal. It was now time to start fighting the demons by trying to banish them from her thoughts whilst she concentrated on becoming a militant Suffragette again.

Letters were swopped with Emily in Morpeth. Both would return to London pronto to meet up. A horse-racing excursion beckoned.

★★★★★★

Being so well known to the authorities, the infamous Miss Davison thought it best not to meet in a public place and preferably somewhere more out of the way than central London. Ruby was too embarrassed to invite Emily to her simple St Johns abode so suggested they meet at May's house on the Lewisham/Blackheath borders, explaining that it was close to where she lived and Emily could get a train there easily enough. But Emily asked if just the two of them could meet. She knew Blackheath. She had been born there, retained links to the area and had a friend in the vicinity who would be happy to be their host.

The two women duly met up. Emily began by telling of a plan to do something at Epsom racecourse. Ruby was quick to point out that when it was not being used for racing, the grandstand at Epsom was used by poor people who had set up home there. They temporarily decamped to the streets while a race meeting was on, and the rest of the time the Epsom authorities turned a blind eye to their lodgers, who were effectively unpaid security people, which was especially useful now that racecourses were Suffragette targets.

"It is not arson I have in mind for Epsom," said Emily with a mischievous smile on her face. "And it is not to be a furtive action. Like your wonderful Monument coup, it is to be seen by a crowd. But rest assured no member of the public will be put at risk. I would like some assistance from you but as you may be aware I am no longer a paid official of the WSPU. Christabel took it amiss when I broke a Whitehall window during a Conciliation Bill truce with the government. She sacked me. I am now an independent. So your assistance must be unofficial. I would not like you to be sacked too so your involvement would be merely to offer advice. You would not be at any risk of committing an offence."

Ruby appreciated that Emily was asking her to act in secrecy. Nobody else was to know about her involvement. It was now clear why May's presence had not been required. Ruby considered the ramifications if she was found out by her employers; expulsion from being a paid WSPU worker, a return to Chiesman's with nicer clothes and better hair, and if that didn't work, a Bermondsey factory. She didn't know why, perhaps it was being star-struck by the infamous and heroic Emily Davison, but Ruby found herself readily agreeing to take part in the enterprise. A long discussion followed ironing out the detail before it was finally agreed that Ruby would meet Emily and her flat-mate, Canadian Mary Richardson, who was another of the WSPU's most militant and independent women, bright and early on Derby Day. Their target was to be the Derby itself.

★★★★★★

The plan was for Emily and Mary to travel to the racecourse

separately from Ruby. They would meet her at the Tattenham Corner entrance to the course but make no sign of acknowledgement. Once they spotted each other, Ruby would make her way on to the course and they would follow behind at a discreet distance. They were to appear not to know each other. This would protect Ruby from any problems with the police after the event. Ruby was both bemused and not a little excited by these cloak and dagger tactics.

There was never any thought of Emily and Mary returning home after the Derby. Even if the attack on the race failed for some reason, they would protest somewhere, somehow. Their day would end with a Black Maria ride and a police station cell in the Epsom vicinity. Consequently they would buy single journey rail tickets. There was no point in wasting money on returns. Emily and Mary duly presented themselves bright and early at Victoria railway station. It had been decided that Mary would get the tickets whilst Emily kept a low profile, sitting on a station bench reading a newspaper. Mary wandered in to the ticket office.

"Two third class singles to the Derby please."

"Certainly miss. Epsom Downs or Tattenham Corner?" enquired the ticket clerk.

Ruby had not discussed railway stations during their planning meeting and Mary hadn't appreciated that there was more than one station, but after a moment's hesitation she presumed they must want the latter of the two proffered. She was about to relay this when the ticket clerk continued in his pompous, preposition-light fashion.

"Epsom Downs, train here, platform four, ten minutes. Tattenham Corner, London Bridge. Epsom Downs for the grandstand. Long crowded walk for ladies. Tattenham

Corner, next to the course or taxi from there to the grandstand, best for ladies."

The man's remarks proved a red rag to Mary's bull. Since when could women not walk or handle themselves in a crowd? And besides neither she nor Emily had been able to sleep last night so they had left home hours before they were due to meet Ruby. Thus time was not of the essence. And it might be better in avoiding police checks if they walked some way to the course. They could get the lie of the land and take a roundabout route if necessary. So they would get the train from Victoria to Epsom Downs, get there in good time and stroll along to Tattenham Corner at their leisure.

"Two singles to the Epsom Downs please."

The Epsom Downs indeed, thought the clerk contemptuously as he resisted the temptation to hunch his shoulders to show the irritation he felt at his advice being ignored. He instead went for a mix of light scolding and sarcasm which, being free of giving directions, was at least relayed in something a little closer to the King's English.

"They won't let you in with that miss," he said pointing at the umbrella that Mary was carrying. "Think it's going to rain from a cloudless sky, do you?"

Since the increase in Suffragette violence against property, major public places no longer admitted women carrying items that could be used for nefarious means, such as walking sticks, umbrellas and muffs. They had to be left at the door. And Mary's most sturdy of umbrellas certainly looked suspiciously unlike the summer parasol that it was being asked to imitate on a fine summer's day. Its true purpose was as a weapon of self-defence should things get a little out of hand later.

Mary ignored the clerk's slight, and politely refused his subsequent offer of selling her a left luggage ticket. The man then told her the price of the tickets before explaining why they were returns.

"Derby Day special excursion fare today miss; return's cheaper than a single."

Mary thanked the man, paid, picked up the return tickets and walked outside to find Emily. An hour and a half later, the last third of which had been spent walking from Epsom Downs station, the two women duly arrived at Tattenham Corner. They were pleasantly surprised to find Ruby had also got to the course earlier than had been agreed, and as soon as she spotted her comrades and made eye-contact with them, she set off. Moments later they were looking out over the racecourse.

What was, three hundred and sixty days a year, the rugged walk-where-you-please wilderness of Epsom Downs had been temporarily covered by a scene that promised something no less rugged, carefree and wild. Ruby was amazed at the view which confronted her. She had never seen anything quite like it, on a racecourse or anywhere else for that matter.

Horse-drawn charabancs, carriages and swaying open-topped double-deckers hurtled along, whilst drivers of motor vehicles were swerving dangerously round them at break-neck speed to show them who was boss. Steam-driven fairground rides, coconut stalls, musicians, clowns, conjurers, boxing, Punch and Judy and all the other fun of the fair were in situ. Shoeshine boys, barbers and the like were also out in force. Ruby saw a man being shaved with slapdash abandon by a barber in a hurry, his arm at risk of being jogged at any moment by the jostling crowd as he passed the cut-throat blade across his customer's neck. A sea captain, ocean liner and iceberg came to mind for a moment before an animated argument nearby regained Ruby's attention. There were plenty of roughs about. Ruby knew she had to be on her guard for pickpockets, con-men and other scoundrels. The only people missing were fortune tellers. Their trade was illegal, but it was not fear of the police that kept them absent. Getting their prediction wrong when there was only one forecast Derby Day punters were interested in, was liable to result in immediate retribution from the disappointed. Ruby's two associates took the whole thing somewhat in their stride, assuming it must be the horse-racing norm.

There was already a fair crowd milling about, many of whom had arrived the day before and slept rough in the vicinity. And corralling this scene was the appropriately horseshoe-shaped racecourse running around the perimeter of part of the Downs expanse. A stone's throw in front of them, at the four furlongs from home marker, stood Tattenham Corner itself. The ticket clerk's warning proved groundless, Mary being allowed to carry her umbrella on to the course with impunity. Most of the stewards who might have challenged her were standing guard at the entrances to the grandstand, leaving a lone colleague at Tattenham Corner. And this man was far too busy with other matters to worry about brollies. He had the impossible task of checking photographs against the faces of the huge crowd. But Emily was not photogenic and looked nothing like her unflattering prison mug-shot, and Ruby no longer resembled a Titanic cashier.

The steward would have been better served looking for incongruously dressed women. On a beautiful June scorcher of a day, the three Suffragettes were all dressed for much colder climes, the theory being that their WSPU flags and copious amounts of Votes for Women literature would be better hid under big coats.

Ruby had tried Douglas Street but being the start of summer the market did not have much in the way of second-hand winter apparel. So given that if things went wrong she may find herself sacked from the WSPU for getting involved in an unofficial Emily Davison stunt, Ruby thought she would treat herself to a new coat with a view to impressing when walking through the front door of Chiesman's looking for a job. She decided to have a bespoke coat made with special large inside pockets for hiding her WSPU stock. She bought the material and was then pleased to give some work to a destitute Deptford tailor to run up the ensemble. The man had given Ruby the briefest of conspiratorial winks when told to provide special inside pockets, assuming his new client to be from the Artful Dodger School of street entrepreneurship. Ruby had not understood the significance of the gesture so had ignored and forgotten it.

Given his client was a Suffragette the tailor had taken it upon himself to work from a photograph of Mrs Pankhurst. Ruby's Derby Day ensemble was thus a hat with deep turned brim, waterproof cotton coat with raglan sleeves, large patch and flap pockets inside and out plus boots. The clothing was not only twenty degrees too warm it looked twenty years too old for her. Though if she continued to do hunger and thirst-strikes followed by being force-fed, it would not be too lengthy a period before the coat no longer looked out of place on her, other than being a few sizes too big.

Also hiding WSPU stock, Mary looked very smart but dressed for autumn in a felt hat with upturned brim, blouse with stand collar, double-breasted half-jacket with fur collar, long jacket, ankle-length skirt and boots.

Emily had brought out of moth balls part of her staid ex-governess Sunday best uniform of hat with feather, blouse with brooch, stand collar and pleated bodice, boots and tailored long jacket. This had WSPU flags and scarf hidden within it as well as 'Votes for Women' sewn into its lining. Added to this was a skirt with central pleat which had been chosen with care as good freedom of movement for the task ahead would be required.

The three women were roasting on a day when every other well-dressed woman at the Derby was in her silkiest finery or at the very least her most comfortable linens and cottons. Emily and Mary were perspiring; Ruby was sweating.

Ruby bought a race-card and made her way to a lemonade stall, with Emily and Mary following at a discreet distance. The three each bought a much needed drink and spoke to one another in front of the lemonade seller as if they were strangers meeting for the first time. They wandered out of his earshot as they sipped their drinks. Ruby lowered her voice to little more than a whisper.

"Do not drink any more. You have wetted your whistle but that will have to do. Once we have got our place on the rails we cannot go to the lavatory because we would not be able to get back through the crowds to regain our position."

Emily and Mary immediately returned their drinks to the stall before wandering back to hear further technical support from their young assistant.

"I have picked Tattenham Corner not just because it is

the most well-known part of the course but because the bend is so sharp here that the stewards will not see you, Emily, until the last moment. And it's the most crowded part of the course so everyone will be so tight packed in that even if a steward does spot you, he will not be able to reach hold of you in time. And this is where all the roughs come, so the police tend to let them get on with it. Most of the police are more likely to be in the grandstand keeping the ladies and gents safe. This is Epsom's steerage."

Aware of Ruby's recent history, Emily and Mary nodded grimly. The trio made their way across to the position that Ruby had selected by the rail on the inside of the bend. Other people who also wanted a great view on Derby Day were streaming onto the course in droves, so Ruby knew they would have people standing tight up beside and behind them in moments, after which they would not be able to discuss anything relating to the matter at hand. This was her last chance to pass on any meaningful information.

"There are fifteen horses running. A few of the outsiders will be starting to tire by Tattenham Corner as the field will have already gone a mile. The better horses will be starting to make their move from the middle of the pack, passing to the outside of those tiring. Emily, this means you will have to walk well out into the centre of the course to ensure you are beyond what might be the widest-running horse for your own safety before you unfurl the flags."

Emily nodded her understanding before Ruby continued.

"But our problem will be timing. If you walk on to the course too soon, officials may spot you in time to bundle you away before the field reaches you. But if you go too late you will be in danger from the horses. Now look there."

With this Ruby turned and motioned towards the raised area of planking behind them.

"That stand is going to be packed with people and as you can see it already blocks most of our view of the rest of the course. And they will be ten deep here right behind us too and most of them taller than us so we will see very little of the race until the field rounds the bend. But once they are in sight, such is their great speed the horses will only be a few seconds away, so by then it will be too late to walk on to the course in safety. I will have to judge when the field is nearing the bend from the noise and the reaction of the crowd further up the course. So when I give you a shove you must, with great haste, duck under the rail and make your way across the course."

People started to huddle around them, which was Mary's cue to begin her working day. She was to go on a charm offensive, moving through the crowd as it gathered, chatting gaily and asking politely if people would be kind enough to take one of her Votes for Women handbills home with them. As for the two women on the rail, it was time to keep the talk off the subject of political protest.

"The Derby is the third race, at three o'clock" advised Ruby, opening her race-card. "We will pick out a horse each in the first two races starting with the one o'clock, cheer them on and mark our card with the result like keen race-goers."

Ruby often felt more at ease with her fellow Suffragettes when the conversation was on Votes for Women rather than social matters. But with Emily it was the other way around. Whilst talking to her during their Derby Day planning she had found Emily rather aloof but now, as her colleague who was about to attempt an audacious coup leaned against the rails as if she did not have a care in the world, Ruby took a shine to her. She found that Emily had a good sense of humour and an endearingly self-effacing manner. And whilst clearly far more bookish than Ruby, she was no intellectual snob; quite the reverse. Emily held court about some of her favourite subjects, such as musical comedy, cats and her family, before Ruby did likewise on one of hers, chocolate. She advised that should Emily ever journey to America she should take some Cadbury's with her. Ruby then lowered her voice to pass on something Suffragette related. She advised Emily on the best sweets, known as black bullets, with which to entice children when you wanted them to take Votes for Women handbills home to their mothers.

Just before the first race Emily mentioned having a ticket for a Suffragette rally that night, which assuming she would be arrested for what she was about to do, would mean her not being able to attend. She asked Ruby if she would like the ticket, but her offer was declined. Ruby already felt weary from the stresses of the day and would just be relieved to see Emily make her protest safely. And besides, her weak foot was starting to ache. Emily nodded her understanding and then mentioned that if Epsom's magistrate gave her the chance of paying a fine she would for once pay it and stay out of prison. She had been force-fed a total of forty nine times and was in no hurry to reach a most terrible of milestones. Disrupting the Derby would be quite sufficient publicity for the cause and she had already promised her sister and niece, who lived in France and to whom she was very close, that she would visit them for a much needed holiday the following week.

The two women managed between them to pick a winner and a second in the first two races, which had thrilled

Ruby rather more than Emily. The new recruit to racing had certainly studied the horses intently each time they had galloped by, but then seemed to lose interest in what happened in the race thereafter, as she became lost in thought. And after the second race Ruby became aware that her new friend had fallen completely quiet. Emily was clearly preparing herself mentally for the mission ahead.

★★★★★★

"They're off!" shouted those with necks sufficiently craned to see the start of the race from atop the raised area behind Ruby and Emily.

As soon as the field set off, some of the crowd who had gathered around the start began running down the course chasing after the horses in the time-honoured tradition of the race. Those fit enough to keep up a decent pace would arrive at Tattenham Corner about seven or eight minutes after the horses. But one spectator had it in mind to be on the famous bend at the same time as the thoroughbreds. Emily had unbuttoned her wintry coat in readiness and felt a moment of relief as the fresh breeze billowed through her clammy clothing. When Ruby gave her a progress report that the horses must have galloped about half a mile, she felt her clothing to check her flags, which were wrapped up and fastened loosely into the inside of her coat, were readily to hand. But she ignored them and instead pulled out her Votes for Women scarf.

The unmistakable groan of disappointed punters started to spread from further up the course to the raised planking area behind Ruby and Emily, as the field made its way down the hill towards Tattenham Corner. The king's well backed horse Anmer was struggling, too far off the pace, close to the back of the field.

"Bloody thing's been got at! It's drugged up to the eyeballs!" and similar shouts of disgust rang out as the bookmakers started to rub their hands together with Fagin-like glee.

Ruby estimated that it was time for Emily to walk out on to the course. She leaned across and whispered in Emily's ear.

"Let's have tea together when you get home from France. No surrender."

And with this she gave Emily a little shove.

"Now or never," answered the brave young woman, but instead of immediately walking onto the course Emily waited, peering up the course until the horses were within sight, before suddenly ducking under the rail just as the leaders of the race flashed by her.

The crowd was so tightly packed and full of excited anticipation of the moment for which they had been waiting all day that nobody noticed the small figure alight on to the course.

The plan had been for Emily to walk out in front of, but safely just to the side of the runners, waving a couple of striking, four feet by two feet, purple, white and green Votes for Women flags and hopefully get the race disrupted or, better still, stopped. But instead of following the plan, Emily had walked on to the course in amongst the horses.

Ruby looked on horrified as Emily showed no sign of whipping out her flags or moving out of the path of the horses. She had her Votes for Women scarf, folded up in one hand. What on earth was she doing? She must have lost her nerve. She would be trampled for sure if she did not duck back under the rail immediately. But to Ruby's great relief Emily then showed remarkable judgement in deftly passing behind the horses in the leading pack, before walking swiftly but calmly into a gap between the leaders and a few tail-enders. She might be safe after all. But the relief was short lived for instead of continuing across to the outside of the course and safety, Emily stepped in to the path of the first of the tail-enders. Ruby recognised it from the jockey's colours as being that owned by the king, Anmer. In that millisecond it flashed through Ruby's mind what her friend was up to. Emily had at some point changed tactics and decided to target the king's horse.

Ruby realised with horror that rather than it being merely a highly dangerous mission, it was a downright foolhardy, suicidal one. Emily must have thought the horse would pass narrowly by her but she had misjudged how the side camber could bring a horse round the bend slightly tighter than expected. Ruby saw Emily try to place the rolled up scarf into the bridle of the horse, but it was an impossible task as half a ton of glossy chestnut thoroughbred bore down on her at forty miles an hour.

Emily shouted "Votes for Women!" as Anmer thundered into her. The collision lifted her off her feet as the horse nosedived then somersaulted forwards with its jockey catapulted into the turf. A flying hoof struck the already unconscious Emily with great force in the head, blood spurting out of her mouth and nose. The power of the initial impact threw her outstretched body yards across the ground, Emily whirling over and over on the turf like a horizontal version of an ice skater performing a spin.

The majority of the crowd were so packed in that they had not seen the incident and continued to watch the race. Those who had seen the horse fall thought it just a racing accident. Moans started to spread through the crowd as they began to appreciate that Anmer was the horse down.

All three of the characters in the drama lay motionless as a small number of people dashed to their aid. An ambulance was called for the woman lying on the quickly reddening turf beneath her.

The incident had taken place by a spot where the public could cross the racetrack to get from the inside of the course to the outside and vice versa when a race was not taking place. The initial mutterings were that the poor woman must have not realised the race had started and been making her way to the railway station. The racecourse steward in charge of the crossing looked on crestfallen. Someone then noticed the inappropriately heavy coat the woman was wearing and suggested the poor wretch might be an imbecile.

A car drove up and Emily was gently laid on the back seat by a man and a woman who turned out to be respectively a local doctor and an ex-nurse. Another woman was also in attendance, apparently seeing what she could do to help. As she ducked under the rail to make her way towards her prone friend, Ruby looked on in a state of shock.

"Deeds not Words! Votes for Women!" was suddenly shouted to the crowd by the woman who had been offering help to the two medical people.

It was Mary. Some of the crowd which were now spilling on to the course suddenly grew hostile, directing a raft of oaths at her before this escalated into violence. A series of blows were rained upon her before a steward stepped forward. It was the man who had been in charge of the crossing, now buoyed by the confidence that it was the act of a Suffragette, and not his negligence, that had caused the accident.

"'ere now, that's enough of that. Have some respect. There's a woman lying over there breathing her last," he said officiously.

There were argumentative replies asking after the health of the jockey and the 'poor 'orse', and suggesting that the woman had only got what she deserved. But some of the crowd looked suitably shocked and sheepish as they removed their headwear as a mark of respect. This allowed Mary to escape from her attackers' clutches and move away to a safe distance before bidding the crowd a fond farewell.

"Emily Wilding Davison will never die; she will live on for ever through all women! Votes for Women!"

"I'll give you votes for fuckin' women!" shouted the angry voice of a punter who had lost a week's wages backing the king's horse.

He beckoned to a couple of like-minded financially embarrassed mates and they started towards Mary. Looking at the menacing expressions on the faces of this trio Mary feared that their extraction of a pound of flesh may be a little too literal for her liking, so she made a run for it. The men responded by starting to chase her. The prize that awaited her if she stayed out in front in this race was the not inconsiderable one of continuing good health.

"Three to one the field!" shouted one wag.

But Mary knew this was no laughing matter. Her fashionable hobble skirt was so narrow at the hem that at first it was difficult for her to take a step of more than a foot at a time. For a few yards she hobbled along like a geisha girl before her hard working lower calves split the skirt which gave them more space in which to move. Mary bent down and grabbed the skirt with one hand to stop it flapping, and held it higher off the ground to give her more freedom of movement, before trotting across the walkway to the far side of the course. A sea of punters, food and drink stalls and entertainments blocked speedy access to Tattenham Corner station so, being eager to keep moving, Mary headed along the outside of the course. A good number of people, who had only come to see the Derby, were also making their way from the course, the majority of whom turned on to the Old London Road, so deciding there was safety in numbers, Mary went with this flow and quickly blended in to the throng.

Though her still relatively restricted movement meant it was impossible for her to escape from her hunters, ironically it was this very limitation that saved her from being more badly beaten. Had she been able to run, the bullies, buoyed by the thrill of the chase would have hunted her down like dogs after a fox and enjoyed beating her to a pulp. But hobbling along she was too easy a target for even the most cowardly of men to fully attack. She was punched in the back, pushed, verbally abused and poked with brambled sticks but managed to avoid being knocked to the ground, so was able to keep moving. Clods of turf were also thrown at her so she stopped to drop her skirt for a moment while she took both hands to open her umbrella, which thereafter was a useful barrier to projectiles.

Back at Tattenham Corner the crowd had trampled over the confetti of hundreds of discarded Votes for Women handbills which Mary had spent hours distributing. Ruby looked at the dirty, foot-marked literature which had clearly been accepted from Mary just to get rid of her before it was cast aside with not so much as a second glance.

Ruby felt bereft at the loss, and it was not just of Emily.

Chapter 20

"The most disappointing Derby. A regrettable and scandalous proceeding. Tea with May (Queen Mary) in the garden."

King George V diary entry

Ruby tried to get to see Emily but watching Mary's troubles unfold had cost her precious seconds so she arrived just after a phalanx of racecourse stewards and police had sealed off the scene of the accident. Ruby was one of hundreds who had spilled on to the course before officials had regained order and started herding people back the other side of the rails. She was in the second row from the front of those crowding up against the steward cordon surrounding the car. Nashey taking her through the cordon to the lifeboat made its inevitable appearance. What she would not give for the big East Ender to be there at Epsom with her right now.

In the reality that confronted her she could not see over the cordon to see Emily so started shouting the obvious questions to the stewards. But it was apparent from the abrupt unhelpfulness of the only man to answer, and the jeers and suspicious looks from those around her, that in being concerned for the health of the woman in the car she was clearly in a minority of one. The atmosphere was charged with anti-Suffragette feeling. Ruby thought it would surely be only a matter of time before someone put two and two together and realised that she was wearing a wintry coat, just like the injured Suffragette and the woman who had been chased off.

A man was allowed through the cordon to join the two people tending Emily. Ruby recognised him as Charles Mansell-Moulin, a member of the Men's League for Women's Suffrage. He was the husband of a fellow Suffragette Edith, who was a friend of Emily's. More importantly given the situation, he was a leading member of the Royal College of Surgeons.

Ruby knew Emily was in the best possible hands and decided that she had no alternative but to leave her brave comrade-in-arms to be attended to, and could only hope that the crossing official's evaluation of her health was unduly pessimistic. The horse was now on its feet and seemed alright, and the jockey was sitting up, so perhaps the collision was not as bad as had first appeared. Emily, whatever her health, would no doubt be transferred into an ambulance and taken away without any information issuing forth. There would be rumours of course, but Ruby was well used to the dynamics of an excited crowd and knew that nothing tangible would be ascertained from the racecourse authorities or even, if she made her way to it, whatever hospital to which Emily was transported.

Ruby wondered if Mary had managed to reach safety. Once the chase had started Mary had only remained in Ruby's sight for a few seconds before disappearing in to the crowd, but it had been long enough to note that in the desire to make a quick getaway she had turned away from the station. So Ruby doubted she would be there, and in a crowd of a quarter of a million people it would be an impossible task to find her, but nevertheless she set off in her associate's footsteps.

Those leaving because they had only come to see the Derby were now joined by others who thought it not worth hanging about. Apparently there was going to be a long delay before the next race and there was even a rumour that the rest of the card might be abandoned for some reason. Some incident at Tattenham Corner; the king's horse had gone down there. Perhaps they'd had to shoot it. But that wouldn't normally cause an end to proceedings. At National Hunt racecourses they were always shooting horses that had hurt themselves in steeplechases and hurdle races.

And slouching off home was many a disgruntled working man. He had taken a day off work he could ill afford to enjoy his bread and circuses, and had now lost his shirt backing the king's horse with cap-doffing loyalty to the Crown which refused him the vote and a decent standard of living.

Consequently thousands were making their way towards charabancs and train stations, and Ruby decided to follow the main stream of the crowd along the Old London Road. Not being encumbered by a hobble skirt she was able to run along overtaking many, asking them as she did so if anyone had seen a woman in a heavy coat running along pursued by a group of men. This brought lots of cheery comments, mostly knowing and crude, querying why a woman should be chased by such a crowd. But Ruby did ascertain from a helpful teenage girl that she had seen a woman, looking tired, flushed and dishevelled, being harried by an angry gang who were pushing and swearing at her, and sometimes striking her. Initially this had apparently led to something of a to-do when some men went to the woman's assistance, but once the mob had explained their actions, they were allowed to continue with their bullying. It appeared from what the girl had said that the mob was growing in size and intensity, like some great storm as it picked up energy and momentum.

Ruby was growing increasingly concerned for the safety of her colleague as she followed the fast flowing river of mankind. At a junction of several lanes and tracks, there was a bottleneck as the Old London Road hordes met the huge numbers who had left the grandstand area and cut across the golf course with which the racecourse shared the Downs. The mass slowed to a halt. Ruby took the opportunity to ask her neighbours in the crowd how she could best make her way home to London from there. She was advised that Epsom Downs railway station was just down the road and that a good number of this crowd were making their way there. She followed the multitude over the undulating bramble filled common land of the Downs, then along a little lane and down a tiny track which quickly became another dam of humanity. Ruby asked what had happened and someone explained that it was just the bottleneck to get into the station.

After five minutes of edging forward in the claustrophobic mass, Ruby spotted a separate little knot of men off to the side of the tiny one-platform station's entrance. An angry mob was shouting outside the porters' room, with the station master in front of them trying to maintain order.

Ruby thought that she recognised a member of the mob as one of the men who had chased Mary, but she was so tight-packed into the crowd that she could do nothing but continue into the station entrance and the small booking hall. Once inside she shouted over the heads of the crowd to the two policemen who were standing at the entrance to the platform, acting as support for a porter who was checking that everyone attempting to get on to the platform had a valid ticket.

"Officer, there is a commotion over at the porter's room."

"That's no concern of yours miss I'm sure," said one of the policemen.

A man in the crowd took this as his cue to have his say.

"Bloody Suffragette's locked in there with a porter; he's only given her safe refuge if you please! She's a mate of the one who's just killed the king's 'orse and the jockey. Should have her up for murder they should, ain't that right officer?" shouted the man as he attempted to use his verbosity as a smokescreen to sneak through the barrier of officialdom without a ticket.

The last thing Ruby had done before leaving the cordon around Emily was enquire about the horse and jockey. She had seen the horse start to be led away with what a stable girl informed her appeared to be no more than a sore shin. And a policeman had told her that the jockey probably had mild concussion but he would be all right. She marvelled at the speed and inaccuracy of Chinese whispers.

"But what does that large body of fine gentlemen plan to do to a lone defenceless woman when she decides she has outstayed her welcome with the porter?" shouted Ruby drily.

The man never got a chance to answer as one of the policemen, who were using their very tightly rolled up raincoats as soft coshes, had just thumped him over the head with gusto as a hint that perhaps he should buy a ticket. Those who had a ticket cheered heartily, those who did not decided it was going to be a long walk home.

It was clear to Ruby that the police were deliberately staying well out of it. Since when was train fare-dodging more important than public disorder and likely grievous bodily harm or worse to a woman? And why were there only two policemen at the station in any case?

As Ruby neared the ticket barrier she allowed herself to be jostled out to the edge of the narrowing queue and then turned and strode out of the booking hall with a view to confronting the mob. She appreciated that for her own safety she must not appear to be a Suffragette. She looked down at her heavy coat. Even a mob would contain someone with enough rational thought to realise that she must be a friend of the woman in the porter's room. It was her only winter coat and come the end of the summer she would not be able to afford to buy another. She walked around the side of the station, which was in the middle of nowhere and seemingly only existed for the benefit of race-goers. The rural location had plenty of trees and bushes in the vicinity, so Ruby was able to hide her coat well out of sight of everyone behind a thicket, hoping to reclaim it later. As she did so she thought it just as well she had not worn her purple, white and green shoes.

She marched round to the mob and asked what the commotion was and whether there was anything she could do. Her working class Hampshire lilt and cheap looking clothes kept her free of any suspicion that she might be a Suffragette. Someone was happy to educate her as to the situation.

"I should be careful. There are policemen in the railway station you know," advised Ruby politely.

"Don't you worry about them; most of the coppers who would be here are up at Tattenham Corner thanks to this one inside's mate," said a man nodding towards the porter's door.

Ruby moved around the crowd, irritating each man in turn by asking him what was going to happen next, which diverted him away from his primary interest of shouting abuse at the woman and her protector on the other side of the door. They all assumed Ruby was a supporter of their cause. It was clear that many of the group were just so much flotsam and jetsam collected by the storm along its path. Few of them had actually seen the incident about which they were having so much to say. Ruby continued to hover about and managed to inveigle herself into the mob sufficiently to gain a brief conversation with the harassed station master. She told him as quietly as possible that having seen the accident she was able to report that the horse and rider were perfectly well. The station master was quick to shout this information to the crowd, which seemed to pacify a few.

She then wandered away from the crowd deep in thought. If she told the lie she had in mind, it might free Mary from her near-captors. It filled her with dread but she eventually told herself that the end justified the means. She ran back to the mob as if fuelled with hot-off-the-press news and shouted at the top of her voice.

"I've just been told by the station newsboy, that woman up at Tattenham Corner's dead! She was a lunatic woman by all accounts! Not long out of Colney Hatch! She wasn't a Suffragette at all! Just pretended to be! Didn't know what she was doing! And her mate here's as nutty as a fruit cake as well!"

It had the desired effect. The mob, not knowing how to

react, started to lose its energy, break up and dissolve. Eager to get these men out of his station as quickly as possible, the station master guided them past the queue, through the ticket barrier and on to the train which had just pulled in at the platform.

Timetables did not exist on Derby Day. Once a train was crammed overfull, a porter would blow his whistle and send it on its way. But on this occasion the station master told the porter at the ticket barrier to hold people there for a moment while he signalled to the driver to take the train away immediately.

The mob thus dispatched, the station master returned to the porter's door, where Ruby introduced herself. The harassed old man was none too pleased to have a second Suffragette to protect. He rapped on the porters' door and informed those within that the mob had gone but to be on the safe side it would be best if they stayed put until the crowd thinned somewhat. Ruby and the station master stood there, a most unlikely couple of security guards.

Ruby was often in the company of women whose interests and pastimes were far removed from her own outside of the political cause which they shared. During her early training, when discussion of matters relating to Votes for Women had waned, there had been many an awkward conversation about the weather and other such inanities between her and fellow Suffragettes. This had led her to become a master of relaxed small talk. Thus she passed away the time by engaging the old station master in everything from whether her Tattenham Corner return would allow her to travel back from Epsom Downs, to asking him what he thought of Jack Hobbs and did Hobbs catch people out at mid-wicket?; to had he heard about a chap called Scott dying in the Antarctic last year? The station master warmed to the young woman and asked her with more an excited schoolboy-like enthusiasm for knowledge than any hint of admonishment, whether she had committed any Suffragette damage to train carriages. She admitted that she had in the past slipped tiny pebbles down between pull-up train carriage windows and doorframes. Thus when some unsuspecting commuter later brought the window up or down with sufficient power the stones would cause the whole pane of glass to shatter into smithereens. The station master was both aghast and impressed. When the old man eventually brought up the inevitable small talk subject of the Titanic, Ruby remembered she had a coat to rescue from the bushes.

Much to her relief the clothing was still where she had left it. On her return she looked round the thinning crowd and wondered if it was time they released the two inmates from their captivity. The station master agreed and rapped on the door to inform the porter and his charge that it was safe to emerge. Mary reappeared, bleeding, bruised, aching and limping from her beating. The station master took one look at the pathetic figure and motioned for her to return back inside and told his porter to get the kettle on. The recuperative powers of a cup of tea were going to be tested, though given that Mary had done nothing but drink cups of tea for the past hour it was the last thing she wanted. But she was too weary to argue.

Ruby sat down, relaxed for the first time all day and immediately slumped. Since her release from prison she had been suffering from several of the many after-effects of hunger and thirst-strikes and being force-fed, and now the day's events brought some of them on. She suddenly felt both hot and cold; and her head throbbed with a chronic headache. It would be another hour before both women had recovered sufficiently to head for home.

★★★★★★

Emily was a fighter to the last. She hung on to life for four days in Epsom Cottage Hospital before finally succumbing to her injuries. Her funeral procession was a huge affair, orchestrated by the WSPU. Ruby had been offered a role as one of the twelve white-clad women carrying laurel wreaths and a banner inscribed 'Fight On and God Will Give the Victory' who followed the cross-bearer. But she turned down the honour. It was time she stepped out of the spotlight. She wanted to pay her last respects quietly, which she duly did in the heart of the throng, dressed in black, carrying a bunch of purple irises. The long line of women marched four abreast through a vast crowd, which covered every inch of pavement and balconies along the route to the service at St George's Church, Bloomsbury.

Ruby looked straight ahead but could not help but occasionally dart her eyes to notice the sea of heads either side of her. They were a mix of men holding their caps and hats in their hands as a mark of respect, and anti-women's suffrage supporters wearing their headgear to show their contempt. Ruby also spotted a few women dotted about but that was all. She pondered that perhaps they were mostly out of sight at the back, concerned about the crush of the crowd. Perhaps, but plenty of women had been on the rails with her and Emily at Epsom. And crowds at meetings and publicity stunts like The Monument being all men were one thing, but this? Ruby had seen the coffin before the procession had lined up. It was adorned with three laurel wreaths inscribed 'She Died for Women'. Yes she had, but did women know or even care?

Ruby followed the coffin to the railway terminus, from where Emily's body was to be transported to her home town, Morpeth, for burial. She had not been invited to the funeral, which she felt was as it should be. She thought herself to be the last person who ought to be there.

She then rejected all offers to spend the rest of the day with Suffragette colleagues. She wanted to be alone with her thoughts. There was great guilt, upset and sorrow for Emily's death, but there was more to what she was feeling than that. She needed to think things through.

Chapter 21

"The perfect Amazon is she who will sacrifice all even unto this last to win the Pearl of Freedom for her sex…To lay down life for friends, that is glorious, selfless, inspiring! But to re-enact the tragedy of Calvary for generations yet unborn, that is the last consummate sacrifice of the Militant!"

Emily Davison, The Price of Liberty, Daily Sketch article, a week before the Derby

The WSPU had not recovered from the huge loss of the 'greatest beggar in London', its chief fund-raiser Emmeline Pethick-Lawrence, and her husband Fred, the erstwhile financial and administrative guru of the organisation, ejected from the society almost a year earlier.

Whilst Parliament had been in recess for the summer holidays, Ruby, who had become well known within WSPU circles for her numeracy skills, had been tasked with the daunting role of being one of a team helping the Pethick-Lawrence's replacements to improve the organisation's financial and administrative matters. But herculean assignment though it was, Ruby was relieved to have a relatively quiet spell during which she spent time doing the less glamorous but very necessary grass roots work of politics.

This gave her time to take stock and reflect. She had

initially considered that it was only to be expected that she felt depressed after the defilement of her force-feeding followed so soon after by the horror at the Derby, but as the summer had worn on her malaise had not lifted. And now, with Parliament, and therefore Suffragette militancy, due to restart she was convinced that her discontent was not simply part of a post-prison and grieving process. Not at least grieving for Emily. She thought that there had to be more to the fight for the vote than escalating violence and publicity stunts. It had become apparent that the WSPU was losing its battle with the government. The increase in violence had turned the public against them. Even Emily's death had achieved nothing. There had not been the expected wave of protest from the public and press, asking why a woman had been driven to risk and lose her life fighting for a just cause. Quite the contrary, she had been vilified for disrupting a major national sporting event.

Ruby decided that she would resign from the WSPU. She would follow the Pethick-Lawrences and many others in the fight for women's rights who had, over the years, quit Emmeline and Christabel Pankhurst's autocratic rule and failing tactics, to join the democratic and militant but non-violent Women's Freedom League. She could not expect to walk straight into a paid position with them but she had come too far to return to factory work slaving for an avaricious uncaring employer. And the fact was that none of her previous employment, or for that matter working as a 'counter-jumper' in Chiesman's, would leave her the time or energy to continue her suffrage work. There was nothing for it, she would have to bite the bullet and settle down to life in the clerical world, which for women meant operating some piece of equipment or another. Monday to Friday, eight till six, would allow her plenty of time to lead a double life fighting the good fight in the evenings and at weekends. The very dullness of the work would at least allow her time to think about the Votes for Women campaign, and sitting at a desk all day would be a good way of resting and refreshing herself after what would, no doubt, be physically exhausting extra-curricular activities.

But first she was off to the East End. Her waning enthusiasm for the WSPU had enabled her to keep a day free for a change, but all her friends and acquaintances were fellow Suffragettes whose lives had been taken over by the fight, so she was at a bit of a loose end. A WSPU friend, Elspeth, had invited her along to help out at one of Sylvia Pankhurst's East End Federation of Suffragettes meetings. Ruby remembered her previous experience of a Sylvia Pankhurst speech in East London. Her initial reaction had thus been to refuse and just take a day off to sit in the park and rest. The last thing she wanted was a busman's holiday. But then she thought that whilst she was in the East End she could visit Nashey.

The day after she had narrowly missed seeing Nash at the Bow bye-election, Ruby had planned to write to him to suggest they meet up now that she was living in London. But she was shocked and not a little embarrassed to think that she had become so wrapped up in the daily round-the-clock fight for the vote that she had never gotten around to writing that letter.

When her friend told her the meeting was back in Bow of all places, it seemed that the stars really were aligning. She dashed off a quick note to Nash informing him that she was now a Suffragette living in South London and was coming to Bow to Sylvia's meeting. But given the short notice and the fact that he was probably no longer living at his cousin's address, she doubted he would receive it in time, if at all. Nevertheless, as Sylvia's bodyguard Nashey would surely be at the meeting so it was with a skip in her step that she made her way along to a political speech for which she would otherwise have had little enthusiasm.

On arrival in Bow, Ruby was immediately informed that Sylvia was not going to appear after all. She had been asked to speak at a big trade union meeting at the Albert Hall, an opportunity too good to miss. But the Bow meeting was still to go ahead with a replacement speaker, personally trained by Sylvia. Ruby cursed under her breath in exasperation. The whole point in going down there was to see Nashey and now she doubted he would be in attendance. And to add insult to injury the other news of the day was that the Home Office had now prohibited Suffragette open-air meetings, and pressure was being brought to bear on the owners of public halls not to rent their properties to the WSPU. Ruby was thus going to attend an illegal open-air meeting, where the speaker was to be someone called Melvinia Walker, a woman of whom she had never heard. It was to be the woman's maiden speech. It did not sound too promising.

Ruby was to assist in chalking pavements publicising the talk, distributing handbills and hold a Joan of Arc placard; all routine stuff. She suspected it would end in the usual punch-up. At the last meeting she had attended the rowdies had thrown fish heads, paper soaked in urine and small stones, and all she and her fellow Suffragettes had got for their trouble was being kicked and trampled black and blue. Even speakers for Irish Home Rule were ringed by police for their protection, but not so Suffragettes. Public order could go to hell in a handcart as far as the authorities were concerned when it came to them. They had become pariahs. What was the point of carrying on? They had lost. Not that the government had defeated them. They had been beaten by no one but themselves.

And it was not love at second sight with Bow as far as Ruby was concerned. On her previous visit there she had been so busy meeting people, helping out, listening to the meeting and getting embroiled in a brawl, that she had taken Bow's assault on her nasal senses with a pinch of salt, albeit that it felt like she needed the smelling varieties. Now her nose wrinkled at the stench of the rotting corpses emanating from the soap-works, the noxious odours escaping from nearby tanneries, and other dubious smells the origins of which she dare not even think about. And the poverty stricken, teeming back streets, courts and alleys she was now seeing, educated her to the realities of the East End. It was somewhat removed from the traffic-choked entrepreneurial scene along the main road through East London which May had guided her along on her previous visit.

So this was the *real* East End, and Bow was where Nashey had *chosen* to resettle. No wonder the Titanic sinking held few horrors for him. If you could survive in the East End you could survive anywhere.

She thought of her father's tales of the old days when he was a lad in Southampton. The horrors of mid-Victorian slum life; the shadow of the workhouse; seemed so alien to her that she had not been able to fully imagine them, until now. And she had often wondered why everything she knew of the old days came from her father because it had been a taboo subject as far as her mother was concerned. But now she understood.

She remembered her child-like excitement when May had suggested a visit to the East End was in the offing. But the realities of East London life were nothing to get enthused about. She felt both relieved and ashamed that her first Suffragette action had been so intensely encompassing that she had barely registered the venue in which it took place. There was relief that at least she had not considered the East End a sightseeing destination; and shame that she had not considered it at all.

The disappointment at not seeing Nashey put Ruby in a bad mood which resulted in her rather going through the motions when it came to fulfilling her duties for the meeting. So it was with some relief when in due course Melvinia Walker stepped up on to her costermonger cart speaker's platform.

Standing on the street behind the cart holding her Joan of Arc placard high, Ruby looked round to see some very scary tough-looking men had surrounded her and the rest of the speaker's entourage. Enough was enough. She was not prepared to get beaten up yet again, especially by men such as these. As soon as the trouble started, instead of trying to use her placard as a weapon as she usually did, Ruby was going to drop the thing and make a run for it, and she would not be coming back, not to Bow, not to the WSPU.

Melvinia started speaking and Ruby was surprised to hear a working class London accent. This was the first time she had ever heard a working woman speak in public. It was unsophisticated but rousing stuff.

"Behind every poor man, there stands a still poorer woman," was her hesitant opening gambit which received light cheers of endorsement from the crowd.

Ruby noticed how the audience was not just the usual all male affair. Very poor looking women, breast-feeding babies whilst older children pulled at their apron strings, were standing there, albeit keeping to the periphery out of harm's way.

The cheers gave Melvinia confidence and before long she was speaking with passion about Sylvia Pankhurst's remarkable impact on the East End in the mere months since she had arrived. The speaker told the crowd how this young woman had galvanised East Londoners and had people go to her regarding their troubles with landlords, employers, government departments and insurance societies, and she had sorted them out.

"They 'ave a poor man's lawyer in Whitechapel's Toynbee Hall but we 'ave a poor man's and poor woman's Sylvia in Bow!" exclaimed the speech-maker.

Cheers rang out. She had the crowd with her and became more evangelical in style.

"Do you remember the Great Dock Strike?"

It had been twenty three years ago but everyone in the audience who was old enough, and even some of those who weren't, shouted "Yes!" to a man and woman. It had been the East End's greatest victory to date.

"A woman whose 'usband broke 'is leg in that strike and 'as been lame ever since, stood in the gutter selling bootlaces but because people sometimes gave 'er money without taking the laces, she got done for begging. She were just in prison for it. Sylvia is working for her!"

Cries of support rang out.

"Girl I know earns six and ninepence a week in a restaurant working till nine every night. She 'as to pay six bob a week rent. Now, I don't know what's to blame. Is it the rent or is it the wages? But Sylvia knows!"

More cheers. The speech went on to tell of the plight of sweated workers such as rope-makers, chicken-pluckers, fur-pullers and women who made wooden seeds which were used to adulterate raspberry jam. And Sylvia was campaigning for them all.

"One of my fellow Suffragettes just told me this young woman 'ere beside me was a poorly paid biscuit-packer in Bermondsey. And now look at her in her purple, white and green. Yes, Sylvia even fights for South Londoners!"

There are was a huge cheer at this joke, as Ruby became aware that the speech maker was looking and motioning at her and a good number of the crowd were following the gaze. It was then that Ruby realised she was the 'South Londoner' of whom Melvinia was speaking.

"But I'm only joking with yer. She only lives south of the river. They tell me she's out of Southampton. But Southampton, South London, East London, Sylvia is working for us all!"

More cheers. Ruby looked across at her friend Elspeth who was catching her eye with a grin. It was easy to see where Melvinia had got her information from. And Ruby had to admit that she had used it brilliantly.

"Working people of Bow, I urge you to join Sylvia's East End Federation of Suffragettes. She is bringing together supporters of the Free Speech Defence League, the Men's Federation for Women's Suffrage, the Independent Labour

Party, the Men's Political Union and the Women's Tax Resistance League. We must all work together for our common causes!"

Huge cheers started up and though nobody had walked over her grave, a cold shiver ran through Ruby. But any further thoughts were halted by Ruby's attention being drawn to a scuffle only a few feet away. Bully boy members of the Men's League for Opposing Women's Suffrage had tried to pull Melvinia's cart away but were soon beaten back by some of the scary looking men whom Ruby had noticed earlier. It became apparent that these men, far from being there as detractors, were there as supporters of the women's movement. And she was standing ringside as the scary supporters club laid into the trouble makers with blows from long thick pieces of tarred rope that had mushrooms of closely twisted rope weighted with lead at the top. Ruby remembered Nashey had mentioned them. If she recalled correctly they were known, with typical dark East End humour, as 'Saturday Nights'. Nashey had said they bludgeoned opponents senseless without too much fear of real lasting damage. They had apparently been by far the softest weapon in his armoury during his villainous days in Whitechapel. She dreaded to think what his most lethal armament might have been.

In the melee, a troublemaker got a good grip on a man's arm and it took a vicious backward pull from the ensnared suffrage supporter to escape the clutches. Unfortunately for Ruby she was a little too close to the action and the flaying elbow of her own supporter, released from captivity, landed bang on the bridge of her nose before skidding into an eye. She was surprised how little it hurt, but she still found her eyes and knees going on strike as she kept an urgent appointment with the cobbles.

The troublemakers were duly run out of town, the suffrage supporters giving them a less than fond farewell courtesy of boots and belt straps.

A crowd gathered round Ruby. Through the fuggy haze of near-unconsciousness she could just about hear men talking above her.

"She'll have a good shiner in the morning," predicted a man with the over confidence of the know-all.

"Yeah but she'll be alright. She's been frew worse. A lot worse," said another as he picked her up.

★★★★★★

Ruby was brought to her senses by the harsh magnesium flash of a camera. She was immediately on the Carpathia sailing into New York harbour.

"Ah, glad to see you're back with us. I'm Norah Smyth. I'm the Fin. Sec. Sorry Financial Secretary. I take all the photographs for Sylvia. Hope you don't mind? You on the ground, having been attacked by bully boys, all good propaganda you understand. I thought we could send copies to some friendly newspapers if the picture comes out right. We still have a few friends in Fleet Street thank goodness."

There was a moment of disorientation before Ruby realised that the Statue of Liberty was nowhere to be seen in Bow. More's the pity, she thought. It might have brightened the place up a bit. She focused on the photographer and answered her question.

"No, no, not at all, only too pleased to be of help I'm sure."

She made the mistake of using a hand to follow the trail of liquid she could feel on her upper lip. She reached her nose and winced.

"Bit of blood coming out of the old snozz," advised Norah. "Nothing to worry about; and those responsible are long despatched. Bow is the most difficult of fixtures for an away team is it not? Foolhardy of them to think otherwise what? Take my advice my girl and stay down for a while. Get your senses back."

"Yeah that's good advice Norah."

Ruby recognised the voice immediately and shot her gaze towards it.

"Nashey!" she gasped as she began to get to her feet.

"What Norah jus' tell you?" scolded Nash.

He bent down, put his huge hands round Ruby's waist and lifted her into an upright position sitting against a wall.

"So you fought you'd come and see old Bow eh and you're straight on the ground. Bit tougher round 'ere than your South London I shouldn't wager? " smirked Nash.

"Bow is certainly tougher on my nose than St Johns but that is the smell of the tanneries I believe," replied Ruby with a gleam in her eye. "Or is it the soap-works? I am sure a man's elbow punching me on the nose in South London would have laid me to the ground just as quickly as it did here."

"Funny cuts," was Nash's failed attempt at a witty response, likening Ruby to his favourite comic paper. "Good to see you ain' lost that tongue a yourn."

Despite the pain from her injuries Ruby was smiling warmly at Nash's wink and about to come back at him with something else when the gooseberry beat her to it.

"Let me take that coat off you my dear, it will ruin on the ground," said Norah softly.

Norah helped Ruby extricate herself out of the coat, before giving the clothing a shake and beating to remove East End street grime from it. She handed it to Nash before bending down to dab at her patient's face with a handkerchief. A few other Suffragettes were still looking on enjoying the little bit of theatre in front of them.

"Best not to miss the rest of the meeting ladies," said Norah, nodding towards the speaker.

The women returned to the audience listening to Melvinia, who had continued speaking throughout. She was reaching her finale.

"Poor woman I know with a babe at her tit got a longer sentence for receiving the other day than some wrong un who forced 'is self on a woman. That ain't right is it?"

"Shame!" shouted the crowd.

"Another woman said to me this morning if I 'ad to choose between electric and the vote I would be wise to choose the electric. But it's the vote what gets yer the electric! It gets yer equal pay, equal chances, better 'ousing and somewhere to 'ave yer kids looked after while you're earning a crust!"

She stopped to take a breath and receive the huge cheers that were coming her way, before making her final thrust.

"There are only two things that matter to me, principle and liberty! For those I will fight as long as there is life in my veins! I am no longer an individual, I am an instrument!"

Roars of approval met the end of the speech.

"Jolly good show!" exclaimed Norah. "What say you Ruby, do you agree?"

"Rather!"

Norah smiled and assisted the young woman to her feet. The crowd started to disperse, trampling over Ruby's placard, which gravity ensured had followed its owner into a horizontal position on the cobbles. Joan of Arc, the patron saint of Suffragettes, in full armour sitting astride a horse, wearing a tabard emblazoned 'Justice', with Parliament in the background, was looking the worse for wear. Another placard in similarly battered condition, adorned with a female Robin Hood, lay next to it. Norah bent down to perform a rescue act. She kept Robin Hood but handed Joan of Arc to a suddenly pensive looking Ruby.

Norah became concerned for the health of the young woman in front of her, who after initially being in good spirits talking to Nashey now appeared rather stunned. Norah would normally have taken her home for a restorative cup of tea, but she had other things on her agenda at that moment.

"I would take you home my dear but I really must get my photographs of the day developed as soon as possible. Sylvia will want to go through the images with me before we pass them on to the press d'you see."

Ruby nodded absent-mindedly. She wasn't stunned. She was thinking of the Votes for Women handbills trampled over at Tattenham Corner.

Nash spotted the faraway look in Ruby's eyes. He had seen it before on the other side of the Atlantic when she had spoken to him of her deceased husband and her family.

"Don't you worry about 'er Norah," reassured Nash as he motioned to relieve her of the Robin Hood placard. "Me and Ruby 'ere knows each ovver of old. We goes back. Me and 'er'll take these 'ere boards back to Jessie's. Giss us a chance to 'ave a good ol' chinwag over a cuppa. We'll 'ang on till Sylvia gets 'ome an' I'll introduce 'er to Ruby. We'll see yer there later I shouldn't wonder."

Norah had been thinking that these two were being terribly forward with one another. The two of them being old friends explained matters. She smiled and bid them a fond farewell as she scuttled off eagerly with camera in hand.

Ten minutes later the two old Titanic pals were ensconced in the front room of Sylvia's landlady, East London Federation stalwart Jessie Payne. They told each other of their lives since Nash had waved Ruby off on her liner home. Ruby was initially amazed that Nash had become involved in women's politics. But he explained that Sylvia Pankhurst was the most extraordinary woman he had ever met, and was going to deliver not just the vote for women but more importantly as far as he was concerned, better living and working conditions for the poor. Having seen Sylvia in action on her previous trip to Bow, Ruby could understand Nash's interest up to a point, though remained somewhat surprised by the level of his enthusiasm.

They chatted for an hour, Jessie keeping what she considered a discreet distance by beavering away in her kitchen and scullery, before Sylvia arrived home from giving her speech in the Albert Hall.

Ruby was rather cool towards Sylvia to begin with, which Nash, remembering how she had behaved towards him when they had first met on board the Titanic, put down to her being her usual aloof self with strangers. But despite herself, Ruby soon warmed to Sylvia, and not just at a personal level. When the conversation strayed inevitably on to politics, Ruby knew instinctively what her future role in life should be.

Chapter 22

"The smallest gleam of political insight would show our muddle-minded politicians that the cause of votes for women is irresistible despite the excesses of a section of its support."

Weekly Dispatch

May's home in Lewisham was to become a safe-house for what would be the increasingly covert WSPU operation. Women 'Mice' would be kept out of the clutches of the police 'Cats' once the looming new Cat and Mouse Act came into force. Consequently when Ruby knocked on the door unannounced there was a little 'who goes there' cloak and dagger stuff before she was admitted.

May pushed herself down the passage of the fine Victorian house in her small indoor wheelchair to meet Ruby. She was delighted to see her young friend. They had not seen much of each other lately what with one thing and another. Ruby was shown into the sitting room and offered a seat. Over the time they had known each other May had come to appreciate that Ruby tended to feel uneasy when servants were around so she did not summon her maid with a view to getting some tea. The two women passed a pleasant few minutes chewing the cud before Ruby told May her big news. She had been to see Mabel Tuke, the Honorary

Secretary of the WSPU, at HQ in Kingsway, and had resigned from being a WSPU paid worker. May was crestfallen and asked the obvious question.

"I will tell you what I told Miss Tuke," said Ruby.

Previously, on the train up to central London, Ruby had practiced what she was about to relay to Miss Tuke but when it had come to it she had got somewhat tongue-tied and left the Hon. Sec. feeling rather perplexed at the garbled explanation for the resignation. But with her friend May in front of her, Ruby made herself understood all too clearly.

She began by informing May that she had come to realise that the WSPU had made a huge error by increasing their level of violence. With this off her chest, she started making points. First of all Christabel stayed in France when she should have returned to England to embarrass the government in what would have been her big show trial. Then she and Mrs Pankhurst ousted the Pethick-Lawrences, their two most important lieutenants. Fred had built the organisation from nothing into a national political party, and it was all funded by the money his wife raised. Without them the WSPU had effectively lost its ability to flourish financially and administratively. Then the violence had been increased even more, losing all the support that had been built up over the years. And Christabel's snobbery ensured the organisation would always be a relatively minor, small membership one, for that's all it could ever be without the masses on board. They had to change tactics but were just beating their heads against a brick wall, blind to what was needed. Christabel made one mistake after another, and instead of issuing orders to countermand her out of control daughter Mrs Pankhurst stood by and let it all happen. All this had brought about the passing of the Cat and Mouse Act. And once this was in operation it would drive the organisation underground to the point where it would surely die. The only part of the Suffragettes still truly alive was Sylvia Pankhurst's East London Federation.

Ruby was standing over May with her left hand splayed out like a starfish. During her rant she had stood up and, starting with her thumb, introduced a new digit each time she had made a point. She was suddenly embarrassed by her aggressive unladylike body language, quickly sat down and looked across at her friend, before looking sheepishly down into her own lap. May's eyes had become a little watery. Knowing her friend's unquestioning love for the Pankhursts and their cause, Ruby was convinced that she had gone too far.

"I am sorry May, I did not mean to upset you but that is how I feel," she mumbled apologetically as she started to give herself the manicure of the nervous.

But moist though May's eyes might have been she was not upset; far from it. Her tears were those of pride. Her young apprentice had come a long way since she had shown that first spark of potential when quizzing the poor young railwayman in the guard's van travelling up from St Johns. She thought Ruby's assessment of Christabel and Emmeline was completely wrong of course but she was delighted with her nonetheless.

May had read a review of a new play by Shaw which was to transfer from New York to London in a few months, the plot of which sounded a little like her relationship with Ruby. Whilst May considered her own success as the professor character, her working class protégé used the silence that had developed between them to dwell upon her mentor.

Ruby regretted that May was so in awe, so stage-struck by Christabel and Mrs Pankhurst that she just could not see anything wrong with their decisions. She wondered whether it had something to do with May's disability. May's life would not have been one tenth as rich and full without the cause that the Pankhurst's had delivered to her. The Suffrage struggle had been May's saviour just as Nashey had been her own. But if someone came to her and argued that everything Nashey was doing was not only wrong but counter-productive to the very thing her whole life was centred round trying to achieve, would she consider their argument for one minute? He was a right old bastard of course, but no she would not, not for a moment.

The fact was that she had to thank the Pankhursts for bringing such light into her wonderful friend's life. And she had to accept, her own. Where would she be without them? She knew the answer; up to her elbows in chocolate biscuit cream in Bermondsey.

May broke the silence by explaining to Ruby that her tears were not of sorrow but joy. She was very proud of her. She then spoke in a theatrically lofty voice so it would be understood that something was being quoted.

"I disapprove of what you say but I will defend to the death your right to say it," she said with a hand raised dramatically. "That my dear is a quote from Evelyn Beatrice Hall. But so that she might be published she pens under the name of a man. We all still have a long way to go, you, me, Evelyn and all women, do we not?"

Ruby smiled knowingly and agreed. She took the moment to explain to May that she now believed the true fight was against poverty, ignorance and all the other elements of an unjust society that held women back from enjoying better lives. She had joined Sylvia's East London Federation to fight for this through the vote. And much to her surprise had been invited to start as a paid worker, which of course she had been only too pleased to accept. May was delighted, not to say relieved, that her young charge was still going to be fighting for the vote for women and wished her the best of luck in her new position.

The two women carried on chatting for an hour or so. It was the first time they had met since Ruby's force-feeding. And though they had swopped long intimate letters about the subject, there was nothing like actually talking about it one-to-one with a fellow sufferer. Both women were in tears by the time Ruby took her leave. She promised to invite May down to Bow for a visit sooner rather than later, when, en-route from Cannon Street, she would wheel her friend through some of the courts and alleys away from the main streets. Here May would see the *real* East End, the *real* problem.

Chapter 23

"I was horrified by the levity displayed by a large section of Members of the House. I could not have believed that a body of gentlemen could have found reason for mirth and applause."

Keir Hardie MP, regarding a House of Commons debate on force-feeding

After debilitating hunger and thirst-strikes, Sylvia had taken the opportunity of spending the political down-time of Parliament's summer recess to recover her health by escaping to Finland for a holiday cum fact-finding mission in the first European country to have given women the vote.

She and Ruby had quickly become friends and the new recruit's obvious intelligence had seen her soon given a role of some responsibility. During Sylvia's absence Ruby had been set the task of arranging a two-week suffrage school; one week in Bow, the other in Kensington. Topics included the industrial position of women, the history of trade union legislation, the franchise movement as a whole and the women's movement going back to Mary Wollstonecraft; women's legal disabilities, and sex education for mothers. The organisation of the school was close to completion by the end of the summer when Sylvia returned to the fold. It was time to resume the fight with the government.

Ruby had acquiesced to an entreaty by Nash that should she ever go back to prison she ought to refrain from thirst-striking in order to preserve her health. She had agreed on the condition that he impart the benefit of his not inconsiderable experience in violence by giving her some useful tips in dealing with future prison torturers.

Meetings at Bow Baths in Roman Road and in Poplar were arranged on consecutive days, at both of which Sylvia spoke. Sylvia was captured by the police at the Poplar meeting, but Ruby was not there to see it as she had been arrested during a near-riot in Roman Road the previous day. In some ways she had been lucky, being arrested and taken away before the worst of the violence had started, after which many supporters had been knocked unconscious, had arms or collar-bones broken or knees badly injured by an increasingly violent police force.

Having refused to pay her fine, Ruby returned to prison and went on hunger-strike. She stuck to her bargain with Nash, which had the benefit of her better retaining strength for the battle ahead. Although she had been warned what to expect before her first bout of force-feeding, there was nothing like experiencing it for yourself to fully appreciate how the process worked. Now she knew exactly how the wardresses, matron and doctor went about their business, she had a few ideas about how to make life more difficult for them. And all her efforts had to be channelled against the torturers' first attack because history told her that she would be too weak to resist them with the same strength thereafter.

She was a whirling dervish of fists, arms, elbows and knees, arching her back and throwing herself backwards, whilst swivelling her hips and thrashing her legs. She managed to wind one wardress with an elbow to the solar plexus which sank the woman to a knee, while another got the back of a balled fist in the mouth. With the opposition struggling temporarily, Ruby managed to avoid getting her feet tied, which allowed her to carry on gyrating like a pommel horse gymnast. It had the desired effect, the chair to which they had been trying to tie her clattering to the floor. The struggle of the bucking bronco was such that the doctor eventually decided he would feed her while she was still not fully tethered. The wardresses had hold of her arms and legs, the matron had the gag in place and held her head, the doctor's assistant had arrived to hold the food jug in one hand and the funnel in the other, while the doctor pushed the opposite end of the tube down the prisoner's throat despite her head still finding some freedom of movement.

"Pour for God's sake man, pour!" shouted the doctor.

The last thing Ruby remembered was thinking how much the doctor sounded like the panicking officers and men launching lifeboats on the Titanic.

The doctor had got the tube down Ruby's throat the best he could, but his best proved not to be good enough. The tube was accidentally passed into Ruby's windpipe. Warm sloppy food was poured directly into her left lung. She collapsed immediately.

★★★★★★

Septic pneumonia could have killed Ruby, but once she had passed its crisis point and her condition started to improve, she made a speedy recovery. The prison doctor who had nearly killed her confirmed far too matter-of-factly that there would be no lasting damage.

"I take you to mean in physical terms merely to the body and not my mind and soul…doctor!" retorted Ruby, spitting out the man's job title with as much contempt as she could muster.

During her first stint in prison, she had thought that the first time one was raped must be the worst, and that she would be able to handle it better the next time. Her second force feeding a few hours later had quickly proved her wrong. But on joining the East London Federation and hearing of how her joyous new colleague Zelie had once attempted suicide in prison, she had not fully appreciated how anyone could come to such a decision. But she did now.

It was thus with a mix of relief and bitterness at the poor timing of it that Ruby heard from the governor that under the terms of the new Prisoners' Temporary Discharge for Ill-Health Act, as from midnight there would be no more force-feeding of Suffragettes. They would henceforth be allowed to hunger-strike until their health deteriorated to the point where it was deemed necessary to release them on licence. Once they were adjudged fit to continue their sentence, they would be rearrested and returned to prison. Ruby would thus have been released shortly in any case under the terms of the Act, but given the circumstances surrounding her present ill-health she was to be released with immediate effect and her prison sentence deemed to have been completed prior to the start of the Act. She would be on licence, as all prisoners realised early were, but effectively free to go about her normal business.

Minutes later a wardress was going through the release procedure.

"Early release I see Martin. For behaving yourself no

doubt. Well done. Please confirm the address to which you wish to be sent home by taxi cab. According to our records you live at 120 Albyn Road, St Johns. Is that correct?"

"Early release for being nearly killed," corrected Ruby flatly. "Yes I live in St Johns."

The wardress, a North Londoner, queried where exactly this was located.

"Is that St John's Gate, down Clerkenwell way?"

"No, it's in between Deptford and Lewisham," said Ruby.

"That's south of the river! I thought you were one of that Pankhurst woman's mob down Bow!"

The incredulity in the voice of the wardress struck a chord with Ruby. Yes, why did she still live in St Johns when her life was now full time in East London? The simple answer was that she spent so many hours working for the cause that she had not found the time to think about moving home. Bow was only a short train ride followed by a similar length tram journey away. And besides, her friend May regularly commuted from Lewisham via St Johns, wheeling herself from Charing Cross station to the WSPU's new headquarters in Kingsway. In comparison Ruby's journey to Bow was certainly no great hardship. But now she thought about it, the cost of the fares certainly ate into the small wage paid her by the Federation. At that moment she decided that on returning from her impending trip to France, she would move to the East End.

Of course she would never hear the last of it from Nashey. He would be sure to say something along the lines of 'about time yer saw sense and moved away from that dump'. She never understood the antipathy that North and East Londoners showed towards South London. It did not seem to be mutual. She had never heard anyone in St Johns deride those who lived north of the river. Frankly she could not tell any difference between north and south but she decided that she would keep Nash on his toes by telling him that she would miss South London terribly. Moving to his neck of the woods was a necessary evil; a sacrifice that she was willing to pay for the cause. She looked forward to the volley of abuse she would receive. Despite feeling terrible from her prison treatment, a serene little smile flitted across her face for a brief moment.

Chapter 24

"No men, even the best of men, ever view the Suffrage question from quite the same standpoint as women…It is helpful and it is good for men themselves when they try to promote women's emancipation; but they have to do it from the outside, and the really important thing is that women are working out their own salvation."

Christabel Pankhurst

When Sylvia had last been released from prison it was on licence as per the terms of the new Cat and Mouse Act. And on the occasions since when she had spoken in public, protecting her from re-arrest and returning her safely to her 'mouse-hole', Jessie Payne's house, had become the bread and butter task of a growing legion of active East London Federation supporters. This band of women and men now went under the name of the People's Army.

Their undertaking was usually a fairly straight forward affair that involved either outfoxing or outmuscling the local constabulary. But now Nash had been tasked with a far more complicated, cloak and dagger mission. And this being out of his comfort zone, he was unusually nervous about it. The only previous time in his life he had taken on something out of his league, he had made a mess of robbing a post office only to return to find his closest friend had been murdered by Jack the Ripper just a short distance away.

His task now was to get Sylvia and the East London Federation of Suffragettes' new assistant financial secretary, one Ruby Martin, safely across the Channel. Once on foreign soil the two women would make their own way to Paris to see Christabel about the rising tensions, philosophical and financial, within the family. It had been decided that Norah Smyth, the senior financial secretary, would stay behind because there was a fair chance Sylvia would be arrested and anyone travelling with her was likely to be too and sentenced to a prison term. It was important Norah stayed out of the clutches of the authorities so she could keep the finances of the Federation ticking over.

Sylvia informed Nash that she wanted to get a ferry from Dover.

"Use yer loaf Sylve, the crushers must 'ave all the Channel ports covered. We'll never get frew Dover."

The term 'crusher' to describe a policeman had completely died out in common usage at least a quarter of a century ago but when his hackles rose, Nash tended to revert to the East End language of his earlier life. Sylvia was used to this and knew full well the point he was making, but thought he was being unnecessarily cautious.

"But Nashey, Annie Kenney has been taking a ferry from Dover every Friday night since Christabel's exile to tell my sister the events of the week and to receive from her the WSPU's orders for the following week, returning with them every Sunday evening. She takes every precaution, is well disguised and has never been stopped. So I am sure we would be quite safe given our propensity for besting the authorities."

Sylvia was lying horizontal in Jessie's front room, feeling very weak from her latest stint of hunger and thirst-striking. The torture was having a terrible effect. Sylvia was thirty one years old, but looked forty. But Nash was not in the mood to spare her blushes.

"Annie! Don't make me laugh. She's just your sister's blottin' paper," said Nash scornfully. "They could 'ave coopered Annie's little pull any time they liked. If they cuts yer sister off she'd 'ave to come back 'ere an' stand trial for smashin' up the West End like yer muvver and the Pefick-Lawrences did. And from what you tell me about 'er, she pitches it in red 'ot. She's already taken the rise out of Lloyd-George in court. Made 'im look a right chump you said. An 'e's the slipperiest of the lot of 'em. What d'yer fink she'd do to someone like Churchill if she got 'im up in court; she'd eat 'im for breakfast. That sister of yourn's in France exactly where the government wants 'er to be."

As this little speech had drawn to a close Nash's eyes had grown wider and in case there was still any doubt as to the strength of his convictions an index finger had been pointed down at Sylvia. And judging by the amount of old Victorian cockney being introduced in to the conversation, it was clear to her that the man standing over her had his dander up. She knew him well enough to appreciate that it was not a good idea to argue with him when he was like this. But more importantly she thought he had a point with which it was difficult to disagree.

She had been so busy setting up the East End Federation, doing good deeds for the local populace, making speeches and protesting in prison, she had taken her eye away from the bigger political picture. Of course Christabel must return to London.

"I am persuaded it is somewhat rum that Annie has been so successful," said Sylvia thoughtfully.

Nash was unsure what the strength of Sylvia's personal relationship was with her mother and sister. He had never met either of them but from everything he had heard from others, he was confident that if he ever met Christabel, the two of them would fall out very quickly. He had heard Mrs Pankhurst give a speech and he could see why so many Suffragettes were in awe of her. She had that certain something. He had heard it called charisma. She reminded Nash of himself in a strange way, not that he considered himself charismatic by any stretch of the imagination. But when she talked people listened, just as they did on the far fewer occasions when he had something to say. But the problem with such power was that people listened to you even when you were wrong. They didn't challenge you. He had certainly made plenty of mistakes in his life which he might not have made if someone had stood up and told him the error of his ways. And he feared that what Mrs Pankhurst was saying so eloquently and persuasively was straight from the mouth of her out of touch Paris-based daughter. The strange thing was, Sylvia hardly ever mentioned her mother or sister, and even when she did it was always completely politics-related. She was loath to talk ill of anyone save for men who wouldn't give women the vote, yet she did make the odd comment about Christabel that might be taken as criticism. He decided to make a little barbed remark of his own to test the water.

"We drive to Harwich and take the boat from there. I'm told you can get a train from the ovver end. Then when you get to Paris you can sort your sister out. I 'eard someone call 'er the ice maiden last week. They ain' far wrong from what I 'ear."

"Nashey it is of no import whether or not Christabel is an ice maiden. But where Votes for Women is concerned she may prove to be an ice*berg*," said Sylvia sagely.

Nash didn't reply. His thoughts were elsewhere. Sylvia realised her faux pas and scolded herself silently.

Chapter 25

"The industrial evils which had formed the basis of much of our appeal were gradually pushed aside… working class women were dropped without hesitation."

Tessa Billington-Greig, Women's Freedom League (and ex-WSPU member)

Ruby's time in service, both domestic and on board ships, where the clock was king, had left her the most punctual of people. She was usually the first to arrive at any gatherings, and so had to spend time making small talk in the homes of middle class Suffragettes, whilst waiting for others to arrive. Being offered tea was always a dilemma. Who knew what a refusal meant? But acceptance brought before her a servant who was herself in a previous life, bowing and scraping above the fine crockery. It was always a relief when such concerns could be replaced with the business of the day.

So it was with amazement that she considered how the middle class Sylvia had so seamlessly blended into working class Bow life without any awkwardness or embarrassment either from her or the East End women around her. Ruby thought Sylvia's looks probably helped her. She had a natural frumpiness that seemed to cross the class divide. You looked at the sad eyed, matronly and, due to hunger and thirst-strikes, old before her time Sylvia, and she looked all too similar to a worn out sweated working woman.

Ruby looked down at her leader and told her it was time to go. Sylvia was so weak that there was no question of her being able to run, leap off costermonger barrows or do any of the other things she had previously done to escape the police. And under the auspices of Cat and Mouse, the 'Cats' had now settled on the simple but effective tactic of encamping outside Jessie's house waiting for their prey. So it was time for a show of force from Sylvia's East London followers. A twenty deep crowd surrounded the front door of 28 Ford Road, and when Sylvia appeared, lying prostrate on a stretcher carried by some of her People's Army, the crowd helped them carry her shoulder high to a waiting car. This already had Ruby, Nash and a driver in situ, and Sylvia was carefully deposited into the back seat to join them. The police could not get near the car as it roared off in the direction of Essex, whilst the crowd enjoyed the usual game of Cat-baiting.

"'ere, why don't yer come and force-feed us! We're bleeding' starvin'!" was today's insult of choice to the police.

And there was a harsh reality to these remarks. There were working people now in prison for their political beliefs, being fed better, nutritionally at least, than they had been at any time in their East End lives, whilst their dependents relied on hand outs from fellow supporters to survive.

The trip to Harwich went without incident. When the narrow streets of the old town gave way to the port area, Nash took this as his cue to alight from the car. A short distance further on a wig-wearing, pillow-up-the-jumper apparently heavily pregnant woman and her nurse followed suit on the quayside. It was hoped that the pregnancy would disguise the difficulty with which Sylvia was walking. The women walked on to the ship followed at a discreet distance by their bodyguard. The plan was for Nash to keep an eye on things from afar.

He soon spotted several plain clothes detectives dotted about on board. He cursed. The Bow police must have contacted Scotland Yard and they had notified all the ports, even Harwich, on the off chance Sylvia had been escaping abroad. The Cats were getting too clever by half. It certainly confirmed his suspicions that the government were simply allowing Annie Kenney to travel to and fro between England and France unhindered.

He thought they must have spotted Sylvia and followed her on board but why didn't they simply arrest her? Were they under orders to let her go in the hope she would stay abroad, out of the government's hair, like her sister? Or had they contacted the Dutch and French Police and were hoping Sylvia would lead them to Christabel? Perhaps he had got it wrong and they did want Christabel arrested after all? Whatever the situation, what could he do about it on board a ship?

These questions were answered in one fell swoop. The detectives slowly started to move towards each other. Sylvia and Ruby were across the ship's lounge, some way from them. Nash, puzzled, moved closer to the detectives. Suddenly all of the detectives moved in to grab a couple of characters Nash had not even noticed. The lead detective pulled out a piece of paper. He told them he was arresting them in relation to diamond smuggling and then read from the paper that in accordance with the new Judges' Law, they could, if they so wished, say nothing.

Nash moved away with the little head shake and lightly amused expression of the incredulous; at detectives having no interest in his charges and their quoting a new law that stated the obvious.

Sylvia and Ruby, deep in conversation about the need to set up nurseries to care for children while their mothers demonstrated, had been thankfully oblivious of the whole affair.

Nash saw the women as far as the train to Rotterdam, where they would change for Paris. Having acted as a porter for their luggage and briefly boarded the train to satisfy himself that the women were not under any threat or surveillance, he did not offer to assist them further, and neither did they expect him to. His brief fulfilled, Nash retraced his steps via an old quayside bar to kill some time whilst waiting for a ship back to Harwich.

The two women duly arrived at Christabel's flat in Paris. She opened the door to them with a tiny Pomeranian dog in her arms. They were shown in and there stood Mrs Pankhurst. It was a shock. They had no idea they were being summoned to see their leader too.

"Thank you for coming Sylvia, and er?" said Christabel flicking her grey eyes at Ruby for a moment before returning them towards her sister. "I was expecting Norah?"

"This is Mrs Martin. You may remember May Billinghurst originally recruited her into the WSPU as a paid worker. But she resigned before joining me in the East End. She is now Norah's assistant with regard to all matters of East London Federation finance."

Sibling rivalry ensured that Sylvia chose not to explain why her senior financial secretary had not made the trip.

Mrs Pankhurst and her eldest daughter duly swopped curt nods, titles and surnames with their new acquaintance.

The welcoming pleasantries were quickly replaced by Christabel regaling her little sister with tales of sightseeing, shopping in fashionable stores, visiting friends and strolling in the Bois de Boulogne.

An exhausted, weak Sylvia was horrified by the gaiety and serenity on display. She just wanted to cut to the chase and talk business.

"You asked to see us?" asked Sylvia.

"Of course I did," confirmed Christabel.

This was followed by an awkward silence. Ruby decided she would fill the void.

"On our way over here we have been discussing the setting up of nurseries to care for children while their mothers demonstrate."

"Yes, yes I'm sure."

"Sylvia's next speeches are going to be based around the slogan 'no vote, no rent'."

"Yes, yes I read the report. Thank you Mrs Martin."

More silence. Sylvia was all too aware that she had broken two of Christabel's cardinal rules. No WSPU members were to take part in any political campaigns other than WSPU ones, and there was to be no combination with men. Sylvia had recently broken both rules by speaking at the Albert Hall in support of the transport workers' strike in Dublin. It was obvious that she had been summoned for a dressing down and she just wanted her sister to say what she had to say and get it over with.

"We have trained working women to make speeches," said Sylvia.

She knew that Christabel's innate snobbery could not let that pass. And so it proved.

"You have a democratic constitution for your Federation; we do not agree with that. A working woman's movement is of no value. The WSPU does not want to be mixed up with them. Working women are the weakest portion of the sex. How could it be otherwise? Their lives are too hard, their education too meagre to equip them for the contest. Surely it is a mistake to use the weakest for the struggle. We want picked women, the very strongest and intelligent. You have your own ideas. We do not want that; we want all our women to take their instructions and walk in step like an army."

Ruby looked at Sylvia expecting her to go back with a fierce sisterly riposte, but it was not forthcoming. Sylvia merely looked back blankly, first at her sister before glancing at her mother. Ruby assumed that Sylvia must be too tired, too ill to argue, but it was not exhaustion which had rendered her mute. She simply felt a sense of tragedy and grief from her sister's ruthlessness and her mother assenting to everything her beloved first-born proposed.

Christabel turned her gaze to Ruby without a hint of embarrassment for what she had just said about the class of women of whom Ruby was clearly a member. It was time to talk money. It was the reason Norah had been summoned to accompany Sylvia, and Christabel's nose was not a little out-of-joint to find herself having to speak to a mere assistant. She took her most haughty tone with the young woman in front of her.

"Moreover your Federation appeals for funds; people think it all part of the same thing. You get donations that might come to us. That's what we say."

Ruby was not going to let her get away with that.

"People have sent money to you on account of our big East London demonstrations for which we have the bill to pay!"

The dictatorial co-leader of the WSPU was taken aback. She was not used to any woman speaking to her like that.

"How much do you need?" she sniffed contemptuously. "What would you think a suitable income for your Federation? You can't need much in your simple way."

"All we can use for our work, like you!" argued a wide-eyed Ruby.

At this point Mrs Pankhurst entered the fray for the first time in an attempt to diffuse the situation.

"Suppose I were to say we would allow you something. Would you…"

She was cut off by her commander-in-chief.

"Oh no, we can't have that! It must be clear cut!"

Sylvia finally spoke, quietly, sadly.

"My East London Federation will be a completely separate organisation from now on. The letters WSPU will be struck from all our publicity materials. And we will have our own newspaper."

The business over, there was a return to an awkward silence. Christabel attempted to fill the void.

"We should sometimes meet not as Suffragettes but as sisters."

It was a meaningless gesture as far as Sylvia was concerned. The family had no life outside of the movement.

Chapter 26

"Women should realise feminism is the whole
issue, political enfranchisement a branch issue."
Suffrage Societies

Sylvia and Ruby returned from France via a deliberately long,
roundabout route, partly to decrease the chances of them being
caught by the docks' police, and partly to give themselves
much needed time to recover strength and health after their
latest stints in prison. They enjoyed making their way through
Normandy on slow relaxing trains, and even spent a little time
sightseeing on the coast before taking a liner en-route from
Naples to America across to Southampton. They would pop
in to visit Ruby's mother whilst on the south coast.

Ruby had arranged the timing of their return to coincide
with her mother's first visit from a new Titanic Relief Fund
lady visitor. Ruby had been determined to be present when
this woman arrived in an attempt to set some new ground
rules about visits. During the planning of the trip to Paris,
Ruby had visited the Relief Fund office in London and told
the lady almoner a little white lie that her mother had flu at
present, and asked if it would it be possible to liaise with the
Southampton office to rearrange the date of the visit. This
was duly done, with Ruby ensuring the visit was changed to
the day when she and Sylvia's ship was due to arrive in

Southampton. Ruby also sent a letter to warn off her sisters in no uncertain terms. Their absence from the family home was required. And thus a brace of birds were despatched by a solitary Suffragette stone.

Ruby would have felt ill at ease taking any other Suffragette colleague, even May to her simple family home for tea, but Sylvia was unlike any other woman she had ever met. She just adapted, chameleon-like, to whatever environment was put in front of her and immediately put everyone at their ease. Ruby's mother, initially so nervous about having the infamous Miss Pankhurst in her home was quickly sharing a joke with her. It helped that Sylvia looked ill, allowing Mrs Turner to snap into clucking mother hen mode. She soon had Sylvia's legs up on a chair in front of the meagre fire in the tiny front room so her visitor could rest weary bones.

There was a knock on the door. Ruby opened it and a stiff-backed young thing stood in front of her. The lady visitor was resplendent in a lace blouse with stand collar, tailored wool suit, finely decorated double-breasted jacket, side-pleated narrow skirt and smart accessories. She was the epitome of the fashionable pyramid turned on its point look, with a huge hat tapering to a narrow hem at the foot.

Mary at Epsom came to mind. Ruby doubted this young woman would have made it to the railway's porter's safe haven and thought she looked rather *too* elegant for the job at hand. Was she trying just a little too hard to impress? Was her fine ensemble a crutch? Ruby looked into the young woman's eyes and had her suspicions confirmed. She saw nervousness and apprehension behind the apparent cool exterior.

"Hello. Is this Mrs Turner's residence? I am Miss Faulkner, from the Titanic Relief Fund."

"Yes, please come in, I am Mrs Martin, Mrs Turner's daughter."

Ruby made no attempt to be less formal with her name and made a point to avoid what would have been the normal attempt at breaking the ice by saying something along the lines of 'I've just popped in for a cuppa,' followed by asking the young woman if she was 'gasping'. Ruby wanted the woman to feel that she was intruding, which undoubtedly she was.

"Myself and a friend are here visiting my mother. It is the first opportunity I have had for some time to see her. We were in the middle of having tea. You are welcome to join us if you wish Miss Faulkner."

"Oh, well I had not expected friends and family. My visit is supposed to be private...," hesitated the young woman as she was shown in to the front room.

Ruby ignored this and made introductions between her mother and the visitor, before matter-of-factly doing the same with 'Miss Pankhurst'.

"Will you forgive me not rising Miss Faulkner?" asked the celebrity sitting across two chairs. "But you will take my second chair won't you?"

With this Sylvia made to lift her legs.

"No, yes, please, don't ..." flustered the young woman.

Ruby had taken a calculated risk. She was aware that introducing a haughty young lady visitor to one of the country's most wanted felons in her mother's house could mean trouble with the committee of the Titanic Relief Fund, but she was keen for this visit to be on her mother's terms.

The young lady soon found herself answering more questions about herself than asking them of Mrs Turner. Her inquisitors soon had the lady visitor confirming that she had just come down from university. What degree did she have? Did she not think it a disgrace that she would not be able to use her degree because that career was closed to women? Did she think it ironic that the new Oriental fashion she was wearing, brought about by the excitement engendered by Scheherazade, had women dressing like slaves in an oriental harem at the very time women were about to win the vote?

Over her second cup of tea Miss Faulkner, keen to take the subject off herself, mentioned that she had two friends who were the daughters of the judge in Mrs Pankhurst's conspiracy trial, and they had since become Suffragettes. This amused the women immensely and the young lady visitor, though appreciating that she was somewhat out of her depth, found herself relaxing somewhat in their company.

At one point Ruby's mother went out to the back yard to use the outside lavatory. Her daughter took this opportunity to apologise for there not being any cake.

"I do hope you are not famished Sylvia," said Ruby. "But mother cannot afford cake or biscuits you understand."

Sylvia was well aware of to whom Ruby was really speaking.

"No poor working class widows can my dear," said Sylvia. "Would you not agree Miss Faulkner?"

The lady visitor felt a mix of intimidation and excitement at being asked such a leading question on such a serious matter by a Pankhurst. She agreed of course and not long into the next cup of tea it was confirmed that she would be writing a very positive report to the Relief Fund Committee on Mrs Turner. Her fellow tea drinkers responded with praise for her taking an interest in the lives of poor people. The young woman reddened and smiled shyly before going on to explain that having come down from university she had been at a bit of a loose end so thought she should do her bit, and what better than to volunteer for the local Titanic Relief Fund? But she admitted to not having had any real clue as to what it would involve. She had received training of course but it was only now that she fully appreciated what her new position entailed. And for the first time in her life she felt of use.

She was asked if she would care to come to one of Sylvia's meetings the next time she was in London. Yes, she would like that. She planned to come to London quite soon as a matter of fact. Addresses were exchanged. Perhaps an acorn had been planted.

Chapter 27

"I have on many occasions…had the prisoners examined by doctors, but in no case have they been willing to certify them as lunatics."

Reginald McKenna, Home Secretary

The rest and recuperation which she had enjoyed in France followed by the success of the trip to Southampton had left Ruby feeling ready to move to Bow. Not that it was any great upheaval moving the few goods and chattels she had managed to acquire since arriving in St Johns with little but the clothes in which she stood up. If she had donned her winter coat she could just about, with some awkwardness, have carried everything herself in one trip on public transport from St Johns to Bow. But it had been an unusually warm start to the summer, and though putting up with the heat was neither here nor there, she was not prepared to again wear that coat when it was not appropriate to do so.

Nash borrowed a pony and cart from his cousins and took it over to South London to help her move, which did not save him from the ribbing Ruby had started planning back in prison. She asked him obnoxiously if his passport had been in order for the trek before pretending to become more serious as she informed him that moving north of the river was a necessary evil. He had immediately recognised the gleam in her eye that told him she was trying to 'have him on', but he reacted anyway, as he knew she would enjoy it. He thus told her in no uncertain terms what he thought.

"No wonder Billingsgate does such a trade. The fish bite easily around here," smirked Ruby. "Ever bin ad?" she added in a cockney accent.

"Don't you come it with me swede!" retorted Nash. "You might hurrrt my feelings."

Of all the words in the English language, 'hurt' was the one that exaggerated the Hampshire lilt more than any other. It was fifteen-all, and they carried on trading quips so it was deuce by the time they had made their way through the Blackwall Tunnel into the East End.

Such had been the success of Sylvia's organisation, that it had quickly outgrown the ex-baker's shop opposite Bow Church. Its more recent HQ had been a shop at the eastern end of the Roman Road with space for a printing press in the cellar. This was the home of the new Women's Dreadnought newspaper. But this premises too had it limitations as a headquarters, especially now that the local council had bent to increasing government pressure to tighten up their procedure for banning known East London Federation supporters from hiring any of their halls. Thus Sylvia had recently acquired a house in Ford Road which had plenty of space out the back, in which a corrugated iron hall with space for 300 standing had been speedily erected. This was soon to be opened as the new East London Federation's centre of operations, to be known as the Women's Hall, with Sylvia, Norah, Jessie and her husband moving in to the house in front.

Ruby moved in as a lodger in a Suffragette-friendly house in Norman Road which Norah had arranged for her. It was handily placed for Sylvia's new house and headquarters as well as the Women's Dreadnought, close to which Ruby and Nash ran an East London Federation stall in the Saturday market. Her new home also happened to be close to the faded grandeur of Tredegar Square which, though it had seen better days, was by some way the most attractive, leafy address in the Bow area. Ruby was quick to inform Nash that it reminded her of South London. Nash gave her a knowing look but otherwise just huffed, allowing the score to reach advantage Ruby.

★★★★★★

There was only so much protection Nash and the People's Army could give to Sylvia. The police had their successes. They had recently captured their prey whilst she had been making a speech in Mile End telling her audience about the Federation's new Dreadnought newspaper, which had just gone to press. She had been returned to prison to continue the remainder of her sentence as per Cat and Mouse.

But now she had been rereleased on health grounds and was soon visited by two of her lieutenants.

Nash was a great believer in letting people make their own way in life, and if some of their decisions proved to be wrong, so be it. He was certainly nobody's nursemaid. But after Ruby's last prison term he had made it clear that he did not approve of her putting herself through such torture. He had received short shrift from Ruby for his opinion, but now, he could not help but pass comment on Sylvia's well-being. He wondered if she should reconsider her desire to make every prison term such an ordeal.

"Actually Nashey I feel better than in the past. Cat and Mouse has ended force-feeding of course, and on this occasion I did not thirst-strike or pace in my cell at night in order to get some sleep and keep my mind strong so as to produce ideas for our new Dreadnought newspaper."

"Oh, so you only did 'unger strike. A right bleedin' 'oliday then. Surprised Thomas Cook don't start it up," came the sarcasm, as heavy as the man who uttered it.

Ruby had discussed with other women how she had felt after being force-fed, but on one occasion had found herself also confiding in Nash on the subject. So she knew he meant well by showing his appreciation that Suffragette prison sentences were not to be made light of, but nobody had suffered more hunger strikes than Sylvia so Nash received a sly but significant elbow in the ribs for his trouble.

"It is good to hear you are feeling in better form Sylvia," said Ruby smiling. "The Dreadnought is why we are here as a matter of fact."

Nash did not understand why Ruby had elbowed him but took it as a hint to keep quiet. This he did, simply tossing a rolled up copy of the hot-off-the-press first edition on to Sylvia's lap.

"Ah, you have read it!" exclaimed Sylvia enthusiastically. "I asked Daisy to arrange its distribution upon my release. What do you say of my vision of new housing, a communal nursery and personalised central heating? And Ruby do you think I have captured the essence of what I was telling you on our journey to France about 'No vote, No rent'? I will call for East Londoners to withhold paying their rent. If we cannot force the government to act, landlords who are not receiving their rent will do our job for us."

"The housing, nursery and heating are wonderful ideas!" said Ruby with the enthusiasm of someone a little too eager to please. "And we also liked your article about providing a cost price restaurant. Tuppenny two-course meals will be a Godsend for the poor. But…"

"The no vote, no rent's why we're 'ere Sylvia," interjected Nash gruffly.

Sylvia immediately picked up on Nash calling her by her full first name rather than his usual abbreviation. He only did that nowadays when he was not in the best of moods. She readied herself for his next sentence.

"We've just come from doin' the stall down the market. All day long all we've 'ad is earache from every cove tellin' us as 'ow your…"

Ruby talked loudly across Nash at this point, fearful the big man was about to be less than tactful.

"Please do not take it amiss Sylvia," she said before quietening her tone, "but we must urge you to think again about asking people to withhold the rent. Fear of losing the home is too deep rooted for working people."

"I understand those fears Ruby. But our splendid People's Army, which enables me to defy Cat and Mouse to make speeches with impunity, will protect rent-strikers in the same way. Bailiffs will not be allowed near the home of a striker."

"We can't be everywhere gell," advised Nash. "Those bastards find a way, just like the coppers do wiv you some'imes. Baliffs 'ave 'ad plenty of practice over the years I can tell yer. A good number of people round 'ere 'ave lost their 'ome some time or anuvver. You tell 'er Ruby."

His co-objector was happy to take up the cudgels again.

"Illness, no work, union strikes; they have all meant

eviction or a moonlight flit to escape the landlord's bullies. I know you have given up a huge amount yourself Sylvia and everyone is very grateful but you are asking too much of the East End this time."

One of the reasons Sylvia had in such a short space of time become so loved and respected in East London was her ability to listen. She did not talk at people. She discussed things with them.

"It is not yet time for such action," agreed Sylvia. "Thank you for correcting me. You two are indeed quite a couple."

Nash nodded with ease. Ruby coloured slightly.

Chapter 28

"Those who take up the sword shall perish by the sword. A cause which cannot win its way to public acceptance by persuasion, by argument, by organisation, by peaceful methods of agitation, is a cause which already…has pronounced on itself its own sentence of death."

Herbert Asquith, Prime Minister

The irony was that whilst Emmeline Pankhurst's charisma and galvanising speech-making around the country allied to her impressive publicity machine continued to successfully politicise an increasingly large number of women, these new recruits were rejecting the great speaker's own organisation. They were joining the suffrage societies of others, be it the militant but non-violent Women's Freedom League, the non-militant National Union of Women's Suffrage Societies, Sylvia's East London Federation or any number of other women's suffrage organisations. Mrs Pankhurst's WSPU was in the autumn of its days.

Christabel's reckless, unwise arson and bombing campaign had made the Suffragettes unpopular with the press, public and politicians of all persuasions. They had lost so much support and sympathy from within the general Suffragist movement that their membership had fallen to just two thousand. And the Cat and Mouse Act had reduced the WSPU's activist arm to being a small covert, underground operation that had lost touch with its fellow members, the public and reality. With what appeared to be a final throw of the dice Mrs Pankhurst had called for a great protest procession to Buckingham Palace to petition the King for the vote for women.

Ruby was concerned this unpopularity and lack of sympathy would leave Mrs Pankhurst and her dwindling number of supporters as sitting ducks for police and bully boy violence that would end in serious bloodshed. She was still in touch by regular letter with May, who had informed her that she would of course be in the procession at Mrs Pankhurst's side. Ruby was afraid that the leader of the WSPU's most easily recognisable lieutenant would be drawn into the centre of the most violent clashes and could be seriously hurt.

Ruby was going to be there because Sylvia had agreed that her East London Federation would show their support for the protest by being part of the procession from Grosvenor Square to the Palace. But they were to be peripheral. Ruby doubted that she would be able to do anything to protect May. Thus she had implored Nash to accompany her to the demonstration so he could keep an eye on May, but Nash was less than enthusiastic about the request.

"Ol' muvver Pankhurst's speeches ain' no good if all 'er mob do is set light to fings and blow fings up. And this Buckingham Palace lark'll just be anuvver punch up with the coppers like that Black Friday you told me about. The WSPU won't even exist in a twelve month. 'er muvver should come an' 'elp Sylvia. The two of 'em togevver would win the vote sharp, but that Christabel's doin' more 'arm than any man, and that includes that cowson Asquith."

"Do not tell your grandmother to suck eggs!" scolded an irritated, exasperated Ruby. "I have got to look out for my friend; just like you looked out for me on board that bloody ship! You didn't know me from Adam but you still saved me didn't you. I owe a great deal to May. I would still be working at Peek Frean's, stinking of biscuit dough, if it were not for her. And she is a cripple for God's sake. We should protect people like her."

Nash retorted that from what he had heard about Ruby's invalid friend she didn't need any assistance from anybody. Ruby responded by telling Nash not to be so stupid which led to further bickering before she finally lost patience with him.

"For God's sake Nashey, stop acting your age!"

Nash perceived that secreted somewhere deep within this rebuke was the most backhanded of compliments. It had the desired effect, Nash grudgingly agreeing to accompany Ruby to the Buckingham Palace demonstration. This was on the clear understanding that he was not prepared to get himself arrested fighting women's battles for them. He would keep an eye out for May and if she got into dire straits he might go to her help if he had a mind to. There again he might not. Ruby gave him her frostiest stare whilst she called him a 'contrary Mary' but left it at that. There was no point talking to him when he was like this.

On the morning of the protest Ruby made an early start to visit May in Lewisham before her friend left for London. She attempted to glean any information she could from her.

How were the WSPU planning to avoid the police cordons? What exactly was going to happen if they got as far as the Palace? Were they planning any specific protest? Press photographers were likely to be their best protection from police brutality; had they contacted the few still friendly newspapers to make sure they would be there?

But May had been surprised not to say a little perplexed to see Ruby. An unannounced early visit on the very morning of the big day in London seemed rather odd. And Ruby seemed nervous, almost too eager to talk about the demonstration. May was already on tenterhooks thinking about the day ahead and Ruby was just making her feel worse. As a result the conversation did not flow. Ruby's questions were met with increasingly short, to the point answers. The conversation was starting to sound like an interview. May wanted to know exactly why Ruby had come to see her but was too polite to ask. Ruby read her thoughts.

"May, you are no doubt wondering to what purpose is my visit."

May feigned 'not at all' with a shake of the head and matching body language before Ruby continued. She told her friend that Nashey was going along to the protest to lend his support. The two of them had become quite close. This freed the conversation from its shackles somewhat as the two women reminisced over their chat about Nashey on the train ride home to St Johns after the Bow bye-election fracas. May then told of how on a subsequent visit to the bye-election she had seen him from afar, but the meeting degenerated into mayhem resulting in him being too busy dealing with troublemakers for her to have had the opportunity to meet him. This gave Ruby her cue. She began hesitantly.

"May, er, I thought it might be nice if the two of you met. It is queer is it not that my two closest friends, both of whom are fighting for votes for women, have never been introduced. I thought perhaps Nashey could meet us at the demonstration this afternoon. Of course I might not see you as who is to say how things will pan out at the Palace, but Nashey is not coming with me. He will only be there as a bystander, so I could ask him to look out for you. To meet you that is; perhaps after the demonstration, or even during it, if that proves feasible."

She considered suggesting Nashey might even be useful if things got a little out of hand with the police but decided to leave it unsaid. She was concerned that May would see through her little plan. The fiercely independent woman may not have appreciated her friend providing a bodyguard for her. She neither expected nor asked for any help. She could look after herself.

But May had seen Ruby's hesitation, borne it would seem out of a little embarrassment. There was also Ruby's earlier nervousness and the sheer poor timing of her visit. And there was that one little tell-tale statement, 'the two of us have become quite close'. Ruby was clearly so excited that despite the inappropriate timing she could not wait to arrange for May to meet her new beau.

May's arithmetic had failed to correctly calculate a couple of twos. May thus showed obvious delight at Ruby's idea and suggested that if neither she nor Ruby were arrested at the protest, the three of them could have an early supper together afterwards somewhere in The Strand. Ruby readily agreed, before apologising that she would not be able to travel up to London with May. She had already arranged to meet Nashey in the East End. They were travelling to the demonstration together. May responded with a knowing smile, nod and comment.

"Of course you are, my dear."

As the two of them said au revoir at the front door, May was not surprised that Ruby had avoided making the big announcement there and then. During supper, with Nashey present would be a far more appropriate occasion. May had only seen him from a distance but thought he was clearly somewhat older than Ruby. She craned her neck to watch her young friend disappear down the hill of Granville Park as she gave due consideration to the age-gap. It was quite common within the middle classes of course. Gentleman often had to work their way up to a certain level of seniority in their profession with its subsequent means before they could show an interest in a middle class lady. And what of those rumours of Sylvia and Keir Hardie? And theirs was an even greater age-difference than that between Ruby and Nashey. A political cause certainly appeared to bring people close together who perhaps might otherwise have remained mere friends. A large age-gap did however appear less customary within the working class. But Ruby did not appear to show much interest in men of her own age. Plenty of young men, of the middle as well as her own social class, had shown an interest in her but she soon intimidated them with her way of looking them straight in the eye and speaking plainly. It was a shame in as much as, with her good looks she could surely have bettered herself. But one had to admit that from everything people said about him, Nashey appeared to be quite a fellow. The two of them were each quite unique in their own way so perhaps it was a good match.

At the bend in the road that would take her out of sight of May, Ruby felt the urge to look back up the hill, and saw May still at her front door watching her. The two women swopped awkward little waves before Ruby disappeared from view to busy herself cutting through the busy traffic of Lewisham town centre. As she made her way up the hill to Lewisham station a frown crossed her face. There was something not quite right about May's reaction.

★★★★★★

Aldgate East was the closest underground station to Bow, and a relatively short walk from Cannon Street, so it was the spot where Nash and Ruby had agreed to meet. They would get the tube from there to the West End.

Ruby had spent the time on the train to London considering May's overly positive response to the conversation about Nashey. It was as the train pulled out of London Bridge that the penny finally dropped. The realisation shocked her, but it didn't stop a schoolgirl's smile spreading across her face. Minutes later Nash hove into view as she made her way along Aldgate High Street. He was never one for greetings. 'Hello' and words to that effect were not in his vocabulary. As Ruby approached to within a few feet of him smiling fondly and about to wish him a good morning, he gave the slightest of nods of recognition and started talking.

"First tube I ever got in me life were back in eighty eight.

Weren't called the underground then mind, we called it the sub; subterranean see. It were steam trains under the ground in them days! Filthiest fing you ever did see!"

"Are you telling me you didn't get on a tube till you were a grown man? Scared of all that nasty smoke and soot before that were you?"

Ruby had said this with a big smirk on her face. She was being deliberately obnoxious and looked forward to Nash coming back with one of his usual retorts. It was just a question of whether he called her a 'cheeky little cow' or a 'cheeky little mare'. But he surprised her.

"I didn't 'ave no money to throw about on trains. And there weren't nowhere in this world I wanted to get to so fast I wanted to 'urtle towards it down a tunnel like some ruddy great mole. Anywhere I wanted to go I walked and I got there when I got there."

His voice then changed in modulation, taking on a more serious note.

"Only reason I got a tube then were cos I were chasin' after some cove."

Ruby was giggling to the point whereby she missed the subtle change in the conversation.

"Chasing? From what I hear you were usually the one being chased back then; by the coppers you crooked old devil. Who were you chasing anyhow?"

Nash's face suddenly darkened. He didn't answer.

Eighteen eighty eight. Ruby winced silently. It was the year of the Ripper murders. She had heard the rumours about Nash's hunt for the killer. She knew to tread carefully. They had become close friends but she appreciated this was off limits.

"I will never go horse-racing again," she said seriously. "Or get on a ship. I had to get on one to get home of course and I got on those boats for Sylvia's trip, but I will not do it again."

There was a pause while the two of them looked at each other grim-faced before Ruby continued.

"Come on let's walk some of the way to the Palace. I want to show you the Monument, where me and May got ourselves arrested that time."

She expected Nash to just nod and that would be the end of the conversation until they reached The Monument, where she would bring the mood back up by regaling him with the tale of her exploits in the vicinity. She was confident he would enjoy hearing about May using her wheelchair as a battering ram against the policeman. But Nash surprised her for the second time in quick succession.

"Spose you've 'eard the rumours about me and the Ripper? I never did catch the cowson yer know. I found out who 'e were right enough, but then 'e were dead in any case. The murders stopped and I finished lookin' for 'im a course. People put two and two togevver and got five. I just let it be; me reputation as the man who did for the bastard did me a few favours over the years."

Nash then thought it was time to return to happier matters. The Monument's close proximity to his old St Botolph's Church hunting ground meant that he had seen the great obelisk many a time, but he would not let Ruby know that. He thought she would enjoy being his guide. He gave Ruby a reassuring wink to change the dynamic.

"So let's see this bleedin' Monument a yourn. It'll better be good after all the earache I've 'ad from you these past months about where the infamous Billings'urst and Martin gang used to roam."

This was Ruby's cue to return to obnoxiousness.

"Get yer facts right you old codger, I'll have you know it was the Martin and Billinghurst gang. And note there is no 's' in Billinghurst but there is an aitch."

"Cheeky little mare."

Chapter 29

"She (Mrs Pankhurst) had the dynamic quality that got things done, though she herself did not possess any great executive ability. The Suffragette cause gave full scope to her dramatic power without demanding from her the difficult task of discovering precise solutions."

Sylvia Pankhurst

An hour later Ruby and Nash had stopped at the Lyon's Corner House in the Strand for a much needed cup of tea. They had got a tram from The Monument to Charing Cross, and whilst on board had whispered conspiratorially to each other to confirm their plans for when they got to the demonstration. It had been agreed that they would split up, with Ruby joining the protest while Nash would blend into the crowd to keep a watching brief, in particular keeping an eye out for May. If all went well, the three of them would meet up afterwards by the arch at the far end of the Mall from the Palace.

With the business of the day dealt with, Ruby now wanted to enjoy a quiet, sociable half an hour with Nash in the café. But their lives were so wrapped up in the fight for the vote that the conversation almost inevitably soon touched upon it again. Ruby looked around the café before speaking with the mix of a knowing smile and enthusiasm laced with a touch of sadness that reminiscing about a fondly remembered deceased friend brings.

"Emily was sitting in this very café when she heard about Asquith blocking the Conciliation Bill four years ago. She went straight to the nearest building site, picked up a brick and hurled it through the first government building she came to in Whitehall."

Nash nodded and snorted in such a way as to show he was impressed.

"Bit of a gell wernt she," he said, it being more statement than question.

"She was one of only two people I have ever met who feared nothing or no one," continued Ruby, leaving the obvious unsaid. "It's a shame you two never met. I think you would have gotten along. You are chalk and cheese of course but she reminded me of you in some ways; aloof to those who did not know her, a great friend or foe to those who did."

Although they each knew the other was the only person in the world with whom they could share the subject of the Titanic, they also appreciated each had a second skeleton in their respective cupboards to whom nobody had a key. But Nash lacked the diplomacy and tact of Ruby. He blurted out the question before he realised what he had said.

"D'yer fink Emily topped 'erself for the cause?"

Ruby looked daggers at Nash for a moment then contemplated her lap. Nash realised his mistake.

"Time we got to the protest, you're gonna be late," he growled, the off-hand manner failing to hide the awkwardness he felt.

Nash looked down, overacting a patting of his coat pockets in search of a tip for the café staff. He could sense Ruby was glaring back at him, he guessed with the grim determination he had witnessed on board the Titanic. As he looked up to face her she started talking.

"What do you think I am?" said Ruby slowly, quietly, indignantly. "If I had thought for one moment she might die, I would have refused to take her to bloody Epsom."

Her tone then transformed into a tired, resigned one.

"It was appalling bad luck. Over the sticks jockeys have falls like that all the time. It was the kick in the head that did for her. She would not have knowingly died without writing a farewell message to her mother. She said that they were close; on all matters except her Suffragette work that is. And she told me a few minutes before the accident that she was looking forward to visiting her dear sister Laetitia in France the following week."

Nash thought he should say something but was not sure what. He was desperate not to say the wrong thing. He thought it safest to keep to the technicalities of the incident.

"Tattenham Corner's down'ill I 'ear. Spose the 'orses were on 'er quicker than she fought."

Ruby shook her head wearily before answering.

"She was supposed to duck under the rail in good time. She watched the first two races most intently. Too intently methinks for someone with little interest in racing. I believe she was pleasantly surprised by how close we were to the horses as they raced by. My suspicion is that on seeing our good position on the rails she decided to change tactics to try to stuff her Votes for Women scarf into Anmer's bridle. The king's horse passing the winning post at The Derby in front of its owner and a packed grandstand, with the whole world soon watching on Pathe News, with Votes for Women coming out of its mouth like a postcard cartoon. It would have been quite the coup indeed."

Nash knew all about impulsive judgements costing a life. His had cost the life of a young prostitute all those years ago. He stared out of the window of the café nodding grimly to let Ruby know he was listening as she continued.

"But the idea would have been to nought if the horse had been running well and bunched in amongst other runners as it should have been. Emily would then not have been able to approach it and perhaps would have refrained, though I daresay she may have approached another horse. In any case she only had a split second to decide where to stand and misjudged it. We should have stood at the start of the race and disrupted it with our flags there. We should never have been at Tattenham Corner. It was too dangerous. It was all my fault."

Nash knew that no words from anyone could dissuade someone from such feelings of guilt. But he said something anyway.

"No, it's bastards who don't let people 'ave wot they've a right to cos it don't suit their politics who's at fault gell." He nodded towards the door and winked to change the mood. "Come on, let's go and keep that friend of yours out of mischief and save a few copper's shins while we're aboud it."

They left the café and within seconds were at the south-east corner of Trafalgar Square, where the world's smallest police station stood, a one-man affair which was really just a spy-hole. It enabled a policeman to spot crowd trouble brewing in the square and telephone through to Cannon

Row police station to warn them to ready themselves for action. Such a sneaky little device was a red rag to Nash.

One of his recent jobs for the cause had been to visit every post office in the East End and pick up however many gun licence application forms he could cajole out of each postmaster. He then got old East End women to complete them and send them in to the authorities. It was just a prank to play on the minds of the government but it appealed to his sense of humour, and he had even managed to get some press coverage out of it.

Nash banged on the glass door of the spy hole. The policeman ignored him, so Nash banged again harder. It was clear to the bobby that a spy-hole was not of much use if someone was going to stand in front of it blocking the view. Grudgingly he opened up.

"'ere officer, seen any old grannies with shotguns 'ave yer? Or ain' they arrived yet?" sneered Nash.

"You be on yer way or I'll nick yer!" warned the policeman.

"You're on yer own boy. All your mates are down the road waitin' to beat up poor defenceless women…"

Nash was about to goad the policeman further by telling him it would take a lot more than a 'thin streak of piss' to nick him, but Ruby, still seething from her café recollections of the Derby, was in no mood to listen to a load of male bravado.

"Stop buggering about Nashey! We've got bigger fish to fry than this tuppeny ha'penny copper!"

Nash grinned knowingly at the policeman as he nodded back over his shoulder towards Ruby whilst keeping his eyes on the constable, before he allowed her to pull him away roughly by the arm. Ruby frog-marched him to the left of Nelson's Column, to move around a small meeting taking place in the square, which for once had nothing to do with Suffragists, Ireland or industrial relations.

"Woss 'appening over there?" asked Nash.

Ruby peered over and after a couple of seconds surveying the scene spotted the answer.

"Oh, it's Mr Brailsford, one of our journalist supporters," she said, her mood brightening. "Looking at the banners, he is speaking for International Peace. He was at one of our meetings recently. I spoke to him about force-feeding. Then we got on to Cabinet ministers. I mentioned the Secretary for Foreign Affairs being the weakest of those who favoured Votes for Women and that started Mr Brailsford off about Mr Grey needing to be decisive about Europe. I glazed over and managed to collar Daisy Lansbury to come and rescue me."

Nash's attention span had also been exceeded. He was staring at the monolith across the road.

"Woss that bleedin' eyesore?" said the new architecture critic.

"That is the arch at the start of the Mall, where we are going to meet up with May after the demonstration. Someone told me King Edward had it built to remember his mother by. He died before it was finished."

"Shouldn't need no bleedin' arch to remember yer ol' gell by should yer? Not surprised 'e snuffed it, 'avin' to stare at that fing all day," commented Nash. "Mummy's boy was 'e? Didn't fink muvvers should 'ave the vote though did 'e."

Ruby could see the conversation in the cafe had left Nash in what she called one of his 'tricky' moods.

"Woe be-tide any policeman who gets in your way today," she said with a knowing look. "I will meet you back here when the protest is over."

It was time for the two of them to separate. Ruby had to climb the steps at the side of Admiralty Arch to Carlton Terrace, from where she would make her way through St James' and along to Grosvenor Square to meet up with her East London Federation colleagues. As with greetings, Nash tended not to offer farewells. Ruby thus merely widened her eyes and raised her chin in smiley acknowledgement as she took the first of the steps. But she immediately stopped and turned. The big step had given her considerable additional height. She leaned forward on tip-toes a little awkwardly, holding onto Nash's coat lapel for both balance and purchase, and kissed him with an ambiguous peck full on the lips.

"Keep yer 'and on yer 'apenny boy," she said with a saucy grin as she pushed away and turned.

And then she was gone, taking the steps at speed before running through Carlton Terrace. She was late for meeting up with the East London Federation but that was not the only reason she was running.

Nash walked up the Mall pondering what had just happened. As he approached the Palace he could see the area to the right hand side of it by the entrance to Green Park packed with sightseers. He decided this was neither the time nor place to consider such things. He would give it some thought later.

Crossing over Pall Mall, Ruby came upon the Crimean Memorial. She was stopped in her tracks by a notice declaring that a statue of Florence Nightingale was about to be added to it. Ruby didn't know how she felt about that. It was good that there was to be a statue of a woman. Was it to be the first such statue in London? She would not be surprised. If there was one already, would it not be in

Trafalgar Square or Whitehall? Thanks to Suffragette protest marches she knew both places quite well and could not remember seeing a woman's statue there except the one of that queen from Roman legend opposite Big Ben, which she thought of no account. But why was Florence Nightingale to be part of yet another memorial to man's inhumanity to man? Why couldn't the great nurse be remembered outside a hospital?

Ruby's thoughts turned to her leader. If Sylvia won the vote for women, would they put a statue up to honour her memory? It would be well deserved of course but she was convinced Sylvia would not want such a thing, the cost of a statue being better spent on educating poor women and their daughters.

Ruby continued to muse about the rights and wrongs of a statue to Sylvia until a church bell brought her back to the reality of the day. It was time to get a move on and join the subject of her thoughts and her East London Federation supporters at Grosvenor Square.

Spending so much time with Nash had made Ruby late meeting up with her Federation colleagues, so they had already set off by the time she arrived at Grosvenor Square. She chased after them and joined the back of the procession as it started to make its way down Park Lane towards Buckingham Palace. This took them into the loop of Hyde Park Corner which was soon encircled by a huge presence of mounted and foot police at Wellington Arch. The police enveloped the procession and corralled it.

Sylvia, who had finished her previous prison sentence and was thus a free woman for once, had a huge meeting of her own planned in the East End's Victoria Park in three days' time. So not wishing to risk arrests the East London Federation accepted their fate without putting up a fight. It was effectively the end of their participation in the day's proceedings. Being a back-marker, Ruby had just enough time to spot what the police were up to and managed to drop off the end of the procession before capture and head in the only direction not full of constabulary, westward into Hyde Park.

Mrs Pankhurst's WSPU group had also predicted the police tactics and managed to circumvent the cordon by turning off Park Lane and making their way through back streets and over Piccadilly into Green Park. This also outflanked a second police cordon on Constitution Hill. They then headed through the park towards the Palace.

Now on her own, Ruby headed west towards the Serpentine, continually looking south to see where the police presence ended. Once she could see no more police she headed south out of the park and into Belgravia. She didn't know that part of London at all, so was soon lost, but being dressed in purple, white and green from head to foot she was unwilling to risk drawing attention to herself by asking anyone the way. She knew the Palace must be to her left so when in doubt she headed in that direction. Whenever she came across any road of size, it was full of police, so she kept to back streets. Finally she came to a narrow street heading towards the Palace which had no policemen around. She took it, then several more little thoroughfares which got her into Buckingham Gate, which led into Birdcage Walk. Suddenly she was back in the fray, with a huge crowd, apparently sightseers, coming towards her as it was harried away from the Palace by mounted police and cavalry troops.

She leapt to the side and hid behind a tree to keep out of harm's way.

★★★★★★

Nash saw a large group of young men on and around the Victoria Memorial in front of Buckingham Palace, with a long line of police between them and the Palace railings. There was no sign of the expected large number of Suffragettes. He took a position on the edge of the crowd and waited. Nash's ocean-ravaged feet had been fine all the time he had been walking from Bow to The Monument, but they had started to tingle irritatingly as soon as he had sat down on the tram and felt worse in the café. And now, standing still outside the Palace the tingle soon became an itchy ache. He was not usually one for small talk, particularly with other men, but he felt the need to make his feelings felt, to the world if not to anyone in particular.

"Christ almighty. Standin' round 'ere like two of eels. Me plates are killin' me. I fought there were sposed to be fousands of Suffragettes comin' down 'ere?" he exclaimed loudly for anyone within a twenty yard radius to hear.

And then as if on Nash's cue, the first WSPU woman darted out from the throng to attack the police line.

"'ere are!" shouted a nearby man excitedly answering Nash's complaint.

The woman was thrown back into the crowd of young men who shouted at her that she ought to be burnt as they beat her up. More women made similar attacks, in an uncoordinated piecemeal fashion and met the same fate.

Mrs Pankhurst and her main band of followers then took

337

the police by surprise by suddenly arriving out of the trees of the park. They passed behind the police line, now holding back the crowds on the Victoria Memorial, and got up to the gates of the Palace. An inspector ordered some of his men to turn round and deal with the women.

Less than fifty yards away and bang in front of the Palace, Nash had a grandstand view of proceedings. He spotted a woman sitting in a strange looking contraption right in the thick of the WSPU followers, which he assumed to be May.

Ruby was well off to the side of the action, more than double Nash's distance away. She could just about see over the heads of the on-rushing crowd to the scene outside the Palace. She saw Mrs Pankhurst close to the Palace gates and then glimpsed May's wheelchair for a moment before it was engulfed in the throng, but could see no sign of Nashey. Ruby's attention was then taken by seeing Mrs Pankhurst grabbed from behind by a huge policeman, who carried the WSPU leader off with his arms around her, the petite frail-looking form dangling almost a foot off the ground. The policeman made for a Black Maria parked a few yards from Ruby. As they passed within ear-shot she heard her ex-leader shout to a knot of reporters who had gathered nearby.

"Arrested at the gates of the Palace; tell the king!"

Ruby was impressed by Mrs Pankhurst's appreciation of gaining publicity for the cause in even the most trying of circumstances, before her attention was drawn to the flash of a wheelchair in the crowd.

Nash continued to watch the events unfold. The huge crowd was mostly sightseers and anti-Suffragette young lads looking for trouble. He was surprised at how few WSPU women were actually there. Cat and Mouse had obviously

338

reduced their numbers even more than he would have guessed. He shook his head in knowing frustration as things appeared to be panning out exactly as he had predicted. It was just another pointless punch-up. He then saw several policemen crowd round the woman in the wheelchair. Nash made no attempt to go to her aid. May would be arrested and that would be the end of it as far as he was concerned. And Ruby would just have to lump it.

But briefed not to arrest the infamous Cripple Suffragette, May and her contraption were lifted up above the policemen's heads. Nash looked on, still not moving. And then May was tipped out of her wheelchair and on to the ground from some height.

Ruby cursed Nash. Where the hell was he? Is he another Lowe, leaving people to their fate? Bastard! She dashed out from behind her tree, running almost under the hooves of a mounted policeman. She saw the horse out the corner of an eye as she dived to safety. Getting up, grazed wrists were surveyed as an image of Emily flashed into her mind for a moment.

She looked up to see May still lying on the ground. Thankfully the police appeared not to have followed up their assault with any further violence against her. Ruby picked up her friend as best she could and woman-handled her into the tricycle. May, though still dazed, immediately wheeled herself to the Palace railings and took out a length of chain from beneath the blanket she had managed to retain on her lap, and manacled her contraption to the railings. It was only then that she looked up and saw the identity of the woman who had helped her.

"Ruby! My dear!" She smiled and nodded towards a

number of policemen a few feet away. "I seem to have a guardian angel."

Ruby frowned. May had obviously received a blow to the head. She was not making any sense. But Ruby's gaze followed her friend's nod nonetheless, so she saw the reason why the police had not followed up their assault on May. The group who had tipped her out of the wheelchair were far too busy tackling a huge violent man.

There was only one thing Nash disliked more than the police, and that was bullies. And bullies in uniforms really were beneath contempt. On seeing May dumped to the ground Nash had instinctively reached inside his left pocket for his lethal old marlin spike only to curse when he realised he had deliberately left it at home to make a point that he was not going to get involved. But he already had his Saturday Night dangling from his right hand. As he had broken away from the crowd he had been cheered by some of the young men on the memorial as it was assumed he was an anti-Suffragette heading into the fray to perpetrate damage on some woman or another. He had thus been left a clear passage as far as the police line. One of the policemen had broken ranks to stop him only to find a Saturday Night making a terrible mess of his helmet. Nash had made for the gap in the line left by the now horizontal policeman and gave the bobby either side of the gap a backhand and forehand of his weapon. A few more blows and he had broken through the police-line but not before he had lost his armament in doing so. The group who had tipped May out of her tricycle had been about to drag her off by the hair, when Nash had waded into them. They were all severely chastised by an East End confection of fists, head butts, elbows and straight fingers to the Adam's apple.

Ruby was standing watching Nash in full flow when a passing sentry punched her in the face without reason. She was lying prostrate on the ground when a group of policemen came up and unchained May's tricycle, removed its occupant and smashed up the contraption. They refused to arrest May, simply carrying her away from the Palace railings and dumping her by a tree on Birdcage Walk. Ruby dragged herself to her feet and retrieved the only one of May's crutches still intact, which had been left within the remains of the wheelchair, before joining her friend. Neither woman had seen what had happened to Nash but his absence from the scene suggested he must have been hauled off by the police. They waited for the mayhem to abate before flagging down a motor taxi. The cabbie had been none too keen to take the battered and bleeding women as they were obviously a couple of Suffragettes. But when offered a fare all the way to distant Lewisham, his reticence disappeared and with his help Ruby managed, with some difficulty, to get May up and into the back seat.

Nash had eventually been overpowered and was one of two men amongst the sixty eight people arrested and taken away, but in the pandemonium at Cannon Row Police Station he was charged with nothing more than disturbing the peace. His huge frame was then wedged painfully into a tiny wire cell within a Black Maria for the thankfully short trip to Bow Street Police Station and Magistrates Court. He was given a fine but refused to pay it. He thus received a custodial sentence, which as a perceived bully boy Votes for Women supporter rather than a Suffragette per se, he would serve as a second division category prisoner; a common criminal.

Chapter 30

"The Liberal Party has always been ready to raise an outcry on behalf of oppressed peoples; and yet they refuse, through their leader Mr Asquith, to apply their own principles in the cause of the liberation of millions of women."

Weekly Dispatch

The Women's May Day in the East End's Victoria Park had been billed as a festival and council of war. There were to be nine platforms and forty speakers. Sylvia had star billing, but there were numerous other notables on the cast list. These included Henry Nevinson, one of the founder members of the Men's League for Women's Suffrage who was a disillusioned ex-WSPU follower and now ardent Sylvia supporter; George Lansbury; and Miss Winson, vice chairman of the Woman's Suffrage Party in Philadelphia, whose visit had been set up by Ruby getting in touch with her old Titanic buddy Margaret Brown.

The procession to the park started in Canning Town and then swept into Old Ford Road in Bow, where Sylvia was waiting for them at the Women's Hall. Sporting a black eye from her Buckingham Palace experience, Ruby was one of a score of Sylvia's followers who had chained themselves to their leader and to each other, before they set off at the front of the procession towards Victoria Park. Outside the park gates fifty detectives were dressed in disguise as costermongers but they weren't fooling anyone. The procession was keeping an eye on them when the uniformed police cleared a space as if to let the women through as they neared their destination. But without Nash and his knowledge of police tactics and instinct for danger, the procession didn't spot that it was the start of a well-coordinated attack. The fifty detectives waded in with sticks. They dragged Sylvia and her guard of chained women to the park's boating enclosure and locked its gates behind them. The police inspector in charge demanded the keys to the chains' locks whilst his subordinates tore at Sylvia's neck where they expected to find the keys. When these were not forthcoming, truncheons were used to smash the locks. Ruby tried to hinder the operation, receiving blows from police sticks for her trouble. She kept her arms high to protect her bruised face so her legs and torso took the brunt. Other women had their faces punched, hair pulled, arms twisted and thumbs bent back, all accompanied by lurid epithets from their tormentors. And there was a particularly terrible scream of pain as a child, who had playing innocently in the park, had its knee broken in the melee.

Sylvia was flung on the floor of a taxi accompanied by swearing, punching and arm twisting by the four detectives who jumped into the seats of the cab. They cursed the East End and its people before asking the woman lying at their feet why she had come to live amongst these 'roughs'. Sylvia answered by reminding them that they had canvassed all the *roughs* as they called them in Ford Road, trying to rent a room from which they could spy on her, and had offered a small fortune for it, yet at every house they had been refused.

"It's all in the game," muttered the least violent of the men shamefacedly.

"You'll never get the vote!" said the most aggressive of them.

"Oh, yes they'll get it," retorted his colleague sagely.

★★★★★★

Sylvia was now being given sentences far in excess of that which would normally accompany the offence for which she had been found guilty. The stroll to her local park with some friends had seen her sentenced to three months in prison for incitement. But nine trips to prison in as many months had taken a terrible toll on Sylvia's strength. This latest prison term thus soon left her so weak that she was quickly released on licence.

Just before her arrest Sylvia had moved in to the house in front of the Women's Hall, but she was now in no fit state to look after herself. Jessie and her husband, who were due to move in to the Women's Hall house with Sylvia in the near future, were still living in Ford Road, so a double bed awaited Sylvia in their front room. And knowing how ill and in need of complete rest her returning lodger was likely to be, the local alpha female had put her door knocker out of commission by tying it up with her husband's muffler.

Sylvia had been offered a taxi ride to Jessie's house by the prison authorities but she had declined. It had been arranged that Ruby would be waiting for her in a cab at the prison gates. They had a little detour planned. A black and blue Ruby duly picked her up and as the taxi entered Bow they were met with an avenue of cheering, waving East London supporters. Once she was back in residence, the police would not allow Sylvia to leave without attempting to re-arrest her under Cat and Mouse so if she was going to make a speech any time soon it had to be now, en-route home. A meeting had thus been arranged outside Bow Public Hall to coincide with her release, ironically next door to the old police station, which unlike the new one, Sylvia had never had cause to visit. The taxi pulled up by the hall and though she was too weak to stand she delivered a speech from a sitting position, while a small group of police detective Cats looked on debating amongst themselves whether she was in breach of the terms of her release. Given that they were considerably outnumbered by Sylvia's tough East End supporters, they decided that on balance she was within her rights to speak to a few friends on an informal basis en-route back to her place of residence.

Sylvia was so frail that her speech had to be a short one. And with the police listening to every word, she was careful not to hint at attempting to give a future speech any time soon. But the crowd were captivated. They cheered and knew that sooner rather than later their heroine would be endeavouring to speak, not just to them but to all the friends and neighbours they would be hoping to indoctrinate and bring along to the next meeting.

A few days of rest and recuperation later Sylvia decided that she had recovered sufficiently to ask Norah, Daisy, Zelie, Ruby and the rest of her local leaders to organise a big meeting back at Bow Public Hall. The venue would be hired from the council by someone with no known Suffragette contact. The meeting was to be held outside of working hours and arranged at short notice, the theory being that in such a space of time they could get a big turnout organised quicker than the authorities could counter with a well concerted response.

The following weekend the hall was packed beyond capacity and thousands were waiting outside as the meeting time approached. The problem was now the perennial one of how to get Sylvia from her mouse-hole in Ford Road, to the meeting without her being captured and returned to prison by the Cats as soon as she stepped foot outside.

Nurse Hobbes arrived at 28 Ford Road. She was a regular visitor, tending to Sylvia's medical needs. A car suddenly pulled up outside with a suitably theatrical screech of the tyres to ensure that every detective in the vicinity heard and saw it. This was the cue for Ruby, head down and disguised as Sylvia, to rush out of the house and into the car, which immediately sped off towards the public hall. Despite a wig and padding as her disguise, Ruby did not look that much like Sylvia but it was only a few feet through a crowded avenue of supporters from the door of number 28 to the car so the police barely got a fleeting glimpse at the fast moving woman. It was hoped the detectives would assume the blur was Sylvia trying to disguise herself. It worked and Ruby's car was duly chased by police vehicles all the way to the hall.

Her duties completed, Nurse Hobbes apparently then left the house. She was wearing a now ill-fitting high-collared coat, her hat was pulled down over the eyebrows and ruddy cheeks enjoyed an upgrade of rouge. She did not look that much like Nurse Hobbes, but more importantly she looked suitably unlike Sylvia Pankhurst to warrant a second look from detectives still watching the house, who were convinced their prey was already in a car chase with colleagues. The disguised woman hobbled round to the public hall as quickly as she could to find an affronted Ruby telling hundreds of policemen what she thought of them. Couldn't a woman visit her local public hall without being accosted by seemingly half the Metropolitan police force? She was not aware that she was living in Russia. And in any case, did she look like Sylvia Pankhurst? She thought not!

The crowd, relieved that their heroine had not been caught, had great fun at the police's expense. It had been three years since the police had failed to capture the East End's second most famous ever criminal, Peter the Painter, after the Siege of Sidney Street, and in the interim the small-time anarchist had assumed near-mythical proportions. And this three hundred strong police presence complete with horses was the biggest turn out of constabulary seen in East London since.

"'ere, yer caught ol' Peter the Painter at last 'ave yer?"

"Who'd 'av fought it eh, ol' Pete's a woman!"

"No wonder they never caught 'im till now!"

"Caught 'er yer mean!"

"ere, I should watch out if I were you boys, she might 'ave an automatic rolling pin stuffed up 'er jumper!"

One of the policemen continued to hold Ruby firmly by the arm, shouting at her above the crowd's jokes that there was still the little matter of her driver's reckless driving. A colleague advised him that a driving offence was the least of their worries given the size of the crowd they had to deal with, so it might be a good idea to let her go. This the first policeman grudgingly did, after which Ruby walked through the hall entrance just as the disguised Sylvia was making her way quietly through the crowd. Sylvia entered the hall just in front of Ruby and was soon spotted by a detective. He grabbed her but was immediately set upon, first by Ruby, then by a number of men and thrown bodily out of the hall. The door to the hall was closed and locked, and men stood guard by it while Sylvia delivered a rousing speech to those lucky enough to be packed inside, about the vote and the need for a democratic mass movement.

With the speech delivered, the door to the hall was reopened, to reveal dozens of police detectives armed with sticks and a sea of uniformed policemen. As far as the authorities were concerned, Miss Pankhurst may have managed to get in to the hall and speak to hundreds, but she was not going to be allowed to leave it to do an improvised al fresco speech to thousands from atop a costermonger's cart. She was going back to prison. But there were organisational skills within the apparent teeming chaos of East London slum life, and this meeting was nothing if not well planned. Astutely positioned high velocity fire hoses were now turned on the police, who were pushed back. Police horses started to flex their considerable muscles, causing the crowd to take avoiding action. Zelie was knocked unconscious in the melee. Ruby didn't notice this, which was just as well as an image of Epsom had already flashed into her head.

"Puss!" "Puss!" "Puss!" was chanted by an angry crowd.

"Cat's never did like water did they!" shouted one wag whilst Ruby and a couple of other Federation women ushered the object of the Cats' desire out of a side door with a view to getting her back unscathed to her mouse-hole.

Her thoughts still not entirely on the job at hand, Ruby mistakenly led them down an alley that was a dead end. They could not return whence they had come; the long boot of the law would be heading up the cobbles towards them at any moment. Ruby started to thrust her shoulder against doors as she passed them. A dilapidated old stable door barely hanging on to its hinges gave and the four women bundled themselves into the darkness within. They shot the bolts of the door and blew their cheeks out in relief. But it was short-lived. A policeman shone his lantern into the stable through a gap in its wooden slatted wall and moments later he was trying the door but the rusty old bolts held. The policeman's half-hearted attempt at entry suggested to Ruby that he hadn't seen them, which appeared to be borne out by him abandoning his search and going on his way.

The four women waited till close to midnight before Ruby thought it safe to go and raise help. She returned with Willie and Edgar, George Lansbury's sons, and a hand cart piled with sacks of firewood. The men quickly hid Sylvia under a blanket amongst the cargo. Ruby whispered to the other two women to set off in the opposite direction and if they saw policemen they should act suspiciously to try and get themselves followed, drawing the Cats away. The Lansbury boys and Ruby then set off with the cart. They were almost back to the yard next to Jessie's house when the chief constable of Bow and some of his officers, who were shining their lanterns into every nook and cranny, spotted them from a distance. The cart was then crashed against a gate post in the hurry to get it into the yard, whilst Sylvia, who really was too weak for such shenanigans, managed to scramble awkwardly from beneath her cover and ease herself down to the ground as Ruby shut the yard gates behind them. The boys bundled Sylvia into her mouse-hole just before the police arrived. They challenged Ruby and made no attempt to hide their suspicions, but they had no search warrant.

Chapter 31

"I am sure that however strong public opinion outside might be today in favour of letting them die, when there are 20, 30 or 40 deaths in prison you would have a violent reaction of public opinion."

Reginald McKenna, Home Secretary

The police encampment outside Jessie's house was now stopping everyone who attempted to enter or leave it, irrespective of who they may or may not appear to be. The days of disguises and decoys getting the better of them were over. A new tactic to get Sylvia out of her mouse-hole and to her next port of call without being arrested was required. A many-deep crowd gathered around the doorstep of 28 Ford Road to stop the police from getting anywhere near it.

The Cats were not unduly concerned. They had expected something like this. The Pankhurst woman's supporters had done this before. The plan was no doubt to drive a car up to the door and bundle her into it. But detectives in a fleet of cars were ready to block the road in both directions. There was no escape.

But as Sylvia was still in no fit state to travel, yet due to speak at Canning Town Public Hall, it had been arranged that she would be transported by the not inconsiderably grand method of being carried shoulder high to her appointment in a bath-chair. This most ostentatious mode of transport also had the benefit of putting the slumped Sylvia on show for East London to see what the government was doing to a defenceless young woman. But lest the local constabulary made the mistake of taking this defencelessness a little too literally, there was an impressive crowd of People's Army men and women including Ruby in attendance, who surrounded the bath-chair all the way to Canning Town. So the Cats did not get the cream.

Almost a year to the day that Ruby had seen Emily Davison die at the Derby, her blood ran cold as she listened to Sylvia's speech.

"The popular suffrage movement with the East End at its active centre must make itself felt by the Cabinet. The objection of Asquith and others that the demand is not democratic, and the movement is not of the masses, must be swept away. A deputation to the Prime Minister must be elected from the East End. Asquith would probably refuse to receive the deputation. We should go in procession to interview him nevertheless. I should accompany the deputation. I should be rearrested of course. Then I should not only hunger and thirst-strike in prison, but continue it after release until the deputation should be received. Asquith might maintain his refusal to the bitter end; he has always been stubborn. In that case I must carry on the fight. I do not want to die and leave all that we hoped to do, yet I am willing to die if it might help to ensure the victory."

Ruby remembered old WSPU stalwart Olive Fergus once telling her of an incident in which she had been embroiled a few years back. Olive and a colleague had been on their way to do some chalking of propaganda on any pavements they could find close to Parliament which did not have a police presence on them. They had been walking down Downing Street when they had come across the then new Prime Minister Mr Asquith and a few other politicians, without a policeman in attendance. It had been too good an opportunity to miss. The two women had quickly cut Asquith off from his entourage, and had walked either side of him, asking polite questions about Votes for Women. Olive had told Ruby how she would always remember Asquith's expression. He appeared not to be annoyed, or flustered or intimidated. And certainly wasn't listening to them. He ignored the women and simply strolled along, eyes straight ahead with the most supercilious, smuggest of smiles on his face.

The man had not taken these women, or any women since, seriously. Ruby believed there could be only one outcome. Sylvia was going to die.

The matter was discussed by all and sundry. Ruby met up with Norah, Zelie, the Lansbury family and all the leading lights of not just the Bow branch of the Federation, but those of other branches set up by Sylvia in Bethnal Green, Limehouse and Poplar. George Lansbury spoke to the Pethick-Lawrences and other important people in the women's suffrage movement. Sylvia's closest friend, Keir Hardie, the founder and ex-leader of the Labour Party, had meetings with the government's Chief Whip Percy Illingworth, and the Chancellor of the Exchequer David Lloyd-George, but had not been able to manoeuvre something similar with the Prime Minister.

Everyone was very concerned about the situation but nobody knew how to resolve it. If there was one person more stubborn than the immovable object in 10 Downing Street, it was the irresistible force that was Sylvia Pankhurst. Ruby decided she needed to get a message quickly to Nashey in Brixton prison. When mere rational argument was not enough, he was the only person she knew, who might just conceivably, by sheer force of intimidating personality be able to talk Sylvia out of committing suicide. He had, after all, stopped a Titanic cashier from giving up on her life.

The problem was that Nash, as a division two common criminal would not be allowed to receive any letters, and ex-convicts, of whom she was one, were not allowed to visit their fellow felons in prison. So as most of Ruby and Nash's mutual acquaintances had a criminal record through their Suffragette work, one of Nash's cousins, who had never served a term at his majesty's pleasure, was asked to pay the prison a visit. The cousin duly passed on Ruby's dictatorial message to Nash. It was along the lines of come off hunger-strike; pay your fine; follow the rules; get out of prison as quickly as possible; let me know when you are about to be released and I will meet you at the prison gates; Sylvia is starving herself to death for the cause.

★★★★★★

Mr Payne's scarf was still wrapped round his home's doorknocker so Sylvia could get some peace and quiet, but someone was banging on the door heavily with their fist. It could not be good news. Jessie shouted from behind the door.

"Who is it?"

"Ruby and Nashey," answered a deep rough voice which made it clear it was that of the latter.

Seconds later a horizontal Sylvia looked up from her sick bed through eyes red with blood to see more than six feet of towering inferno standing over her. She had heard of his arrest, imprisonment and hunger-strike so was surprised someone as fit and healthy as Nash was out of captivity quite this quickly.

Nash considered women to be the equal of men and as far as he was concerned that meant they got no special favours. No opening of doors, no standing up for them on the tram unless they were 'expecting', and no saving them from the most severe dressing down when they deserved it. Sylvia was very poorly but that was not going to save her from being told the error of her ways in no uncertain fashion.

"Christ almighty, look at the state of yer! Yer look fifty if you're a day! You ain't gonna do Votes for Women no bleedin' good dead are yer! Look at that poor lit'le cow at the Derby last year. Fat lot of good that all did!"

It was clear Nash was not in the best of moods. But Sylvia was not above using a little of the lowest form of wit to put him in his place.

"Thank you Nashey. A woman likes a man to inform her when she is not looking at her best. It keeps her up to the mark."

Nash gave Sylvia a knowing look before replying.

"Sharp ain't yer. Mind yer don't cut yerself."

"And it's good to see you out of prison Nashey", retorted Sylvia. "I heard you were in Brixton. It must have been awful for you to be incarcerated *south* of the river."

Nashey turned and gave Ruby an old fashioned look. It was clear the women from Southampton and Manchester had some time previously enjoyed a good chortle together at the xenophobic East Londoner's expense.

"Never mind that chaff," was his rather more Saturday Night than rapier-like response.

There followed a colourful debate on the present situation vis-à-vis Sylvia's present hunger and thirst-strike in relation to the fight for the vote. A considered and scholarly argument put forward by Sylvia, a somewhat less intellectual but coherent, in its own way, one proffered by Nash.

"You're doin' the same bleedin' fing as that sister a yourn. Banging yer 'ead against a brick wall just cos yer can't wait five minutes. Women'll get the vote when it suits that bastard Asquith. An' it'll suit 'im right enuff when 'e knows 'e can get the vote fru for working men who'll vote for Liberals an' kick the Tories in the balls. An' that'll be soon the way it's goin'. We've nearly won. There ain' gonna be no more Black Fridays. Beatin' up a few ladies is one thing, they ain't gonna beat up the likes of me and fousands like me from the East End carryin' our Saturday nights and worse with us are they? We're like the Micks. We pose a freat. The Micks'll get what they want and we'll get what we want. You mark my words."

Sylvia usually enjoyed a good colourful argument with Nash over his unsophisticated, cynical views on politics but on this occasion she was too tired and too ill to take him on for long. She simply responded by telling him that there must be more to politics than what suits the prime minster at any given moment, and the threat of physical force. Doctrine and fairness must be at the heart of a democracy. Irrespective of which political party would gain out of it, and not withstanding whether the working classes carried a greater physical threat than middle class women, it was simply time that women got the vote. The women of Wyoming had got the vote almost half a century ago. New

Zealand, a British colony, had been the first country to give women the vote. Australian women also had the vote. And some European countries were already franchised too. And closer to home women on the Isle of Man already voted in their domestic government. She would not wait any longer. Her father had helped women secure the vote at local election level when she was still a girl, and she had waited the rest of her life since to acquire the vote at national level. It was now women's time. It was her time. She was determined to die a martyr for the cause if necessary.

Ruby could see Sylvia was too ill, yet too determined to continue her hunger and thirst-strike, to warrant the continuance of the debate, so ushered a perplexed Nash out of the room.

★★★★★★

As Sylvia had predicted, Asquith refused to accept a deputation from the East London Federation so she arranged for a night march from the East End to Parliament, with herself carried in front of the procession. She also sent another request to the Prime Minister asking for an audience. She had grown so weak that Ruby was desperate for her leader's plight to get more publicity so the impasse might be resolved. Ruby had thus agreed with Nash that the People's Army would supply only limited security for Sylvia's latest appearance in public. It was a terrible risk but they had decided that on balance it would be better if their leader was rearrested and returned to Holloway. The government could not afford to have a Suffragette die in prison. They would have to do something.

Sylvia was duly taken out of Jessie's house on a long

carrying chair with poles for the shoulders of four bearers. She strove to cheer and hearten the waiting crowd outside but as she beseeched them to keep up the fight should the matter prove fatal, the crowd fell silent, women streaming with tears, men removing their headwear and bowing their heads as a mark of respect.

The procession had only reached Grove Road in Mile End where, as the road narrowed a parked motor taxi partly blocked the way causing the ranks of followers to thin out. The cab had been placed there deliberately by the police, whose plain clothes detectives swept forward. An inspector on horseback seized Sylvia by a wrist and the chair bearers were hurled aside by his officers.

"You are arrested Miss Pankhurst!" he said attempting victorious but merely achieving melodramatic.

But the procession carried on through Poplar, Whitechapel and the City, down Ludgate Hill and along Fleet Street. A police line spread across The Strand outside the Gaiety Theatre. But they were no longer dealing with middle class women. This was a group of tough East End men and women carrying serious weaponry, with Ruby and Nash at their head. The procession broke through the police ranks and continued their march to Parliament. On arrival they were informed that the second request to be seen by the Prime Minister had also been refused.

It was illegal to make political speeches on Parliament Square so in an act of open defiance the procession did just that, while the police stood by and allowed it. Nash nodded at Ruby with grim satisfaction on his face. She knew what the nod meant. The authorities were clearly conciliatory to a multitude who carried a threat.

Chapter 32

"Millicent Garrett-Fawcett's mistake was always asking and expecting too little of them (government ministers). Perhaps because she had been the wife of one of them."

Sylvia Pankhurst on the widowed president of the National Union of Women's Suffrage Societies.

Such was her state of health that Sylvia was soon released from prison, with wardresses having to accompany her in a taxi to Bow. A crowd had gathered in Ford Road after the prison pickets had telephoned through to tell people that their leader was on her way. Norah had a car at the door, waiting to take Sylvia to Westminster. Jessie helped her lodger into number 28. Sylvia washed her face and changed the dress she had worn night and day in prison. Like an athlete about to start the race of their life, Sylvia appeared emotionless as she concentrated all her being on the task at hand. She got into the car, not noticing the women weeping on the pavement. For once there were no Cats about as, whatever her behaviour on her release there was no possibility of Sylvia being returned to prison in her present condition.

The car duly drew up outside the Houses of Parliament. The light-headed Sylvia pondered why the statue of Richard Coeur de Lion, a Frenchman from seven hundred years ago, was outside the House. But better to be associated with him than with the mass murderer of the Irish, Oliver Cromwell, who had the only other statue in front of Parliament. A long forgotten king who could barely speak a word of English and a mass killer who had also cut a king's head off; was that the best English and British democracy had come up with over the centuries? My God it was time for a change.

Keir Hardie, and disillusioned Liberal MP and women's suffrage supporter Josiah Wedgewood came out to meet the car. There was also a little crowd of East London Federation women led by Ruby. Hardie had tried to gain admittance for Sylvia into the House but she was still banned from entry due to a previous incident when she had been ejected for throwing a stone at a painting of an old Speaker. Hardie begged her to stay in the car while he hurried away to try to talk with the Prime Minister.

Policemen were guarding the steps of Strangers' Entrance so the car trundled a short distance along to a little square door to the left. Ruby and other supporters carefully got Sylvia out of the car and gently laid her down. A police inspector soon came over and informed her that she could not stay there. One of his officers was about to seize her when George Lansbury and Henry Nevinson came running out of the House to relay that Asquith would receive a deputation from the East London Federation. He would receive six women on Saturday morning. Almost everyone began to cheer.

"We are winning! At last we are winning!"

Ruby was a lone voice of caution.

"I will believe it when I see it," she said sceptically. "Asquith is not worsted yet. It is only because he is worried how the death of Sylvia would look to the press and public."

359

But within the week Ruby was voted in by the East London Federation as one of the six women to represent them on the deputation to see the Prime Minister. She tried to refuse her nomination, feeling awkward that she was not an East Ender or even a Londoner, and she had only been involved in the East London movement for a year. But her supporters countered that even Sylvia herself was not a Londoner and had only been in the East End for a couple of years. The fact was that Ruby was a good speaker and had done as much as any East Ender for the cause. She also brought something different to the group, as unlike the other members of the deputation she was young and single. And as well as having different work and life experiences, she was also more genteel. None of the other women had any experience of dealing directly with wealthy people as she had done in service and on board ships. And thanks to her friendship with Sylvia, she also understood politics that much better than the rest of them.

Ruby eventually agreed to be a member of the deputation. On the big day she wore her smartest outfit even though it meant she was overdressed for the time of year, just as she had been the last time she had worn it, at Epsom.

Julia Scurr had been given the job of leading the deputation. She had been what she considered to be a quiet housewife until galvanised by the Suffragette movement and was now a vigilant Poor Law guardian. She made and received the introductions, and was first to speak. Sylvia had prepared Julia's statement on themes that she knew were close to the women's hearts.

"Parliament is constantly dealing with questions affecting the education and care of our children, with the houses in which we live, and more and more with every item of our daily lives," she began in slightly stilted fashion, concentrating on sounding her tees and aitches. "Our husbands die on the average at a much earlier age than do the men of other classes. Modern industrialism kills them off rapidly, both by accident and overwork. We can here speak with much feeling on these matters for we know by bitter experience the terrible struggle with absolute want that our widowed sisters have to face through no fault of their own. We feel most earnestly and emphatically that it is gravely unjust to pass legislation in matters of this kind without consulting the women of this country. We would further point out that whilst women are taxed on exactly the same basis as men, and like men are obliged to obey the laws, they are allowed no voice in these questions."

Jessie Payne then told of her terrible life as a sweated worker; a cigarette packer in a factory where she had earned less than a shilling a day. Men had been allowed time for lunch but women were not, and had nowhere to eat so had to consume their food in the lavatory. She emphasised that men's trade unions would not tolerate such conditions.

Summoning up all her resolve, she went on to tell of life with her mentally retarded daughter. Having a conscientious objection to her little girl being vaccinated she had gone to the local magistrate for an exemption order. He had laughed and informed her that in the eyes of the law she was not the parent. Only a father could apply. It had been a terrible insult. Her daughter lived into adulthood and on one occasion became unmanageable to the point where Mr Payne had felt compelled to take her to the workhouse. When she had arrived the next morning she found her daughter had been

361

placed in a padded room. She had asked the doctor why her daughter was in such a predicament and was informed that a mother had no voice in the matter. Only the father had that right.

Fearful of becoming emotional, Jessie had not been able to make eye-contact during these revelations, but now she sniffed a big breath through her nostrils and looked up to hold the Prime Minister firmly in her gaze whilst she read out her prepared statement.

"Our demand is for the form of franchise for women you have repeatedly said you could best understand and with which you would be most in sympathy. It is the form of the franchise which you have declared your intention of establishing for men in the near future. It is the one for which your party is supposed to stand; a vote for every woman over twenty one. This demand is supported by an enormous volume of working class opinion throughout the country, especially in our own district."

This was Mrs Bird's cue to take over the baton. A mother of six and wife of a transport worker earning twenty five shillings a week, she declared herself better off than thousands for some men earned as little as eighteen shillings a week yet had more children than her. She described how men simply laid money on the table and then it was up to women to pay all the bills and make ends meet. She listed examples of the accountancy and administrative skills required to keep the worst ravages of poverty at bay.

"You can tell we don't get a living, but an existence and we have to leave our children to the mercy of the streets."

It was perhaps more a social history lesson for the Prime Minister than a political speech but no less powerful for that.

She handed over to Mrs Savoy, a sweated brush-maker who was jolly and brave despite suffering from dropsy and palpitations. She told of being paid a penny farthing for each brush, which required two hundred holes, and took her almost two hours to make. She suddenly placed one of her brushes firmly on the great shiny table that separated the deputation from the Prime Minister and his entourage. It made a clatter which startled the politicians as if a small bomb had just gone off in front of them.

"I do all the work. I keep my home. I ought to have a vote for it!"

Mrs Daisy Parsons, a frail little woman, told of how she had worked full time since she was twelve years old to keep her mother and younger siblings out of the workhouse, and was now with a husband on a small wage on which she cared for her own children as well as an orphaned niece.

Ruby told of the plight of her mother, left poverty stricken by the appalling administration of the Titanic Disaster Fund. Then, having mentioned that she too had been on board the doomed ship, which she had only planned to mention to gain some gravitas, she found herself going off-script. She likened the collision with the iceberg and the lack of lifeboats to the WSPU's movement since 1912, the initial huge mistakes being terrible but not irretrievable. She distanced the East London Federation from the WSPU, and claimed that those aboard the Votes for Women ship would be saved by Sylvia Pankhurst's organisation. They were the lifeboats and they were going back time and again so there were no longer merely thousands, but millions on board.

She then caught Jessie glaring at her which caused her to wonder whether this was all rather too theatrical for the circumstances, so changed the subject by reading out her statement.

"With regard to Miss Sylvia Pankhurst, we ask for her unconditional release from the sentence that will have her return to prison under the auspices of the Temporary Prisoners' Discharge Act. We feel that Sir Edward Carson, the Ulster Unionist, has not only made inciting speeches but he said that the Irish streets would be flowing in blood. We feel that that his incitement has been greater than hers yet he is not in prison. We feel that the vote must be won shortly. And Miss Pankhurst is giving her life for the purpose of fighting for this vote."

She then went on to tackle the issue of police brutality.

"When we go along in procession suddenly without warning we are pounced upon by cowardly detectives and bludgeoned and called names when nobody is about. There was one old lady of seventy who was with us the other day, who was knocked to the ground and kicked. She is a shirt-maker and is forced to work on a machine so she has been in the most awful agony."

Ruby motioned to her face, which still showed a yellow tinge of bruise from the sentry's fist outside Buckingham Palace.

"And as you can see, I was punched in the face when I was merely a spectator at a procession recently. And three days later I was struck repeatedly around the body by police sticks in an unprovoked attack. These men are not fit to control the country while we have no say in the matter."

Asquith replied that their delegation was more representative than others he had met. And if the change to women's suffrage had got to come he and his government must face it boldly and make it thoroughly democratic. It appeared that he finally recognised he could not maintain his resistance to women's suffrage much longer and stated his position now for equal suffrage was closer to Sylvia Pankhurst and the East London Federation than Christabel and Emmeline Pankhurst's WSPU.

"I tell you quite frankly that I have listened with the greatest interest to the statement read by Mrs Scurr and to the special, individual experience of the various members of the deputation, by which the statement has been reinforced. It is a very moderate and well-reasoned presentation of your case and I will give it very careful and mature consideration. I am not going to enter into anything of argument here, but I think the substance of the case you have presented comes to this. The economic conditions under which women labour in any community like, for instance, the East End of London, are such that we cannot get substantial and intelligent reform unless women themselves have a voice in choosing representatives of Parliament. And you have each given me special illustrations, drawn from your own experience, to show that this is not a rhetorical statement, but does correspond to the actual facts of East End life. I will take all these things into consideration during the recess which is upon us and will write to you with my full response in due course. And this statement will be laid out in public come the next Parliamentary season."

An hour later the women were walking up Whitehall together discussing the meeting. They were enjoying the moment as they neared Trafalgar Square but were in no mood for a long, serious debate. Most of the women had not slept a wink the previous night with a trip to Downing Street and a meeting with the Prime Minister looming over them, and they had used up a lot of nervous energy both prior to and during the appointment at number 10. They were pleasantly surprised by how cordially Mr Asquith had received them and were delighted the meeting had appeared to go so well, but were also relieved it was all over. They now just wanted to have a little time to relax and take a breath before reporting back to Sylvia and their other East London Federation colleagues. Like everyone else, Ruby was in high spirits but that did not stop her from sounding a note of caution about the Prime Minister, just as she had on the last occasion she had stood outside Parliament.

"If Mr Asquith is so reasonable, why have women had such a fight these past ten years? The Liberals could have given women the vote when they won their landslide eight years ago but they did not. And it was Asquith, more than anyone else, who stopped it. And he has been blocking it ever since. Look at the way he scuppered the Conciliation Bill. We will only get the vote when it suits him, you mark my words."

The canny East End women were well aware that the vote was certainly not won yet, but it was time for a few old Londoners to let off some steam by having a joke at the expense of a young Hampshire woman.

"Now, where 'ave we 'eard all that before ladies? Don't your jaw ache Mrs Nash?" mock scolded Jessie Payne.

The other women laughed and expected a quick riposte, but the usually quick-witted Ruby just coloured, which was pounced upon by tough East End women with tough East End humour. Ruby quickly recovered her composure and started giving as good as she got, suggesting Nashey was far too old for a lovely young thing like herself so perhaps an old married woman such as one of them would like to have him as their bit on the side? But Ruby had at some point in the recent past made the mistake of telling her Federation friends that she had enjoyed a cup of tea with Nashey in the Lyons Corner House just before the Buckingham Palace protest. As the women approached the tea room, this came back to bite her.

"Who's for a cuppa tea then ladies?" asked Jessie. "Only we can't go in Lyons' 'cause that's Ruby's special place from 'er trip to Buckingham Palace, if you get my meaning."

The wink and knowing nod that accompanied this remark ensured that if any of the other women had not immediately comprehended Jessie's meaning, they soon did.

Chapter 33

"We want it (the vote) far more for its symbolic value – the recognition of our human equality that it will make…When we have done that, then we will help the men to solve the problems of the 20th century. Plainly they can't settle them without us."

Christabel Pankhurst, WSPU

Soon after the East London Federation's meeting with Asquith, Sylvia had gone along to a working breakfast at the House of Commons with the Chancellor, Lloyd-George, at which he offered to support a Reform Bill which included women's enfranchisement, claiming he would resign if it failed. This was with the proviso that militancy stopped. But when this was relayed to Christabel, she had refused to comply.

Realising that she was now not only fighting the government but the equally powerful force of sibling rivalry, and with Parliament about to begin its summer recess, Sylvia conceded that nothing more could be achieved for a couple of months. Thus she and Norah packed themselves off to Ireland to investigate the troubles there. Ruby had also been invited along but had declined the offer. She had no desire to travel by ship again and apparently had something to sort out in London.

Nash was pondering what to do for the best during the

summer. Six months ago, during the Christmas break he had made himself scarce. With Sylvia having taken the opportunity to travel abroad to spread the word, he had spent a month away from the Suffragette scene, helping his cousins with their wood-cutting business. It was the least he could have done given that they had provided him with a place to stay when he had returned to the country from America.

He remembered how he had been looking forward to spending some time away from intelligent women. He had felt the pull of his old world of pubs, beer-drinking, betting, swearing, spitting, crude jokes and 'taking the rise'. But most of all he looked forward to waxing lyrical about any subject which took his fancy without the need to back up his assertions with any evidence, logic or other intellectual properties. The bald statement beckoned.

He had therefore been surprised to find that soon after being back in that world he yearned to return to his Suffragette work. Yet it was not as if the work was overly interesting. Whenever he was not acting as a bodyguard for Sylvia, he and Ruby would spend the day working together which, though interspersed with the odd plot and exploit to counter the police, was often filled with the relatively mundane chores of grass roots politics.

In early January, on hearing that Sylvia had arrived back in the country Nash had immediately rushed back to the Suffragette fold. But he had been surprised to find Ruby rather distant towards him. It was if she had been annoyed with him for something. But she had gradually thawed and during the following months they had got along better than ever. They had become close.

And recently, what with his imprisonment, Sylvia almost

starving herself to death and Ruby and the others seeing Asquith and receiving a hint of progress towards victory, it had been a remarkable few weeks. So much so that he had not returned his thoughts with any great depth to the matter which had dominated his thoughts whilst he had been in prison. Why did Ruby kiss him on the lips that day in the West End? He had seen her kiss a few women on the cheek in greeting or parting, but even that was not something she did as a matter of course. The two of them had got into the habit of bumping each other when they were messing about and joking together, and she would pat him on the chest or shoulders from time to time, sometimes when she was caringly scolding him for something or another. But that was a far cry from kissing. Perhaps she had just been worried that he would get into trouble protecting May. And such concerns had proved well founded. After all he had ended up in prison. And those steps beneath Admiralty Arch and the great difference in their respective heights had made the kiss difficult; perhaps she had just meant to give him a reassuring kiss on the cheek and misjudged it. After all it was only really a peck and she ran off pretty quickly straight afterwards. Perhaps she was embarrassed by the mistake. And when she had met him outside Brixton prison, there had been no second kiss. She had been all business, telling him what Sylvia had been up to. The first thing he had intended to do when released was ask Ruby about the kiss but the shock of hearing that Sylvia was slowly but surely committing suicide had driven such thoughts from his head. And since then life had been such a whirlwind for both of them that he had not thought it the right time to talk of such matters, and nor it would seem had Ruby. In fact, she had seemed a little reserved with him lately, though not in the way she had been when he had returned from working for his cousins. Ever since she had got back from the meeting with Asquith her behaviour towards him had been more one of awkwardness than frostiness.

He had considered whether he should simply leave matters as they were. But he knew full well that he could not. It was time he admitted to himself why he had gone to Halifax. Why the past year had been the happiest of his life.

He was on his way to see Ruby when Jimmy Pearson ran round the corner and bumped straight into him.

"Oi woss your game?" demanded Nash.

"Get yer aris round to the Women's Hall sharp!" shouted Jimmy as he set off running again.

"Eh?" shouted Nash after him. "Wot for?"

"Sylvia's back! 'cause of wot's 'appened!" shouted Jimmy over his shoulder and then he was gone.

Nash looked blankly down the street at Jimmy's disappearing back, wondering why Sylvia would have returned from Ireland so soon. And then it dawned on him.

They had won! The government had finally caved in. He wondered if all women had got the vote or just those who owned property. And surely he now had the vote too. Asquith would not have given propertied women the vote who would vote Tory without also giving it to working men, who would vote Liberal. He started to run. He was fifty yards from Sylvia's new home in Old Ford Road when he had to stop to catch his breath. It was then that the dawn was replaced by an eclipse. How could the vote have been won while Parliament was on its summer recess? It must be something else.

"Christ! Mrs Pankhurst must have turned her toes up!" he exclaimed out loud to no one but himself and a passing stray. "All those terms inside must 'ave finally done for 'er!"

He rushed on to find the front door to the house was a-jar so let himself in and walked down the passage past the front room to the back. There was nobody about so he carried on through to the adjoining Women's Hall, to find Sylvia standing there surveying her empty new headquarters.

"Nashey. It is good to see you even in these circumstances. Have you heard the news? We are at war."

Nash nodded gravely. He had never met the woman, and she had become almost as much opponent as colleague in some ways, but nonetheless he felt a terrible sense of loss. And she had been his great leader's mother too after all.

It was only when Sylvia started telling him about Germany declaring war on Russia three days ago, which had caused her to cut short her trip to Ireland, that he realised he had completely misunderstood the situation. As usual Sylvia had read the political runes correctly. Germany had now declared war on France and invaded Belgium. These being Britain's allies, Britain had been dragged into it.

The implications did not immediately register with Nash. He had been so wrapped up in the fight for the vote that he had not paid much attention to anything else. As far as he was aware, suffrage, industrial unrest and Ireland had dominated the headlines. Where had this war come from? And what did Germany declaring war on Russia and the French have to do with Britain anyhow? But he accepted that Britain was always shouting the odds and going to war with somebody. His brother-in-law had been killed in the Zulu War, and he had lost relatives or mates fighting for queen or king and country in some part of the world or another at regular intervals throughout his life. Joining the army had been one way out of the slums for them at least, and most of them had come home in one piece.

Nash's first emotion had been relief that Mrs Pankhurst was not dead, but his overriding thoughts were of how easily he could get 'the wrong end of the stick'. If he could mistake the impending outbreak of war, firstly as winning the vote and secondly as the leader of the WSPU dying, what chance did he have of understanding what Ruby's feelings were for him?

His first utterance on hearing that Britain was at war lacked delicacy but it was an honest reflection of what, other than thoughts of Ruby, was on his mind.

"What's this all mean for Votes for Women then Sylvia?"

The usually imperturbable Sylvia was a little taken aback but quickly recovered.

"Well Nashey, I am a pacifist. Being a militant politician and a pacifist are not mutually exclusive. Though I should say that I do regret some of the violence in which I have become embroiled these past few years. And being a pacifist, I trust the Federation, of which I hope you will remain a loyal member, will not become involved in the war effort and instead spend much of its time helping the poor of the East End as best we can. For it is the poor who always suffer in these matters is it not. We will probably have to rush forward our ideas about mother and infant welfare centres, a cost price restaurant and helping the unemployed and sweated. And my latest idea is to provide a second hand clothes redistribution centre."

Nash nodded as Sylvia disappeared into the hall's kitchen.

"I am making tea of course. What else at such a time. Make yourself at home Nashey," she said, before raising her voice to be heard as she continued from the scullery. "The usual Parliamentary procedures will no doubt be suspended though we will continue to lobby for the vote whenever it is appropriate to do so. I have already spoken to mother. The WSPU intend to suspend their suffrage campaign to assist in the war effort. I told her I would do no such thing. She took it amiss of course. Emmeline Pethick-Lawrence tells me that the Women's Freedom League will continue to lobby for the vote. My estimation is that the gaining of the vote will be postponed by a few months until the war is over but victory for Votes for Women is close to being won."

Nash was not one for crowding close to someone when they were getting on with a task, so he remained in the hall. He had picked up on Sylvia hoping that he would continue to be a loyal member of the Federation. He wanted to reassure her that, whilst he was clearly someone who had waged many a one-man war against opponents over the years and had a slum dwellers wariness of outsiders, he had no particular axe to grind against his fellow working men and women of Germany. This was a politician's war. Not his.

"Don't you worry Sylve, this war ain't my fight!" shouted Nash through to the kitchen, his voice echoing in the empty space. "An' I ain't no jingo neiver! I'm with you gell!"

During this high decibel exchange Nash had not heard Ruby slip unobtrusively into the room behind him. She stepped forward, her right hand gently taking hold of his left and spoke quietly.

"And I am with you both, boy."

Author's Notes

The events in this novel are accurate retellings of what occurred, and on occasion I have used almost verbatim dialogue from contemporary records.

I used poetic licence on rare occasions. The introduction of the Cat and Mouse Act was in reality rushed through Parliament by the government a little earlier than in my story. The struggle to avoid arrest under its auspices became such a chore that I delayed its inception, as describing this constant battle would have slowed the narrative.

Gladstone's statue in Bow, which still has red hands to this day, had the 'blood' added somewhat later than Nashey does the deed.

May Billinghurst was not involved in the Monument protest.

Officer Lightoller, Officer Lowe, Margaret Brown, Annie Kelly, Mrs Lightoller, May Billinghurst; Sylvia, Emmeline and Christabel Pankhurst; Emily Davison, Mary Richardson, Norah Smyth, Melvinia Walker, Jessie Payne and the other East London Federation women who were seen by Prime Minister Asquith were real people.

Ruby and Nashey are fictional characters. Ruby is used either as an additional character, or occasionally as a replacement of a real person. For example, both The Monument and Derby Day protests were actually two-woman affairs. Ruby is added as a third character. Ruby replaces Norah as the woman who argued money with Christabel in Paris. And in being one of the deputation of six women who met Prime Minister Asquith, Ruby replaces Mrs Watkins, to whose memory I apologise.

Sylvia did have a large bodyguard. He was known as 'Kosher Bill', a Jewish, 6 foot tall, ex-boxer.

Key Dates of the Suffragette Campaign:

1903

Women's Social and Political Union founded in Manchester by Emmeline Pankhurst.

1905

First militant incident at Free Trade Hall Manchester. Christabel Pankhurst and Annie Kenny imprisoned.

1906

February – Emmeline Pethick-Lawrence joins WSPU. She and husband Fred become co-leaders of the organisation, respectively chief fund raiser and financial secretary.

Liberals sweep to power in landslide general election victory.

May – Deputation representing a number of suffragist societies including WSPU seen by new Prime Minister, Campbell-Bannerman. Told to be patient.

June – Christabel Pankhurst becomes WSPU Secretary. Decides organisation will become militant.

Autumn – WSPU moves HQ to London. They decide to oppose all government candidates at bye-elections irrespective of their personal views on women's suffrage.

1907
February – Police brutality. 60 women arrested at demonstration outside Houses of Parliament. Newspapers condemn government.

March – 130 women sent to prison. Start of bye-election work. Emmeline Pethick-Lawrence selects WSPU colours: Purple for Dignity, White for Purity; Green for Hope.

May-October – 3,000 meetings. Regular heckling at Cabinet minister speeches.

September – WSPU splits over autocratic Pankhurst leadership and use of violence. 70 leave to form Women's Freedom League, which is militant but democratic, non-violent.

October – Votes for Women newspaper launched by Fred and Emmeline Pethick-Lawrence.

1908
Majority of MP's including most of Cabinet in favour of women gaining vote in some form but...

April – Henry Asquith becomes Prime Minister. He is strongly opposed to women gaining the vote.

June – Women's Sunday in Hyde Park. 50,000 participants; 500,000 line the streets. Mary Leigh and Edith New smash windows at 10 Downing Street.

October – WSPU leaders arrested following 'rush' on Parliament. Mrs Pankhurst requests political prisoner status which is refused.

1909
July – Miss Wallace Dunlop becomes first hunger-striker.

August – Home Secretary Herbert Gladstone orders force-feeding of hunger-strikers.

September – Hunger-striking widespread.

1910
January – Lady Constance Lytton's appalling treatment in prison becomes national scandal. Home Secretary Herbert Gladstone replaced.

Truce awaiting the Conciliation Bill. Peaceful protests only.

March – Home Secretary Churchill grants Suffragettes class one and a half prisoner status, giving them special privileges without granting them political status.

June – Conciliation Bill introduced into the Commons. It would enfranchise only propertied women; over 800,000 would get the vote. The Bill passes with big majority but Asquith refuses to give time for its further passage.

November – Asquith refuses to consider further progress of Conciliation Bill until after next general election (31 January 1911).

Black Friday. March on Parliament in protest against Asquith's action results in 6 hours of serious police brutality. Many women badly assaulted. Home Secretary Churchill refuses enquiry.

December – Mary Clarke, Mrs Pankhurst's sister, dies from brain haemorrhage brought on by fight for the vote including her arrest on Black Friday.

1911
WSPU renews truce awaiting another Conciliation Bill. Most protests peaceful.

April – Census boycott by many suffragist societies.

June – Huge Coronation Procession by WSPU and many other suffrage societies. 60,000 march. Friendly cheering crowds.

November – Asquith kills Conciliation Bill by stating intention to introduce a manhood suffrage bill. WSPU see this as trick and betrayal.

Start of Guerrilla warfare. Widespread window-smashing of government offices in Whitehall. 223 arrested.

December – Arson used for first time as means of protest.

1912

March – Big window breaking attack on Downing Street, the Strand, Knightsbridge followed three days later by greater attack on West End shops. Shocks and alienates public and press opinion.

Police raid WSPU HQ. Mrs Pankhurst and Pethick-Lawrences arrested. Christabel Pankhurst escapes arrest, flees to Paris in self-imposed exile.

May – Mrs Pankhurst and Pethick-Lawrences tried for conspiracy, given nine month prison sentences.

October – Sylvia Pankhurst arrives in Bow to campaign for George Lansbury at Bromley and Bow bye-election.

Pethick-Lawrences criticise increased violence as self-defeating; are expelled from WSPU and join Women's Freedom League.

1913

January – 'The Speaker's Coup' – government introduce Male Suffrage Bill with amendment to give votes to women. Speaker rules amendment out of order. Government seen as dishonest or shambles, dependent on whether or not they knew action would be taken. Speaker suspected of collusion.

Arson and other violence increases. 250 acts of arson or destruction take place in 6 month period.

Public opinion alienated against WSPU. Suffragettes roughly

handled, beaten up. This atmosphere allows government to rush through Parliament a morally dubious new Act.

April – Prisoners' (Temporary Discharge for Ill Health) Act passed. Quickly becomes known as 'Cat and Mouse Act'.

June – Emily Davison dies from injuries sustained at Epsom Derby.

June 1913-June 1914 Sylvia Pankhurst is imprisoned ten times and hunger strikes each time. Her East London Federation of Suffragettes successfully galvanises working class support.

WSPU membership dwindling while other Suffrage societies' numbers increasing significantly.

1914
January – Sylvia Pankhurst expelled from WSPU after meeting in Paris with her mother and sister. East London Federation of Suffragettes becomes autonomous organisation.

May – Buckingham Palace demonstration is last significant act of WSPU.

June – Sylvia Pankhurst threatens to hunger-strike to death. Deputation from her East London Federation seen by Asquith. He appears conciliatory.

July – Lloyd-George meets Sylvia Pankhurst. He offers to

back a Reform Bill including women's enfranchisement with proviso there is end to militancy. Christabel Pankhurst refuses to end WSPU militancy.

WSPU's membership has dwindled to just 2,000 members.

Non-militant National Union of Women's Suffrage Societies membership reaches 100,000.

August – Britain go to war. WSPU suspend their campaign. Many other women's suffrage societies continue.

The Gaining of the Vote:

1917
All-party panel set up to consider the franchise. Votes in favour of women getting vote in some form, against them getting it on same terms as men. Cabinet supports motion. House of Commons votes in favour of the legislation.

February 1918 – The Representation of the People Act gives women vote if they are: over age of 30 and are either householders, or married to householders, or have obtained university degree or occupy property paying £5 a year rent. Women form 42% of electorate.

Millie Garrett-Fawcett, president of NUWSS, leads deputation of 22 women's suffrage societies to meet the government. Three reasons *claimed* for women gaining vote: 1- Their war work; 2- The right of women to participate in post war reconstruction; 3- The absence of "that detestable campaign that disfigured the annals of political agitation in this country (the Suffragettes)."

Large percentage of female workforce in the war, notably munitions workers were aged under 30, and remain without the vote.

1928

The Representation of the People Act gives all women over age of 21 the vote; the same as men.

"The right honourable gentlemen the Chancellor of the Exchequer, would like it to be known, he does not agree with this legislation."

Winston Churchill. Hand written note on The 1928 Representation of the People Act original document.

Acknowledgements

I wish to thank my wife Jenny Fairweather for her assistance in editing this novel, and in particular for restraining me from imposing on the reader too many keen historian's 'information dumps'. For example, you have her to thank for not reading close to half a page every time someone's clothing is described.

I also wish to thank the staff of the following libraries for their assistance in helping me find what I was looking for: Manchester Central (Women's Suffrage Collection), Women's Library, London (Papers of Rosa May Billinghurst and Millicent Garrett Fawcett), Kent County Maidstone Central (pretty much every book written about the women's suffrage campaign) and the National Maritime Museum (everything worth reading about the Titanic).

And thanks to a Parliament's archivist for the snippet about Mr Churchill's note on the 1928 Representation of the People's Act.

Likewise I offer warm appreciation to the authors/editors of the books which I found particularly useful. Fran Abrams (Freedom's Cause: Lives of the Suffragettes); Melanie Phillips (The Ascent of Woman); Jill Liddington (Rebel Girls); Antonia Raeburn (The Militant Suffragettes); Constance Rover (Women's Suffrage & Party Politics in Britain); Midge McKenzie (Shoulder to Shoulder); Diane Atkinson (The Suffragettes in Pictures).

The memory of Constance Lytton (Prison & Prisoners) on whose force-feeding Ruby's first torture was based is remembered with great respect.

And a special thank you to the memory of Sylvia Pankhurst (The History of the Women's Militant Suffrage Movement and other books).